THE DOCTOR'S FORBIDDEN FLING

BY
KARIN BAINE

THE ARMY DOC'S SECRET WIFE

BY
CHARLOTTE HAWKES

MILLS & BOON

Karin Baine lives in Northern Ireland with her husband, two sons, and her out-of-control notebook collection. Her mother and her grandmother's vast collection of books inspired her love of reading and her dream of becoming a Mills & Boon author. Now she can tell people she has a *proper* job! You can follow Karin on Twitter, @karinbaine1, or visit her website for the latest news—karinbaine.com.

Born and raised on the Wirral Peninsula, England, **Charlotte Hawkes** is mum to two intrepid boys who love her to play building block games with them and who object loudly to the amount of time she spends on the computer. When she isn't writing—or building with blocks—she is company director for a small Anglo/French construction company. Charlotte loves to hear from readers, and you can contact her at her website: charlottehawkes.com.

THE DOCTOR'S
FORBIDDEN FLING

BY
KARIN BAINE

To Barbara

Hope you enjoy the book!

Love Karin
x

**MILLS &
BOON**

Published in Great Britain 2016
By Mills & Boon, an imprint of HarperCollins*Publishers*
1 London Bridge Street, London, SE1 9GF

© 2016 Karin Baine

ISBN: 978-0-263-91495-5

Our policy is to use papers that are natural, renewable and recyclable products and made from wood grown in sustainable forests. The logging and manufacturing processes conform to the legal environmental regulations of the country of origin.

Printed and bound in Spain
by CPI, Barcelona

Dear Reader,

There has been no greater loss in my life than that of my mother. It changed my life beyond recognition, but thankfully I had the love and support of my husband and family to help me through it.

When I pictured my heroine, Violet, going through that grief as a teenager I knew the kind of strong but damaged woman she'd become further down the line. It will take someone like cardiologist Nate, who has always known her better than anyone else, to reach behind that tough façade and help heal her wounded heart.

The best part of writing this book was my research into the Dempsey family's ancestral home. It was a good excuse to travel the country, taking afternoon tea in stately homes and imagining all the drama and romance going on behind closed doors.

I thoroughly recommend reading this with a cup of tea and a slice of cake—or two!

Karin xx

For Tammy. From one special snowflake to another.
Our field trip was epic! xx

Special thanks to my IT guru, Cherie,
who dragged this technophobe kicking and
screaming into the twenty-first century and
managed not to throat-punch me in the process!

As always, I couldn't have told this story without help.
A big hug to my editor, Laura, to Chellie, Susan
and Alison, and an extra squishy one for Amalie
for her author guidance too. xx

Books by Karin Baine

Mills & Boon Medical Romance

French Fling to Forever
A Kiss to Change Her Life

Visit the Author Profile page
at millsandboon.co.uk for more titles.

**Praise for
Karin Baine**

'The moment I picked up Karin Baine's debut medical
romance I knew I would not be disappointed with her
work. Poetic and descriptive writing, engaging dialogue,
thoroughly created characters and a tightly woven plot
propels *French Fling to Forever* into the must-read,
highly recommended level.'
—*Contemporary Romance Reviews*

'This is a wonderfully written book and one I could not
put down and had to finish. You will not be disappointed
in Karin Baine's writing.'
—*Goodreads* on
French Fling to Forever

CHAPTER ONE

In Violet Dempsey's experience the family room in a hospital department was where good news and hope came to die. It was in one of these seemingly innocuous side rooms she'd learned of her mother's fate and now she was waiting to hear of her father's too. He was fighting for his life in the cardiac care unit down the corridor while she was staring at the wall waiting for that ominous knock at the door.

She knew how crucial the first few hours after a heart attack were and she'd spent them trying to organise a flight back to Northern Ireland from London. Even that relatively short drive from Belfast to the Silent Valley Hospital in County Down had seemed like an eternity when her father was so close to death.

Their relationship was strained to say the least, since she refused to conform to her role as the daughter of an earl, but that didn't mean she didn't care. After watching her mother's struggle to fit into society life, Violet had simply decided to take her own path rather than the one her father had paved for her. They'd barely spoken since.

The tap on the door still made her jump even though she'd been expecting it. This was the reckoning. Life or death. Her stomach clenched as the door opened and the harbinger of impending doom swooped in. Except this was no po-faced stranger invading the already claustro-phobic space.

'Nate?'

He was taller, broader and better groomed than she remembered but she'd recognise that dimpled smile any-where. The hardest thing she'd ever had to do was walk away from that handsome face twelve years ago. She had no clue what he was doing here but he'd always had that knack of knowing exactly when she'd needed him.

'Hello, Violet. Or should I say *Lady* Violet? It's been a while.' He closed the door behind him and took the seat opposite her. It was so like Nate to plonk himself in the middle of her problems without a formal invitation.

'It has, but as I recall you were never one to stand on ceremony. Violet is just fine.' She hoped he was teasing her rather than trying to rile her when he understood bet-ter than anyone how much she hated her title.

They hadn't parted on the best of terms, on any terms really since she'd left without a word of explanation. Al-though he would have just cause to turn his back on her after what had happened, or even want a showdown to confront her about her behaviour, she was counting on him cutting her some slack in the circumstances. The old Nate would always have put her needs first and it was odd enough trying to come to terms with the fully formed man version of her childhood companion with-out finding out he might've completely changed charac-ter since their last meet too. Especially as she was just as attracted to Nate the adult.

The dark blond floppy hair had been tamed into a dapper short back and sides, the boyish face now defined with a sleek jawline and dusted with enough stubble to be fashionable and sexy. The son of Strachmore Castle's domestic staff had apparently swapped his hard-wearing flannel shirts for more tailored, expensive attire. He could easily have moved in her family's circle of friends now. If either of them had ever wanted that. One impulsive teenage kiss had effectively ended their friendship and sent Violet scurrying off to London before she committed to something that could never have worked.

Nate cleared his throat and she realised she'd been staring longer than an old friend ought to. The heat started to build in her cheeks as she recalled their last meet when they had ventured into new realms of their relationship.

'So... I assume you're here at your father's behest? He told me he was the one who phoned for the ambulance.' She steered the conversation, and her mind, away from dangerous territory. There was nothing like the thought of disapproving parents to pour cold water on certain heated moments that should be left in the past.

Nate leaned forward in the chair, forcing Violet to meet those hazel eyes she'd forgotten were so easy to get lost in. 'It was Dad who found him, but that's not why I'm here. This chat is of a more...professional nature. I'm a doctor here. Your father's cardiologist, in fact.'

She opened her mouth to tell him to stop messing about, then closed it again when she saw how serious he was. There was a ghost of a memory of the sister in charge mentioning a Dr Taylor but she'd never imagined this scenario in her wildest dreams.

'I didn't even know you'd gone to medical school,' she blurted out before she realised how bad that sounded. Cold. As though the spoilt brat with the privileged upbringing had swanned off and never looked back. That their time together had meant nothing to her.

It wasn't that she hadn't cared, or thought about him, over the years. Quite the opposite. She'd been afraid she'd become *too* interested in the life and times of Nate Taylor. For the sake of her new independent life away from her family's estate, she'd deemed it necessary to sever all ties with the one person who could've convinced her to stay.

'I mean, I keep contact with home to a bare minimum.' She wanted to justify her ignorance of his success in her absence. Of course she wasn't vain enough to imagine he'd spent all this time tending the grounds with his father, waiting for her return. She simply hadn't thought of him as being so…ambitious.

'I decided medicine would be a better paid, more respected profession compared to following family tradition into service.' There was that same old chip on the shoulder that had dominated conversation between them for hours in the old boathouse. Obviously their determination to branch away from the routes their parents had chosen for them had shaped both of their lives. For the better.

'You've certainly done well for yourself.' Not that it made a difference to her. Nate was a good person at heart, no matter what salary he brought home. The very reason she'd needed to create some distance between them. He'd deserved better than getting mixed up in the hell that was society life when her main goal had been to escape it.

'I'm sure I've surprised a few people round here by working my way out of a minimum-wage lifestyle. Now, I hear you've gone into nursing yourself so I'm sure you'll understand the seriousness of your father's condition.' He was definitely pricklier than she remembered and not above shaming her by displaying greater knowledge of her achievements than she had of his.

Violet's inner teenager with the schoolgirl crush couldn't help but wonder if he'd specifically sought out that information about her, or if his mother had simply been bending his ear. As the housekeeper at Strachmore, Mrs Taylor liked to keep her finger on the pulse, and that extended even as far as London. Every now and then Violet fielded prying phone calls from her father's well-meaning employee and, although she tried to keep details of her new life to a minimum, snippets of her successes and failures tended to slip through. The failures mostly related to relationships when the purpose of these communications was primarily to see if Violet had found herself a husband yet. Not in this lifetime. To her, marriage meant giving up everything you were to make another person happy and she'd seen first-hand the damage that could do. The fact she was here without her mother was proof enough it didn't work.

'Mental health is more my area of expertise.' Violet had felt so powerless after her mother had taken her own life she'd wanted to train in an area where she could make a real difference. It could be a challenging role at times but one that brought its own rewards. She was doing her best to emotionally save lives, if not physically like Nate.

That little nugget apparently was news to him, as his raised eyebrows finally gave an indication he felt something more than indifference to her.

'I guess that's…understandable and admirable.'

The compliment was hard won. Not that Violet had chosen her profession to gain brownie points from anyone, but Nate seemed reluctant to give her credit for getting off her backside to work instead of languishing in that house. It was another reminder they'd left those summer afternoons planning their escape far behind.

'Us kids done good.' For old times' sake she decided to praise them both for doing exactly what they'd said they would and breaking free from their parents' hold.

Although, her father would've been appalled by her

murder of the English language after paying for her elocution lessons. That was exactly why she'd relished doing it so frequently during her adolescence. Credit where it was due though, those hours spent improving her pronunciation had probably made her transition to London easier than sounding like a Northern Irish Eliza Doolittle. Perhaps she owed the old man some credit even if it had felt as if he was trying to force her to be someone she wasn't at the time.

'And yet here we are…'

She knew he was trying to get her to focus back on what was happening here and now but the words held a different meaning for her. No matter how hard she tried, she would never be able to completely separate her world from her father's.

'Okay, give it to me straight. Is he going to make it?' At some point she was going to have to apologise for running out on him but that would mean having to explain why she'd done it. It wasn't the time or place for that intense personal conversation, given the reason they were both here.

The scowl marring Nate's brow was further indication that her father was as bad as she'd feared. 'As you know, your father has suffered a myocardial infarction—a heart attack. He was unresponsive when the paramedics arrived and they had to resuscitate him on scene.'

It was no wonder Mr Taylor's message had been so fragmented and frantic. Technically, her father had died. She really didn't know how to feel about that. Since her mother had passed away Violet had resented him—for the way he'd treated her and for not being the one to have gone in her place. Now she was faced with the possibility of losing him too, things didn't seem so clear-cut. When you stripped away the bad memories and anger, he was still her father. She was starting to understand why her mother hadn't been able to simply walk away when the going got too rough. Sometimes having a conscience could be a terrible thing.

'A heart attack,' she repeated. Even though she'd heard it from others, coming from Nate somehow made it more real.

He nodded. 'It's been confirmed by blood tests. The increased levels of cardiac enzymes have indicated the presence of damage to the heart muscle. We'll continue taking bloods every six to eight hours as well as running electrocardiograms, ECGs, to monitor his heart's electrical activity and make sure there are no further complications. The next twenty-four to forty-eight hours will be crucial. Our first line of treatment would usually be emergency angioplasty to widen the arteries and allow easier blood flow to the heart. Unfortunately your father has proved…opposed to that idea.'

Nate didn't sugar-coat it. He didn't need to. They both knew she preferred straight talking to well-meaning platitudes. That way she wouldn't get hurt by hidden truths further down the line. Such as finding out her mother's overdose hadn't been as accidental as she'd first been led to believe.

It was a typical response from her father to ignore advice and insist he knew better than everyone. This time it could cause his own death instead of someone else's.

She closed her eyes and took a deep breath, batting away those old feelings flooding back and that helplessness at not being able to shake her father into facing facts. It hadn't worked for her mother so her chances after all this time were slim.

'Do we know what caused it?' She knew nothing of his lifestyle these days but she doubted his love of whiskey and cigars had diminished since she'd last seen him. He was a man who did as he pleased and sod the consequences.

'There's no family history of heart disease that we know of and no current health problems, I understand. We'll know more after we run a few tests. For now, our priority is limiting the damage to the heart.'

'I'm sorry I couldn't give the nurses any more information.' She grimaced, imagining the low opinion the staff were already forming of the absent daughter who couldn't give them any insight into her own father.

'It's all right. I understand things have been…tricky between you both. We've pieced together what we could in the meantime.'

No doubt the Taylors' close relationship with her father had played a part in gathering that information. Violet didn't begrudge the bond the families had, but it sometimes made her feel inadequate, superfluous to requirements. Indeed, no one had ever needed her until now. Even now she wasn't sure how her presence would be received by either side of the class divide.

'Can I see him?' No matter how fractured their relationship had been since her mother's death, or how frustrating he was, he was the only family she had left. Just because she wasn't the daughter he wanted didn't mean she'd stopped caring about him. It simply made it more difficult.

Nate bounced back up onto his feet. 'I might be able to pull a few strings and get you a couple of minutes with him.'

The way he'd been reacting to her she was surprised he was willing to do anything other than list the facts of her father's condition. She figured this one must be for old times' sake—the days before things had got complicated and she'd made him despise her.

Determined to make the most of this breakthrough, she followed him into CCU, bobbing up and down like a meerkat keeping watch for predators as she tried to locate the patient. Nate strode through the ward with an air of confidence and authority she'd never seen in him before. It suited him. She had a sense of pride in him as patients and staff alike sat up straighter as he walked by. Finally people other than her had realised his worth in this world.

She zoned out the blue flashes of nurses zipping by and the hospital beds occupied by ill strangers to hone in on her father. He was in the top left-hand corner of the room, by the window. At least he'd only have one immediate neighbour to complain about when he was back to his grouchy self. The Earl Dempsey would not be happy to find himself on an NHS ward surrounded by the great unwashed when he woke instead of some private hospital he'd happily pay through the nose for. Tough. When all was said and done, Nate and his colleagues were all that was keeping him alive.

'He's a little out of it at the moment due to the morphine we've given him to reduce the pain.' Nate led her to the bedside and for the first time in her life Violet felt sorry for her father. The man who'd virtually driven her mother to death in the pursuit of gaining a higher status in society now looked like any other old man lying there in his hospital gown, his white hair matted to his head and tubes and wires covering every inch of him.

She couldn't miss the monitors charting his vital signs, the IVs pumping life-saving drugs into his system, or the oxygen mask keeping him breathing, but she didn't cry. Nate's shoulder was safe from her tears these days. That display of emotion was reserved for the privacy of her own home where no one could witness her weakness. There was no way she was going to end up like her vulnerable mother, letting others take advantage of her. She was stronger than that. She'd had to be.

'What are his chances?' Violet was so matter-of-fact, so devoid of emotion, Nate was concerned she might be in shock and he'd have to treat her too. Then this night really would be complete.

Until now, he'd only seen her act this coldly once before. He knew she hadn't visited home since leaving for university but this was still her father lying here on the brink of death. The girl he'd grown up with had years of fear and hurt built up inside her because of this man, whether she loved him or not. There ought to be some sort of reaction to finding he could die without ever resolving the past.

He'd held back from saying those things that had sprung to mind the minute he'd known she was in the building, all of them prefaced with 'why?'. He'd had no choice but to pick himself back up and get on with life after her disappearing act but that didn't mean he'd stopped asking himself what he'd done to drive her away.

Seeing her again brought conflicting emotions to the fore. That broken-hearted teenager who still haunted his relationships would probably always hold a candle for her but with that came the hurt of her abandonment and that dismissal of his feelings for her.

Instead of acknowledging his declaration of love for her, or reciprocating, she'd walked away and refused to see him again before she'd left for London. It had been the only time she hadn't turned to him for advice, or confided her plans. The only time she'd turned her back on him instead of leaning on him for support. Although her rejection had cut him deeply, he'd tried to turn it into a positive. If he'd carried on in that vein, as an emotional crutch for her, he would've remained stagnant at Strachmore in his parents' footsteps. They'd given the best years of their lives to the running of the castle, sacrificing everything else in their loyalty to the Dempseys.

Despite his father's view that they owed the family some sort of non-existent debt that included tying the next generation of Taylors to the Earl's needs, Nate had sworn not to get drawn into that trap. His parents might have conceded some of their freedom to maintain their positions but he was pretty sure sacrificing their firstborn hadn't been included in the terms and conditions of their contracts. This was his life, and he'd had ambitions beyond the Strachmore estate.

Violet had been the one flaw in that plan. He'd probably have given up all of his hopes and dreams to be with her. It still hadn't been enough. *He* hadn't been enough. Her actions had been confirmation he needed to do something with his life beyond the estate and he owed her for giving him that final push. That was partly why he'd insisted on speaking to her himself tonight.

He'd often imagined the moment their paths would cross again. Every medical exam he'd taken and passed with flying colours had been his way of getting his own back, proof he had been worthy of her after all. He mightn't have been born into money but with hard work he'd earned it, along with a good reputation. She would've seen that for herself if she'd shown any faith in him and stuck around.

There were many points in his career where he'd been spurred on with the thought of being able to flaunt his success some day. As if she were a loser in a game show and he were showing her what she could have won. If money and status had been all that mattered to her when he'd only had love to give, he knew she'd be kicking herself to find out he had it all now.

He'd be lying if he said he wasn't curious as to how the years had treated her too. If her mother's death had changed her emotionally, life in London had certainly transformed her physically. Although she'd hate it, her noble heritage shone through in every step she took. The once waist-length raven hair was now styled in a sleek bob, and her skinny frame, although still slender, definitely had curves in all the right places. She was every inch the sophisticated woman about town even in her casual butt-hugging jeans and silky polka-dot blouse. However, her new look and altered attitude couldn't hide the real Violet from him. Those blue eyes, the colour of a stormy winter's night, were as troubled as ever and he couldn't bring himself to confront her about the past when she was already in such turmoil.

It could wait until they were both ready to talk and stop pretending seeing each other wasn't a big deal. She might've moved on, consigned everything they'd had together to the past, but he still needed an explanation as to why she'd turned her back on him so he could close that chapter. Violet's rejection had marked the one failure in his life and that wasn't something he found easy to live with.

Although he wanted answers, for now he'd have to put his personal feelings aside and treat her as he would any family member of a critical patient. In the old days he wouldn't have thought twice about throwing his arms around her and giving her a much-needed hug, but they weren't here together through choice. Neither were they angsty teenagers united in rebellion against their parents. They were adults, virtual strangers who knew nothing of each other's lives. He chose a clinical approach to appease this edgier version of the girl he once knew and try to maintain some sort of professional distance from the case.

After dealing with the Earl, he had a renewed appreciation for what Violet and her mother had contended with. The frustration at not being able to do his job and perform the angioplasty because of his patient's non-compliance had made him want to scream. In some ways he understood Violet's decision to leave him to his own devices; it was easier than standing by and watching him self-destruct. Even in the jaws of death he thought he thought he knew better than those around him. As if he imagined continued denial would somehow defy fate.

'He's not out of danger yet but he is in the best place. We've administered clot-busting drugs quite early so it should restore the blood flow and reduce the damage. In my experience, the earlier we treat the patient after a heart attack, the better chance of survival they have.' Although he performed this procedure day after day, it was never routine. Every patient was individual, reacted differently to medication, suffered varying degrees of muscle damage and experienced all sorts of complications on the road to recovery. All he could do was fight with all the drugs and technology he had available to him and the rest was up to fate, or the stubbornness of the patient.

'I don't wish him any harm, you know. Despite everything. I'm not heartless.' Violet leaned across the bed and for a split second Nate thought she was going to reach out to her father. At the last second she withdrew again.

'I know. I'm sure he knows it too.' He might have had his doubts about that when she'd abandoned her life here with him in it, but she'd proved that rumour wrong by simply being here. Clearly she still cared for her father, and Nate had no doubt somewhere deep down the feeling was mutual. The trouble was they were both too stubborn to make the first move on building that bridge. He'd seen how the loss of her mother had affected Violet and he dearly hoped there was still time for her to connect with her father, to get closure if nothing else.

Nate had had his own parental issues but he still checked in with them on a regular basis. He just made sure he kept enough distance to ensure they didn't interfere in his life and he didn't get roped into drama at Strachmore. Until now.

The steady blip of the monitors suddenly flatlined as the Earl's heart rate dropped. Nate swung into action as the alarm rang out to summon the crash team. A second arrest was always a possibility when patients were at their most vulnerable after the first. Especially when they'd refused life-saving treatment. In Nate's head he'd thought bringing Violet in could somehow prevent the worst from happening. Instead, she was here to witness it for herself.

'Violet, I'm going to have to ask you to leave.' He motioned for help to get her out of here. Saving a man's life wasn't as pretty as they made out in the movies and he certainly didn't want family members in the audience for the performance.

'Nate?' She didn't have to say anything else. The trembling bottom lip caught between her teeth and wide eyes expressed her plea eloquently enough.

'I'll do everything I can. I promise.' He was forced to block out that haunting image of her silently begging him to save her father so he could focus on the job at hand. He didn't want to be the one to have to deliver that earth-shattering news to her for a second time.

Sweat beaded on his forehead as he charged the defibrillator that had been wheeled to the bedside.

'Stand clear.'

The first shock Nate administered to try and kick-start the heart again was for the Earl, and Violet, and a second chance for their father-daughter relationship. He started CPR, thinking of his own parents and their ties to this man with every chest compression.

So much for not wanting anyone relying on him. Now both of their families were depending on him to save the day. And a life.

CHAPTER TWO

NATE LEANING OVER the bed, pumping her father's chest, was the last thing Violet saw before the ward doors swung shut, closing her out of her father's struggle for life. A nurse steered her back towards the cell she'd vacated only minutes earlier for another interminable wait. With her pulse racing, her insides knotted, she didn't have it in her to resist a second incarceration.

There was nothing she could do but take a seat in her still-warm chair. Everything was in Nate's hands now. Literally. She trusted his word to do his utmost to save his patient; he'd never let her down before. It had been the other way around. When he'd kissed her, told her he loved her, she'd run away rather than confess she felt the same. It was the one thing she couldn't give him, dared not give him, when she'd watched love destroy her mother.

She admired Nate's professionalism after the way she'd left things with him. There was an aloofness about him she wasn't used to, but she guessed she'd been the one who'd created that by going to London without telling him why. Perhaps it was water under the bridge for him and not something he was keen to be reminded of. In fairness, she probably deserved a lot worse than the cold shoulder and she didn't think she'd be quite so civilised if the situation had been reversed. Whatever his thoughts on seeing her, she was grateful to him for not calling her out on what had happened. She didn't want to deal with any more emotional fallout today. For someone who did her best to keep her feelings on lockdown, this had been a doozy of a day already and she couldn't face any more demons from her past.

Yet, here she was relying on him the same way she had every time her parents had fought, feeling sorry for herself and wondering what the future held. This time her thoughts were consumed with becoming an orphan at the age of thirty instead of being married off to another family who valued reputation above all else.

There was a tentative knock on the door and the same nurse appeared with a tea tray. 'I thought you could do with a cuppa.'

'Thanks.' Violet accepted the offering with a forced smile. Despite the fact she hadn't eaten anything since receiving that fateful telephone call, her stomach was in too much turmoil for her to even face the plain biscuits presented to her with the tea.

'You need something to keep your strength up. You'll be no use to your father if you faint from hunger.'

Violet honestly didn't know what use she'd be to her father whether she was conscious or not, but her new shadow stood waiting and watching until she took a nibble at a biscuit and a sip of tea. Only then, her care of duty fulfilled, did the nurse leave her alone again.

The next time the door opened some time later, it was Nate who entered. She told herself the little flip her heart did was in anticipation of finding out her father's fate. It had absolutely nothing to do with the sight of Dr Taylor with his shirt sleeves rolled up and his perfectly groomed hair now ruffled and unkempt as if he'd just got out of bed. It was clear neither he nor her father had had an easy time of it.

'We got him back.' Nate immediately ended her suspense and she let go of the breath she'd been holding since he walked in.

'Thank you.' Her voice was nothing more than a whisper, her throat burning from the tears she couldn't shed. Until today she hadn't realised how much it meant to her to know she wasn't alone in the world.

'We'll keep him under close observation. A second arrest was always a possibility after the stress his heart has been under today but he's stable now.'

Nate's dedication was a blessing. Especially when her father had treated him with nothing but disdain when they were growing up. He thought associating with those below one's station was degrading and it had been to blame for Violet's 'rebellion'. In hindsight, she wondered if he'd seen how dangerously close they'd come to having a proper relationship and that had coloured his view of their friendship. Nate would never have lived up to her father's idea of a noble son-in-law to carry on his title. Not that he would've wanted it either. He hated Strachmore as much as she did. In the end the Earl's campaign to keep them separated had been a wasted exercise on his part. Violet had no intention of settling down with anyone, whether she loved them or not.

'Thanks for keeping me in the loop. I know you're probably needed elsewhere.' She was under no illusion that this particular cardiologist was assigned to her only. He'd undoubtedly done her a huge favour by personally informing her of her father's condition. For reasons known only to him when he'd made it clear he hadn't forgiven her for her sins.

'Do you need me to order you a taxi? Is there somewhere you need to be?' He eyed her small *I-left-in-a-hurry* luggage, probably keen to ship her out of his territory as soon as possible.

She'd barely packed enough for more than tonight, but that had been out of sheer panic rather than optimism.

'I'm fine here for the night if that's allowed? I can pull a couple of chairs together.' She hadn't thought beyond getting here before it was too late, never mind overnight accommodation. Since it was still touch and go, her personal discomfort didn't seem that important.

'You can't sleep here. I'm sure you're exhausted.'

There was a pause and a heavy sigh before he continued. 'I'll give you a lift back to Strachmore and get the keys from my mum to let you in.'

Nate sounded resigned to homing her for the night, as if she were a stray dog he'd picked up on the side of the road and was stuck with until help arrived. This was how things had always been between them—Nate finding solutions to problems of her own making. Except back then he'd always seemed to enjoy coming to her rescue.

'Honestly, I don't want to hold you back any longer. I'm sure you have other patients to see and this means I'm close if anything happens during the night.' If she was honest she wasn't sure her family home would be any more inviting than this windowless broom cupboard.

Nate dipped his head, looking decidedly sheepish. 'My shift finished hours ago. I'm all yours.'

A shiver played across her skin, teasing every tiny hair to attention. It was her guilt at keeping him at his post through some misplaced sense of loyalty manifesting. Definitely not a physical reaction to him offering herself up to her.

'I can't ask you to—'

'You didn't. I'm volunteering.' He was already grabbing her bag and robbing her of her refusal even though he made his offer sound as if he'd had no other choice.

He paused by the door and fixed her with those soul-reaching eyes. 'The night staff will phone you, and me, if there's any change. I'll get you back here in a flash if it comes to it.'

'Only if you're sure?' She'd finally run out of excuses not to go home.

Violet waited in the car while he paid his parents a visit. She hoped it was quick. The longer they were travelling companions with this elephant from the past, the more likely they were going to have to acknowledge it. She wasn't ready to face that, or the Taylors. Not that she held any ill will against the pair—after all, they were the ones who kept this place running—but she was tired and definitely not in the mood for grand reunions or lectures. Nate had left the engine running and the heater on so he clearly didn't intend to loiter either. He was probably every bit as eager as she was to put today behind him.

She shifted in the leather bucket seat, which was marginally more comfortable than the hospital waiting chairs. The mode of transport she was being chauffeured around the countryside in was still something of a shock to her system. To see the boy who'd spent his summers working umpteen jobs to save cash had splashed out on a bright red sports car was more surprising than if he'd turned up on an ancient motorbike and sidecar. It was almost as though he was sticking two fingers up at everyone who'd treated him as a second-class citizen in his youth and told him he'd never amount to anything beyond Strachmore. Ironically, the youngest member of the Dempsey family relied on public transport to get her from A to B. It was more practical for city life but it also had the added bonus of ticking off her father.

She watched Nate stride back to the car in the muted evening light. He could easily pass as the master of the big house now he'd swapped his ripped jeans for those tailored suits. Although, he would probably look good in anything. Or nothing.

Whoa!

Those teenage hormones she'd thought she'd left behind long ago had apparently resurfaced and mutated into adult ones. It had been a long, emotional day and clearly she was misinterpreting his reluctant kindness for something…sexier.

She cleared her throat as he opened the car door and climbed back into the driver's seat. If only she could clear her mind of the images she'd planted there as easily. Her wayward thoughts weren't helped by the fact his tall frame was packed so tightly into the car, his thighs were almost touching hers.

'Mum's in a tizzy about not having the place cleaned for your arrival. I assured her I'd roll the red carpet out for you myself but we'd best get out of here before we run into a cleaning mob brandishing mops and dusters.'

Violet ignored the barb, simply grateful he'd run interference for her, when Mrs Taylor was probably bursting with questions for her. 'I'm sure the house is as spotless as ever with your mother at the helm. I only wish I could clone her and take her back to London with me.'

Unlike Strachmore Castle, her poky flat was never going to make the cover of any magazines but she worked hard to pay the rent. That meant more to her than gleaming silver and polished marble floors ever would.

Nate threw the car into reverse and rested his arm along the back of her seat as he kept watch out of the back window. The smell of soap and hard-working doctor enveloped her and for a moment she was tempted to snuggle into his solid chest. He could give her comfort and a whole lot besides. Exactly why she should stick to the idea of him as only a friend, or her father's doctor, and not someone who'd taken the lead role in her first erotic imaginings.

'Do you know how long you'll be staying? I mean, is someone holding the fort for you while you're here?' He trained his eyes back on the dark road leading from the cottage up to the main house, so Violet couldn't tell if he was fishing for personal info or making polite conversation.

'I'll stay as long as I'm needed. I have a lot of personal leave I can use.' She preferred to keep busy with work rather than take duvet days where she had nothing to do but dwell on things beyond her control. It wasn't the first time her superiors had warned her of possible burnout if she didn't take a break from her caseload so they'd be only too happy for her to take some time off.

'If you need anything my parents will be here to help.'

He was leaving himself out of the equation but it was a long time since Violet had relied on anyone having her back. For good reason. She'd needed to learn to stand on her own two feet to make herself stronger than her mother had been.

'Thank you. I know you've gone out of your way to help me and I wouldn't want to get your other half offside by holding you hostage to my problems.' Okay, she *was* fishing. He'd been her first crush, her first kiss, it was only natural that this curious cat was wrestling a green-eyed monster at the thought of him going home to another woman. One who wasn't afraid to make compromises.

'There's no danger of that. I'm a confirmed bachelor.'

Those words had the same effect as if he'd thrown a bucket of ice-cold water over her as she jumped from one conclusion to another. She'd been so caught up in her feelings for him she'd never contemplated how much his could have changed for her, or for women in general. Suddenly his new grooming regime started to take on a whole new meaning. 'You're not—'

'No, I'm not gay, Violet. I thought you of all people would realise I'm attracted to women.' He turned and, though Violet couldn't see his face clearly in the dim interior, she imagined he was looking at her lips, remembering *that* kiss too.

She'd managed to block it out for over a decade but here, so close to him again, it was all she could think about. That first tentative exploration of each other had soon given way to a raw passion she hadn't experienced since. These days she approached any romantic entanglements with a certain degree of cynicism and caution, which meant she was always holding back. In that moment with Nate's lips on hers she'd given no thought to consequence or complications that could arise. That had come later when she'd tried to imagine a future together and failed. He didn't belong in her world and vice versa. Ironically they seemed to have traded places anyway.

As the stately home loomed into view of the car headlights, the butterflies in her stomach turned kamikaze, dive-bombing her insides until there was a chance she might hurl over the expensive leather upholstery. At least it was wipe-clean.

'Home sweet home.' Nate's attempt at humour was a welcome distraction from the memories assaulting her from the second the stone pillars of the eighteenth-century house came into view.

Her father, spit forming at the corners of his mouth when she defied him by sneaking out to a concert with Nate.

Violet hiding in the old servants' quarters when she was supposed to be dining with the Montgomery family, whose son had been deemed a suitable match for her at the age of seventeen.

The empty pill bottle by her mother's bedside.

Dark humour was definitely the cure for dark memories.

'In case you can't see it, I'm giving you the death stare.'

Nate gave a hearty chuckle, letting the serious doctor mask slip for a glimpse of her old friend. 'Nostrils flaring, mouth puckered up like you've just licked a lemon, eyes narrowed to mere slits—I can picture it now.'

Violet flattened her lips back into a thin line with a huff. She could hear the smugness in his voice that he still knew her better than anyone even after all of this time.

They pulled up into the driveway and the sound of the handbrake meant there was no more stalling.

'Thanks for everything. I can let myself in.'

'No can do. I told you I'm under instruction to escort Lady Violet inside her ancestral home. Don't forget, under different circumstances I could've ended up as your official errand boy.'

He was being facetious. Violet knew he would never have played the skivvy any more than she would've been the boss lady. Still, it conjured up more interesting images if they'd chosen different paths.

She let out a long sigh and admitted defeat. Having a surly Nate here was infinitely more bearable than having Mrs Taylor fussing around her, or setting foot back inside alone. It was one thing going home to an empty flat at night but an entirely different game coming back here where the ghosts of her past roamed the hallways.

Nate really needed to work on that keeping-at-arm's-length ethos where relationships were concerned. He'd thought he'd built up a tolerance to all things Dempsey since his teenage heartbreak. One glimpse of those big blue eyes and he was taking on the duties of the whole domestic staff who'd once resided here—the chauffeur, the butler and housekeeper all rolled into one. He told himself his promise to light a fire and see her settled in was the only way to keep his parents at bay and Violet's discomfort to a minimum. They meant well, their subservient role so deeply ingrained in them the very thought of Lady Violet returning to a cold, empty house brought them out in a cold sweat. He knew this would be difficult enough for her without an audience and he still had a duty of care via her father.

Despite their history, or possibly because of the one they'd had pre-kiss, he still felt an obligation to help her. Perhaps he wasn't as far removed from his heritage as he liked to think. He'd really been the only one Violet had had to turn to when things had got rough and it would be callous for him to abandon her now for the sake of his own pride. He simply hadn't been able to leave her for the night in that waiting room, expecting her to bed down where she stood. In a fit of madness he'd even briefly contemplated taking her back to his house rather than expect her to face this place alone.

Ultimately he'd done enough damage to his relationship boundaries already. She was only back in the country five minutes and he'd already landed himself firmly in the friend zone. Not a position he wanted to be in with any beautiful woman. Especially one he already had an emotional history with. One who'd dumped him without a second thought. Then there was the double blow to his ego with the whole gay thing. He knew one teenage fumble probably hadn't made a long-lasting impact on her but he'd assumed it had been enough to define his sexuality.

Now he'd slipped back into a supporting role there was no way he was ever going to win top billing as Violet's leading man. If he'd once imagined taking her back into his arms and replacing that inexperienced make-out session with a more confident approach to recover his male pride, he'd stuffed up the minute he'd insisted on staying to talk to her about her father. Friends or lovers—there was no in between for him when it came to the women in his life. He didn't even want to peek inside people's personal baggage, never mind help them unpack it, and yet that was exactly what he was doing now. The pressure was on him more than ever to save his patient and return everyone back to their normal status quo. As soon as he'd done the gentlemanly thing and seen her settled in, he could walk away with a clear conscience. He'd proved the better person by not exacting revenge.

'You put the kettle on and I'll get the fire started.' He opened the heavy front door with a reverence the stately home deserved even if the current owner didn't. It was a beautiful building, full of history and wonder. Unfortunately it also held negative connotations for those entering it tonight. While Violet had been the princess held captive in the tower, he'd very much been the lowly serf kept in his place by his master. He'd dealt with a lot of those issues through hard work and determination but he couldn't help feeling Violet still had to face hers. Although he still had an axe of his own to grind with her, he wasn't totally unsympathetic. It was best he try to make this as normal as possible for her. As if they were walking into any other family home and not the country pile of her ancestors. Easier said than done when there was a huge chandelier dominating the space in front of them.

'We do have modern-day conveniences like central heating.' She was still resisting his attempts to phase her into her surroundings gradually with his assistance, but he was used to dealing with difficult patients and bolshie family members.

She was more defensive than he remembered. He guessed years of independent living had toughened her up. A definite plus given his aversion to needy people outside the workplace.

'And kettles?'

It amused him to watch her flounce away the way she used to when his teasing went too far. It was further proof her fiery spirit was very much alive. She was going to need it to see her through the next days, whatever they held.

'Milk, no sugar,' he called after her as he headed for the study.

It was the closest and smallest room on the ground floor, and easier to heat. The pale blue walls and ornate white ceiling of the entrance hall were pretty and in keeping with the period pieces dotted throughout but they didn't make the cool atmosphere any more inviting. Okay, they had no practical need for a fire but there was something homely about a real fire. It was cosy and welcoming, something this house was sadly lacking.

He could sense the disapproving stares of past earls staring down at him from the walls as he trespassed into the inner sanctum. They all had the same stern features of Samuel Dempsey. Nate wondered if not smiling was another one of the house rules Violet had deigned to disobey. Ruling with an iron fist might have worked in the olden days but, as far as he'd seen, all it had succeeded in doing in recent times was shatter the family.

'Is this where they found him?'

He hadn't heard Violet enter the room as he'd knelt to set the fire in the hearth. It wasn't until he turned around again that he understood why she'd sounded so pained.

Her father's papers littered the mahogany and brass writing desk and spilled onto the floor, his chair toppled over in the corner of the room with a whiskey tumbler lying next to it—the contents of which had seeped into the antique rug long ago.

'I'm so sorry, Violet. I had no idea. We can move into the drawing room and I'll get this tidied up.' Regardless of the painful history between them, he would never have purposely exposed her to this scene. He took the rattling cups and saucers from her shaking hands before she slopped the tea on the expensive furnishings too.

'It's all right. It was just a shock.' She righted the heavy chair and Nate set down the tea things so he could help.

They both bent down to reach for the upturned glass at the same time, Violet's bracelet clinking against it in the process. He reached for her wrist, curiosity getting the better of common sense.

'Is this the one I bought you?' It was only a cheap turquoise bead bracelet with a dainty seahorse charm hanging from it. So unlike the diamonds and pearls her mother had favoured on occasion. He was surprised it had stood the test of time, even more so to find she still wore it.

A trace of a smile lifted the corners of her mouth. 'Yes. From the day at the aquarium.'

The day things had changed between them for ever.

'You were fascinated by those damn seahorses.'

She'd stood for ages watching them as if she'd found

her peace there and he'd wanted her to have a souvenir of that summer afternoon together. He hadn't known it would be their last.

'They're just so…serene. I envy the simplicity of their life. And, of course, it's the male who gives birth. The female seahorse has a much freer life than most women, she transfers her eggs and goes back to her own place— the onus isn't on her to carry on the family line.' It was a tragic narrative of Violet's childhood when she'd been jealous of a fragile species trapped in a tank. At least now she was free of some of her burden even if it had cost Nate a piece of his heart in the process.

He flicked the charm up with his thumb so it rested on his nail. So small, so inexpensive, so evocative. If that day had meant nothing to her, if he'd meant nothing to her, why would she still be attached to it now? He felt her pulse quicken beneath him, met her eyes with his, and they were back in that bubble where nothing mattered except the chemistry.

He didn't know who'd leaned closer to whom but suddenly they were no more than a breath away from kissing. Violet's eyes fluttered shut, her lips were parted and waiting for him. There was nothing he wanted more in that moment than to give into temptation. Despite how much she'd hurt him in the past, he'd wanted to do this the minute he'd seen her again but this was typical Violet behaviour. She couldn't drop him and pick him up when the mood took her. Not any more. Especially when she still hadn't done him the courtesy of an apology or an explanation, never mind simply acknowledging what she'd done to him.

Unfortunately physical attraction couldn't always override common sense. A kiss was much more than that when it was with your first love, the woman who'd broken your heart without a backward glance.

He let go of her wrist and stepped away from temptation. As he began to collect his thoughts away from her lips, the Earl's collection of antique clocks chimed the late hour and sounded the death knell for this...whatever the hell it was.

When he didn't swoop in and ravage her, Violet was afraid to open her eyes and face him. She'd done it again—gone with her heart instead of her head. Thank goodness one of them had been thinking clearly this time. She shuddered at how close she'd come to making another monumental mistake when she'd yet to address the last one she'd made with Nate. Her world was complicated enough now without resurrecting old emotions like zombies wandering through her life with no real purpose except causing eternal misery for everyone in their path. She needed to remember that every time she was tempted to lose herself in his embrace, that one place she was able to forget her troubles.

In her defence she'd been under a lot of pressure today and Nate had been her one source of comfort, the only familiar thing from home that didn't make her want to run screaming. Even in his current indifferent state. She blamed her faux pas entirely on stress. Apparently making moves on hot doctors was a side effect of tangled emotions no one had warned her about. They hadn't covered that in her course. Then again, Nate was the professional—he should've known he was in danger simply by being in the room with her.

In fact, he seemed to have found the best treatment for her particular case by continuing to pick up the de-

bris around them and ignoring the latest addition to the
elephant herd now parading around the room.

'No wonder Mum was so frantic about getting this
place tidied up before you set foot inside. I guess they
just locked up the house once the ambulance left.' Nate
in cleaning mode was as efficient as his mother and Violet decided to follow his lead. Time and distance hadn't
made this any more feasible.

They worked quietly together, sifting her father's correspondence into manageable piles. The quicker they got
this sorted, the easier it would make it for Nate to leave.
She knew him well enough to know he'd see this out
until the end, when he'd fulfilled his obligation to her
and his parents.

'Violet?' After some time he drew her attention to a
stack of letters headed with bold red lettering.

'Mmm?'

'These are all bills. Most of them final demands.'

'Let me see.' She snatched a few from his grasp and
confirmed it. All correspondence, most of it threatening
action against him, was leading to the conclusion her father was in dire financial trouble.

She collapsed into the chair with such force she almost toppled it over again. This was too much for her
to handle on top of everything else today. Somehow she
was going to have to fix this. She just had no idea how.

'You had no clue this was going on?' Nate spoke softly,
as if he was afraid of spooking her even more.

The façade her father had presented to the world all
these years had duped many into thinking their fortune
was never ending. She'd known differently.

'The place has been leaking money for years but I
didn't know things were this bad.' Her father's spending and refusal to admit they were in trouble had been

the source of many an argument in the house before her mother died. The worry and uncertainty about the future had certainly contributed to her mother's fragile state of mind but he hadn't taken any responsibility then and he wasn't likely to do so now.

'What? There's no magical pot of gold hidden under the floorboards?' Nate pretended to be surprised the place didn't run by reputation and superiority complexes alone.

'Unfortunately not.' She lifted the stack of bills and slammed them back down on the table. This wasn't his problem. Hell, it wasn't even hers.

Whatever happened to her father, Violet knew she was going to have to be the one to sort this out. She should have known better than to come back. It had been inevitable that she'd get sucked back into her father's delusions of grandeur and the repercussions of stark reality. Perhaps she should have done as she was told at seventeen and agreed to marry Lord Montgomery's son. At least she might've been in a position now to help financially, possibly with her mother still around too.

This new discovery threatened to undo all the progress she'd made in her new life. Nothing had changed in her absence, she'd simply avoided dealing with it. She was back to being that frightened girl, lonely and overwhelmed by the burden her father had put upon her.

She wanted to confront him, scream and cry, and walk away for ever. Now she could do none of those things. She was stuck here. Again.

'I'll worry about these tomorrow, as soon as I know he's made it through the night. Then I might go up there and kill him myself.'

Nate arched an eyebrow at her with a smirk. 'Now, I know you don't mean that. I told you, there's help available. It's a shame you Dempseys are too damn stubborn for your own good. You don't have to do this on your own.'

Deep down she knew he was talking about his parents or some other official source of financial advice but it gave her more comfort to imagine he was still in her corner. 'You're the only person who was ever there for me, you know.'

Reuniting with Nate was the only light in this darkness and she wanted to run towards the safety she knew was there. For a little while she didn't want to think about tomorrow, or the next day, or the next. He could help her forget, take her to that happy place away from all of this mess. What was one more mistake when her life was crumbling around her? All she had to do was convince him, and herself, this wasn't the big deal it had been when they were teenagers.

Suddenly she was tired of being strong, of bearing the weight of Strachmore on her shoulders alone.

'Stay with me tonight, Nate.'

Nate's body reacted to the invitation before his brain kicked in and listed all the reasons this was a bad idea. He ignored all parts of him straining to make the decision for him, knowing Violet would regret this in the morning, as he would. For altogether different reasons. This was his chance to exorcise that painful rejection for good, but he knew her well enough to understand what this was really about. Her way of dealing with difficult matters had always been to divert her attention elsewhere, put off tackling the hard stuff for as long as possible. Violet was the Queen of Procrastination and he'd always been the Fool, keeping her entertained and distracting her from the hardships within the castle walls.

Not any more. He'd made certain he was King of his own castle since those days.

'I think it would be better if I went home.'

She'd let him know he wasn't good enough for her before and he wasn't going to be the consolation prize now.

She stood up so she was close enough to invade his personal space and trailed a fingertip down the front of his shirt. 'Don't tell me you haven't thought about this, about us—'

She didn't need to say any more. He was already picturing them together in bed, giving into that chemistry he'd never been able to forget.

He took a deep breath to purify his thoughts and make sense of hers. She'd taken an emotional battering today and he'd never take advantage of her when she was so vulnerable. Lord knew he wanted her and it was an ego boost to know it was reciprocated this time but it didn't change circumstances. *Friend or lover?* He reminded himself he couldn't be both and remain sane. He'd breached the professional boundary long ago and only friendship had remained before he'd ended up in no-man's land—a minefield he had to tiptoe through, full of the sort of explosive situations he'd happily avoided since he was nineteen.

'We're both adults, single, with no illusions this would be anything more than sex. I need the distraction.' It was confirmation of exactly where he stood with her and that wasn't any place of importance. She might as well have been hiring an escort for the evening for all the emotional significance she afforded him.

Normally that kind of detachment wasn't a problem. In fact he welcomed it. It stopped things becoming too messy. However Violet wasn't a faceless one-night stand. Uncomplicated sex should never involve the woman whose rejection had made you so cynical about relationships in the first place.

'Unfortunately, sharing a bed is not the modern-day equivalent of hanging out in the boathouse pretending real life isn't happening around us.' His heavy dose of honesty transformed Violet's coquettish eye-fluttering into a wide-eyed, open-mouthed, I've-just-been-slapped-in-the-face expression.

He was pretty sure he'd worn that same look once before and he took no satisfaction in being the one to cause it this time.

'You're right. I don't know what the hell I was thinking.'

He could see the shame clouding her eyes already. That wasn't what he wanted either.

'There's nothing I'd enjoy more than taking you to bed right now, but I think it would be a mistake. For both of us. Get some sleep and I'll see you in the morning.' He knew she didn't want to be alone, but he didn't intend falling into that old pattern of being at her beck and call again. He'd invested too much in that before and paid the consequences.

'You always were the sensible one.' She gave him a wobbly smile and Nate knew he had to get out of here before the tears really did fall. When she finally did give into the real emotions she was trying to hide from, he knew he'd never be able to leave her.

'And you always were the impulsive one.' He'd lost count of the number of times he'd had to talk her out of doing something stupid—like running away or sabotaging her father's dinner parties with laxatives. It was probably the reason she hadn't confided in him about moving to London. She hadn't wanted to be talked out of it.

This proposition was most likely a cry for help rather than an unyielding need to have him in her bed, but it didn't make it any easier to resist.

'Goodnight, Violet.'

He wondered if she'd ever regretted walking away as much as he did now.

CHAPTER THREE

THE TROUBLE WITH the countryside was the quiet. There was no traffic noise to drown out Violet's thoughts and nowhere to go to escape her shame. She'd spent most of the night replaying the moment she'd made a complete fool of herself with Nate. Lord knew what he thought of her throwing herself at him like some nympho desperate for a quick lay. She shuddered, the cringe factor at an all-time high as she recalled the look of disgust on his face as he rejected her advances. All he'd done was show her some kindness, more than she deserved, and she'd implied she was only interested in his body. Nothing could be further from the truth. Well, okay, his body had been on her mind since she'd first seen him suited and booted but she'd needed him for so much more than that. She'd tried to use sex to get him to stay when she was really yearning for his company.

After one bombshell too many, her common sense had been blown to pieces. There was no other logical explanation for her behaviour last night. These past years of being so strong, so independent had skewed her idea of friendship until she'd seen it as a weakness. Until yesterday, when Nate had reminded her how good it was to have someone in your corner fighting your battles with you. In her messed-up head, sleeping with Nate had seemed like the only way to recapture that fantasy world they'd had when they were young but he'd called her on it. She had no right to expect anything from him when she'd been the one to burst that bubble in the first place. What had been the point of walking away then if she was simply going to drag him back into all Strachmore's problems now?

In the cold light of day Nate's refusal to stay had probably been the most sensible option but her ego was still a little bruised. Clearly he'd done what she'd ultimately wanted for him at the time and moved on from her. She should be happy about it. Not wondering what, apart from her badly executed proposition, had turned him off her. That one kiss had been so full of love and passion for her she hated to think she'd killed it stone dead with her actions, even though she'd acted in what she'd thought was in both of their interests.

At least *not* sleeping with Nate meant minimal embarrassment when she would inevitably run into him again. The good news this morning was that her father had made it through the night and was as well as could be expected for a man determined to be in control of his own destiny at any cost.

Now that the sun was up she was keen to get to the hospital and see him but her thoughts were as muddled as ever when it came to her father. Last night she'd been afraid for him, and herself, as far as his health and finances were concerned. Yet there was also that lingering resentment that he'd brought her back here, unintentionally or not. These rose-covered walls and four-poster bed might be the stuff of little girls' dreams but to her this had always been a prison, a place that had robbed her of her freedom. Even as an adult she was still trapped here.

She tossed off the covers and climbed out of bed, her

bare feet sinking into the thick wool carpet reminding her she wasn't in Kansas any more. The wooden floors throughout her flat served a dual purpose—minimum cleaning and a stand against her old-fashioned upbringing.

She wandered down the halls trying to find the beauty in her opulent surroundings and failing. The shiny, gilded trinkets and ornate antiquities were exquisite but at what cost? She would've taken a childhood in a one-bedroom council flat if it had meant she could've had her mother back. Not so her father. Even when his wife had begged him to downsize to stem their outgoings, he'd refused to part with the family silver or make any concessions to give her peace of mind. If anything, he'd become more extravagant, throwing lavish parties to prevent the rumour mill churning with stories about the depleted family coffers. Her mother had been expected to be compliant in the façade, playing the glamorous, gracious hostess while quashing her anxiety with a cocktail of drugs.

Violet slid her hand over the smooth mahogany bannister leading down the staircase. It took her to a happier period when the house was her playground and this was her slide taking her from one floor to another. With few friends outside her preparatory school, she'd had to make her own entertainment when she'd been waiting for Nate to finish working in the grounds with his father. At least with him she'd never had to pretend to be something she wasn't. She shouldn't have tried to do that last night by making out she was some sort of good-time girl.

Perhaps he'd seen right through her façade the way he'd always been able to and realised she'd simply been acting out of fear. That thought was preferable to the one where he didn't find her attractive any more and enough to spur her on to get dressed and face the day ahead.

* * *

So many elements of what happened last night had been playing on Nate's mind. The most persistent one being Violet's indecent proposal and why he'd turned her down. He doubted she felt any more for him now than she had back then and surmised she'd been trying to use him as a sticking plaster over the wound coming back here had reopened. He knew he'd ultimately made the right decision. Going down that path again would only have led to that same dead end it had taken him years to navigate his way out of.

In hindsight her flight to London rather than take the next step with him had probably been for the best. Nothing had changed since then. Except they were no longer best friends and self-preservation was a higher priority for him now.

The discovery of the Earl's debts had added to his disturbed sleep; he was worried not only for Violet but for his family too. Regardless of his own thoughts on Strachmore, or the people who resided there, his parents were very much a part of it. Any financial problems would affect them too when it was their livelihood, and their affiliation was the only thing keeping a roof over their heads. The cottage was the only perk of the job as far as he could see and one that would certainly vanish along with the Dempseys. Strachmore's problems were also his now. He couldn't stand by and watch his parents lose their home simply because he and Violet had unresolved issues. They were all going to have to work together to find a solution. The future was going to have to be more important than the past.

He'd made Samuel Dempsey his first port of call on the ward rounds this morning to follow his progress. All had been quiet since the last dramatic intervention to restart his heart so Nate hoped this was the start of his recovery. There was no associated arrhythmia, with the heart beating too quickly, too slowly, or irregularly, which could sometimes occur after a heart attack. It would take a while to assess the full damage done to the heart and how much tissue would be able to recover but, for now, he was stable.

That was more than could be said for another one of his elderly patients, who'd suffered severe heart failure and had undergone stenting of his coronary arteries yesterday. The balloon catheter supposed to inflate/deflate timed by the patient's heartbeat and support the circulation hadn't been beneficial in this case. After examining him, Nate had had to concede that a large part of the heart muscle had died and nothing more could be done. A younger patient might have been a candidate for further surgery but it had been decided at the morning multi-disciplinary meeting not to pursue any further investigation. Already weak, the patient wouldn't have survived another round of intrusive surgery. It wasn't the outcome he wanted for any of his patients, no matter what their age or circumstance. He absorbed every loss as though it were personal, his failing. If anything happened to the Earl he'd never forgive himself for letting Violet or his parents down.

After seeing in-patients, outpatients and performing a pacemaker insertion, he'd come full circle back to CCU. Deep down he'd known Violet would be here.

'Hey, Dad.' Violet was glad to see he was a bit more with it and his pallor was a lot less grey today. She'd been sitting around for hours waiting for all the tests and scans to be completed before she got to see him. Making her own way to the hospital this morning had seemed like a better plan than car-sharing with the man who didn't want to sleep with her but it also meant no string-pulling visitor privileges.

'Violet? What are you doing here?' His eyes were flickering open and shut as though he wasn't sure whether or not to believe what he was seeing. It was no wonder when she'd spent so long out of the country, and his life.

'The doctors have told you what happened, right?' She didn't want the responsibility of breaking the news to him; he wasn't invincible. He'd probably call her a liar if she tried.

'A heart attack.' He nodded and closed his eyes again. She couldn't tell if he was tired, zoned out on drugs or annoyed she was here. Probably all three. She was the last person he'd want to see him weak and out of control.

'I wanted to make sure you were all right.' It was weird saying that when she'd barely let him enter her thoughts until recently. He'd been out of sight, out of mind, to enable her to move forward. Until one phone call had forced her to acknowledge he was still part of her life whether she liked it or not.

She stood by the bed, arms folded and doing her best to sound strong, as if admitting she'd been scared for him would somehow give him power back over her.

'I'm grand.'

And people wondered where she got her stubborn streak from. There was no point telling him how close to death he'd come. He knew. He simply wouldn't admit it to her or himself.

She waited for something more—a complaint about sharing a room with the general public, a request for water, an acknowledgement of what it meant for her to be here. Nothing. Not even an attempt to keep his eyes open.

Violet took deep breaths to try and quieten the urge

to treat this as some sort of therapy session, unleashing years of unresolved issues in a verbal tirade while he was strapped down and forced to listen. He was still a sick man and she was living with enough guilt without having to shoulder the blame for his possible relapse. She'd waited this long, she could hold out a little longer to say her piece. Preferably when he and Strachmore were back on their feet and she'd bought a return ticket to London.

'And how are we doing today, Lord Dempsey? You were asleep when I came by earlier.' The sound of Nate's voice close to Violet's ear made her jump. Lost in her inner raging, she hadn't heard him approach, hadn't expected him to purposely come within five hundred yards of her after last night.

Even while she was trying to find the courage to face him her cheeks were burning. Looking him in the eye after her epic seduction fail was akin to watching your drunk antics at a wedding back on video. Except she didn't have alcohol to blame for losing control of her mind and there was definitely nobody getting married around here.

'I feel like I've been hit by a truck, Doctor.'

Violet could only shake her head in disgusted wonder as Rip Van Winkle bypassed her with the truth in favour of the medical professional. It said everything about their lack of communication and trust.

'Your body went through a lot yesterday so you are going to be quite sore for a while. We'll give you some more pain relief to make you more comfortable in the meantime. I don't have a problem with you calling me Nate if you prefer, Lord Dempsey.' He was smiling as he reached for the chart at the end of the bed with no obvious signs of long-lasting trauma after her little display last night. Things could've been awkward but he apparently wasn't going to make an issue of it. Not in public at least.

'Why would I want to do that?' Her father was making an effort to sit up now, scowling as he did so.

Violet's stomach sank with the realisation he didn't know who it was who had saved his life. Nate deserved some sort of recognition. 'You remember Nate, Dad? Bill and Margaret Taylor's son? He's a cardiologist now.'

'For now we need you to rest but as soon as you're feeling up to it we'll need to get you moving, even if it's just to sit in the chair by the bed. It's important we get the blood flowing around your body again.' Nate ignored her attempts to big him up and went about his doctory business.

Violet couldn't help the eye-rolling when she might as well be talking to the walls today for all the notice anyone was paying her. Perhaps she'd actually died of embarrassment when Nate had walked out last night and this was actually her ghost standing by the bedside whom no one could apparently see or hear.

'Nathaniel?' He was peering at Nate, his face screwed up in a sneer. Yeah, the penny had finally dropped.

Nate gave a curt nod. 'There appears to be some narrowing of your arteries, Lord Dempsey, and we will have to look into the possibility of a surgical intervention before they become blocked again.'

'You had a lucky escape this time, thanks to Nate.' She wanted to fend off the vitriol she could see was already building with his strength.

'I want to go home.' There was no thanks or recognition this man had saved his life, only demands.

Violet didn't know why that should surprise her. Owing his life to someone he'd looked down on for most of his life would mean admitting his stereotyping had been wrong. That chaos theory would rip his entire belief system apart. It was about time.

'I'm afraid you can't just yet. We need to build up your mobility gradually so you don't overdo it. Trust me, we want you recovered and out of here as soon as possible too. We need the bed.' Nate still managed to crack a joke even though it was probably killing him as much as her not to bite back.

'And when you do, you're going to have to cut back on the whiskey and cigars, Dad.' It was time he took responsibility for his own actions to save his own skin if no one else's.

'Just like your mother. Trying to tell me what to do. Who asked you to come back here anyway?' The old curmudgeon closed his eyes and lay back down. Conversation over as far as he was concerned.

Violet's blood was boiling. All anyone had tried to do was help him and all they ever got in return was verbal abuse. The olive branch she'd held out was being whacked around her head with every dismissive utterance.

'This is for your own good. If you don't want me here, if you don't want Nate involved, then start looking after yourself.' In all the years she'd spent with her own patients, she'd always been able to tread carefully and keep her temper in check in the toughest circumstances. Right now it was stretched to snapping point. There'd been a very good reason she'd left her personal baggage in a different country—it made her a different person. A weaker one.

He didn't bat an eyelid.

'This is something we can discuss once your father is up to it. Lifestyle will be something we'll cover during rehabilitation. I think we should let you rest now, Lord Dempsey.' Nate addressed her directly for the first time since he'd sneaked in and it was to undermine the stance she was trying to take here.

She swung around, hands on hips, and tried to communicate via the medium of dirty looks how ticked off she was with him. The patient gave a grunt next to them, which Violet knew amounted to another dismissal. The chance to get everything off her chest had passed and she wasn't best pleased about it.

Nate did his own spot of mime, nodding towards the door. She had no option but to follow when he turned on his heel and walked away from the volcanic eruption she was building up to. She didn't attempt to quieten the fast click of her footsteps out into the hallway after him.

'What?' She was mad at him, her father and, most of all, herself for ending up back in this situation.

He held one hand up in surrender, with the other resting on the door handle of that dreaded family room. 'Can we talk?'

'Not in there.' She was already on the edge without being forced to relive that nightmare again.

'That's right. It'll be safer for me if we go somewhere more…public.'

She heard the tease in his voice before she noticed the glint in his eye and the dimples blossoming in his cheeks. It was too hard to stay mad when he was giving her his best 'naughty puppy' look. Violet groaned in defeat. It had been too good to be true to think he would let last night's shenanigans sink without a trace.

'What can I say? I was clearly in the midst of some sort of breakdown. I promise not to try and jump your bones today. I'm sure there's some sort of medical ethics involved where you're not allowed to bring that up without my permission.' The only blessing about this continued humiliation was that, by turning it into a joke at her expense, they'd broken the ice before it had time to fully form between them.

She was loath to admit it but she needed him as a friend if nothing else. It was one thing being strong and independent when you were able to leave all of your troubles at work, quite another when they followed you home at night and invited their mates round to party. A familiar, if not overly friendly, face was the only thing stopping her from being completely overwhelmed and jumping on the first plane back.

'That really only applies if you're my patient…'

'I'm sure with the stress I'm under that's a definite possibility. So, if we can forget that ever happened…you wanted to talk?' If her father was going to continue playing dumb she was going to have to get back to Strachmore and make a start on that pretty red paper trail. She knew she wasn't going to like what she found at the end of it.

Nate gestured towards the empty plastic chairs in the corridor. It wasn't exactly the cosiest set-up for a heart-to-heart but there was every possibility she'd break her promise if they were holed up in that confined space again together. That white doctor coat suited him. It said he was in charge and that was irresistible to someone whose own confidence was floundering more with every second she spent back here.

'First off, I wasn't trying to interfere in there. I know you have a lot of things to sort out with your father but it's going to have to wait.'

She was so intent on watching his lips and imagining how differently things could've turned out last night, it took a few seconds for his words to register. 'Sorry. What?'

'We need to keep his stress levels to a minimum

while he recovers. The lectures can wait until we get him through the other side of this. Trust me, we'll be giving a few of our own on his lifestyle before he leaves.' He rested his hand on top of hers, probably the way he offered his support to all family members who walked these hallways. Violet wondered if his touch had the same effect on them. The bolt of electricity shooting through her at the point of contact was powerful enough to make the heart defibrillators redundant.

She slid her hand out from his so she could think clearly. 'You're asking me to back off?'

'For now, yes.' He could just as well be talking about the inappropriate thoughts she kept having about him.

Back off. Stop picturing me wearing nothing but my stethoscope.

She reluctantly agreed. The strength of her willpower would surely be tested over the next few days. In both areas.

'Now, I don't want to tread on your toes any more than I already have but I was thinking about Strachmore.' His scowl seemed only natural. It pained Violet every time she thought of the place too.

'Did the nightmares keep you awake last night?' She thought he appeared a little more rugged this morning and had hoped that spurning her advances had kept him awake with regret.

Oh, wait. That had been her.

Nate gave her his version of the death stare. It didn't have the same menacing effect when he puckered his lips at her. She was simply tempted to help smooth them out again.

'I'm serious. I had a few ideas of what you could do to generate some income.'

'I'm listening.' So far her only plans had included

selling up or torching the place for the insurance money. Both of which had her conscience screaming 'Cop out!' She'd probably find herself haunted by the ghosts of past earls for eternity if she surrendered their legacy so easily. Besides, she was none too fond of playing with matches. There was always a chance of getting burned.

'Okay, so, I was thinking more long-term financial stability. A way of making the estate self-sufficient. You have beautiful gardens, large banqueting areas and floors of empty bedrooms. It's the perfect wedding venue. Stately homes are all the rage these days and not only for receptions. You can apply for a licence to actually hold the ceremonies on site—' Nate had obviously given this a lot of thought in the space of a few hours. No doubt it was a ploy to get her out of the country quick smart before she put him in any more awkward situations.

'That sounds…complicated.' She rubbed her temples, the mere thought of tackling this bringing on another tension headache.

'Perhaps, at the beginning, but once everything is in place I'm pretty sure the bookings will come flooding in.' He made it sound so simple.

'Where do you even begin with that sort of thing?' It sounded like a lot of hard work that would keep her here far beyond a couple of weeks' paid leave. She didn't want to start something she'd be expected to see through to the end. Her idea of helping was to get the bills paid while her father was laid up, not take on a whole new set of problems on his behalf.

'You'll need public liability insurance for a start, and then the licences for alcohol, entertainment, et cetera. There'd have to be a fire-risk assessment, maybe some planning permission depending on how far you want to develop this.'

'I'm not sure I do. I'm not sticking around, remember?'

'I know. I'm just brainstorming ideas that will keep the place afloat so you don't have to come back.'

'Of course.' Violet took a direct hit in the feels. This wasn't Nate trying to ease her burden. He just didn't want her hanging around.

'You don't have to jump right in at the deep end. There's no reason why you couldn't test those waters first by opening the place up to the public. You could run tours of the house or hire out the gardens for photographic shoots. There's endless possibilities.'

And an infinite number of new headaches to deal with.

'I suppose it's worth looking into.' Especially if it meant she could absolve herself of further responsibilities or reasons to return. Coming back had only managed to upset the new life she'd created for herself and Nate had made it abundantly clear there was nothing left for her here. If only this weren't such a Herculean task to take on herself it could've proved the answer to all of their prayers.

'I've spoken to my parents and they're on board with whatever decision you make. After all, Strachmore is their home too. There's just one problem…'

'Of course there is. You're sure it's just the one?'

'Well, one particular obstacle which could shut the whole project down before it gets off the ground.' The way he was fidgeting with his tie gave away his sudden nerves, which didn't bode well for Violet. She thought he was supposed to be bringing her solutions, not more reasons to get wound up.

'Which is?' She sat on her hands so she didn't give into her instinct to stick her fingers in her ears. She had to hear this if she was to find some way out of this whole mess.

'Your father. We'll need his say-so on everything.' Not even Nate's apologetic smile could salve that slap in the face.

The man who'd let the castle crumble around him was the only one who could save it. If he weren't so completely blinkered by his self-importance there might've been a chance that plan might've actually worked.

'That's the end of that, then.' Enough people had wasted their time and energy trying to wake him up to what was happening around him for Violet to know this was a lost cause.

'I get this isn't going to be easy but it'll be worth it in the end. You'll finally be able to leave Strachmore behind.'

She couldn't fault his logic. It was the lack of emotion she was having trouble dealing with. He apparently wanted this all neatly tidied up so he could wash his hands of everything she'd brought to his door.

'That's what we all want, I guess.' Unfortunately, even if she had been at her ass-kicking, emotionally detached, sleeping-at-night best, this was going to be a monumental task. If by some miracle she could engage her father in conversation long enough to convince him of the plan, the practicalities alone would cripple her.

She needed help. She needed Nate. All that was left to do was swallow her pride and admit it.

'I know you can do this, Violet.' He had more faith in her than she had in herself. Or perhaps it was wishful thinking on his part, pre-empting the words that were going to come out of her mouth next.

'I don't think I can do this on my own. Will you help me?' She almost choked on the words that went against everything she'd strived for in adulthood. This was the second time in less than twenty-four hours she'd showed him her weakness.

By asking Nate to sleep with her, now begging him to bail her out, she made her new life into a sham. She'd flown back into town as a city slicker, an independent career woman who hadn't relied on anyone to help her make it in the Big Smoke. Now she was back to being that simpering, frightened girl she'd done her best to escape.

A wave of nausea crested over her as she waited for what seemed like an eternity. He'd turned down her request last night and she wouldn't blame him for doing the same again. He didn't owe her anything and he certainly didn't need this clingy, emotional side of her any more than she did. She'd simply hoped Nate would be the one person who wouldn't hold the past against her.

'I'm sorry. I shouldn't have asked. You've done so much for us already and I know you're busy—' She tried to back out of this with her last scrap of dignity intact.

His brow was furrowed in contemplation and she could almost see his refusal making its way from his brain to his lips. This smart idea had been right up there with asking the man she'd unceremoniously dumped years before to jump into bed with her.

She got to her feet and scouted out the nearest toilets so she could have a good blub in private. It was her own fault she didn't have a friend in him now when she'd run out on him when he'd needed her the most.

'Wait!' Nate shot out a hand and grabbed her by the wrist, pressing against her bracelet and temporarily branding her skin with her seahorse charm. It was a reminder of everything she'd thrown away and apparently could never get back.

It was too late. The old Nate wouldn't have hesitated to offer his support.

'Don't worry about it, Nate. I've dumped my problems on you once too often. I'll put in a few phone calls myself tomorrow—the bank, Citizens Advice, the Samaritans…' She forced a smile past the lump in her throat and her trembling bottom lip. Even though she'd been content on her own for a long time, somehow the thought of not having him by her side now made her feel more alone than ever.

CHAPTER FOUR

'I'LL HELP. WE'LL FIGURE this out together if that's what
you want?' Nate hadn't known what he was going to say
until the words were out of his mouth. He hadn't known
he was going to reach for her until she'd tried to walk
away. Now it was too late to take any of it back. His conscience had got the better of him again when it became
clear how desperate she was for him to stick around.
Once upon a time he'd been in that very position, wishing
she'd stay with him at any cost. Just because he'd been
left in the cold it didn't mean he should do the same to
Violet. He would never intentionally hurt her when her
family had done such a sterling job of that throughout
her entire life.

He'd hesitated with good reason. The 'no' had danced
on his tongue where he couldn't quite catch it. This was
everything he'd sworn to stay away from—Violet, Strachmore, and a commitment to be there for someone for
more than purely physical reasons. It might've been easier to draw that line if they had slept together. But he
couldn't bear to see that dejected look on her face again
if he rejected her a second time.

Violet bit her lip and nodded her head. From everything he'd heard over the years, she'd had her life all figured out without assistance from anyone. He knew she

must've been out of options to turn to him for help after all this time apart. A huge step backward for her. Lord knew he wasn't in a hurry to go back to the Dark Ages either, where everything revolved around her father's will, but he had to consider the long-term benefits. One pride-swallowing favour could render him guilt-free for the rest of his days from everyone who might expect something from him in the future. This would be a one-off.

He resigned himself to whatever fate had in store for him next as punishment for not learning his lesson the first time around. If he approached this new relationship with Violet with the logical side of his brain instead of that useless emotional one, he might just come out of this with what was left of his heart in one piece.

'Okay, then. First things first, we'll need to pay off the most pressing bills before applying for any licences. We can't have them cutting off the electric, or, God forbid, your father's champagne-of-the-month subscription before he gets home.'

Another nod. She was going to have to move from the back seat and take over some of the driving duties if his involvement here was to remain short-lived. He was assisting her in her hour of need, not enabling her to ignore the problem.

'How do you want to proceed with this, Violet?'

She was going to have to make decisions for herself and not get too comfortable with him being around. Once his idea was up and running, so was he. He'd thought he'd found his 'Get out of Jail Free' card by coming up with this venture in the first place. A pair of storm-coloured eyes had been his undoing yet again. Perhaps he could persuade her to start wearing sunglasses and prevent any further forced promises being made in a hypnotic trance.

Violet inhaled a deep breath as though she was girding herself for the challenge ahead. The first good sign she was in this with him. 'We should sit down and go through the paperwork together to see exactly what we're dealing with.'

It was the logical first step and the proactive approach he wanted to see from her. However, it also meant spending more time together. Inevitable, he supposed, and also the main reason he'd initially resisted volunteering for being her second in command. He'd already proved how weak-willed he was when it came to Violet, barely surviving the last test of his strength.

'If you have everything with you now we could go through it in my office. I have some time before my cardiac clinic.' His attempt to avoid a repeat of their previous one-to-one at Strachmore earned him a raised eyebrow and a grin.

'I understand why you don't trust me not to rip your clothes off if we're left alone for too long, but I'm afraid I don't carry my father's shame around in my handbag. We'll have to come up with an alternative venue. Somewhere with a glass partition, perhaps, to protect you from unwarranted advances? Or would you prefer I was immobilised and trussed up *à la* Hannibal Lecter?'

It was his turn to give the dirty looks. He was simply taking necessary security measures to make sure this remained a platonic meeting.

'Let's not make this weird, Nate. I'm sure even you've been knocked back on occasion without being made to feel like a sex fiend by the other party.'

She was right. By shying away from being alone with her he was turning this into a bigger deal than it should be. There'd been instances where he'd turned down advances from patients and colleagues alike and he'd carried on without giving it a second thought. He shouldn't treat this, treat Violet, any different from anyone else. That was what had got him into trouble thus far.

'I can't say I've ever encountered that particular problem myself...'

He hit the jackpot with that one—a *'tut'* and an eye-roll combo.

'Well, Mr Smooth, I defer to your superiority in these matters. What shall it be? My place, yours, or somewhere neutral? Say, Belfast City Hall? It's a bit of a drive but there'll be plenty of people around to keep you safe.' This snarky Violet put him more at ease than the meek version even if she was making him the butt of her jokes.

If he was honest, he'd seen enough of Strachmore this last couple of days to last him another lifetime. The city hall was tempting but that merely compounded the theory he didn't trust her, or himself, not to act inappropriately. That only left one other option.

'My place it is. I can swing by after my shift to pick you and the paperwork up. Maybe even grab some takeaway to eat while we work?' He was going on the theory that at least if they were at his house they'd be playing by his rules. There was no chance of any last-minute sleepovers and absolutely no reminders of their shared past. He would set the boundaries and time limits on tonight's escapade.

'That would be great. I'll pop in and say goodbye to Dad and head back to get things organised.' The smile back on her face was because of him. Her peace of mind came at the price of his but at least those eyes had their sparkle back.

'And I've got a waiting room full of patients to attend. Unless there's any emergencies I should be away around seven p.m.' He made a move to get back to Outpatients, where he was confident in his decision-making process.

'Thanks, Nate.'

Why did every pat on the head from Violet seem like a reward and a step back at the same time?

Violet couldn't sit still. She'd changed, twice, carefully applied, then removed, her make-up, and cooked a lasagne. All so she wouldn't come across to Nate as though she was trying too hard. This wasn't a date, it was an intervention of sorts. Yet the butterflies in her stomach were the same ones she'd had when she'd waited for him to take her to their fake prom.

Sure, she'd swapped her baby pink swing dress for jeans and the grey hoodie she usually wore for jogging, but it was the same sense of excitement making her fidgety at the prospect of spending the evening with him.

Until yesterday she'd forgotten the effect he had on her. It was entirely possible her subconscious had locked those memories away with the bad ones, fearing they were equally damaging to her equilibrium. Her London-based liaisons held no element of surprise when she was the one calling the shots. Having the upper hand enabled her to bail when things got too serious. Just as she had done with Nate. That had been a bigger step for her than leaving home, but one that had also given her the courage to protect herself first and foremost in her following relationships.

Now she was back to hanging around this big house waiting for Nate to rescue her. Except this time he was whisking her from a mountain of debt instead of the school dance she'd been dreading and taking her to his place instead of the old boathouse.

That had been the night her feelings for him had begun to change. He'd dressed in his best shirt and tie to escort her to their alternative prom. To this day no one knew she'd ditched the fancy hotel venue her classmates had attended for an evening in the draughty wooden shack. She'd been more comfortable there, safer, than in a room full of her peers.

Sweet sixteen and never been kissed but in his strong arms as they'd danced to the mix tape he'd made specially, she'd thought about it. He'd been the only one who'd taken her pleas that she hadn't wanted to go to her prom seriously but still wanted to make the night special for her. He'd always known what was best for her and it would be easy to sit back and let him make those judgement calls for her now, but deep down she realised those days were long gone.

She'd seen it in his reluctance to get involved, felt it when she'd had to ask for help rather than have him pre-empt it. It was down to her that things had changed between them and she hadn't regretted that decision until she'd had to come back and face him. It had been easier not to miss that close relationship when she wasn't seeing him every day.

She covered the lasagne dish with aluminium foil and put the salad ingredients into a portable container. This way she was simply bringing dinner to a friend's house, leaving no room for misunderstanding when Nate wasn't paying for the food they'd eat together.

She'd been listening for a car horn to sound his arrival and hadn't expected him to ring the doorbell. Neither had she expected to see him waiting on her doorstep. All he'd needed were the bouquet of flowers and box of chocolates accessories and she'd found her dream date.

Not a date. Crisis management.

If she kept telling herself that they might both come out of this unscathed.

'Hey.' He scuffed his shoes on the stone steps the way

he always had when they were kids, eager to get away from here as soon as she was ready before her father spotted him.

'Hey. I've just got to grab a few things and I'll meet you at the car.' She knew he was only standing here out of courtesy, being the gentleman her father had always told her she'd deserved.

After a quick dash inside to collect the makings of dinner, she joined him in the car.

'What's that?' He sniffed the air and peered at the mini tower of food containers on her knee as if she were using his vehicle to transfer toxic waste across the country.

'Dinner. Lasagne, to be more precise. I can't take credit for the salad but I made everything else from scratch.'

The car swerved as Nate turned to stare at her. 'Since when could you make more than burnt toast?'

Violet reached across to straighten the steering wheel so he didn't run them off the road. That split second of closeness made her heart beat a little faster. His breath was hot on the back of her neck, his frame strong around her and his spicy aftershave so enticing she wanted to sink back into him. She didn't.

'I know it was our secret snack of choice in the days of sneaking into the kitchen but the single life called for something more exciting and nutritious. The lack of a social life gives me plenty of time to experiment in the kitchen after work.' She was rambling now but since she was practically sprawled in his lap things could get awkward quickly if they let silence descend.

'I...er...think we're good now.' He gave her the nod to extricate herself from his side of the car.

Their brief encounter had given her more than a warm feeling inside. A tingling sensation had started at the top of her thighs and was steadily making its way south. It took a few seconds staring at the upturned dish in her lap before she made the connection.

'Ack!' The bottom of her sweatshirt and her jeans were now coated in a hot tomato and minced beef marinade. Thankfully the pasta layers had remained intact between the foil and the dish so she was able to rescue it with a quick flip.

'What's wrong?'

'I spilled dinner. Don't worry, I caught most of it.' In her lap, which was now stinging beneath her denims. She tried not to make a scene and draw even more attention to her stupidity.

Hs curiosity deepened his forehead into a frown when he cast a glance in her direction. 'Are you all right?'

'Fine,' she said through gritted teeth as molten lasagne lava singed her flesh.

'We're here now anyway. I'll take a look once we're inside.'

They pulled up outside a very modern, very secluded two-storey glass building overlooking Dundrum Bay. Nothing like the city-based apartment she'd pictured him in.

'I had no idea you lived so close.' Even more surprising than this sophisticated bachelor pad with only the local wildlife for company was the fact Strachmore was merely a ten-minute drive away.

'Only for this last couple of years. I've worked all over Ireland but when the position opened up in Silent Valley, I decided to move back. It turned out I missed the peace and quiet out here. And it's still far enough away to deter my parents from dropping in when they feel like it.'

Violet imagined no one got beyond the gates without some sort of personal invitation. She tried not to think about those who had passed through here and took comfort in the fact she'd been personally chauffeured door-to-door by the owner.

Nate climbed out of the driver seat and walked around to her side of the car. He opened the door and took possession of their dinner remains in one hand. Even as he helped her out with his free hand, it was obvious he was assessing the extent of her injuries.

Violet groaned as the cool air made contact and increased her discomfort.

'That's it. Get inside and take your clothes off.' Nate opened the front door and practically shoved her inside.

'I bet you say that to all the ladies,' Violet snarked with a grimace.

In a different situation that line would've got her hot and bothered for other reasons. Now she was simply cringing at the turn this night had taken already. It wasn't the civilised evening she'd planned.

'Only the ones who turn up on my doorstep with third-degree burns.' He chivvied her upstairs to the bathroom while he carried the source of tonight's humiliation to the kitchen.

Violet eased her jeans down to reveal angry red welts across her thighs. They were throbbing so badly now as she sat on the edge of the bath she wasn't sure how she'd ever put her clothes back on again.

She took a towel from the rail and ran it under the tap before draping it across her sensitive skin. The relief was only temporary as the heat from her burns began again in earnest.

There was a knock on the door. 'Violet? Are you okay in there?'

She wondered how it had come to sitting in her underwear in Nate's bathroom nursing a lasagne scalding.

'Umm…have you got any antiseptic cream I can use?' With any luck a dollop of cold cream and a few glasses of wine would help her forget this had ever happened.

'In the bathroom cabinet but I think I should take a look first. Can I come in?'

Her mortification was complete as Nate joined her, fully dressed, in the confined space.

'May I?' He hunkered down in front of her asking permission to see her mishap for himself.

She slowly lifted away the towel covering the last of her dignity. In keeping with her not-a-date mantra she'd forgone all sexy, lacy underwear in favour of the comfy cartoon knickers one of her friends had given her for Christmas. Her cheeks burned as much as her thighs.

'Ouch. It looks painful but you'll live. It mightn't feel like it now but it's pretty superficial. You won't require hospital treatment, although you should really keep those burns under running water for a few minutes.' He reached for the shower attachment over the bath and turned the tap on.

As Violet swung around to put her bare legs into the bath she was grateful he hadn't made her strip and get into his fancy-pants shower cubicle in the corner with more nozzles and buttons than she'd know what to do with.

Nate rolled his sleeves up as he administered the cooling jets of water to the burn site. After a few minutes of relative silence her teeth began to chatter from the cold.

'I think that should do for now.' He patted her dry with another towel then retrieved a tub of cream from the bathroom cabinet.

There was such a calm, gentle manner about him Violet could see what made him a great doctor. He applied the cream in soothing strokes, not batting an eyelid at her choice of underwear. It was unnerving having him so close, paying such attention to delicate parts of her. He was tender and considerate, and Violet was forced to clamp down on inappropriate thoughts as arousal took hold of her.

Nate was still intent on treating her burn, apparently oblivious to the erotic nature his touch had taken on in her corrupted mind. If his strong fingers massaged any further up her thigh she might spontaneously combust. And probably not very quietly.

As if reading her thoughts. Nate withdrew and got to his feet. 'We'll get you some painkillers but you should be fine. I wouldn't try and get your jeans on again though— they'll rub too much against the skin.'

'I'm not prancing around your house all night in my undies. Imagine the gossip.'

Nate looked as horrified by that suggestion as she was. Clearly all that electricity had been surging in one direction only.

Nate was having difficulty putting out of his mind that image of Violet wandering through his house in the altogether, not least because she was already half-naked in front of him. 'I'll go see if I can find you something to wear and throw those clothes in the washing machine before they stain.'

He needed space, and a reality check. Violet might not be his patient per se, but he definitely shouldn't be thinking about the softness of her skin while he was treating her. Not even her novelty underwear was helping to rein in his wayward libido. It reminded him he was one of the few who'd ever seen that fun side of her. A reminder there was more to her than glamour and pain.

He retreated to the sanctuary of his bedroom where

there was nothing to stimulate his Violet fantasies any further. Except the huge bed with the black leather headboard dominating the room. He turned his back on his pride and joy and yanked the wardrobe open. He'd known nothing in here would ever fit her but he'd taken the time out to compose himself before more than his trousers became uncomfortable.

The rows of dry-cleaned shirts and trousers were practical for a busy doctor but not much use for a slender burn victim who needed covering for both of their sakes. He paused flicking through the rails when he came to his lab coats and scrubs but apparently even they were too much for his over-sexed imagination to handle. He snatched a white shirt from the hanger. The sooner he covered her up, the sooner they could carry on with the real reason she was in his house.

It took a few seconds for his befuddled brain to clear so he could remember what that was.

She was still perched on the end of his bath where he'd left her, looking for all the world as if she were in that post-coital, comfortable-wearing-nothing stage. Except he hadn't had that pleasure and nothing about this was comfortable for him.

'Here. This should be long enough to wear as a dress with the bonus of letting the air around those burns.' He practically threw the shirt at her in his haste to get away. He even contemplated going back to the en-suite in his bedroom for his own cold shower.

When his stomach began to rumble it gave him a different body part to focus on. 'Just throw your clothes in the laundry and I'll see if I can rescue what's left of dinner.'

He reconstructed the layers of pasta as best he could and plated it up with the well-tossed salad. Violet reap-

peared in the doorway as he was setting it out on the dining table and diverted his appetite elsewhere.

The shirt skimmed the tops of her thighs, covering her
curves and brightly coloured underwear, but it did nothing to hide those long, toned legs. He'd never be able to
wear that shirt again without seeing her in it or smelling
her sweet perfume.

He sat down at the table and took a long drink of water,
trying to drown that persistent idea that this was how
she'd look the next morning if she'd spent the night. All
that could save him now was that folder of truth spell-
ing out in great detail why he shouldn't get involved with
the sexy heiress. She came with more than just overnight
baggage.

Violet could see it written all over Nate's face that he
wanted this night to be over. They ate dinner in virtual
silence although she suspected neither of them had much
of an appetite. Despite her efforts to make this a casual
arrangement it had all the hallmarks of an awkward first
date, or a really bad seduction attempt. After her last
botched come-on, it wouldn't be beyond the realms of
possibility for one to accuse her of faking a lasagne-
related injury so she had an excuse to strip. If only she'd
planned this. Or, Nate had been interested in her half-
naked body.

'That was delicious. My compliments to the chef.' He
cleared away the dishes in his obvious hurry to get down
to the real business of the evening and send her on her
way before she caused any more embarrassment.

'Thank you, and mine to the doctor.' Although she was
still in some discomfort, the pain had considerably sub-
sided, with only the occasional flare-up of mortification.
She hoped she'd recover sufficiently to put her own

clothes back on, dirty or not. She didn't fancy doing the walk of shame home in Nate's shirt under false pretences. That was normally only a liberty taken after spending a night together. Naked.

'Let's see what the damage is.' He'd retrieved the folder of paperwork she'd left in the car so they were able to finally get the evening back on track and prevent her from forming any more ideas of how she could get him into bed.

Violet spread the bills and threatening letters over the table, glad she had him beside her to help get her through this.

'We've got household bills, unpaid credit cards, bank statements…'

They sorted the final demands into easier-to-handle piles. Her father would be apoplectic if he suspected they were going through his personal things but this was for his own good as well as hers. Perhaps one day he'd re-alise that.

'I'm sure some of these companies might be sympa-thetic and suspend payment for a while if you contact them and explain your father's current circumstances. I don't think they would deal with me since I'm not family.'

'I'll phone around first thing. It's worth a try.' It would help her if they could find some way to stagger the pay-ments so she could work her way through these gradually.

Nate frowned as he gathered a handful of scarlet bills. 'Unfortunately, there are quite a few of these which re-quire immediate payment before you find yourself cut off from civilisation.'

Electricity, telephone and rates bills were ones she couldn't afford to ignore even if her father had.

'And the credit cards are going to need at least mini-mum payment made on them. Not to mention the loans he's taken out with sky-high interest rates.' It took every scrap of courage inside her not to rip everything up and pretend she'd never seen it. Instead, she created a new 'red alert' pile to be dealt with in the morning.

'There's definitely no emergency fund anywhere to buy some time?' Nate's optimism had long outlived hers.

A thorough read of the bank statements confirmed her father had been living on a wing and a prayer for quite some time. No doubt his good name had given him more leeway than most but little else.

'I'm afraid his finances are as dire as my own.'

'Can I help?' Nate reached for the nightmare she was holding in her hand but she snatched it away from his grasp.

'No!' She'd put upon him enough, let him pry further into the family secrets than anyone, but she had to draw the line somewhere. Asking Nate for financial assistance would be the final insult to all involved. Her father would never forgive her and she didn't want Nate to feel even more used than he already did. If she could find any other way to bail out Strachmore than borrowing from him she would.

'It's only money, Violet. Something I can help with.'

It's only money.

How many times had she heard those words from her father? Enough to know it was never *'only money'*. It annoyed her more hearing it from someone who'd worked hard to make his fortune, not inherited and squandered it. It was more than money, it was a matter of pride.

'Thanks but I don't want to go down that road. I can cover a few of the smaller debts for now and I have an idea of how to raise the rest.' She didn't have much in the way of inheritance other than headaches and a useless title but there were a few things she could sell that her father had absolutely no say in.

'I don't like the sound of that.'

He had his arms folded across his chest, his pride probably wounded by her refusal of help, but Violet hadn't relinquished total control just yet. Nate was her support but it was important she didn't compromise her own principles to suit him. Otherwise, that made a mockery of everything she'd railed so hard against. She might as well be married in that case.

'Thanks to my mother I'm still a woman of certain means.'

'You can't—'

'I'm going to sell her necklace. It's only jewellery after all.' Suddenly the ball was firmly back in her court.

'I won't let you do that.' Nate couldn't stand back and watch her throw away the only thing of worth left from her mother. Not on behalf of someone who didn't appreciate her and certainly not when there was an alternative on offer.

Money he had, could give her easier than anything else when it held no emotional attachment for him. It could solve the problem and let him off the hook a hell of a lot quicker if she'd accept it.

'You won't *let* me? Who the hell do you think you are telling me what I can and can't do?' Violet leaned across the table to blast him as she battled for control. With that passion she could've been the CEO of her own company, defending her assets in the boardroom.

Assets he was getting a good view of every time she leaned over.

'Your friend. I know how much your mother's things mean to you.' He walked around the table beside her so this supposed *friend* wasn't getting excited with every glimpse of her white cotton bra.

'I have some of her other belongings, which don't represent the problems that kept her awake at night. Expensive jewellery was Dad's way of showing off money he didn't have, not an expression of love for my mother.' She had that defiant tilt to her chin she used to have when she was challenging her parents' authority.

Nate didn't want her to think she didn't have anyone in her corner. He was there, yelling advice from behind the ropes.

'I don't want you to give up something you love just to make a point to your father. You might come to regret it.'

'Been there, done that.' She was talking about him. He could see it in that wistful smile and he wanted to believe she'd loved him once. It meant everything to him to know she might've regretted leaving him. That he hadn't imagined the strength of their bond and he'd been more than part of the fixtures at Strachmore.

All of the anger he'd been holding against her for these past years seemed to fade and render his resistance to touching her futile. He reached out to tuck a wayward strand of hair behind her ear.

'How did we end up here, Vi?'

Things could've worked out so differently if she'd been brave then and given them a chance regardless of what anyone thought. He'd been so in love with her all she'd had to do was give him the word and he would've gone anywhere with her, done anything for her. Now he was a man on his own, too scarred to let anyone into his life.

'I don't know but sometimes I wish I could go back.'

With Violet standing here in his dining room wearing nothing more than his shirt and a smile, this was as far from those innocent days as they got. 'I can't say I'd rather be anywhere else.'

He leaned in to kiss her, reasoning twice in twelve years wasn't going to wreak too much havoc. He simply wanted to find out if her lips were as soft and sweet as he remembered. They were.

He should've left it at one gentle peck on the lips, enough to reconnect and erase the bad feeling left with her departure. When he opened his eyes and saw her lips parted for more, felt her hands slide around his neck in submission, he couldn't recall any reason to hold back. They both wanted this. In some ways they needed it to enable them to finally move on.

He slipped his arms around her waist and pulled her closer to deepen the kiss he'd waited too long to repeat. As Violet pressed her body against his it soon became clear this was more than one innocent smooch. His erection grew ever stronger with every flick of her tongue against his, every breathy moan of acceptance.

With his hands at her waist he lifted her off the floor and set her on the edge of the table. Violet gave a yelp against his mouth in surprise but wrapped her legs around him to keep him in place. With one sweep of his arm he cleared the papers from the table to the floor so he could lay her down. He went with her, kissing the exposed skin at the open V of his shirt. She was a feast he intended to enjoy guilt-free.

Violet's limbs had turned to jelly with that first brush of his lips on hers and made her forget they were in the middle of an argument. Her thoughts were hazy with desire but she'd known he'd only been trying to help as always. She'd been the one to let emotions get in the way by almost letting slip the extent of her feelings for him in the past and lighting the touch paper for this chemistry that had been bubbling between them since she'd come home. If she was honest it had always been there and it had been a long, hard fight to keep it at bay, and not always a successful one.

That second kiss had nothing to do with the past. This time around they were acting on pure carnal instinct. Having sex on a dining table was as animalistic and far from emotional entanglement as she could hope for.

As if to illustrate her point, Nate was reaching beneath her shirt to remove her panties and making her wet with want for him. Her skin was so sensitive every brush of his fingers sent a shudder rippling through her in anticipation. She couldn't distinguish her scald marks from the rest of her skin burning up with his every touch.

He stepped back and tossed her underwear over his shoulder with a grin, leaving Violet squirming on the hard wood surface. She didn't care how uncomfortable this was, all that mattered was the ache he'd created inside her and how soon he was going to cure it.

Not any time soon, it seemed, as he began a torturously slow ascent along her thigh using his mouth and tongue. Her body was on high alert—her nipples hardening, her arousal heading to meet him—as he teased her with a sample of everything he could do for her. To her.

Violet braced her hands on the table, fighting off the too early waves of ecstasy trying to drag her into oblivion. She wanted this to last as long as humanly possible because in all likelihood it could be their first and last surrender to temptation.

Somewhere in the distance she heard a faint buzzing sound. She hadn't figured Nate to be into anything kinky but, spread-eagled before him, it wouldn't be right to start getting prudish now. She heard Nate groan and bit back one of her own. He was certainly taking his time. If he was into that tantric nonsense she was going to have to take matters into her own hands pretty soon.

'I'm really sorry, Violet.' The sound of his voice and the cold air hitting her where his hot lips had once been pulled her sharply back from the brink.

'Hmm?' She was struggling to sit up, her body limp with desire and Nate-tending.

'I have to go. I'm needed at the hospital.' He waved a battery-powered device at her, which was unfortunately ending their evening, not getting it off to an exciting start.

'You've been paged?' She came close to banging her head on the table in frustration.

''Fraid so.' The bulge in his trousers and his sad eyes said he was as disappointed as she was that this was over before it had begun.

Violet scrabbled to sit up, her hands sliding on the remnants of the bills scattered around. Her guilt receptors kicked in immediately. Putting her own needs first had saved her sanity in the past, but in this case she'd lost sight of what was most important. They were supposed to be working on helping her father, taking steps to make sure she could escape at the end of all of this. Getting jiggy with Nate certainly wasn't doing anything to fast-track those plans.

He was integral to all aspects of her life here and she didn't want to jeopardise any of that. She should be doing everything she could to try and get her father back in his rightful place instead of finding reasons to keep her around.

'It's probably for the best. You're my dad's cardiologist…you're helping me with Strachmore…that has to be more important than this…us.'

Nate was left breathless with the full impact of Violet's comment. It was bad enough that he'd been physically pained at having to call a halt to this moment of madness but Violet's reaction had body-slammed him and stolen what was left of those feel-good endorphins.

He was acceptable in his professional capacity treating her father, helpful in his role as financial advisor, but, when she'd stopped to think about it, not good enough even as a temporary bed partner.

Of course, hooking up with Violet hadn't been a good idea; he'd known that from the first time they'd almost done this. He'd simply got carried away with the revelation she might've loved him at some point. If he'd been thinking with his head he might've realised that had made her even more callous for leaving him.

'I have to go straight into surgery so I'm afraid I won't have time to take you home. I'll leave money for a taxi. Make sure you lock the door on your way out.' This time he wasn't going to sit around brooding about why she didn't want him. He had a job and a life outside Lady Dempsey's whim.

CHAPTER FIVE

VIOLET HAD KEPT herself as busy as possible in the days following Lasagne-Gate. She'd managed to sell her mother's diamond necklace back to the jewellers her father had originally bought it from, for probably a fraction of what he'd paid for it, but it had eased some of the financial burden heaped on her shoulders. For the best part of forty-eight hours she'd had the phone attached to her ear, fending off the bailiffs before they descended on the castle to seize the family silver. It had taken a lot of time, talking and money but she'd managed to pacify most of the creditors chasing her father. For now. Unfortunately none of it had managed to keep Nate from her thoughts for long.

If the hospital hadn't paged him she had no doubt they would've rocked that dining table all night long. That call had given her the clarity to remember how much sleeping together could complicate things. Even he seemed to have had a change of heart since then, reverting to that aloof Nate she'd encountered on that first night. There'd been no mention of the fact they'd almost done the deed at his house, neither had there been an invitation to finish what they'd started. It was a shame her body wouldn't let her forget the sizzling after-dinner entertainment.

She and Nate had kept interaction about Strachmore

matters in strictly public areas since that night but it
didn't prevent her from thinking about what they'd done
in private. His talk of fire-risk assessments could have
well been about the physical effect he had on her. A five-
minute chat these days was enough to leave her hot and
bothered when she could still feel his lips inching along
her inner thigh. It wasn't fair only one of them appeared
to be suffering, and it was confidence-crushing to find
he had no lingering desire to see that night to a conclusion. Even if her conscience had played a part in bringing matters to an end.

Unresolved sexual tension aside, this past couple of
nights had been tough. It didn't cost her a second thought
to come home every night to her London flat but Strachmore seemed to amplify her loneliness. The chimes of
antique clocks echoing through the empty house taunted
her, reminded her of the time that had passed between
her and everyone here. She couldn't get it back and some
day her lone occupancy of the castle would be permanent.

When she was with Nate there wasn't a moment to
dwell on the past, or the future. With him, it was all
about the present. She missed his company at night, especially when she had absolutely nothing to come home
to. He was part of the reason she was spending longer at
the hospital. It certainly wasn't all about being in her father's presence. She was as sympathetic as anyone could
be for everything he'd gone through but his self-pity was
exhausting.

He was still in some pain and Violet knew a lot of his
bad temper was down to fear and frustration. It didn't
make it any easier for her to come here two or three times
a day and bear the brunt of his complaints. Especially
when she was working so hard behind the scenes to make

his life as uncomplicated as possible when he got home. That revelation was another headache waiting to happen. She knew he would explode when he found out and she would have to justify the fact she'd cared enough to try and alleviate some of his stress. Samuel Dempsey never asked for help and he certainly wouldn't appreciate it.

Even now Violet could see a commotion around him at the nurses' station. Over the past couple of days he'd progressed to bathing on his own and taking short walks around the room. She suspected they'd come to rue their encouragement of his mobility. Now they'd all be in the line of fire.

'Dad? Is everything okay?'

She fought the urge to turn on her heel and let someone else deal with him. That selfish attitude was probably part of the reason Strachmore was in the mess it was. She'd had to put herself first at eighteen but that meant the Earl and his bloody-mindedness had been left unchecked for too long. He hadn't been accountable to anyone in her absence and it was a big ask to expect him to take on any advice now. They were both going to have to shoulder some responsibility for the current state of affairs and take steps to rectify the damage. As much as she longed to have this all neatly wrapped up so she could get back to her own life, Violet wasn't convinced she was strong enough to make a difference.

'I'm fed up with being poked and prodded every day in this…this torture chamber. How am I supposed to rest when I'm woken every five minutes for scans and tests? There's absolutely no respect for me here and I've had enough. I want to go home.' He slammed his fist down on the desk and Violet jumped, along with several of the nurses.

If her prayers were answered she'd disappear into the bowels of the earth any second now and not have to face these people as her father spat abuse at them. It was different when she was the one subjected to his tirades—she was family, had grown up listening to them—but these people should be exempt.

'The doctors and nurses have worked tirelessly to get you well again. You've got to understand these tests are necessary—they're not done out of spite.' Sometimes it was like talking to a petulant child when she tried to reason with him. When he was in one of his rages there was no logic involved, only emotion. The overriding one usually being anger. In these circumstances it was liable to kill him.

'I was explaining to your father that we want to move him onto a main ward to continue his recovery. We would prefer to continue the ECG monitoring for a few more days there before he goes home.'

She hadn't seen Nate standing in the melee until her father had turned to glare at her impudence. But there he was, standing toe to toe with him and trying to run interference for her. Even when he seemed to be avoiding her his chivalry still shone through.

'Do you know who I am?'

Violet cringed as he played the nobility card. The one that had done nothing but bring her embarrassment over the years.

'Yes, Lord Dempsey, and I assure you you'll receive the same standard of treatment as all of our patients.' Social status had never held any sway with Nate either. It wouldn't need to, given his professional approach to his work. Violet was certain every one of his patients was treated with the utmost respect no matter what their background, perhaps even despite it in cases such as this.

'That's what I'm afraid of. Thanks but no, thanks. I want to go home to a clean bed where the staff are paid more than the minimum wage to take care of me.'

'Dad! That's completely out of order.' Not to mention factually incorrect. It showed how delusional her father was when he was under the impression his staff were being paid more than a qualified cardiologist.

'I appreciate this is a difficult time for you but we need to take precautions for the good of your own health. Your physical activity needs to be increased gradually and we would like to make sure you attend cardiac rehabilitation.'

It could've been another run-in between the pair when Nate was nothing more than a schoolboy, given the manner in which her father continued to speak to him. Not once had Nate been forced to raise his voice to make his point even though he was surely wounded by the insults flying around. Violet had never seen anyone stand their ground with the Earl in full flow. Even when she'd mounted her great rebellion she'd done it over the telephone rather than face to face.

'I'm sure those are matters which my own doctor can facilitate. He's a man with over forty years of experience. I trust *him*.' Another dig at Nate, both personally and professionally.

Not that her father would've taken any more notice of a different staff member, Violet was sure, but this continual slight against Nate was very hard even for her to stomach. By denying his achievements he somehow rendered her own unremarkable. The great Earl would never admit he'd been wrong in trying to force them into their society pigeonholes or congratulate them on their successes. Until now Violet hadn't realised she'd been waiting for his approval.

* * *

Nate had dealt with his fair share of obstinate patients over the years. People had different coping mechanisms when it came to facing their own mortality and sometimes that manifested itself against the very staff treating them. Usually he took it in his stride. After all, who was to say he wouldn't lash out if he were the one on the other end of the stethoscope? Today he was finding new limits to his tolerance he didn't know he was capable of.

In the space of ten minutes his integrity and his professionalism had been called into question by someone who'd known him since he'd been a child. That was the problem, he supposed. His parents' employer was still judging him on the nonconforming teen he imagined had robbed him of his daughter. It was ironic that Nate hadn't gained anything from that loss except the successful career that was now being maligned. Regardless of how hard he tried, those from Strachmore would never see him as anything but the next generation of domestic staff. The only difference was the Dempseys weren't paying him to take this abuse.

He'd even had to battle his own family to pursue his chosen career. In their eyes by going to medical school he'd thrown away the honour of working for the aristocracy. As if their allegiance meant he should've sacrificed his prospects too. They hadn't understood his resistance to doing manual labour so a privileged family could sit comfortably on their pedestals. There'd been no support, financially or otherwise, as they'd seen him as some sort of traitor.

That attitude had created a distance between Nate and his parents. He'd hated them at times for their blind devotion to the Earl when they'd effectively disowned their own son for the sin of ambition. In a roundabout way they had been part of his success when his anger had driven him to reach the pinnacle of his career. These days he accepted them for who they were in the hope they would some day do the same for him. He'd learned it wasn't healthy to hold on to grudges or look for answers where there was none, and taken back control of his life by simply accepting circumstances beyond his control. No matter how much it jarred.

'In that case all I can do is ask you to wait until we have your discharge papers ready. We need to have it in writing that you are going against our recommendations by leaving before your treatment here is complete. There's also the matter of arranging your medication before you leave.' If it was merely a case of one stubborn patient showing he was still in control of his own fate, Nate would sign off and move on to the next patient who actually wanted his help. That was practically impossible when Violet was standing opposite worrying her bottom lip with her teeth.

'I will not linger here a second longer than is absolutely necessary.' The Earl continued to bluster, his cheeks reddening as he pointed a knobbly finger at Nate as though he were holding him to ransom. It was the other way around. As tempted as Nate was to have Security bundle him out of the door, he couldn't bear to be responsible for anything happening to Violet's only surviving family member.

'That's entirely your prerogative, but it would be in your best interests to wait for the reasons I've stated. I would also ask you would do so quietly to prevent any further disruption to your fellow patients on the ward.'

His thoughts were also for Violet, who was standing with her arms wrapped around her waist in a self-comforting gesture being completely blanked by her father.

The more distressed he could see her becoming, the harder it was for Nate to keep his own temper in check.

'How dare—?'

'Dad! He said he'll sort it. Go and lie down before you do yourself any more damage.' Violet cut him off as he launched into another rant, her hands now planted on her hips.

The strength of her bravery was belied by her trembling bottom lip, which only Nate seemed to notice. The Earl, whether exhausted by his own ire or his daughter's, finally returned to his bed with a grumble.

Violet visibly relaxed when the argument was brought to a close. Nate had never been privy to the rows she must've witnessed at Strachmore and, although he'd been dismayed at times by his own parents' behaviour, he'd never been afraid in his own home. He had seen the fear in her eyes as she'd confronted her father about his attitude and Nate had just witnessed how vile this man could be. Although he'd tried to back off before he and Violet acted out any more erotic scenes on his furniture, he couldn't seem to stay away.

If he'd truly meant to keep his distance he could've transferred Samuel Dempsey's care elsewhere and reduced the chances of running into his daughter, but Nate was very much a part of this dysfunctional relationship. Despite the constant reminders he would never be a suitable match for Violet, it had been hell trying to put that night at his place out of his mind. The handprints left on his table were a frustrating reminder they were physically compatible, combustible even, if not couple material.

Now today's drama was over they were left staring at each other pretending there wasn't a conflict of interests going on. He had history with Violet, and her father, which he was doing his best not to let cloud his judgement. Unfortunately whatever happened with this patient was always going to affect his personal life too.

'You can't let him leave.' Violet was imploring him to intervene with those big expressive eyes. He preferred the dark glittering sapphires when she was in the throes of passion to the all too familiar worried baby blues.

'Now *you're* trying to tell *me* what's for the best?'

She'd almost bitten his head off for daring to do the same over the matter of her mother's jewellery. A matter that he still wasn't happy to lay to rest.

'I'm serious, Nate. You said yourself he should stay here. He's not ready to go home.' Everything in her tense body language said she wasn't ready for it either. If he could've chained her father to the bed rather than subject her to any more of his outbursts, he would've found a way to do it. They both knew her father's return to Strachmore would throw everything they'd been working towards into chaos.

'My hands are tied, I'm afraid. He's an adult, of, allegedly, sound mind. I can only advise him to remain under my care, not force him. This is clearly also an extremely volatile environment for him and staying won't benefit him or the other patients around him.' He hated himself for doing this to her. While she was doing her best to be strong, Nate had seen enough of her telltale signs to see she was struggling.

'What am I going to do with him? I'm a mental-health nurse, I'm not qualified for cardiac care.' Violet kept glancing across to his bed, where he was still grumbling and slamming his things around. It was impossible to tell which of them was more stressed here.

'I'll get in touch with his GP, see if he can't persuade him to stay where he is. Failing that, between me, you and my parents, we'll have to muddle through.' Another commitment he'd made just so he could put that smile back on Violet's face. There was also that niggle about not being able to perform the angioplasty making him uneasy. It was the first time he'd been unable to complete his duty of care to the full.

'You'll come and check on him?'

'We'll probably have to find some covert way of doing it but I won't let you take this on alone.' At least then he could keep an eye on the Earl's recovery and watch for any complications arising from his refusal of conventional treatment.

'You won't *let* me, huh?'

'Well, I thought on this occasion you might concede a small piece of that iron will.'

They exchanged wry smiles over the private joke. The origin of which was rooted in that night at his house. Not long after they'd argued over Violet's stance on selling her mother's jewellery, they'd ended up locking tongues, and almost a lot more besides, on his dining room table.

He began to regret his decision to wear a tie today as the air seemed to dissipate and leave him struggling to breathe. It made no difference if they were alone or in a ward full of people when it came to chemistry. Violet was staring at his lips and he could tell she was recalling the last time she'd yielded to him.

The silence that fell between them crackled with tension and unfinished business. It didn't matter to his libido that both members of the Dempsey family had judged him and found him wanting. He was programmed to enjoy the benefits of a physical relationship without any emotional messiness and he shouldn't start changing the rules now. It was his pride keeping him awake at night imagining what could've been instead of living it.

'Dr Taylor, you're needed in Room One.'

Nate was reminded he was supposed to be working, not trying to figure out a way he could sleep with Violet without compromising his principles. He gave the nurse a nod of acknowledgement.

'I'd best get on and do what I'm paid for. Don't worry, Violet, I'll make sure your father has the best care whether it's here or at home.' The promises tripped off his tongue as easy as denial and insults flowed from Samuel Dempsey's. They were both trapped in a pattern of self-destructive behaviour that could jeopardise their future if they weren't careful. Sooner or later they were going to have to make changes in order to survive. For Nate that would entail cutting out more than whiskey and cigars.

True to his word Nate had sent in a crack team of physiotherapists and dieticians to speak to the Earl. Neither Violet nor the forest's worth of advice leaflets had been enough to convince him to stay put. As usual, they'd all had to bend to his will and accept he was going home. He'd offended so many people along the way, there was a certain amount of relief mixed with Violet's trepidation.

Regardless of their lengthy estrangement she still felt the need to apologise to everyone he came into contact with for his abrupt manner. She should have been firmer with him, tried harder to make him modify his behaviour, but the truth was she was still intimidated by him herself. If he objected to her interference and really cut loose on her, she wasn't sure she would turn out to be any stronger than her mother.

She'd given up any right to tell him what to do when she'd left home at eighteen and vice versa. There was no way she would've accepted him swanning back into her life and trying to run it for her after all this time either.

The difference was, she wasn't putting other people's livelihoods in jeopardy with a blinkered approach to her finances. She'd made damn sure she had no dependants for that very reason, when it had cost her so much to simply take responsibility for herself.

It was late afternoon before they were ready to leave, much to her father's continued agitation. He didn't seem to grasp the fact that a crotchety old man going against medical advice wasn't the top priority on a ward full of seriously ill patients.

Not even the whistling porter who came to escort him from CCU escaped his wrath.

'I'm not a cripple,' he said and kicked the wheel of the wheelchair in disgust.

'It's only to take you to the door, Dad. Bill's picking us up outside. The physio said gentle exercise only, remember? You don't want to end up exhausted before you leave the grounds.' She imagined by this stage they were all glad to see the back of him from the department.

He was already out of breath with the effort it had taken to get dressed but he eventually got into the chair with a huff.

'A lot of fuss about nothing, if you ask me.'

She hadn't asked him, because that had the potential for her to lose her temper and demand to know why it was impossible for him to thank Nate for saving his life. They might get into hostile territory sooner than anticipated and run the risk of shattering the fragile remains of their father-daughter relationship, dooming Strachmore for ever.

As they made their way through the corridors she hoped to catch a glimpse of Nate, but he undoubtedly had his hands full with clinics and surgery. His skill in his field still astounded her, and she appreciated the time he'd dedicated to helping her even if her father didn't. He'd borne the brunt of her parent's rudeness through no fault of his own.

She wondered how much of that bitterness was actually apportioned to her. Her father had always associated her belligerent attitude with Nate's influence rather than his own tyranny. There was the possibility he blamed him for encouraging her to break out on her own. In which case she was going to have to set the record straight with a few home truths.

She'd never stopped to consider how her new start in London might have impacted on those she'd left behind. It had been easier to believe they'd all carried on as normal instead of adding more ballast to her burden of guilt. Only now were the consequences of her actions, her cowardice, becoming clear.

The next step was for all those who'd messed up to hold their hands up and admit their mistakes so they could start to move on from past transgressions. Even Nate, who appeared to have his life together, hadn't managed to let go of all responsibility to Strachmore. She owed it to him to enable that final break but just not yet. She had an inkling she was going to need his support more than ever now she was faced with living under her father's rule once more.

The Taylors did enough fussing over her father to enable her to take a back seat for a short while. When they were fawning over him his level of churlishness significantly decreased and gave Violet a reprieve from her 'tightly coiled spring' act every time he opened his mouth.

Bill had kindly arranged for his bed to be moved down to the ground floor to save him from having to take the stairs and Margaret had prepared a light dinner following his new dietary regime. It was only when the couple went home that the interminable silence fell at the dining table.

Of course he'd refused to take a dinner tray on his lap, insisted on keeping things 'normal' with the formal dining, regardless of how ludicrous it was with only the two of them seated around the massive mahogany table. She suspected this charade was more for his benefit than hers. He looked like the king of his castle perched at the head of the table even if he mightn't feel it.

'I've missed Mrs Taylor's cooking,' she said to break the tense atmosphere spoiling her appetite.

'There was nothing stopping you coming back if you missed it that much.' He didn't miss a beat as he scored a point against her in between spoonfuls of soup.

There was nothing to be gained by getting into a fight now, when he was still wearing a hospital band around his wrist. They could get into the whys and wherefores of their non-relationship when he was fully recovered and she wasn't afraid of causing him to relapse.

'I've been so busy with work I haven't had much time for holidays.' It wasn't completely untrue. She'd simply omitted to tell him he was the reason she didn't take any.

'For twelve years?' He paused mid-slurp to raise a bushy white eyebrow.

She'd never been a particularly good liar.

'I didn't think I'd be very welcome.' She wasn't even sure she was now. At the minute his attitude towards her labelled her as more of an uninvited guest rather than the prodigal daughter returned to the loving arms of her father.

'I never asked you to leave in the first place.'

This was exactly the sort of backwards-and-forwards blame game she'd hoped to avoid.

'Well, I'm here now. I have some time off to take while

you recuperate.' The way her nerves were stretched she might very well need some extra time to recover herself when this was all over.

'Why the sudden interest in me now? Or did you only come back to claim your inheritance? I'm sorry if I ruined your plans but it seems I'm going to stick around a while longer.' He resumed sipping as though he hadn't completely ripped her good intentions to pieces.

Violet could barely find the words to refute his allegations. She'd never expected to have to justify caring for him. 'I… I… That's not fair. I only came back for you. To make sure you were all right.'

'Unfortunately for you, and me, I'm fine.'

She was sure her frown matched her father's as she struggled to work out what the hell he meant. Were things so bad that he didn't want to be here any more? Was that the reason he'd refused treatment and insisted on leaving hospital too early? A chill blasted through her at the thought of losing another parent to the jaws of that black dog that had hounded her mother to her death.

'You're not fine. You're recovering from a heart attack and you're drowning in a sea of debt. All I want to do is help you.' Her voice hitched as she held out that olive branch. Despite everything, he had to be her main priority now or she would end up truly alone for ever.

He very carefully set his spoon down and fixed her with that withering stare that made Violet want to hide under the table. 'What do you know about my personal affairs?'

Only now, faced with the prospect of telling him what she'd been up to over the past few days, did she realise how intrusive he'd find her actions. She gulped. 'We found the bills and final demands when we were tidying up. It wasn't as if we were snooping.'

'What do you mean "we"? Who else has been prying into my private business?' He was red in the face, building up to one of his eruptions, and Violet braced herself to take the full force of it.

'Nate. He has some really good ideas about what we could do here—'

The fist came down hard on the table, rattling the dishes and the cutlery in its wake. Even Violet was shaking from the impact.

'Who the hell do you think you are coming back here and rifling through my things? Nothing at Strachmore is any of your business. You made that clear when you ran away, Violet. And it certainly has nothing to do with *him*.'

'I understand why you're angry at me. I stayed away too long, I realise that, but why do you hate Nate so much? He saved your life.'

'I didn't ask him to.'

There it was again, the unmistakable sound of a man who'd grown tired of living. She'd dealt with enough suicidal teens in her time to take his comments seriously and not simply dismiss them as attention-seeking. Lord Dempsey would never willingly admit defeat unless there was something seriously wrong.

'Dad—'

The doorbell chimed before she could query his state of mind any further or tell him how selfish that kind of thinking was.

'You'd better get that. Or do you expect me to struggle all the way to the front door and back?' Apparently the invalid card was only valid if it involved her guilt.

Violet made her way to the door on somewhat shaky limbs. Trying to get her father to open up would be like death by a thousand paper cuts—slow, with each new wound more painful than the last. Whoever was on the other side of this door, be it the Taylors or a door-to-door salesman, she intended to drag them inside to interrupt the direction the conversation with her father was taking. Neither of them were ready to tackle that head-on without building up their strength first.

'Hi. I thought I should pop over and see how the ground lay. Should I get my flak jacket from the car now or have you laced his tea with sedatives already?' Nate greeted Violet with a joke in an attempt to hide the nerves that had kept him from knocking on the door for the past ten minutes.

He'd stayed in the car with the engine running, contemplating whether or not to get involved in the Dempseys' domestics. He'd had no doubt the two of them under the same roof was causing friction when it was in their nature to rub each other up the wrong way. The reservations had come when he'd pictured himself in the middle of it. In the end, his conscience had rapped on the door for him. He couldn't leave Violet to manage his patient and his moods alone. Not when he kept promising her otherwise.

'Oh, Nate. You're a sight for sore eyes.'

He had no room for preening when he saw Violet was visibly shaken and as pale as the alabaster statues in the entrance hall behind her.

'What's happened?' The whole idea had been to make this a casual visit but he was well versed in emergencies too.

'He's angry about me being here…about our meddling in his affairs…and he's saying such morbid things. It's as if he's upset he's still here.' Violet was hanging on to his arm as she rambled. There was absolutely no danger of him leaving now.

'Okay. We knew he wasn't going to react well when

he found out we'd been digging into his financial status. As for the rest, depression or anxiety isn't uncommon in heart-attack survivors. He'll be feeling weak and vulnerable. Something which your father definitely won't be used to. He might need to start a course of anti-depressants. I'll have a chat with him and see if I can get a handle on his mental state.' Another reason Nate would've preferred he'd prolonged his hospital stay. There were so many possible after-effects, and not all of them physical, aftercare was a vital part of recovery. He'd been denied giving that and Violet was the one suffering as a consequence.

'That would usually be where I come in.' Violet sighed as she stepped aside to let him in, looking as dejected as she was describing her father.

'Hey, it's not your fault. You're too close to see this objectively and you're doing your bit simply by being here.' He hooked a finger under her chin to lift her head up and was tempted to kiss her worried mouth to bring them both some comfort.

It seemed an age since they'd last done that, their night together almost nothing more than an erotic fantasy now. He'd wanted that intimacy again, even for the briefest moment, to remind him it had been real, that she'd wanted him once as more than someone to bail her out when the going got tough.

'Who is it?' The dulcet tones of a crotchety Earl soon put paid to any romantic notions, reminding Nate of his professional responsibilities.

The medical stuff was within the remit of his normal day-to-day life. Whatever this was with Violet certainly wasn't. He let his hand fall down to his side again and took a deep breath. 'I guess it's time to face the music.'

Violet led the way towards the dining room with no real urgency in her step and he could see her steeling herself before she went in. It had never been the homely environment he'd been lucky to have even before his strained relationship with his parents, but the atmosphere here was so tense and thick with resentment it wasn't conducive to anyone's health.

'Hello, Lord Dempsey. I was just down visiting my parents and I thought I'd see how you were settling in.' It was a little white lie to soften the idea of his trespassing where he wasn't wanted. In all these years he'd never just 'popped in' for a visit, even when he'd been only a stone's throw away.

Samuel Dempsey eyed the offer of a handshake with a suspicious glare. 'I don't need to settle in. *I* live here.'

'I know Violet has been very worried about you—'

All concerns were brushed aside with an ungentlemanly snort.

'Worried about her inheritance more like. Is that why you're *really* here? Violet tells me you've both been helping yourselves to things while I've been fighting for my life.' He leaned back in his chair, arms folded across his chest, giving the impression he was enjoying this power play. It was as though he saw this as a game, where they were competing for the title of top dog and there could only be one winner. Nothing could be further from the truth. Nate wanted them to work together to make sure he was still fit to rule his kingdom.

'That's not what I said. We were simply trying to get things organised for you coming home.' Violet made a futile attempt to clear their names. Futile because her father wouldn't even look at her while she was talking, keeping his beady eyes firmly tableside on Nate.

'I've got your number. You're teaming up to snatch this place from under me. I see you riding around in your fancy car pretending you are somebody. Well, let me tell you, class isn't something you can buy.' The blue veins were pulsing beneath his flushed skin as he raged against his imagined foes.

Nate had to count to ten in his head to keep his own temper in check. It wasn't his place to make this any more personal than it already was by pointing out the Earl's faults in turn. Class didn't always equate to decency and it was entirely possible to have one without the other.

'Please don't do this again, Dad.' Violet's small plea was so full of fear it instantly made Nate think of her caught in the middle of her parents' battles. He didn't want to put her in that position again and he certainly didn't want to inflame the situation any further.

'It's okay, Violet. Your father's entitled to say how he feels in his own home.' It was a shame he'd never let his daughter do the same. Still, it wasn't his family, or his battle.

'Damn right I am. Just as I'm entitled to some privacy. I shouldn't have to put my personal correspondence under lock and key every time I leave the house.' For a man so predisposed to dramatic outbursts, he was doing a good job of making his near-death experience sound like a trip to the shops. Painting Nate and Violet as a pair of opportunistic burglars in the process.

'Perhaps I should leave.' Nate made eye contact with Violet. Her father wasn't showing any signs of having given up on life, at least not to him. If anything he seemed to be fighting to hang on to everything he had.

'Good idea. I've been perfectly capable of taking care of myself for the past I-don't-know-how-long. I don't need anybody's help now.' The Earl was clinging desperately to his independence.

Nate could sympathise to some extent with his stubborn stance against them. They were essentially trespassers who'd taken it upon themselves to get involved in his affairs. But he could also see that Violet was simply doing what she thought was best for him. This had moved so far beyond the professional excuses he'd made for coming here tonight he was in danger of having his say on the matter. Something that probably wouldn't please either side and would only drag him in deeper.

'Everyone in this room knows that's not true. You have no money coming in and nothing to cover the debts you already have. I've managed to cover a few of the most urgent bills but you need to generate some sort of income.' Whether it was because she'd found strength in numbers or she was so exasperated, Violet was starting to find her voice. She didn't need him; she hadn't done for some time. Nate imagined it was a case of reverting back to type because she had so much unfinished business with her father. And him.

'I didn't ask you to pay for anything. I suppose the money came from Dr Flash here? Well, the Dempseys don't need anyone's charity. Especially not from domestic staff.'

'I paid with my own money. I sold Mum's necklace, if you must know. One of us had to get our priorities straight.'

Nate could only stand and watch as Violet threw herself under the bus to save him from further abuse. Now she had her father's full attention.

'How could you?' He visibly paled and sat up straighter in his chair with her full disclosure, acting as though it were a betrayal rather than the huge sacrifice Nate knew it had been for her.

'What's the alternative? Wait for the bailiffs to seize it anyway in lieu of payment? Or do you have a Swiss bank account somewhere you've forgotten to mention?'

Violet was in full flow now. There was no reason for Nate to intervene when she was managing so beautifully without back up. She needed to have her say. It had been a long time coming.

'Does her memory mean so little to you that you can sell it for a few pieces of silver?'

'If you knew Mum at all you'd realise she hated those gaudy baubles you insisted on buying her. It was sentimental things like the clay bead bracelet I made at primary school she wore every day, not expensive statement jewellery.'

Not unlike the bracelet she'd worn on her own wrist for over a decade. There was a flutter of something he didn't want to recognise in his chest at the thought he'd held the same special place in her thoughts. It felt a lot like hope.

'Your mother was a good woman. She deserved the best.'

'But at what price, Dad? She knew you couldn't afford that kind of expense and worried herself to death over it. I think she'd be only too happy at the idea of using it to make a difference here.'

It was the first time Nate had witnessed something approaching shame on the Earl's face before he hung his head. 'I know you blame me, Violet, but your mother was a sick woman. I can't change what happened in the past.'

Violet dropped to her knees and reached for her father's hand. 'But you can do something about the future. We can open Strachmore to the public and bring enough money in to cover all your outgoings here. Nate's been looking into the idea of hiring part of the place out as a wedding venue.'

Just when it seemed as though they were making progress, Samuel Dempsey got to his feet, almost knocking his daughter to the floor in the process.

'Over my dead body! This is my home. It's not for sale or rent and neither is my pride.'

Nate immediately went to Violet's aid and helped her up to a more dignified position. It was too much of an insult against her good intentions to simply let him get away with this one. He turned, fully prepared to wade in and add his voice to Violet's cause, only to find the Earl had his eyes closed, refusing to entertain further discussion. He truly was the most infuriating man to try and get through to.

Then Nate noticed his hand move to his chest, then grab his left arm before he fell to the floor with a sickening thud.

'Dad!'

His expletive was drowned out by Violet's shout.

Along with the Earl's sickly pallor and clammy skin, all the signs pointed to another cardiac arrest. Nate should've seen this coming but he'd been too caught up in other people's emotions to keep his doctor head in the game.

Although the Earl had dropped like a stone he'd thankfully avoided hitting the table on the way down and there was no indication of any head injuries. Nate loosened the shirt around his neck and tilted his head back to check his breathing. Nothing.

'He's not breathing. Phone 999.' He delegated phone duties to prompt Violet into moving. He couldn't afford to have her in shock too. Far from helping, his meddling had simply caused more catastrophe. He should've left well alone and they might all have carried on down their own paths they'd chosen a dozen years back. Oblivious to each other's emotional dysfunction.

If he hadn't still been hung up on Violet and insisted on getting involved in her father's treatment in the first place this could've turned out differently. The Earl might've accepted help easier or sooner without all of this added stress.

Leaving the past unresolved now seemed a better option than being directly responsible for his death. If the worst happened there was no chance Violet would ever forgive him, never mind love him.

CHAPTER SIX

VIOLET STAMMERED OUT the address and the details of what had happened to the switchboard operator. It was difficult to focus on what was being said on the other end of the phone when she was watching Nate pump life back into her father's chest for a second time. The difference now was there was no defibrillator to shock the heart back into rhythm. He was literally the only thing standing between her father and certain death.

'The ambulance is on its way.' Sooner rather than later, she hoped. Every second counted now in bringing her father back.

Violet was helpless in the fight, watching her father's body jerk with every violent chest compression needed to keep the blood circulating around his body. It was her fault they were all in this situation. If she hadn't come back in the first place, or dragged Nate into their family politics, her father might still be recovering in his hospital bed. Not lying here on his dining-room floor literally heartbroken because of the accusations she'd thrown at him. This was what happened when she finally stood up to him.

He'd never forgive her for this. If he made it through. She'd never forgive herself if he didn't.

'Did they say how long on that ambulance?' Nate was

breathing heavily, sweat beading on his upper lip, with the continued effort of CPR. It was easy to forget how physical a task it was doing the heart's job when it was out of commission.

'Five minutes. Apparently there's one not too far from here.'

Nate nodded and turned his attention back to his patient.

Watching him work, his hair falling over his forehead as he tried to prolong life, was impressive and mesmerising. She, on the other hand, was standing here like a spare part with no active role in saving her father's life.

'Do you want me to take over for a while?' Her mouth was dry at the mere thought of undertaking such a crucial task but Nate needed a break and she needed to do something useful.

'Are you sure?' His serious face told her he wasn't going to leave his post unless she was confident she could do this.

'Yes.' She knelt down beside him on the floor, not giving her brain time to start overanalysing everything that could go wrong.

'Remember, you need to be forceful to be effective. Ready?' He scooted over so she could move closer for the transfer.

'Yes.' No.

She'd never performed CPR on an *actual* person, only synthetic dummies whose fate didn't affect anyone. If she screwed this up she'd have her father's death on her conscience for ever as well as Strachmore's fate.

She locked out her arms and linked her fingers in preparation, throwing her weight into the first compression when she took over.

'One, two, three…' She counted out each chest pump to keep the timing regular and her brain occupied.

'That's good. Nice and steady.' Nate laid a hand on her back to support her and used the other to grab his phone from his pocket.

Her father's skin was cold beneath her fingers and she tried desperately not to convince herself it was already too late but Nate wouldn't give up and neither would she.

'Come on. We can do this,' she told him in the hope he would suddenly bat her away and tell her he could do this on his own. This was the first time she'd actually been in a position to help him and she prayed it wouldn't be the last.

'Apparently the ambulance is coming up the drive. I'll go out and direct them here if that's okay with you?'

'Sure. Hurry.'

Her arms were beginning to tire with the tension and repetitive movements but adrenaline was keeping them moving. She could hear the sirens, see the shadows of the ambulance lights dancing through the windows, but she didn't relax until Nate returned with the crew, giving them the lowdown on events to date.

'We can take over from here.' Nate gave her a reprieve and took over the compressions while the paramedics set to work with the oxygen and defibrillator.

'Stand clear.'

This time Violet was there to witness the shocks as they were delivered in between Nate's chest compressions as everyone crowded around to save her father's life. They had him hooked up to so many machines and life-saving equipment he might as well have been in the hospital.

After the second shock was administered there was a renewed flurry of activity.

'We've got a pulse.'

'Lord Dempsey, can you hear us?'

'Open your eyes for us, Samuel.'

'Dad?' Violet held her breath, waiting for confirmation there was still a chance he could make it. Nate came to her and put her mind at ease with a squeeze of her hand.

'He's breathing on his own again. You did an excellent job, Nurse Dempsey.'

'We made a good team, Dr Taylor.' Her limbs were shaking as the tension began to ebb from her body, only to be replaced with shock at what she'd just undertaken. They were a long way from celebrating just yet but they'd done their bit to get him this far.

'I'll ride with you in the ambulance in case there are any complications. We might have to operate this time to prevent this from happening again.' Not even Nate's warmth could prevent the cold chill that ran down her spine. They were right back at square one, with the stakes higher than ever. This time she was directly responsible for putting her father in hospital and it was down to Nate again to save the day.

Nate had been more forceful about the need to perform emergency angioplasty as soon as they reached the hospital to prevent any more attacks. This latest episode had obviously shaken the Earl as he'd agreed without much of a fight this time. Now Nate's blue scrubs were sticking to the sweat on his back. He performed this procedure as a matter of routine but not usually on people who thought he'd somehow forged his qualifications, and not with old girlfriends sitting outside waiting for news.

With the Earl awake and aware of everything going on around him, Nate was under pressure more than ever to prove himself. He'd never been more aware of the small risks involved in this minimally invasive treatment, or his responsibilities during it, as he stood over Violet's father.

'Okay, Lord Dempsey, you'll be awake during the procedure but you shouldn't feel anything with the local anaesthetic we've given you. You can even watch what's happening on the monitor beside you.' He usually tried to make his patients more at ease by remaining on first-name terms but he didn't want to antagonise his patient before they started.

'Thanks.'

They'd administered a mild sedative along with a local anaesthetic but Nate was still pleasantly surprised at how co-operative the patient was being, considering his earlier mood. Well, at least less combative than he'd expected. He'd had visions of having to strap him down to stop him taking a swing at him for bringing him back to the hospital.

'We're just going to insert a catheter into the small incision we've made in your wrist. That will allow us to inject X-ray dye into the arteries so we can get a clear picture of what's going on in there.' He could make a better assessment of how to proceed when he could see the problem for himself instead of guessing.

Once he had the nod, Nate carried on as he would normally do. There was nothing out of the ordinary about this case if he could set personal history aside and stop thinking about how much was riding on this being a success. Potentially this was his chance of winning the Earl's approval, essential in making his and Violet's lives a little easier. It mattered to him to be accepted when he was spending so much time at Strachmore. With Violet. There was also the matter of professional pride when this was his patient who'd been readmitted only a matter of hours after leaving.

With the help of the monitors, he concentrated on feeding the thin, flexible tube through the blood vessels until it reached the coronary arteries on the heart. It was an intricate process, one which he'd honed over the years. Hence, his continued irritation when people dismissed the skills he'd worked hard to perfect.

'You can see on the screen that your right coronary artery is almost completely blocked, preventing blood flowing to that particular section of the heart.' It was clear now exactly what was causing the problem and, providing there were no objections, he could repair it.

'What's next, Doctor?'

If the Earl's co-operation had taken him by surprise, being referred to respectfully in his professional capacity was nearly enough to knock him off his feet.

'The best thing to open the artery is to insert a tiny balloon and inflate it to let the blood flow. I think in your case we'll also need to use a stent too. It's a small mesh tube that helps support the inner wall of the artery to make sure it remains open once we remove the balloon.'

'Whatever you think's for the best.' He deferred to Nate with his eyes closed, either too tired to argue or too squeamish to watch.

It enabled Nate to relax a tad without being scrutinised as he threaded the guide wire into the affected artery. The balloon was inflated to widen the artery and squash fatty deposits against the artery wall, the stent expanding with it. Once the stent was open, he was able to deflate the balloon and remove it.

'And that's us finished.' The whole thing had taken just over an hour, a typical time for the procedure but, under the gaze of Lord Dempsey, it had felt like a never-ending test of his abilities.

'Already?' Lord Dempsey was straining to make sure he'd been true to his word.

'Yes. We'll send you back to CCU to monitor you overnight but with any luck you should be back home again tomorrow.' He removed the catheter and the lab nurse applied pressure to the site to prevent any bleeding. Job done with a great degree of satisfaction and relief.

'Thank you, Nathaniel.' The Earl reached out to shake his hand and Nate stood a little taller in his comfy Theatre shoes.

'I think you need to thank your daughter too. She was very much part of the team keeping you alive until you got here.' She deserved some positive recognition from him for once too.

'Violet?'

'She helped me perform CPR until the ambulance reached you. That is one lady determined to keep you around for a while longer.' Nate wanted to put to bed the ridiculous idea that she wanted him out of the way. No devious gold-digger would have worked so hard to bring him back from the dead.

'I'll talk to her.'

'I think it's about time you did but, please, hear her out this time. She only wants the best for you, and the estate.' He'd held his counsel too long and in his eyes both he and Violet had proved their true intentions over the course of the evening. Despite their resistance to Strachmore and all it stood for, they'd both made a commitment to them in their own way.

He stripped off the lead apron that he'd worn to protect against the X-rays and tossed his surgical gown aside, keen to report back to Violet and share this feeling of after-surgery euphoria with someone for once.

* * *

Violet was biting what was left of her fingernails. She inspected her once-beautiful nails, now raggedy, the candyfloss-pink varnish starting to flake. It was funny how quickly frivolous things such as her weekly mani-cure became insignificant in the grand scheme of things. Nate had reassured her that her father's was a relatively straightforward procedure and she had every faith in him, but her father's health was so precarious she couldn't relax until she saw them both coming out of Theatre.

'Did everything go okay?' Her father was awake, Nate was smiling, but she wanted confirmation all had gone to plan.

'Like clockwork. We're just taking your father back to CCU, if you want to come with us?'

He was so handsome in his scrubs, made even more so with his amazing life-saving skills, Violet was liable to follow him anywhere. Overcome with relief and grat-itude, she launched herself at him for a hug. She found solace in the smell of sweat and soap, which told her ev-erything about how hard he'd worked over the course of the last hours. Now the drama was over she wished they were able to take time out in one of their old haunts to decompress and simply enjoy each other's company. Somewhere she wasn't constantly faced with reasons she shouldn't want to be with him.

From the corner of her eye she saw her father struggle to sit up. She instantly let go of her hold around Nate's neck and stepped away from the hunky cardiologist. Even though she was proud of him, it was her natural response to back off, knowing her father would never approve of such a public display no matter what the circumstances and especially with someone he deemed beneath him.

'How are you feeling, Dad?'

'Sore.'

If she'd expected Nate to flick on her father's humility switch while he was in there, she was sadly mistaken. She couldn't bear for him to take umbrage against Nate for any residual pain after all his hard work.

'I'm sure Nate did everything he could—'

'I didn't dispute that. From what I saw in there Nathaniel is a very, very skilled physician but I think I'm entitled to express my discomfort after everything I've been through. Now, if you don't mind, I need some rest.'

Violet could only stand open-mouthed as he was wheeled away.

When she finally regained control of her paralysed body parts she turned to stare at Wonder Doc. 'Did I imagine that or did my father just pay you a backhanded compliment?'

If so, it was a breakthrough of epic proportions. She'd never heard him praise anyone for anything. It was probably the closest thing to an apology they'd ever hear from him. Violet was pleased on Nate's behalf that he was finally being recognised for his achievements even if she wasn't likely to receive that honour herself.

Nate gave her a wry smile to warm her frozen limbs. 'I told you I was good at what I do.'

'Yes, yes, you are.' That brought all things non-medical to Violet's corrupted mind, forcing her to break eye contact before he saw her lustful thoughts for himself. She knew how good he was at everything he did—she'd had a sample for herself. That taster had only made her crave more.

Nate gave a nervous cough and she got the impression those wayward thoughts hadn't been confined only to her head.

'It's late but you can go to CCU and say goodnight before you leave if you want.' Apparently he'd decided to go with the relatively safe ground of dealing with her father compared to that minefield of their relationship and the boundaries they'd come close to redrawing.

'I'm not sure that's such a good idea. I don't want to push my luck and end up in another row with him after that bombshell. I don't want a repeat of what happened at the house.' Their cosy chats didn't have a great track record. For all the good she'd done so far trying to help, she was tempted to simply let his world collapse around him rather than take any more responsibility for his ill health.

'You saw him for yourself. He's quite mellow at the minute. For him. Although, it might be wise not to mention Strachmore. At all.'

'Message received loud and clear.' Violet pondered his advice. There'd been enough excitement for one day, but surely five minutes spent bedside saying goodnight couldn't hurt? It might even put her mind at ease to see him settled at the end of such a traumatic twenty-four hours. Then she might stand a chance of a decent night's sleep.

She set off after the porter towards the coronary care unit safe in the knowledge Nate had fallen into step next to her. She was getting too used to having a sidekick with her during her trials and tribulations. When she finally went back to London she was probably going to have to get a dog or something to pour out her troubles to even though it would be a poor substitute for this man, who knew her better than she knew herself at times.

'I'm just popping in to make sure you're comfortable before I head home.' Violet approached her father's bed with as much caution as ever. There never was any warning of what mood he'd be in from one minute to the next, and he was bound to be tired and cranky after the evening he'd had. This wasn't the time or place to start pointing out his flaws and mistakes again. With any luck he'd begin to realise them for himself some day.

'I know you would rather I'd died instead of your mother. I do too.'

It was such an out-of-the-blue statement coming from him it stunned Violet into silence. Not so long ago it would've been true, she'd have preferred to have lived without him instead of her mother, but she'd moved past that. Nobody could change the past and it had been her mother's decision to leave them when all was said and done.

The greatest surprise, other than her father considering anyone else's feelings, was that he'd expressed something approaching remorse. She guessed facing his own mortality had finally awoken his conscience from its long slumber.

'Why would you say that now when we've done everything we could to keep you here tonight?'

He'd never shown any emotion over her mother's death, not even in the immediate aftermath. He'd done what he'd always done: pretended the bad stuff wasn't happening around him and carried on as usual. That had included hiding the truth from her about the overdose, leaving it to others to break that news to her. Hearing him express a wish to swap places with his dead wife at any point was unexpected, out of character, and made him more human. It went some way to softening the hard stance she'd taken against him because of his apparent indifference to her great loss, but he should be celebrating the fact he was still here tonight.

She eyed Nate, hoping he knew where the hell that had come from. Perhaps he'd done some counselling alongside the heart repairs—a full mind and body MOT.

'Lord Dempsey, are you feeling okay?' Nate's frown

didn't tally with insider knowledge of his patient's sudden attack of conscience. Now he'd witnessed that morbid decline for himself he might be able to prescribe something to lift his mood.

'I know you only came home through a sense of duty, Violet. I've barely heard from you in over a decade, for goodness' sake. I could've died tonight without us ever clearing the air and I think it's time we had this talk before it's really too late. You've made it pretty clear you thought I was responsible for you losing your mother but do you honestly think I ever wanted to be here without her? I blame myself for her death as much as you do but I can't change what happened. Lord knows, I wish I could.' He bypassed Nate's question to continue his train of disturbing thoughts, his eyes red with stubborn unshed tears.

Nate pulled the curtains around the bed, giving them some privacy. It merely added to Violet's sense of emotional suffocation.

It was the first time her father had taken any responsibility for her mother's death, everything Violet had wanted since losing her. Seeing his distress as he did so didn't bring her the peace she'd always imagined. Quite the opposite. It was distressing to discover he'd been hurting all this time on his own too. Perhaps if he'd been this open with her back then she wouldn't have been so desperate to leave and they could've used their combined grief as a base to evolve their relationship instead of leaving it to stagnate.

'All you had to do was love us.' Her voice became smaller as the tragedy of her loss got bigger.

'I did. I still do. I never meant to hurt you or your mother but I always wanted to do the best for Strachmore too. Generations of my family kept the castle through war and unrest. I couldn't be the one to let it all slip away. I didn't realise it was your mother I'd truly failed until it was too late.'

'Why couldn't you have said this at the time to your teenage daughter who thought she'd lost the only parent who cared for her?' Until now she'd only ever seen the dark side of him and had run from it at the first opportunity. This guilt, this expression of actual emotion had come too late for her mother, perhaps even for her. Everything she'd thought she'd known about her father and her parents' marriage had coloured her view on every relationship she'd ever had. It had even cost her one with Nate.

'I dealt with things the only way I knew how—with a stiff upper lip. I was devastated, but what use would I have been to you if I'd fallen apart too? I might have gone about things the wrong way but I was the one who had to be strong. I've come close to death too many times this week to take anything for granted. I don't want to die with you still hating me. It's difficult enough knowing your mother went feeling that way about me. I'd do anything to change places with her. I've wanted that since she passed but I can't undo the past. Nathaniel has given me a second chance to at least try and make amends with you.'

Silence fell in the small cubicle, heavy with unspoken apology. She wouldn't have expected him to break down and beg for forgiveness but seeing him contrite like this was unnerving in itself. It was a bittersweet moment. This was the conversation he should've had with her mother, explaining his actions and exhibiting signs of humanity—capable of making mistakes and now owning up to them.

The logical part of her brain knew her mother must've had mental-health problems beyond her father's churlish ways to do what she'd done. Violet had chosen to ignore that fact and diverted all the anger she felt as a result of her mother's actions towards her father. It wasn't going to be easy to shift her perception of her father overnight and she needed time to process everything. With his round-about apology she wasn't certain what he expected from her in return either.

'I don't hate you and I'll be here for as long as you need me. We'll discuss this again when you're feeling better. Now get some rest.' She was desperately fighting her own tears, her breath catching on the lump of emotion wedged in her throat. She didn't want to cause him any more pain than he was obviously already in.

She leaned over and placed a kiss on his cheek. An act she'd never carried out without being prompted. He wanted her forgiveness, and she would willingly give it if she thought they could move on, but she couldn't help feeling as though she was walking into another trap.

'Are you going to be okay?' Nate had snatched his keys from the dining-room floor where they'd fallen from his pocket during the fight to save the Earl and now he was saying his goodbyes on Strachmore's marble steps.

He and Violet had taken a taxi back together, since he had to get his car, but she'd been non-communicative during the journey home. She was entitled to some quiet after another fraught day. He'd inadvertently intruded on her heart-to-heart with her father and been as shocked by the outcome as she was. However, he didn't want her to sit brooding all night, feeling guilty about what had happened, or dwelling on her father's state of mind. None of this was her fault.

'I never saw that coming,' she said, staring off into the distance. 'He was grieving in his own way, still is, and I left him alone. I'm supposed to be a mental-health expert and I didn't even consider that a possibility.'

'You couldn't have known when you were in a different country. I would say he's been very good at keeping his feelings to himself when my parents didn't pick up on it either and they see him every day. Hell, he's my patient, if you want to start pointing fingers at people who should have seen he was having trouble coping with his grief.' Perhaps if Nate hadn't known the background to their estrangement he might've picked up on other reasons for the Earl's mood swings besides his relationship with Violet. Blame wasn't going to solve the problem, only more of the plain talking he'd witnessed tonight.

'That's the point, I wasn't here. I was feeling sorry for myself in London, learning to treat people with mental issues when my own father was mourning the loss of his wife. Hating him all this time makes me the awful person I thought he was.' Her eyes rested on him again, two oceans of blue crashing with waves of sorrow.

He grabbed her by the shoulders, desperate to still those troubled waters. 'Stop this. It's obvious he wants you to stay here—that's why he's telling you all of this. He's trying to leave whatever has gone on between you behind so you can now both start to look forward. You've both suffered and I'm sure you've both said things you've regretted but now's the time to let the healing begin. These plans for Strachmore could mean a clean slate and a chance for you two to start building bridges if we can get him on board.'

A strengthening of Violet's relationship with her father would not only bring them some peace of mind, it could also give Nate some space from the happenings at the Dempsey household. He was already in way over his head and if he could hand over the reins so much the better. When all was said and done he wasn't going to be part of Strachmore's legacy any more than he was going to be a permanent fixture in Violet's life. These were all simply temporary arrangements due to circumstance. Not even his first love took priority over his sense of self-preservation. At least, not long-term.

'And I want that but not at the price I suspect I'll have to pay. What if I'm simply swapping one prison for another? I ran away so he wouldn't be able to force me to marry and keep me tied to this place. After that emotional outpouring I'll be the bad guy again if I leave again. I don't want him under the illusion I'm staying indefinitely. Whether he chooses to go along with this wedding idea or not, I've still got a job and a home in London I have every intention of returning to.'

Her torment was pretty much the same as his own. Somehow they had to find a way to fulfil their promises but still maintain their hold on their lives pre-heart attack. Ones which hadn't included Strachmore or each other.

'Everything's still raw at the minute. You can clarify the situation tomorrow and discuss what you both expect to come from this.' When everyone had had a good night's sleep and some time to think about exactly what they'd committed to.

'I don't know how to do that without disappointing him again. I want Strachmore to succeed but I'm not sacrificing everything else for it.'

'Tell him you're glad he got everything off his chest but your personal circumstances haven't changed as a result. Set very clear boundaries so you remain in control. If you don't have a firm date for going back to work, make one and don't break it.' That would prevent them both from falling any deeper into this quagmire of guilt and responsibility they'd unwittingly stumbled into. With an end date they'd be able to claw their way back out at some point and carry on as though this had never happened.

'He's always been such a dominant force I don't think I can cope if he starts talking about dying again. I'm afraid I'll let him guilt-trip me into staying permanently. I'm so weak.'

He could feel her shoulders sag under the weight of her burden. Nothing tonight seemed to have eased it for her. He gave her a gentle shake in an attempt to awaken that fighting spirit he'd seen in her earlier.

'Emotionally and physically exhausted perhaps, but you're certainly not weak. You took over CPR tonight without hesitation when I began to tire, pumping your father's heart as though it was your own life depending on it. Does that sound like a woman who can't handle a crisis to you?'

That raised a faint smile. 'I did surprise myself.'

'You didn't surprise me. I've always known how amazing you are.' He let go of his grip on her shoulders to cradle her face in his hands. With only the shine of the moon lighting the darkness, bathing Violet's heart-shaped features in its silvery glow, she'd never looked so beautiful.

With adrenaline and pride still coursing through his veins post-op, he leaned in for a kiss. He'd gained some respect tonight and it was enough to bolster his ego. Although he might never find total acceptance, her soft lips against his would be sufficient reward.

Violet accepted his tongue into her warm mouth, met him with her own. Somehow she tasted sweeter now he knew there'd be no complications in getting involved. She didn't want to stay at Strachmore any longer than was necessary or any more than he did. They could both walk away at the end of her stay without any ill feeling or recriminations this time.

They wanted each other—that much had never really been in doubt. Everything preventing this attraction reaching its natural conclusion was an obstacle constructed by his own pride.

'Are we really going to do this?' Violet already knew the answer but they'd both changed their minds so often she didn't want either of them to end up disappointed. Her head was so full of every word spoken, every life-changing decision that had been made over the course of the evening, she needed to be free of her thoughts for a while.

Nate was encouraging her to leave as soon as feasibly possible, removing that last obstacle before they got naked with each other. They were going into this with their eyes open and their hearts closed this time around. Neither would expect more than the other was prepared to give, avoiding any guilt or misunderstandings. Exactly how she preferred to conduct her love life.

'I guess so.' Nate interrupted her inner conciliation with what she was doing with his husky breath in her ear. It instantly revitalised her weary body, awakening every nerve ending and hitting each erogenous zone simultaneously.

Why was she still waiting?

'Shall we take this inside?' She was breathless; the cold night air and Nate's trail of kisses over the sensitive skin at her neck conspiring to make her shiver.

'Only if we can skip the acrobatics on the fixtures and fittings and go straight to bed. I've been on my feet all night.' Nate grinned as he backed her over the doorstep and kicked the door shut with his foot.

'You're just full of brilliant ideas, Nathaniel Taylor.'

She wasn't about to object to some tenderness after the day she'd had. A night lying in each other's arms sounded perfect to her.

'I think this is one of my best ones yet.' He growled and grabbed her backside. She flung her arms around his neck as he kissed her again, keeping them locked together as he hoisted her up around his waist.

'I thought you said no acrobatics?' It did a girl's ego good to be picked up so effortlessly and carried upstairs as though she weighed nothing. Even more when she could feel the hard evidence of her seducer's arousal pressing into her.

'I'm simply making sure I have you where I want you. The door is shut, my phone's off, and I'm not due back to work until tomorrow. No more interruptions. Tonight is ours. I'm reclaiming it.' He fastened his mouth to hers, sealing that promise he would do everything to drive her demons away for a while at least.

'Well, in that case, giddy up, Taylor.' She dropped her hand to slap him on the ass, giggling at the surprise on his face.

'Oh, it's like that, is it, Dempsey? You think you're the one calling the shots here?' He halted their journey at the top of the stairs, pushing her up against the wall and rendering her limbs useless.

'Uh-huh,' she mumbled, daring him to prove her wrong.

Now he had her pinned between the hardness of his body and the brickwork, his hands were free to do just that. He slid the sleeve of her white peasant blouse off her shoulder, exposing her skin to more soft kisses. Her insides turned to mush while everything on the outside stood up and begged for more.

'You sure about that?' he asked with a devilish grin

that caught her breath as she waited to see what else he had in store.

'Hmm, mmm.' She nodded, temporarily struck dumb as he slipped his hand inside her bra.

Her nipples were as hard as diamonds now at the very idea he was claiming her body for the night as he palmed her breast with an authority to make her gasp. She could afford to relinquish a little control if it meant feeling this good.

He teased her at first with a flick of the tongue over her puckered pink flesh, only increasing the pressure, and the enjoyment, when she bucked against him demanding more. There were no more thoughts buzzing in her head except those of the carnal kind as Nate drew her nipple into his mouth, sucking her towards oblivion. She was caught between a moan and a gasp as he took her to the crossroads between pain and pleasure.

She'd been right not to let this happen when they were young. If she'd known this would be how it felt to be in his bed she might never have left home. At least here and now she was free to savour this for what it was without trying to predict what happened next. She'd take an orgasm and one hell of a memory to keep her warm in her old age over a doomed relationship any day.

'You're a stubborn so-and-so. I guess we'll just have to take our turn at going on top.' He peeled her back off the wall and carried her towards the bedroom. It was just as well when she knew her trembling legs would never have carried her there on their own.

He dropped her gently onto the bed and proceeded to strip her clothes away, leaving her panties to the very last. If sexy was a handsome cardiologist tugging your underwear down with his teeth she'd hit the jackpot. It was like watching her wildest, most erotic dream play out for real. Except someone had censored out the best bit.

She teased her fingers along the ridge in his trousers, making it his turn to moan. And strip. He stood strong and proud, meeting all of her expectations as he sprang free from his confinement.

'What about contraception? I don't have any with me.' The pained expression as he made the confession said he'd put an end to this now, regardless of his own discomfort, if protection was an issue.

'It's okay, I'm covered.' She might've been offended he was so frightened of somehow getting trapped if she hadn't been on the pill since her first real boyfriend for the very same reason. A pregnancy didn't go together with her independent woman stance.

Nate's relief was there in his smile, and every other part of his body she could see was willing this to happen. There didn't seem a valid argument for holding back any more when they were clearly ready to take the next step. One they'd both waited a long time for.

He joined her on the bed, covering her lips and body with his. She rubbed herself against his erection, her softness yielding to his long length until they were joined together in one quick thrust. He exhaled a shaky breath in her ear as she settled around him. The sound of his contentment echoed the same sense of satisfaction travelling from her well-tended lips to her curled toes. This moment was everything she'd expected it to be, everything she'd feared it could be.

He was kissing her again, tending her lips at a leisurely pace, reminding her they had all night to indulge this fantasy when her body was craving everything he had now. She trembled with need, her urgency to reach that final peak increasing every time he drove into her.

Her mind drifted between this plane and the next, only the pinch of Nate's fingers on her flesh keeping her anchored in the present for now.

As their bodies slammed together she made the mistake of looking into his eyes. Regardless of the fact this was supposed to be a one-time-only deal, those eyes were shifting from brown to green, reflecting emotions that weren't included in the terms and conditions. They should've made some sort of 'no kissing on the lips' rule, like Julia Roberts in *Pretty Woman*, to prevent this from being any more than sex. Except they weren't strangers who'd hooked up on the sidewalk and the kissing damage had been done a long time ago.

She tightened her hold on Nate internally and externally, hitching her legs around his waist and clenching around him. They needed to start treating this like hot, dirty sex, not childhood sweethearts who'd finally consummated their feelings for one another.

She clung to him, dug her nails into his back, picking up the pace and trying to stop this from turning into something it wasn't. His irises were now only full of desire, dark with lust and need, his breathing erratic as she pushed him towards surrender. This was all about one thing now—sexual release—and that was exactly how she preferred it.

Nate's entire body shuddered against her as he cried out. Finally Violet was able to give herself completely over to the moment as their bodies rocked together one last time. All of the tension and stress she'd been carrying inside flowed away as she threw herself into that welcoming abyss.

She didn't even know she was crying until Nate wiped her tears away.

'Hey. Was it really that bad?' Not once had he seen

her break down during everything she'd faced since coming back here. Although she'd come close to cracking at times, she'd held it together with every new challenge her father's illness had brought her. To see her break now pained him when they'd shared something amazing together. Society ranking had meant nothing when they were rocking each other's world and he hoped these weren't tears of regret. Not when he expected her to be soaring up on the clouds with him after what they'd experienced together.

'No. It was really that good. You made me forget all the bad stuff.' She gave him a watery smile.

'My reputation remains intact.' He lay back, hands behind his head, his ego as satisfied as the rest of him.

'Definitely. I guess it all caught up with me for a moment.' She turned her face away from him as though she was embarrassed she'd let him see her cry.

Nate turned on his side and pulled her close. There was no reason for her to feel ashamed when lesser mortals would have struggled long before now. Still, he didn't want to draw any more attention to her tears when she was uncomfortable about it.

'In that case it's my duty to keep you occupied—body and soul. I do believe it's your turn to go on top.' He rolled over, taking Violet with him so she could feel as though she was back in control for a while.

He'd spent a long time imagining this time with her and he didn't want anything to spoil it for either of them. They'd already shared the lows of today, they were entitled to enjoy a few highs too. Tomorrow they'd have to face all of those same problems keeping them tied to the estate, but tonight was still theirs.

CHAPTER SEVEN

THE RIGOROUS BEDROOM workout might have taken Violet's mind off everything except what Nate was doing to her body, but it hadn't helped her sleep any easier. She sat up watching his broad chest rise and fall in peaceful slumber as the sun rose.

He had a body made to help a girl forget—those perfect pecs, lickable abs, and…damn she needed him gone. Lying here naked together wasn't going to help matters one iota. Bedding him once had been exciting, eye-opening, leaving her curiosity and body satiated, but ringing the bell for round two was only asking for trouble. It had been easier to tell herself this would be a one-off before she'd known how good they were together.

This wasn't her usual casual affair where no feelings above the waist came into play. Never mind he was involved in everything going on between her and her father, now he'd seen her cry, for goodness' sake. She never cried, not in front of anyone, and certainly not during sex. It was a wonder he hadn't bolted out of the door at the sight of the first tear. In fact, it was kind of disturbing he hadn't. If this was purely sex, why was he still here?

Nate rolled over, the sheet falling lower to display that sexy 'V' of his torso leading to the danger zone. She dragged her eyes away with more discipline than she'd known she possessed. Good sex was like any other addiction—hard to resist when it could make your troubles fade away so easily and leave you feeling invincible. It was the side effects you had to watch out for. Emotional attachment had a way of sneaking into temporary 'fixes'.

She sneaked another peek at Sleeping Beauty, who was definitely beginning to stir beneath the covers. There was absolutely no chance of going cold turkey when she was going to be exposed to said addictive substance every day here. Only the sound of the front door opening stopped her from falling off the wagon before she'd even got on it and taking one last hit of that Nate Taylor good stuff.

'Cooee!' It was closely followed by the morning call of the lesser-spotted housekeeper.

Violet had forgotten the Taylors had more than one set of keys between them. They always rose with the larks to start their duties and let themselves in so as not to disturb the Earl before he was ready to wake. Apparently those same rules didn't apply to her. She wasn't used to having to answer to anyone except herself these days.

'It's only me!' Mrs Taylor called again, louder this time, as though she was getting closer.

There'd be no way of passing this off as anything casual if Nate's mother caught them in bed. They'd never hear the end of it. Although her father had begun to warm towards Nate, if he found out about this all hell would break loose.

'Wake up!' she whispered and shook her bed partner awake.

'Hmm?' His eyes fluttered open with a moan that almost made her care less about getting busted. Almost.

She scrabbled around the floor for her discarded clothes and hastily threw them on. She might think more clearly if she wasn't naked. Or lying next to Nate's impressive morning glory.

'Your mother's here.'

That woke him up and killed his libido quicker than a bucket of ice-cold water.

'What?' He bounced up, wide-eyed now and with that same look of panic he'd had when she'd once caught him skinny dipping in the lake. Unfortunately Violet hadn't had as clear a view of his assets then as she did now as he hopped around the room trying to get dressed.

'Violet? I wanted to make sure everything was all right. Have you seen Nathaniel this morning? I see his car's still parked outside—' Mrs Taylor voiced her concerns from somewhere on the stairs.

Nate muttered all the expletives running through Violet's head at the same time. The first rule of secret liaisons was to be discreet. History should have told them privacy wasn't an option around here.

'How the hell are we going to get out of this one?' He jammed his feet into his shoes, the muscles in his back flexing with tension. He'd always been a completely different person when he was around his parents than when he was with her. In this case his frustration was most likely directed at himself and her for letting this happen.

'I've got an idea. Stay here.'

He was so straight-shooting he might well stomp out and announce what they'd done to shock his mother and get her to back off. Violet didn't want them making this into a big deal simply because they'd been interrupted.

She stepped out of the room before he could grab her and tiptoed to the top of the stairs. 'Hello, Mrs Taylor. Nate stayed over in the west wing last night. It was late when we got back from the hospital and he'd left his car here. I thought it would be better for him to stay than drive home when he was so exhausted. I'll give him a call and perhaps you could make us something to eat in the meantime?' She hated using her position here to suit her agenda, the lies made her sick to the stomach, but in this instance she deemed them necessary, for everybody's sake.

'Of course, dear.' Mrs Taylor beamed, no doubt thrilled at the idea of resuming her duties to the family in the Earl's absence. Violet couldn't imagine one without the other any more, nor did she want to. The Taylors were part of Strachmore and would hopefully take the reins when she was no longer here.

Violet waited until Mrs Taylor scurried off towards the kitchen before she turned back. Nate was fully dressed now and standing by the door with a scowl to sour the milk his mother was probably pouring on their cornflakes. She suddenly found the need to justify her actions. After all, this was his family she was bossing about.

'I thought it would buy us some time.'

'Sure. There's nothing Mum loves more than playing the faithful servant. I guess I'll see you downstairs for breakfast in five.'

It was her turn to be dismissed and she didn't enjoy it one bit. The fairy tale was well and truly over and now they were back to that upstairs-downstairs divide that had always dominated their lives.

Nate doubted there was anything more cringeworthy than a post-coital breakfast with an ex and your mother. When had his life got so messy? Oh, yes, the second Violet Dempsey had walked back into it wearing skin-tight jeans and a worried smile.

'I'm so glad things went to plan with your father at the hospital. I hardly slept a wink last night.'

Nate declined a second cup of tea. He'd only agreed to this charade so his mother's suspicion was kept to a minimum and he wouldn't be expected to pay penance for defiling the Earl's daughter.

'Neither did I, Mrs Taylor.' Violet's reply was innocent enough for his mother's ears. To his, it was a reference to something definitely inappropriate for the breakfast table. Something that was now reminding him of everything they'd done last night instead of sleeping, in all its X-rated glory.

'Speaking of which, I'm going to have to nip home and change before I go into work and check on him.' He drained the last of his tea and took a big enough bite of toast to reassure his mother he'd eaten. Her fussing wasn't confined solely to the Dempseys' welfare but he didn't have to pay for the privilege.

It hadn't sat well with him when Violet had requested she make breakfast for them. Deep down he knew it had been a ploy to save their blushes, but it had succeeded in also reminding him of his place too in the scheme of things. Although he still couldn't quite believe they'd finally slept together, he wouldn't let his ego get too inflated. He was always going to be the son of the hired help, no matter how big his pay packet.

'Thanks for everything you did last night.' This time he knew she was deliberately trying to make mischief as she fixed him with those ever-darkening sapphire eyes.

She pursed her lips together to blow the steam from her china cup and Nate's mind immediately connected her actions to scenes of a sexual nature. He jumped up from the table, lucky it was only his knee banging against the table in the process.

'You're welcome. Any time.' They hadn't discussed what happened next with regard to this new development in their relationship, but something told him it was going to take a great deal of willpower to prevent it happening again. That something was going to require a long cold shower to get rid of.

At least she hadn't seen him off to work with a packed lunch and a kiss in that we've-slept-together-so-let's-set-the-wedding-date fashion some were fond of after one night in bed. He'd met enough of those to recognise the hope of commitment even with a promise of none. He should be happy Violet didn't have it, not lingering on his Dempsey-induced inferiority complex. It left the bedroom door open for another casual hook-up with no expectations beyond those four walls. If she was agreeable, continuing the more physical side of their relationship for the time she had left at Strachmore could be the ideal way to work out their residual issues and finally get closure.

Today's status update: *Lover.*

It had all but killed Violet sitting so close to Nate this morning, pretending they hadn't spent the entire night getting to know each other more intimately than ever before. While they'd swapped their private thoughts and feelings in their younger days, it was nothing compared to what they'd shared together in bed. Sex with Nate had been the only positive experience she'd had since coming home, and the most fun.

She didn't know what new discoveries she'd make regarding her father from one day to the next but so far they'd all taken an emotional toll. Her time with Nate had been cathartic, a chance to wind down and remember how it was to be a young, carefree woman. She could do with more of that. More of him.

His mother's interruption this morning had prevented them from analysing their actions and discussing where they went from here. With her body still zinging from their tryst, she hoped he was on the same page she was as far as letting this thing run its course. The only commitment she'd intended making was to her job back in London with a phone call today.

Although her father's altered attitude was a revelation, she'd discovered for herself it hadn't made him Dad of the Year overnight. His old, grouchy self was very much alive and kicking when she'd been to see him this morning. She'd left him talking to the rehabilitation team and come back to make a start on making Strachmore accessible to the public in the hope he'd agree to give the idea a chance. The first step was a deep clean of the areas she thought might appeal to history buffs. Mrs Taylor ensured the main house was spick and span but it had been some time since anyone had paid any attention to the old servant quarters.

This part of the house where her ancestors had housed their domestic staff had always intrigued her and she'd used it as a hiding place at times, safe in the knowledge her parents would never venture there. The major flaw in the architecture here was the lack of ventilation. She stripped off the denim shirt she'd found in her closet so she was cooler in her strappy white singlet as she worked, moving from room to room with her duster and mop.

It was like being in a time warp once you set foot on those stone steps. The period pieces of furniture and personal effects left from days gone by were still in good condition under their thick layer of dust. From the huge wooden table in the servant hall where the staff would've congregated for their meals, to the sparsely furnished bedrooms, they'd all played an important part in Strachmore's history.

She was cleaning down the worktops in the room

where the butler used to polish the household's shoes and boots when she thought she heard footsteps. The idea of seeing past residents had never frightened her, but she held her breath as the steps grew closer and louder.

'Thank goodness, it's you.' She let out a relieved sigh when Nate stepped into view, but her heart didn't beat any slower. He was the quintessential gentleman today, again dressed in his dapper charcoal-grey fitted waistcoat and trousers. Although, she preferred him wearing only a sheet. Or not.

'Everyone seems so happy to see me today. It makes a change. Even your father managed to be civil.' He joined her in the small space, stealing more of her oxygen.

She bustled away to the farthest side of the room to clean the sink so she could breathe again. 'You saw my father?'

'I did. I can't lie and say trying to discuss treatment was a fertile exercise, but he has agreed to see a grief counsellor.' He skirted around the leather-covered bench in the centre of the room to come towards her.

She scrubbed the sink a little harder and tried to avoid his gaze. Her morning had been productive but less than glamorous. If she was to convince him another tumble in the sheets was a good idea she wasn't going to do it covered in dirt and sweat.

'That's great. I really appreciate you doing that for him. It will help him move on.' And her, if they could start some dialogue over what had happened to her mother without blaming each other.

'I really do think he's beginning to soften, though, and it shouldn't be too long before you can persuade him about the benefits of Project Wedding Venue.' He slipped his hands around her waist and made her drop her scrubbing brush.

Was he simply more tactile because he was celebrating their future liberation from Strachmore, or making a move? She wasn't sure if her now supercharged libido was interpreting his actions to suit her needs.

'I…uh…can't wait. That's partly why I'm down here. I thought if we got this cleaned up we could do house tours to break us in gently.'

'You are rocking this domestic goddess thing you've got going on.'

Her mouth was dry now and it wasn't down to the dusty atmosphere. He was nuzzling her neck, holding her tight and giving her the unmistakable sign now that he was interested in picking up from where they'd left off last night. Every step she took with Nate, as much as she wanted it, was also a test of her courage. It was a step further from her comfort zone, and one closer to keeping her here.

'There's so much to do to get the place ready. The paint's peeling everywhere, it'll all need to be redone. Then there's the structural repairs if we don't want to be sued by people getting hit by pieces of loose masonry.' All things that could be remedied easily but suddenly seemed so important to excuse her current state.

'Don't worry—I'll help. We'll all chip in when and where we can while we're waiting for approval from up above.' He spun her around to face him and she forgot why she cared so much about her appearance when he so clearly appreciated it.

He was kissing her neck, grazing her earlobe with his teeth and generally turning her into a puddle of hormones.

'I didn't think I'd see you today. I thought you'd be busy with work.' She was sure he'd be able to feel her pulse throbbing violently beneath his lips.

'I've no patients scheduled for the next few hours. I thought we could take the time to discuss our new *arrangement*.' He dropped a feather-light kiss on her lips.

'What's that?' Violet was burning so hot for him all these wooden fixtures and fittings were becoming a serious fire hazard, but she wasn't going to be the one to make the rules. After the way things had ended the last time between them she wanted this to be his call.

'We had such a good time last night, I don't see any reason to keep us from doing it again. I'd go as far to say we should do it every night before you leave.'

Before you leave. They were the crucial words she wanted to hear. That way there was no room for misunderstandings when her time here was done.

'Every night, huh?'

'Maybe every day too if we feel the need.' He would definitely have the need for her in his arms, night and day, now he'd established a clear time frame. His commitment would end the minute she was on a flight back to London and that was an even bigger aphrodisiac than seeing Violet get her hands dirty.

He'd spent the morning flitting between arousal and annoyance every time he'd thought about last night and this morning. So much so he'd been in danger of becoming distracted. For the sake of his patients, and his sanity, he'd needed to come and see her here. He hadn't known what action he should take regarding their tryst, whether it was better to draw a line under it or repeat it. One look at Violet had made it a no-brainer. Literally. That wasn't the part of his body doing his thinking any more.

'It might make my time here more bearable, I suppose...' She was teasing him now. He could see through that flimsy shirt she was as turned on as he was.

'I think I'll make that my new tagline on my business

cards. Dr Nathaniel Taylor—making life more bearable for over thirty years.' He hadn't come here with sex on his mind, only a desire to see her, but the time limit they'd just set meant he didn't want to waste any more time talking.

He planted his lips on Violet's with an urgency he'd never felt with anyone but her. It was an all-consuming need to be part of her, have her be part of him, which he could indulge now he knew there'd be no consequences or regret.

They were a flurry of hands and clothes as they tore at each other's clothes. The waistcoat had been a spur-of-the-moment decision this morning, one he was now cursing for its many, many buttons.

'Sod it.' He tore it open, the damnable buttons pinging around the room in the process.

'Shouldn't it be my clothes you're tearing off?' Violet helped him undo those of his shirt in double-quick time so he was topless, and halfway to where he wanted to be.

'Don't worry, you're next.' He whipped off her shirt in one swift move to find she'd gone commando, her perky breasts greeting him without restraint.

Violet writhed beneath him as he buried his head in her cleavage, revelling in her softness. She was opening his belt, unzipping his fly and letting his trousers pool around his feet. When she gripped his erection in her surprisingly strong hand he had to grab hold of the bench behind him before the instant rush of blood from his head caused him to black out. When she knelt and took him in her mouth there were fireworks in the darkness behind his eyelids.

With her hands gripping his hips, his hands pulling her hair, she took him to the edge of oblivion and back time and time again.

'Come here.' He urged her up beside him to make this afternoon delight last longer than he was currently anticipating. She kicked off her own jeans and underwear and pressed her naked form against his fevered flesh.

'You know, we're not the first people to make out in here. Rumour has it this was the favourite spot for one of the most notorious butlers who worked here. He had a reputation for seducing the kitchen maids and he carved his initials wherever he made his conquests. They're all over the house. See?' She traced her finger over a set of initials scratched into the leather-covered bench.

He could see where this was going. 'You got a penknife on you?'

'There's an old kitchen knife on the window sill.'

He hurriedly carved a crude NT into the wooden cabinets on the wall. 'Now we're making history too.'

'There? Really?'

He pulled her over beside him. 'Well, the randy butler's already claimed the bench and we've done the furniture thing already…'

As much fun as it was marking his territory, he wanted to finish what they'd started. He braced himself against the cupboard doors, caging Violet against the cupboards. His beautiful sex monkey hooked herself around him, permitting their bodies to forge together with ease.

They were so in tune with each other she met his every thrust, kept pace with him until they reached that glorious peak together. Their combined cries of ecstasy were loud enough to wake the dead and Nate was glad they were far enough from the main house to be heard. He didn't often get carried away in such a fashion where anyone, including his mother, could catch him *in flagrante*. His reputation was his livelihood but when he was with Violet nothing else seemed to matter. A dangerous game to play in real life but thankfully this was nothing more than a holiday fling, giving them the excuse to take a walk on the wild side for a week or two.

Once they got their breath back and their clothes back on, Violet returned to the scene of the crime to inspect the graffiti.

'He must've had a lot of fun during his time here. I've seen these initials in the wine cellar, the laundry room and the stone archway at the back of the house.' She studied the carving, lost in thought, as though she somehow envied the freedom of a paid servant.

Nate didn't want her to relate this moment between them to feelings of regret when that was the very thing they were trying to avoid.

'I reckon we could give the horny butler a run for his money. Let's set ourselves a challenge to reclaim every nook and cranny where he's made his mark with one of our own. It shouldn't be Strachmore subordinates only who get to have all the fun. I think it's time the lady of the house got to play too.'

This became more like an illicit romance between servant and mistress with every clandestine meeting in the big house. He could live with that as long as they kept treating this as an exciting fling with a definite deadline. There was no better way to do that than to make love in every room of the house, erasing every bad memory associated with the place in the process. It was therapy on an enjoyable level for both parties, ensuring they chased the pain away with lots of pleasure. A way of closing out the past and opening up their hearts for the future. One that couldn't include each other.

CHAPTER EIGHT

VIOLET DIDN'T KNOW much about *BH* but he'd certainly
been a busy boy and *NT* had been doing his best to rival
him. Of course, they'd been discreet in recording their
exploits for posterity, careful not to vandalise valuable
historical artefacts, and they'd had fun along the way.
In all, these last two weeks exploring, and supposedly
renovating, the forgotten rooms at Strachmore had been
some of the best days of her life.

Her father was growing stronger every day, thanks
to his work with the physiotherapists and Mrs Taylor's
close attention to his diet. Violet had made it clear she'd
be returning to her job at the end of the month and that
had been sufficient to prompt him into sitting down with
her and Nate to discuss the ideas they had to make the
estate self-sufficient. He'd eventually agreed in principle
to their suggestions and put his signature to the required
paperwork for now.

Nate's cool, calm explanation of the proposed changes
and the expected benefits had been a crucial part of ne-
gotiations. Having him as a third party helped prevent
a lot of the emotional obstacles from getting in the way.
In the end her father had even offered to sell a few of the
paintings he had in storage so she could hire an events
manager and whoever else it took to make this thing work

in her absence. She might even come home every now and then, now there were a few more attractions, and a few places still left for *NT* to conquer.

There hadn't been a conversation between her and Nate about the possibility of her coming back, or reconnecting if she did. It didn't seem such a stretch to carry on with what they had going on. She wouldn't be a permanent fixture in his life, expecting any more than she did now—great sex. It would be a shame to end things completely when they were having such a good time together. Spending more time with Nate would give her something to look forward to other than TV and pizza at the end of the working week.

She watched him now, schmoozing with the wedding party and the photographer in the grounds, and listened in fascination as he recounted her family's history to the bride and groom. Despite his resistance, he was as much a part of Strachmore as she was. More than ever given their recent antics. She couldn't imagine coming home and not seeing him here.

He waved her over, not ready to leave his post as today's host just yet. The bride and groom were his colleagues from the hospital here to use Strachmore as the backdrop for their wedding photographs. It was a favour both to his friends, and Violet. They got free use of the grounds and it was the first step to gently break her father into the idea of sharing his family home with strangers.

Violet watched the newly-weds smiling for the camera capturing their love for eternity. She wanted to be sick.

'I'd be crying too if I'd been condemned to a life of misery.' She sidled up to Nate, making sure she was out of earshot of the over-emotional couple now dabbing their eyes and hugging. She didn't want to ruin their day but marriage had a lot to do with the misery that had surrounded her ancestral home for so long. Her father's confession of his love for her mother had only served to confuse her views on matrimony further. It had all seemed so black and white when she'd thought her mother's love for her father had never been reciprocated and had cost her her life. The fear of giving everything and receiving nothing in return had kept Violet from falling into that marriage trap.

Now she knew how much her father had loved her and how lost he was without her, it made her question if refusing to admit your feelings was equally destructive. Apparently once love had you in its clutches it was game over, either way, and no amount of pretending or running could prevent it.

'Not a fan of the bride, or the groom?' Nate cocked his head at her as though she were some anomaly of nature for not getting sentimental over the proceedings.

'Marriage in general. You saw what it did to my family. It's all flowers and romance now but she's probably given up all her hopes and dreams to play wifey.' She clung on to that belief her mother had been the only casualty in the marriage—the only one with feelings to consider. The alternative was to admit both of her parents had been at fault and their marriage had been a partnership rather than a dictatorship, with each of them responsible for their own actions. That idea of free will, even as part of a couple, called into question every excuse Violet had ever made for being on her own.

'It's not the eighteen hundreds any more, you know. Women can get married, have children and still work if they choose.' He was being surprisingly pro-commitment for someone who'd taken great care to make sure they didn't have one.

Violet's stomach flip-flopped. Perhaps it was only

her he didn't want around long-term. She hadn't contemplated having to see him with someone else any time she came home, someone he might want to settle down with.

'You didn't strike me as the marrying kind.' At least not since they were teenage sweethearts when the intensity of his feelings for her, and hers for him, had sent her running.

'I'm not. It seems to work for some people, though. My parents would be an example of that, I guess. For the record, I have no problem with the honeymoon part. It's being tied down I take issue with.' Nate confirmed his place alongside Violet on the dark side, enabling her to breathe a little easier.

'I don't know who's in your little black book but I'm sure you could find someone who *isn't* into bondage.' Not that she was encouraging him to start hooking up with anyone else. She'd prefer he did that when she was long gone. If he really had to.

Nate snorted. '*That* I can handle. It's this notion that love can solve problems that galls me when, ultimately, it only creates more. All this nonsense is fine for sentimental types whose only aspirations in life are a semi-detached house and two-point-four children but you're right, some of us have bigger dreams.'

She should've been relieved to hear his matrimonial views were in sync with her own but hearing he was as cynical as she was chilled her insides. He was so changed in his views since a teen and she knew she'd been the cause. She must have hurt him more than he ever would admit. Her selfish actions might well have cost him the happy family she'd always thought he'd deserved. The Dempsey curse had struck again.

For a split second she'd zoned out, light-headed and unsteady in her high heels. Her conscience had clearly taken news of his commitment phobia badly, manifesting her guilt physically. They moved with the wedding party through the gardens and she slipped off to take a seat on the carved stone bench under the eucalyptus tree. She stripped a couple of the long blue-green leaves and crushed them in her fingers. The smell of menthol and pine instantly filled the air. She took a deep breath, hoping it would help quell her rolling stomach.

It was coming up to that time of the month too, which probably wasn't helping this feeling of nausea. She did a quick mental calculation—she'd been here for three weeks, her last period had been before she'd taken time off work… She frowned. That couldn't be right. She was as regular as clockwork, every four weeks. Her calculations made it more than five. She did another tot-up of the dates. It was still longer than she'd ever gone. It had to be down to the stress.

Another cramp doubled her over, surely a clear sign all was as it should be. What was the alternative? She hadn't eaten anything other than Mrs Taylor's nutritious meals, same as her father, so it wasn't food poisoning. That left one glaring possibility. She couldn't be pregnant, she just couldn't.

Nate chose that moment to come and sit beside her. 'Are you okay? You look a little pale.'

He put his hand on her forehead, her skin suddenly clammy now. Her own health hadn't been of any significance when her father had been so critical. Now it meant everything. With horror she recalled the fraught night waiting for news of her father and that whole debacle with Nate at the house. Her routine had gone completely out of the window and she'd been a day late taking her pill. In the circumstances she hadn't thought in a million years she would have to take extra precautions. Sex with

Nate had never seemed an option. Her recklessness had apparently come at a price after all.

How would she ever make her escape from Strachmore now if she was pregnant? She didn't have the support in London needed to look after a baby and work at the same time and she certainly wouldn't be able to afford childcare on her wages. Nate hadn't asked for this either, when she'd promised him this would be nothing more than a fling. She couldn't expect him to take two of them on when he'd made it clear he didn't even want a plus one. Hell, she didn't even want one.

Parenthood had never been in her future plans. It had been too much for her mother to cope with and not enough for her to stick around. Violet didn't want that level of change, or responsibility, causing chaos in the new life she'd made for herself. Her quiet, organised life, where loving anyone except herself was simply out of the question. It was part of the reason she'd been keen to get back to it, knowing she'd be safe from her feelings for Nate there. Now she was in double trouble.

All she could do was throw herself at her father's mercy now, if the worst had indeed happened, and beg him to take in his pregnant, unmarried daughter. Her life was never going to be the same.

'I think I'm gonna be sick.'

Nate had tried to go after Violet when she'd taken suddenly ill, but she'd shooed him back to the wedding party, insisting someone should be taking an active role in the day's events. He'd had no option but to return to the gathered guests when Strachmore's reputation would soon depend on good word of mouth. Someone had to escort them around the grounds and smile in all the right places. Even if he had been desperate to go check on her.

He'd spent most of his waking moments outside work with her these past weeks, and all of his sleeping ones too. If there was something wrong he wanted to be with her, looking after her the way he always did. He guessed that sense of duty towards the Dempseys was simply born into him. That was the only acceptable explanation for why he cared so much.

Once he'd seen the wedding party off to continue their celebrations elsewhere, he sprinted back to the house. He bounded up the stairs calling her name but she didn't answer. Eventually he found her in her bedroom, changed out of the dress she'd bought specially for today back into her casual jeans and grey hoodie. She seemed even paler now she'd removed her make-up, looking lost perched on the end of her princess bed. He was sorry he'd left her alone for so long.

When he saw her suitcase lying open on the bed, clothes strewn all around, he went into full panic mode. 'What's wrong? Is it that bad? Do you need me to take you to the hospital?'

'I'm fine. Actually, I'm not. I'm far from it but I don't need to go to the hospital. I need to go home.'

She wasn't making any sense and was starting to freak him out.

He knelt on the floor and took her hand. If he'd known she'd react so strongly against the idea of marriage he'd never have suggested bringing his friends here. Her commitment issues were clearly greater than his. In a moment of sentimentality he'd even contemplated how Violet would have looked in a wedding dress. Beautiful and elegant as always, he supposed. If she hadn't run away, breaking his heart, or he'd been enough for her to contemplate staying, they might have had this one day for themselves. It was a shame their parents' actions had skewed their view on marriage for ever when people like his co-workers today seemed to find their happiness in it.

'You don't need to go anywhere. The condemned couple has left the building. We are officially bridal-party free. If it's an allergy to weddings you have, perhaps we can go hang out in the divorce courts to counteract the toxins.' Usually his naff jokes were enough to make her smile, but not today.

'It's not that. Thank you for setting that up today,— they really seemed to enjoy it. It's just…it's just… I can't do this.' She dropped her head into her hands and sobbed her heart out.

This was it—she was going to run again before he was ready to accept it was over. He was supposed to have two more weeks with her. Now she was cutting their time together short he was left with that same sick, empty feeling inside as before. He needed some warning before he was back to his 'work, eat, sleep' routine with none of the fun in between and no one to come home to at the end of the day.

'Do you need me to get you anything?'

'A pregnancy test?' Violet gave a forced laugh, but there was nothing funny about it.

'Don't joke about something like that.'

'I'm not. I'm late.'

Nate dropped her hand to steady himself before he fell over. This couldn't be happening. 'But you're on the pill, right?'

'I think I missed one the night I flew in from London.' Her grimace sucker-punched him in the gut.

'You've been under a lot of stress too though.' He slowly got to his feet, still trying to come up with alternative theories. Ones that wouldn't tie them together for the rest of their days.

'I've been queasy and light-headed today. We both know if there's a possibility the worst could happen, it will. I should have known things were going too well.' The tears started again and it was obvious she didn't want this any more than he did. Neither of them had signed on for parenthood; they hadn't even been able to commit to each other for longer than a month, for heaven's sake.

'We'll get through this. Somehow.' The sickness was spreading to him now, his stomach twisting into a tight knot of anxiety.

A baby, their baby, was going to affect so many— him, Violet, his parents, the Earl... Nobody was going to take the news well. Why should they? He'd messed up big style. He should've taken extra precautions to prevent this happening, but he'd been too lost in his own desires to consider the consequences. Now he'd ruined Violet's future, the one she'd worked so hard to ensure didn't include him.

'I don't expect you to take this on. That's why I'm leaving. This was my mistake. I'll deal with it on my own.' She wouldn't look at him and turned her attention back to throwing her clothes haphazardly into her case.

A vice gripped his heart and squeezed. If there *was* a baby he wanted to be part of its life, wanted to be included in any decisions concerning *their* child. He didn't want Violet to deal with this on her own, regardless of how she did or didn't feel about him. A child needed two supportive parents to have the best possible start in life. To make sure it wouldn't ever feel abandoned, as he had when he'd attempted to improve his lot in life.

'Let's not jump too far ahead of ourselves. First things first—we get a test.' If their lives were about to change for ever they should really find out for sure. The delay would also give him a chance to figure out how to get her to stay. Indefinitely.

The sight of Violet packing to leave had crushed him almost as much as finding her room empty had when she'd first gone to London without an explanation. This was much, much worse. That had been puppy love, a childish infatuation. Now he knew how powerful real love was. The kind that was ripping him apart from the inside out at the thought of her leaving again. She was taking an even bigger part of him with her this time. Literally.

This baby might not have been planned but that didn't mean he didn't want it or wouldn't take responsibility for it. All of those steps he'd taken to avoid emotional attachments had led to the biggest one of all—fatherhood. He got chills every time he thought about it. Twelve years ago this would've been everything he'd wanted. Violet's rejection had changed all that, clouded his view on relationships even more. He'd dodged commitment as if it were some deadly disease when all along he'd still been devoted to Violet. She was the only woman he'd ever imagined spending his life with. Still was.

Unfortunately, the last time he'd confessed his feelings for her she'd skipped the country. He doubted ruining her life with an unplanned pregnancy was going to do anything to improve his chances of her loving him back. She'd only just begun making progress with her father and this news could set them back at loggerheads. Nate knew the Earl's reputation was everything to him and he would never want to sully Violet's name because of his selfish mistake.

The journey in the car to the chemist for the pregnancy test had given him the space and clarity to decide what to do.

'Marry me, Violet.' He loved her. No matter how much he tried to deny it, in the midst of this chaos, the strength of his feelings for her were abundantly clear. Until now he'd refused to admit it and run the risk of repeating the past. Although he'd never be the great love of her life he'd hoped to be, he'd always supported her. He'd always been afraid of marriage but now it seemed the best solution for all three of them. They needed each other.

'Don't be stupid.' A marriage proposal wasn't helping her dizziness as she glared at Nate and back at the screen. She knew it was a knee-jerk reaction to the reading when he'd told her what an awful idea he thought marriage was only hours ago. He didn't love her and she doubted he'd even entertained spending the rest of his days with her until they'd sat on the edge of her bed watching the digital screen spell out their future.

Pregnant
2-3

There was no mistaking her symptoms now, the damage apparently done at the beginning of their supposed fun fling. She gave a strangled laugh. It was either see the irony of that or start crying again.

'I mean it. This baby needs a father and I know how you feel about marriage but you need a husband. Hear me out—' He put a hand up to stop her as she bristled. 'It can be in name only, or you know we can keep the physical side going since we've both enjoyed it. What I'm saying is, love doesn't have to enter the equation. I don't expect it to. But I have a house you and the baby can live in, I can provide for you, and your reputation remains intact.'

He looked so pleased with himself as he shredded her heart into tiny irreparable pieces.

The man she'd apparently never stopped loving, the father of her unborn child, was offering her a marriage of convenience. It somehow seemed worse than the arranged marriages her father had proposed to maintain his social status. Probably because she knew she was in love with Nate and she'd ruined her chances of him ever feeling the same way about her. It was the reason she'd made certain she would leave the country again for London, a place she'd hoped to be able to forget him. Now she would have a permanent reminder.

Nate would always do the right thing, that was who he was, and it was the only reason he *would* want to marry her. She'd wreaked havoc in his life once too often and it wasn't fair to lumber him with a wife and child he'd never wanted. Neither did she want to give up her job to fake a happy marriage, following in her mother's tragic footsteps after all.

In an ideal world her baby would have two doting parents, madly in love with each other, providing the happy, family environment she'd never had. Marrying Nate would simply be perpetuating that myth that money and good name were all that mattered. She would rather raise this baby alone than with a father who was only there out of a sense of duty. The next generation of Dempseys deserved more after the trouble she'd caused to emancipate herself from society rules in the first place.

'It wouldn't work, Nate. We'd only end up making each other miserable. Marriage isn't for us. It's for people who love each other and are willing to give up everything to be together. Forget about me, forget about the baby, and just pretend I never came back. That this never happened.'

The vertigo was back, her head spinning with snap-shots of these weeks they'd spent together and memories of her parents' tumultuous relationship. Neither of them should have to compromise who they were simply be-cause they'd made a mistake. In her case, it was falling in love with a man who could never love her back after everything she'd done to him.

'That's impossible.' Nate rested his hand gently on her stomach, staking a claim on the life growing inside her.

She slapped it away. It would be easier for him to walk away now before this was about more than a bunch of cells. 'Not if I'm in a different country. I don't want you in my life, Nate. That wasn't the deal.'

She was shaking with nerves as the lie left her lips, hoping he couldn't see through it, or if he did he'd realise this was her way of letting him off the hook. She wanted Nate in her life more than anything but not through a sense of responsibility. This was her way of trying to pro-tect him, sacrificing her desires again and putting him first before her own needs. No matter how much it hurt.

Violet had taken a sledgehammer to what was left of his heart and pounded it until it was nothing but a big red stain he would never be able to scrub away. He was will-ing to give himself to her body and soul, something he'd never thought he would do, something he'd never imag-ined he would *want* to do. Everything he had worked to achieve seemed to have been building up to this moment and asking Violet to share it with him and their baby. Yet, she still didn't want him. The house, the job, the car—none of it was enough to convince her to be with him. None of it seemed to matter without her.

'I know this wasn't what either of us had planned but I'm simply trying to make the best of the situation.' He was doing his damnedest not to get too emotional and make her even more skittish than she was. She didn't respond well to intense personal discussion, as he'd found out to his cost. Her default setting was to run and hide rather than confront the truth; he'd seen it so many times before. She'd disappeared for twelve years after one kiss between them and he knew if she went back this time he'd lose her for ever.

'I just want you to go, Nate.' She sounded tired, resigned to life as a single parent already and he was being forced into the role of absent father. He didn't want to make things even more difficult for Violet than they already were by arguing with her, even though he was dying inside with every push further away. Neither could he, in good conscience, simply walk away after getting her into this condition in the first place.

He wanted to be there as she blossomed during her pregnancy, see their baby on the screen as it happened, not in some grainy printout he'd been sent as an afterthought. That role of a supportive father was important to him. It was something neither of them had really had growing up. Violet's father had been more concerned with his place in society than her feelings and Nate's parents' priority had always been Strachmore.

His childhood hadn't been carefree either, but an endless round of chores and lectures on being respectful. He'd practically had to make himself invisible so as not to offend the Earl. That wasn't conducive to making a child feel wanted or loved. More like an unpaid, unappreciated skivvy. Perhaps if they'd both been accepted for who they were by their own families they wouldn't have the problems they had connecting now.

If Violet didn't want him in her life there wasn't much he could do, but he had to at least try to be a part of their child's. That wasn't going to work long distance and he was willing to make sacrifices to get her to stay if it prevented their baby becoming another statistic of a broken relationship.

'I'll go and I promise not to come back unless you want me to. On the condition you stay at Strachmore until you're due back at work. I want you to be one hundred per cent sure that this is what you want.' His feet were blocks of wood, heavy and clumsy, as he reluctantly made his way to the door. He'd thought knowing she was leaving would be easier than finding out after she'd gone. He was wrong. However, whenever it happened, Violet walking out of his life was always going to be the worst thing that would ever happen to him.

'I am.' She threw one last knife into his back and killed the last dregs of hope stone dead.

CHAPTER NINE

'I'M SURE IT won't be much longer now.' Violet tried to pacify her father, who'd already picked up and set down the one magazine sitting on the waiting-room table. She understood how difficult it was to manage time when dealing with emotional patients, but she also knew how much of a short fuse her father had when he was kept waiting for an appointment. Especially when grief counselling wasn't something he was totally on board with.

He checked the clock again and gave a huff but at least nothing had been thrown in the interim. It was progress but she was still tense sitting here in the hospital with him. Her heart picked up the pace again as the thought of bumping into Nate came to mind. It had been over a week since she'd seen him at the house. He'd kept to his word to stay away as she'd known he would, enabling her to spend her last few days at Strachmore trying to figure out her next move.

'I haven't seen Nathaniel for a while. Did something happen between you two?' Her father picked up on the very subject matter making her unhappy.

Although she was glad he'd chosen conversation over berating the staff to fill the time, every time she thought of telling him about the baby her heart fluttered in her chest and she felt as though she might pass out.

'He's a busy man and we've probably taken up too much of his time at Strachmore.' She had no wish to take up any more of it by making him pay for her mistake. Whether she stayed at home or went back to London, she had to plan the rest of her life without him in it. The thought alone made her light-headed.

'I'm not blind, Violet, nor am I stupid. That boy has been in love with you for years and vice versa, unless I'm very much mistaken. He's hardly been away from Strachmore these past weeks and I doubt that's solely because of me. Now, he's suddenly incommunicado. Something clearly happened between the two of you and, whatever it is, I don't want it to affect your decisions about coming home in the future. I know I drove you away in the past but I really want you to at least visit.'

It was a huge step for him to admit his past behaviour towards her and let her know he wanted her to be part of his life again but, oh, how she wished he were right about Nate's feelings for her. He might have been in love with her when were kids but time and distance, not to mention her actions, had changed that. She fidgeted with the sleeve of her shirt, knowing she in turn should be honest with him, regardless of how petrified she was at the prospect of having to tell him she was pregnant. He might have mellowed slightly since his heart attack and subsequent procedures but that didn't mean his principles had changed.

The Earl's daughter was pregnant by the son of the housekeeper and it didn't get much more scandalous than that when it came to society gossip. This would be a real test of his priorities but she couldn't put it off much longer. Her condition would soon become apparent if she did come back in the future. It wouldn't be fair on her father to disappear again without telling him why.

She took a deep breath. And another. 'I'm pregnant.'

She braced herself for the backlash—shouting, screaming, crashing furniture—all of his typical reactions to such news would be justified this time. Most of them she'd done herself since sending Nate away.

'And he's not stepping up to his responsibilities?' Only when he'd jumped to the wrong conclusion did his face take on that red hue of impending rage.

'No. It's not that…he even offered to marry me.' She was quick to defend Nate; he'd done everything right. Except love her.

'What's the problem, then?'

'I don't want to get married because it's the right thing to do. I'm sorry, but I'd rather be on my own than in a cold marriage put on for appearances' sake.' Her reasons for turning Nate down might seem a tad insensitive in light of the present situation but it was the truth. Perhaps if there'd been a bit more of that between her parents, or between her and Nate, things could've turned out much differently. If she'd been honest with him about the strength of her feelings for him in the first place they might've actually stood a chance together.

Her father's frown turned into a half-smile. 'Marriage always was your sticking point. That doesn't mean you can't still be together. Times have changed, so you keep telling me.'

She was surprised he'd paid any heed to her word against that of his ingrained sense of tradition. An illegitimate child would have devastated him not so long ago but he was clearly working hard on keeping their relationship alive.

'I can't be with someone who doesn't love me. It wouldn't be fair on me, or the baby.' She rubbed her hand over her still flat-belly, wishing only happiness for the life growing inside her.

'I don't believe that for one minute. Only a man in love would put up with your irritable father and do everything he has to secure Strachmore's future. I think it's *you* who doesn't want to commit.'

'Well, he's never said it,' she huffed, upset at the accusation she was the one at fault here. As far as she was concerned she'd done everything right to ensure Nate had been treated fairly. Not many women would've given him the green light to walk away. Especially when they were head over heels about him and carrying his child.

'Have *you*? You know, if I could change things I'd make sure your mother and I had really talked about how we felt. I'd make damn sure I listened. Don't throw something special away because you're scared to face the truth. You'll spend the rest of your life regretting it.' His teary blue eyes were a reflection of her own but she feared they'd both left it too late. She'd pushed Nate away, said some horrible things to ensure he'd stay out of her life. Unfortunately, given his silence since, she seemed to have succeeded in her quest.

'You're not mad at me? About the baby?' She was going to need at least one person to be there holding her hand when this bundle of trouble arrived and turned everything upside down. If she had her father's support it would ease some of her stress and help her enjoy this pregnancy more. So far it had been all tension and sickness and she was still waiting for the so-called blossoming to start.

He sighed.

'It's not what I wanted for you but it's not the end of the world. I just want you to be happy.' He reached over and gave her hand a squeeze, the only loving gesture she could ever remember getting from him. She cursed her hormones as the tears tipped over the edge of her lashes. She wasn't sure she'd ever be truly happy again.

'Lord Dempsey?' The receptionist called him for his appointment, drawing them both out of their heart-to-heart and on their feet.

'Whoa.' Violet had to sit down again as all the blood in her body seemed to rush to her head at once.

The receptionist rushed over to check on her. 'Are you all right?'

'She's pregnant,' her father answered for her, rubbing her back, already playing the role of protective grandfather.

'Just a little dizzy. My heart's racing a little but that's been happening a lot recently.' She didn't want to make a fuss and somehow have Nate get wind of it, but she was a bit breathless and seriously feeling as if she was about to faint.

'At least you're in the right place. I'll put in a call and get them to check you out in A and E.'

Violet could only nod as she struggled to stay conscious.

It wasn't long before she found herself stretched out on a bed with electrodes stuck all over her body, hooked up to an ECG machine. They'd gone over her medical history, and taken blood samples. She didn't know what they were expecting to find but the longer she lay here worrying what was happening, the faster her heart rate seemed to get. It was beating so hard she could easily have just finished running a marathon rather than simply have had an intense conversation with her father. She rested her hands on her invisible bump. It was still early days into her pregnancy and she was trying not to freak out about the fact she was already in hospital.

The doctor studied the printout of her test with a frown, which wasn't helping her relax at all. 'Your heart rate is higher than we would like. At the minute it's beating so fast the heart muscle can't relax between contractions and the lack of oxygen is what's causing the dizzy spells.'

'Will it harm the baby?' That was all that mattered right now. She mightn't have planned on this baby but neither did she want anything to happen to it. It was all she had left of Nate now.

He shook his head. 'There's nothing to worry about. We do want to send you to CCU, though, so they can keep a close eye on you during treatment.'

If she didn't laugh at the irony she'd cry. It was the one department in the building she was virtually guaranteed to see the man she'd been trying to avoid. There was no way her baby daddy was going to remain a silent partner once she and junior rocked up on his turf. He was going to have plenty to say about looking after herself and his child. Fate was going to make sure they had one last showdown before she left for London this time.

London. It had been her salvation, her road to independence, but now going back to her empty apartment felt like a punishment for her mistake. She had family here, and friends. And Nate. All she had in London was her job. She'd been so busy building walls to protect her heart she'd isolated herself emotionally and physically from anyone who'd tried to get close. It wasn't the ideal set-up for a woman raising a child on her own. What if there were any more complications during the pregnancy? She had no one to lean on there because that was the way she'd wanted it. Impending motherhood had since changed her views on complete independence.

These past weeks had reminded her how good it felt to have companionship, to be loved, to be *in* love. Even having her father waiting patiently outside for news she and the baby were safe was a turning point in their relationship, an insight into the family life she could have had here. Returning to a one-bedroom flat, pregnant and broken-hearted, wasn't something she was looking forward to. She was going to miss Strachmore and everyone associated with it.

Nate was on his way to do the rounds on the coronary care unit, having just finished fitting a pacemaker for one of his patients. It was best to keep busy to stop him from running up to Strachmore to see if Violet was still there. He'd given her his word he wouldn't go near her to give her space to think, but the distinct lack of communication indicated his plan to get her to stick around had backfired. As she'd told him in no uncertain terms, she didn't want, or need, him in her life. He didn't even know if she was still in the country.

This time he wasn't simply going to accept her decision. He would follow her to London if it meant he could at least see their child grow and flourish. Without Violet and the baby here he wasn't sure what was keeping him here anyway. The house he'd been so proud of owning now seemed too big for a single man, too empty. The rooms should be full of toys and plans for the future, not a reminder of everything he'd lost. He didn't know how he was ever going to get over her this time, knowing what they could have…*should* have had together. Too bad his peasant status had let him down again. It was a stigma he would never be able to overcome to become worthy of the Earl's daughter. Or perhaps he'd simply have to face the fact that she'd never loved him anyway and he'd been the one using his upbringing as an excuse. Either way she didn't want him, and he was lost without her.

If only it were as easy to fix his broken heart as those of his patients. He'd gladly volunteer as a guinea pig for any new research looking into replacing emotionally battered hearts if it meant an end to this misery. He hadn't even been able to share the pain of losing the woman he loved and his baby when no one had known they'd existed, including his family. This was only supposed to have been a meaningless fling; there'd been no reason to broadcast the fact they were together. He'd had no way of knowing this would change him for ever. Somehow he was going to have to break the news to his parents they were soon to become grandparents and they might never see their first, and possibly only, grandchild.

Thoughts of Violet and the baby had tormented him for days; he'd been wondering if some day another man would take over *his* role as husband and father. He knew without doubt he could never replace what he'd lost, but that didn't mean Violet wouldn't love someone else, someone acceptable. If she didn't relent about seeing him again to at least discuss future arrangements, he might have to move away too. He didn't think he could face Strachmore again or hearing any stories coming out of it. He'd been here before, knew the pain he'd go through to come out the other side and the only thing to get him through was hard work.

In fact he was obsessing over his personal life so much it was encroaching on his professional one. He would've sworn he'd seen the Earl walk past when the CCU doors had flashed open at the end of the corridor. Impossible. He would've known if his patient had been readmitted.

Still, it would put his mind at rest to check with the senior nurse in charge.

'Has Samuel Dempsey been admitted again, by any chance?'

'No, but he's here with his daughter. She came in yesterday.'

'What? Why didn't anyone tell me?' In the fearful haze clouding his brain he'd forgotten this had been a secret affair. His colleagues had no idea this woman in jeopardy was everything to him.

The nurse frowned. 'She said she didn't want us to contact anyone. We've put her in Room One—'

Nate didn't wait to hear any more. He was already haring off to find Violet, regardless of whether she wanted to see him or not. People weren't admitted to CCU on a whim, especially pregnant women. If Violet, or the baby, were in danger he was going to be there for them regardless of her objections.

He burst into the side room and, while he was glad to see her again, the sight of her lying in the hospital bed, small and pale, was almost his undoing. The heart monitors that were part of his everyday job now took on a sinister new meaning as they charted her progress.

'Nate!'

Perhaps he should have given her some warning before crashing in here as he watched her heart rate spike on the screen. He reached for her charts to find out exactly what was going on. 'Are you and the baby okay?'

'We're fine. I didn't sleep very well last night so they moved me in here for a little more peace and quiet.' Despite the circumstances and how they'd left things the last time they'd seen each other, she actually looked pleased to see him.

'Why didn't you phone me?' He directed his question at her father, sitting by the bedside, not a figment of his imagination at all. It was more of an accusation that he'd been purposely kept out of the loop. Probably by the man who'd made it his life's work to interfere in hers. So much for the new leaf they'd supposed he'd turned over.

'I told him not to. I've caused you enough grief over the years. It's not fair to keep involving you in my problems.' Violet's admission saved him from beginning a new battle with her father even though it was completely without foundation. He'd never backed away when she'd needed him.

'Why not? This is my baby too. I *want* to be involved.' A second too late he realised he'd blown the big secret. She might not have wanted her father to know her predicament before she'd gone back to London and now Nate would have his reaction on his conscience too.

'As I told her you should be. Now, I think it's about time you two had a serious talk about your future, about this baby.' The Earl's lack of punch-throwing and willingness to walk out of the room, leaving him alone with his daughter, led Nate to believe Violet had already broken the news of the addition to the family.

'You told him?'

'I didn't think I'd be able to hide it much longer. He took it better than I could ever have dreamed of.'

'Clearly. I'm still standing.' It would've been a different story twelve years ago, pre medical school, if he'd knocked up the Earl's daughter. The long road to cardiology had been worth it to be accepted on some level, if not as part of the family.

'Actually, he didn't seem that surprised. I guess we weren't as discreet as we thought we'd been.' That twinkle in her eye took Nate back to a time and a place he was already having trouble letting go of.

'Okay. Let's see what we have here.' He resisted running over and kissing her when he knew for sure she wasn't in immediate danger. It might be pushing his luck too far.

SVT, supraventricular tachycardia, was something he'd had plenty of experience with in his patients, including pregnant women. The complications that could arise were often due to the presence of heart disease, a cause for concern given her father's recent history. Thankfully her ultrasounds and ECGs had ruled this out. She had, however, been admitted with a very high tachycardia rate, reaching between one hundred and eighty and two hundred and forty beats per minute.

'I'm fine, honestly.' Violet tried to convince him there was no need for him to worry, or be here, but he could see her arrhythmia had not yet abated.

'We still need to get that heart rate stable again before you leave.' There was no way she was going home until he knew all was well. A beta blocker had already been administered to no avail. There was always a small chance the administered drugs could cross the placental barrier so it wasn't something he wanted for her long term when there were no obvious benefits in her case. The alternative wasn't something he relished for the mother of his unborn child either.

'They said they might have to take me to Theatre?' There was a slight tremor in her voice belying her nerves even though she was insisting on her indestructability.

Since she hadn't bawled at him to get out of the room he dared to get closer to the bedside. 'If your heart rate doesn't regulate they are planning electrical cardioversion. Essentially this will be delivering a mild electric shock to jolt the heart back into a normal rhythm.'

'The same thing you did to Dad?'

'Something similar. Except without the drama. And you're a much prettier patient.' He couldn't stop himself from reaching out and stroking her hair back from her forehead. This could be the last time he'd see her if she chose life in London alone over one with him. The last chance he had to tell her how he really felt in the hope it could somehow make a difference.

She closed her eyes. 'Nate—'

'You scared me, you know. When they told me you were here I nearly flipped my lid. I know you don't want to hear it but I want to marry you. I want to raise our baby together. I don't want to find out what's happening to you via a third party.' There were eight months left of this pregnancy, never mind the next eighteen years of their baby's life.

'I appreciate the sentiment but a marriage of convenience isn't what I want. It never has been. Forcing you to marry someone you don't love makes me no better than my father when he was trying to pair me off for the greater good. I don't expect you to make compromises in your life to suit me, nor am I willing to do that for anyone. I saw what that did to my mother.'

'I'm not asking you to make compromises. I'm simply asking you to be with me. And what's this nonsense about not loving you? I've loved you since our private prom night in the boathouse and I doubt I'll ever stop loving you. You're the one who keeps running out on me.' He wasn't about to take responsibility for her fleeing the country again when he was the one trying to get her to stay. If she was insisting on leaving because the thought of being with him was so abhorrent, he wanted to hear her say it. It was the only way he was ever going to be able to accept it.

'But…but…you made it sound as though you felt

an obligation to marry me. You never mentioned the L word.' Violet held her breath, the impact of what he was saying too great to comprehend in her current state. He was basically killing her argument for getting on a plane back to London stone dead.

'The last time I did that you disappeared for over a decade. I was trying to prevent another vanishing-woman act. Listen, I know I didn't measure up then and no amount of certificates will make me a qualified member of the aristocracy, but I will look after you and our child. I don't want you to change. I'm not asking anything from you except to give us a chance.'

She thought her heart was going to burst through her chest, it felt so full. Nate loved her; even after everything, he loved her.

'I was scared, that's why I left the first time, why I was leaving now. I thought it was best for you. I watched my parents' love turn to hate with the pressures of society. I didn't want that for you, or us. The strength of my feelings for you was never in question but I didn't want it to be at the cost of anyone's freedom. You didn't sign up for a baby, or a grumpy Earl, or a run-down country estate.' It said a lot that he was still here now she'd reminded him of all the baggage she was lugging with her.

Nate sat on the edge of the bed and took her hand in his. 'I love you. Everything else we can deal with.'

She didn't think she'd ever get tired of hearing him say those words. 'You mean it?'

'I mean every word. I want to marry you because I love you. A baby is just the icing on the cake. I'll move to London with you, leave my job and be a stay-at-home dad, whatever it takes for us to be together because that's what I want more than anything else in the world.' He leaned over and placed a gentle kiss on her lips.

As soon as he touched her the tension left her body, a sense of peace finally descending and releasing her from the burdens of the past. This was everything she'd been waiting for.

After a long, satisfying smooch, Nate got up from the bed. 'I don't believe it.'

'What?'

He was staring at the heart monitor and she automatically feared the worst. No matter who tried to reassure her, having electrodes stuck to her body to conduct electricity to her organs wasn't how a first-time mum wanted to begin her pregnancy. She'd take morning sickness or a craving for pickles over that scenario any day.

'Your heart rate is stabilising on its own.'

Violet followed his gaze. Sure enough the figures were dropping, evening out to where they were supposed to be. Finding Nate *actually* wanted to marry her had been enough to shock her heart into working properly again. Although, she might have to insist he keep his distance for a while longer. If he kept kissing her and things got steamy there was every chance he'd send her pulse sky-high again.

'In that case I guess we can start making plans for the future. We've got a baby to think about.'

She didn't want to spend any more time looking back. Not when she had so much to look forward to. Her life was going to change for ever, probably bring more challenges along the way, but with Nate at her side she knew she could face them head-on.

After all, one kiss from him had been enough to heal her heart.

EPILOGUE

VIOLET WATCHED FROM her bedroom window as the wedding guests filed around the side of the house to the Victorian conservatory. This was it, the day she'd fought against for most of her life in the very place she'd run from as a teenager and she couldn't have been happier. In less than an hour's time she'd be marrying Nate.

With Strachmore now fully licensed to hold weddings, it seemed fitting that theirs would be the first. They'd agreed upon a small affair with only close family and friends in attendance, simple and discreet with none of the palaver she'd always associated with society weddings. Today was about celebrating their love and nothing else. Everything was perfect.

She stroked her small baby bump concealed under her white lace bridal gown. It wouldn't be long before the three of them would become a family. The past four months had been a whirlwind of activity. After a great deal of thought she'd decided she wanted to move back to Northern Ireland, with both families nearby when the baby arrived. Nate had gone with her back to London to help her pack her things for moving in with him while she worked out her notice. With all of their pre-planning she hoped the rest of her pregnancy was going to be more relaxing.

Once the baby was born she would go back to work at a local level and share the childminding with Nate and the excited grandparents anxiously awaiting the new arrival. Everything was slotting into place. She just wished she had her mother here to share it.

A knock on the door interrupted her maudlin thoughts before they could fully develop and taint the happiest day of her life.

'I just wanted to see how my beautiful bride was holding up.' Nate, devastatingly handsome in his wedding tuxedo, stepped into the room and immediately lifted her spirits again. She couldn't help but wonder if he wore one of those mood rings she'd had as a kid, which had some way of telling him when she needed him most.

'I'm fine, but isn't it bad luck for us to see each other before the wedding?' She really didn't want to tempt fate when it had taken so long for them to reach this point.

'I thought we'd broken free of tradition and superstition by now? These days we make our own luck.' He crossed the room in three strides to reach her and slip his hands around her waist. It was all she needed to feel complete again.

'You're right. I'm sure there's a million women out there who'd want to swap places with me at this moment.' She was the luckiest woman alive to be marrying this man today and she wasn't going to let any imagined curses get in the way of that a second time.

'Have I told you how stunning you are yet? I have to keep pinching myself as a reminder that this is actually happening.' He deflected her comment with one of his own, standing back to admire her vintage-style dress.

'This is *actually* happening. We're minutes away from taking our vows in front of all those people out there.' The nerves started to creep back in at the thought of leaving this lovely cosy cocoon with Nate and proclaiming their love in public.

'Well, we've got a little while yet…' He had that twinkle in his eye that said *NT* wanted to make his mark one last time as a single man.

'Do you know how long it took for me to squeeze into this dress? There's no way I'm taking it off again.' The knowledge he still found her irresistible despite her changing body was enough to send shivers of need skating across her skin and make her want to fast forward to their wedding night.

'Who said anything about getting you naked? Honestly, the way your hormones are raging I'm wondering if I'm going to make it back from the honeymoon alive.' His fake outrage widened Violet's smile even further. She couldn't promise him that when they were going to spend the next two weeks alone on a tropical island. They were still making up for lost time.

'So if you're not going to seduce me, what are you doing in my bedroom, Mr Taylor?'

'I have a present for you, soon-to-be Mrs Taylor.' Nate reached into his pocket and pulled out a small velvet jewellery box. He opened it to reveal a delicate silver necklace.

'It's beautiful.' Violet fingered the tiny diamond-encrusted entwined seahorses dangling from the end of the chain he was now fastening around her neck. She'd taken off her bracelet today and had felt naked without it, as if a piece of her were missing.

'I'm afraid I couldn't get your mother's necklace back for you, but I thought you could do with an upgrade from my last gift of jewellery.'

'Thank you.' She knew this was his way of marking the start of their new life together and fading out the past.

'I thought we could have our first dance here too. Without anyone else.' He placed her hands around his neck and took her in his arms. She closed her eyes and relaxed into his embrace, remembering their faux prom where they'd danced in secret and fallen in love for the first time. Nate was all she'd ever needed.

As they held each other tight, their bodies swaying together with nothing but the beat of their hearts keeping time, Violet knew there was nowhere else she'd rather be. She'd finally come home.

* * * * *

If you enjoyed this story, check out these other great reads from Karin Baine

A KISS TO CHANGE HER LIFE
FRENCH FLING TO FOREVER

Available now!

THE ARMY DOC'S
SECRET WIFE

BY
CHARLOTTE HAWKES

Published in Great Britain 2016
By Mills & Boon, an imprint of HarperCollins*Publishers*
1 London Bridge Street, London, SE1 9GF

© 2016 Charlotte Hawkes

ISBN: 978-0-263-91495-5

Our policy is to use papers that are natural, renewable and recyclable
products and made from wood grown in sustainable forests.
The logging and manufacturing processes conform to the legal
environmental regulations of the country of origin.

Printed and bound in Spain
by CPI, Barcelona

Dear Reader,

Thank you for picking *The Army Doc's Secret Wife*—my debut novel for Mills & Boon Medical Romance. I'm so proud and honoured to be a writer within the M&B family. I picked up my first M&B at fifteen—when a school friend lent me one from her collection—and I was hooked.

I love high-octane heroes, and I'm so proud of our soldiers—who are prepared to lay down their lives to protect their country, whether they agree with the politicians or not.

My very own hero is my former Troop Commander—a shy young man who nonetheless was a stickler for discipline. We resisted the sparks of attraction for three years whilst I was an Officer Cadet under his command… But I wondered what would happen if my hero and heroine, Ben and Thea, were caught up in a more emotional situation, with Ben's terrible survivor's guilt over the death of Thea's brother playing a part in the way he responds to her.

The idea of a second chance at love also appealed—especially as my hero walked away for such honourable reasons. But Thea is no push-over. She's a high-flying professional in more than one sense of the term and, having been hurt in the past, has an inner core of steel. As much as she loves her hero, she's determined to help Ben beat his demons before she opens herself up to him again.

I hope you enjoy *The Army Doc's Secret Wife*, and I'd love it if you dropped by my website—charlottehawkes.com.

Charlotte

To my beautiful boys, Montgomery and Bartholomew.
You may never read these books, but—for the record—
one of you is very excited that you're almost able to
read the back of your pirate bubblebath bottle!

To my parents,
for your unfailing love and support throughout my life—
even if you *do* now spoil my boys terribly.

To Flo, my editor, for getting me here.
You whipped me—and my book—into incredible shape.
Don't stop *hmmmmm*-ing!

To my husband, my real-life hero (& Capt.).
Without you, none of this would be possible.
Sorry(ish) about the *Sir* stuff.

The Army Doc's Secret Wife
is **Charlotte Hawkes's** debut title
for Mills & Boon Medical Romance!

CHAPTER ONE

ICY NUMBNESS HAD been sneaking around Alethea 'Thea' Abrams' body from the moment she'd received the phone call. The drive to the hospital was a blur but somehow she must have done it. And now the chill finally took a grip of her shaking limbs, forcing her to stop and lean on the door frame as if to draw strength, as she stared down the military wing's ward and into the side room where Ben Abrams, her husband, lay—still asleep—in a bed.

'I understand you've been fully briefed?' The nurse consulted her notes. 'And that you're also a civilian doctor, working for the Air Ambulance Emergency Response Unit? That'll certainly help a lot. And Dr Fields *has* prepared you for the chance that Major Abrams… Ben… might not recognise you?'

Thea managed a stiff nod, surreptitiously sliding cold fingers around the doorjamb. *Yes, they had warned her it was a possibility.* Words of caution she often had to say to other people, and yet it had still been a shock to hear them said to her. It all felt surreal—like some kind of nightmare. The broken body in that bed was so far removed from the robust, spirited, dynamic Ben she knew.

If she had ever really known him.

'I understand how difficult this is but you need to be

ready. Your reaction could influence how Ben approaches his recovery.' The nurse was kind but firm.

'I understand.' Miraculously, Thea made it sound as if she did, despite the fact that the professional, medical side of her brain appeared to have completely deserted her.

'Are you ready to go over there?'

Thea watched as Dr Fields moved around Ben's bed. There was another man there, an older man who looked vaguely familiar, but Thea couldn't place him. He wasn't interfering, and she couldn't tell whether he was over-seeing or not. An Army specialist perhaps? Not anyone she knew.

Not trusting herself to speak, Thea forced out a cou-ple more jerky nods. The nurse seemed unconvinced.

'Listen, it's a lot to take in all at once. Do you need a few more moments? We can go to the visitors' room—it's just down the corridor.'

Thea shook her head, unable to drag her gaze from Ben, who looked so utterly alien to her, and yet so pain-fully familiar at the same time.

'Just run me through it again.' Her voice was so hoarse she couldn't even recognise it herself. 'Ben was caught in a roadside bomb?'

'Yes—well, two, actually. His vehicle was the fourth in a convoy, and the IED was detonated as the second four-by-four passed. Ben was quite severely injured in the initial blast, severing his arm at the level of the proximal humerus, and he has since undergone successful micro-vascular replantation. However, even with that level of injury we understand he ran to the front vehicles to pull out the rest of his patrol.'

The utter admiration in the military nurse's voice was evident, but Thea just stared at the uncharacteristically still figure in the bed, a maelstrom swirling in her head.

Dammit, Ben—you nearly died. Why do you always have to play the hero?

How was she meant to correlate this with the life-loving Ben who had always lived for his beloved sports?

'He pulled five soldiers to safety—he saved their lives—before the second IED went off, and then he was crushed under a vehicle and knocked unconscious.'

'Which is when he sustained the spinal damage,' Thea stated flatly, her medical brain finally—mercifully—kicking in. She needed to detach herself from her unsteady emotions. It was the only way she was going to get through this. *If only it was that easy,* she thought bleakly.

'It looks bad, but from what we've seen, Ben is strong. If anyone can pull through this, he can. With your help.' The nurse smiled encouragingly. 'Your husband's a hero.'

Your husband's a hero.

Nausea churned in Thea's stomach. Her mouth was parched—too parched to respond. It took her several attempts to swallow, then to flick out a nervous tongue to try and moisten dry lips.

Her husband...

For the first time since she'd heard about the accident and rushed to the hospital Thea felt her pain and fear give way to something even more visceral.

Anger.

The man lying in that bed—her husband—was almost as much of a stranger to her as he was to the nurse standing next to her now. That was if Thea set aside the fact that the last time she'd seen Ben they'd had wild, crazy sex, only for him to walk out on her the next morning. Leaving her abandoned and alone. That was a far cry from the Ben everyone else saw—the self-sacrificing soldier who always seemed to save the day in her brother's war stories. Where had Ben the hero been when *she'd* needed saving?

Instead, she'd had to save herself.

So why, even now, did he still have the power to affect her the way he did?

'I understand your husband has been hailed as a hero before?' The nurse broke into Thea's preoccupation with another encouraging smile. 'Wasn't he awarded the Distinguished Service Order?'

'He was part of a patrol that was ambushed.' Thea forced herself to acknowledge the question, her tongue feeling too thick for her mouth. 'Ben took out at least twenty of the enemy before back-up arrived.'

'I can believe it.' The nurse smiled, shaking her head incredulously. 'And his patrol mates?'

'That's all I know.' Thea heaved her shoulders and fought back tears. She didn't want to talk any more—didn't want to tell the nurse that Ben's patrol mate—her own brother Daniel—had died. Having already lost her parents when she was nine years old, Daniel had been all she'd had, and back then the pain of losing him had been raw. She hadn't asked Ben exactly what had happened, and he had never spoken about it.

'Can you just give me a few moments, please?' Thea asked the nurse, grateful when she nodded her understanding and moved away to give Thea some space.

This was harder than she could have imagined. This one event had opened a floodgate of emotions and memories she'd kept locked away for almost two decades.

After their parents' death it had been just her and Daniel, but whilst she'd stayed with foster families—twice being offered and turning down a permanent home—her brother, seven years older than her, had remained in the children's home. No one had wanted a teenage boy.

Hardly surprising that Daniel had joined the Army the day he'd turned eighteen.

The day Thea had turned eighteen she'd thanked her kindly foster family, packed her bag, and left to be re-united with her brother. Looking back, she realised that moving from the free accommodation within the Army barracks to renting a tiny flat in town for them both must have taken every penny Daniel had—and yet he'd never once made her feel anything other than welcome.

Three years later he'd been killed in that ambush and she'd gone to pieces, fallen in with the wrong crowd. It seemed doubly ironic that Ben—the one person who had tracked her down night after night and dragged her out of illegal warehouse raves, the one person who had stayed with her until the very worst of the grief had started to clear and she'd been able to see that being hell-bent on self-destruction wasn't the way to go—should have walked out on her too, leaving her more alone than ever.

Of all the losses in her life, none had left her feeling as abandoned, as *bereft*, as when Ben had walked out on her. Except perhaps the loss of their baby. *Ben's* baby. Thea pushed away a surge of nausea but couldn't tear her mind away from the devastating memory.

When Ben, barely twenty-five years old, had offered her marriage Thea, just twenty-one herself, and looking for someone to cling to after Daniel's death, had jumped at it. With hindsight, Ben's subsequent walking out on her had been inevitable.

Daniel had once claimed that Ben had always ap-peared older than his years. Something to do with a reg-imented upbringing and a strict Army Colonel father, which had left Ben with an overdeveloped sense of re-sponsibility for everything and everyone around him.

And Ben had honoured the *responsibility* side of their

marriage. His Captain's income had given her security, money to fund her continued education and a home of her own—not that he'd ever returned to it after their wedding night. If he hadn't done all that, where would she have ended up? Certainly not as one of the youngest doctors with the Air Ambulance, that was for sure.

She would have to keep reminding herself that *that* was why she was here. Not because she still cared about Ben, but because she owed him a great debt. However much he had hurt her.

Nothing could ever completely erase the pain of losing the people who had loved her the most, but the one consolation she'd always held on to was the fact that both her parents and her brother had been ripped from her against their will—they hadn't abandoned her.

But Ben was different. He had *chosen* to leave her. Worse still, he had walked out on her the morning after their wedding. The morning after their wedding *night*— when she had thought they had made the ultimate connection.

She'd been wrong.

'Dr Abrams?' Thea hadn't noticed the nurse return, and she swung around to meet her gentle gaze.

'I'll be over at the nurses' station—just let me know when you'd like to go in to see your husband.'

'Great,' Thea croaked.

What the hell was she supposed to say to him?

Her mind whirled. This was a walk of shame and an oh-so-awkward morning-after conversation all rolled into one. And to make matters worse it was five years too late.

She squeezed her eyes shut, as if blocking the memories which suddenly threatened to engulf her. *She had to stop being silly.* No doubt the last time they'd been together—the awkward sex—was the least of Ben's problems right now. Besides, nothing good could come of wallowing. She knew that from bitter experience. It might have taken her almost all of these five years to come to terms with what had happened, but she had finally managed to.

At least she'd thought she had. The moment she'd received that call—shocked that she was still noted as Ben's next of kin—and seen him lying immobile in that bed, her emotions had been whipped into a confused mess.

Ben was hurt. She couldn't ever forgive him for abandoning her emotionally when she'd needed him, but she had to concede that he hadn't abandoned his responsibility to her. Now he needed *her* help, and she couldn't ignore the sense of commitment that struck in her—half buried as it might be. She owed him loyalty for that, at least.

She stuffed the anger back down, feeling calmer as the genuine concern she felt for him slowly started to regain control over her errant emotions. Perhaps seeing Ben through this, helping him to recover, would be the closure she finally needed? She had no choice. It was proving impossible to put Major Ben Abrams into her past any other way.

Thea felt a tiny sliver of resolve harden in her chest— her strong, professional inner core finally peeking its head out again—and she clutched at it before it darted back into the shadows. Tilting up her head, she urged her leaden legs to move in the direction of the nurses' station just as the nurse glanced up.

'Dr Abrams? Are you ready to go in now?'

Thea jutted out her chin and fell back on all her training. It offered her a much needed confidence boost.

'So…' Thea injected as much authority into her tone as possible. 'What's the prognosis?'

It barely took a moment for the nurse to register the difference in her. She shot Thea a look more akin to one colleague looking at another, rather than at a patient's next of kin.

'Fortunately the ambush occurred not far from the camp, and they were able to get a team out quickly to secure the area and recover the casualties. Ben was medevacced to the nearest main hospital, which was when his arm was reattached. The seven-hour operation went smoothly, but there will be follow-ups, of course.'

'And what about regaining normal function?' Thea asked. That sliver of resolve was starting to grow, lending Thea a new sense of determination.

'Under ideal circumstances, with consistent physio and positive rehabilitation, Major Abrams can expect to regain up to eighty-five per cent of normal function.'

Eighty-five per cent of normal function? Ben was a surgeon.

Thea suppressed a shudder. How would he cope with never being able to operate again? What was more, these weren't *ideal* circumstances.

She could see the concern in the nurse's eyes.

'I'm guessing that with Ben's additional spinal injury that replantation prognosis is optimistic? What level of spinal injury is it?'

'Honestly…? We simply don't know at this stage.' The nurse shook her head. 'We know the bomb blast was significant, and that Major Abrams went into spinal shock. So there is spinal cord damage. But the swelling means we have no idea just how extensive the damage is.'

Thea nodded grimly, struggling to keep those icy fingers from curling their way around her heart again.

'I appreciate you're Air Ambulance,' the nurse was

saying, 'but how much do you know about spinal injuries post-emergency rescue?'

'These days it's mainly assessing, securing and stabilising the patient to ensure no further damage during transport,' Thea acknowledged. 'As you say, I don't usually get involved with the post-emergency rescue care. But before I joined the Air Ambulance I did do some work on the Keimen case.'

It was one of the things which had helped to propel her up the career ladder at such a young age. That and her driving need to block out the pain caused by Ben's ultimate rejection.

'The boy whose spinal cord was completely severed and who took his first steps some two years later?'

Thea dipped her head. The work had been cutting edge, and she wasn't surprised that it had caught the nurse's attention.

'I understand they transplanted cells from the part of the brain involved in sending smell signals from the nose to the brain to stimulate the repair of his spinal cord?'

'That's right.' Thea managed a smile despite herself. It had been inspiring to work on that case.

'I see.' The nurse nodded. 'Then you'll completely understand the difficulty at the moment with Major Abrams. As I said, there's still too much swelling to get a clear MRI, and unfortunately we do know that the impact of the second IED and the Land Rover crushing him was significant.'

'So it's a waiting game,' Thea stated as calmly as she could.

As unlikely as it sounded, she could only hope that the swelling was protecting his back and that any injury was as low down as possible. Usually, the lower it was, the better. The sacral nerves, perhaps, at worst the lumbar. But the higher the damage—the thoracic nerves or, God forbid, somewhere within the cervical vertebrae— the more chance Ben might be paralysed for life.

Thea squeezed her eyes shut at the thought. Ben was such a physical guy—not just as a soldier but in his personal life, too. She couldn't imagine how he would react to such news, but she would need to start considering options just in case. He loved sports. *All* sports. Mountain biking, climbing, kayaking—even base jumping. And their fake honeymoon had been a skiing trip—not that they'd gone after he'd walked out.

Before that failed night Ben had promised to take her, after she'd told him that the highlight of her years in and out of care homes had been a charity group who'd taken a bunch of them to some rundown hostel every year.

Thea shook her head before the memory could get a grip. It was those caring, thoughtful moments from Ben which had meant that the same morning he'd walked out—the morning after they'd made love for the first time—Thea had been screwing up all her courage to suggest that one day they might possibly have more than just a fake marriage. Even if it took time.

Odd, the randomness of the memories which now popped into her head...

'Yes, it's a waiting game,' the nurse confirmed sympathetically.

Thea blinked slowly. *Ben didn't know any of this yet.* She stood for a moment, looking down the ward in silence. Life was precious,—so very precious. Why was it that people lost sight of that so easily—including her? *Especially* her.

Abruptly she stepped forward, as if to steel her body as well as her mind, and headed to the side room. As she got closer she could see the traction which stopped

Ben from moving his neck and back, his legs, until they were able to assess the damage. He looked so uncharacteristically fragile that she felt her emotions start to bubble once again.

Ben—who had rejected her not once, but twice, leaving her broken. And yet it seemed entirely fitting that, as she stood by his bedside, across from the nurse as she checked his vitals, Ben chose that moment to wake up.

'Thea? What are you doing here?'

He recognised her!

She blinked back tears as the nurse swung around to pour a beaker of fresh water and offer a straw for Ben to take a sip. He was clearly still groggy from the sedatives, and his brain was no doubt a mush of memories that he wouldn't be able to process or even arrange in chronological order. But the fact that he knew who she was an encouraging start. And, despite the painful rasp, the unexpected warmth in his voice at seeing her had caught her off guard. But it had also made her feel more helpless than she'd ever felt before. It was as if the last five years had momentarily been erased.

She wouldn't cry, she *wouldn't*.

'I'm sorry. I'm so sorry…' His voice cracked as he struggled to speak. 'About Daniel…about the wedding…'

'Shh…don't talk. Just rest.' She blinked furiously to stop the unwelcome tears from falling. Tears of fear, but also of relief.

So much for the concern that he might not remember anything. She should have known better—this was Ben Abrams they were dealing with. She should have known he would fight through.

'I'm sorry about everything…'

His slurred words were barely clear, but she could decipher them.

'I'll protect you, Thea. I'll never leave you again.'

It was absurd that her heart should lurch so unexpectedly. Thea chastised herself. It was the medication talking—she knew that—and even groggy he wasn't saying the three words she had once longed to hear. Though no longer. There weren't *any* words she wanted to hear from him any more.

Caught up in her thoughts, Thea realised too late that Ben was fighting to move his arm and take her hand. His injured arm. As if in slow motion she watched him struggle to raise his head, only for the restraints to stop him. His eyes slid to the damaged limb as it lay obstinately on the bed, refusing to obey the commands his brain was sending out.

This was happening all wrong. She needed to speak to him, explain things to him—not have him find out for himself...especially not like this. In horror, she saw Ben stare at the arm, then down to the other restraints around his pelvis and spine. Finally came the realisation of memory, and it chased long, furious shadows across his bruised face. His eyes met hers one final time.

'Get her out of here. *Now*,' he snarled, his eyes unexpectedly full of accusation and despair and loathing before he abruptly passed out again.

Did he still blame her for that night? That night when she'd barely been able to think straight with grief. That night she'd craved just a few moments of dark oblivion, to forget everything. An oblivion that only crazy, stupid sex with Ben might have momentarily brought.

Emotions rushed to crowd in on her, dense and suffocating. Her initial relief had been swallowed up in pain, anger, frustration, sympathy and misplaced love. They coursed around her body, leaving her weak and nauseous.

Pain gripped her heart. This wasn't about *her*—she

knew that—and yet she couldn't help reliving her utter devastation of almost five years earlier. It wasn't right that this should be the first time she'd seen him since he'd walked out. It wasn't right that he should be lying there so battered and broken. And it wasn't right that—even like this—he still had the power to hurt her.

A strangled sob escaped her throat before she could stop it. Her emotions were pushed to the limit. And suddenly all she could think about was the baby she had conceived as a result of that one incredible night. *Their* baby—although he'd never known. Almost five years on, she could still feel the pain which had torn at her heart the day she'd lost it.

Another sob threatened to break free and she choked it back just as Dr Fields came back into the room.

'It's just the sedative talking.' He looked up at her sharply before softening his voice. 'Think of Ben like any other patient, if it helps. Don't let it get to you, Doctor.'

She bowed her head, unable to speak and yet unable to leave the room.

The surgeon continued. 'His vitals are stable. Rest is the best thing to help his body to heal at this time, and I've no doubt that, despite his initial reaction, seeing you will help to calm any fears he has and help him to be patient until we know more.'

Thea wasn't so sure. But when Ben woke up she'd finally have to tell him. *Everything.* Yes, she definitely needed closure.

CHAPTER TWO

Five years earlier

'SHOULD I...? THAT IS...do you want me to carry you over the threshold?' Ben hesitated at the cottage door, his key still unturned in the lock.

'Sorry?'

Her voice sounded thick, as if she was in some kind of fug. He could empathise with that.

'Now we're married...' Ben shrugged, feeling uncharacteristically helpless. He didn't *do* emotion at the best of times. But Thea's brother—his best friend—had just died. How was he supposed to support her? 'I just wondered...'

He trailed off, hating these alien feelings. His career depended on him being decisive and sure. He gathered the best intelligence he could and made his plan of action accordingly. But how did he gather intel on the right way to help a grieving sister? How did he ensure he said the right thing, *did* the right thing? He didn't know the right protocols. He didn't know the rules. It left him feeling ineffective and uncertain.

But he *did* know it was now his responsibility to help Thea. And that ignoring loss, pretending it didn't exist, didn't make it go away. He knew *that* from bitter experience.

'I don't know if I'm expected to carry you over the threshold,' he stated uncomfortably.

'Oh. No, *Lord, no*—of course not.' Thea shook her head in distress. 'I just want to get into the house and off this street. I can practically *feel* the curtains twitching.'

Ben glanced around. Not a single curtain had moved, but he could understand Thea's discomfort and her need to escape inside.

Marrying someone with whom he'd only been on one date wasn't something he'd ever thought he would do. He wasn't impulsive. At least not in his personal life. But this wasn't about impulsiveness. It was about practicality. It was about fulfilling his promise to Dan—Thea's brother and his army buddy—that he would take care of Thea. The guy had taken a bullet for him—fulfilling that promise was a given.

Ben had taken over payment of the fees for Thea's medical degree, given her access to other necessary finances, but finding her a new home had been harder, given the time constraints. Her landlord had evicted her the moment he'd discovered Dan was dead and she could no longer pay the rent. Finding her a new flat would have taken more time than he had.

The only solution had been to marry her, so that the Army would allocate them a house within the officers' married quarters on the base. With its tight-knit community, and the fact that he was often away on courses, exercises and tours of duty, he'd thought it the safest place for a twenty-one-year-old girl who had already lost her parents at…what had Dan said…eight? Nine?

'I'm just not used to all…*this*.' Thea waved her hand in the direction of the cul-de-sac as Ben opened the door and she practically fell inside.

'Community?'

She shook her head. 'People knowing your business.'

There were boxes in the hallway. He hadn't had time to sort anything out yet, although neither of them owned much stuff. She didn't seem to hang on to personal effects; that was something they both had in common.

'It's…pretty,' she sounded surprised. 'Until the other day, I'd always assumed married quarters just meant a different wing in the barracks,'

'No. Married soldiers get a house either on, or near to, the camp,'Ben dredged up a smile. 'The higher rank the soldier is, the nicer the accommodation. And the quieter the area on camp.'

'Right,' Thea nodded robotically.

He doubted if she had even really seen the place properly when the Housing Officer had marched them in a week ago to take inventory and do a damage report. She had still been coming to terms with burying Dan.

He knew Dan hadn't been able to afford to rent more than a one-bedroom flat for his sister, so she could have a roof over her head. He had always put Thea first.

Dan had been a great medic, but he would have made a great doctor—a great officer. Just as Ben was. The only reason Dan hadn't become one was because he hadn't been able to afford the time out for courses. The guy had signed on into the Army the moment he'd been able to, just to get out of that children's home and earn enough money to send the gifted Thea to uni when she came out of foster care.

He'd given his sister every advantage he hadn't had, and the fact that she was in the third year of her medical degree was as much down to his love and encouragement as Thea's ability.

Now Dan was gone, and Ben had promised to take on the mantle of responsibility. To put Thea first. He'd be damned if he was going to betray the promise he'd made to his dying buddy. But that meant he was also going to have to remember his own promise to himself never to go near the only woman he'd ever felt strongly about.

For one dangerous moment memories of their one incredible date together assailed him. Instantly Ben slammed the shutters on his mind before those memories could take hold and complicate matters. He could *not* afford to go there. He would have to keep reminding himself that he wasn't the right man for Thea. He would only end up hurting her, and she had enough to contend with.

'I thought you might feel more secure here.' Ben forced himself to go on. 'The neighbours are all army spouses too. You'll have a support network when I ship out in a few days—they'll look after you.'

'Yes, it should help,' she agreed flatly.

'Plus, getting something through the Army was the fastest thing I could do in the time frame.'

He saw her wince, regretted his directness. But the truth was he had only been given one month of compassionate leave. One month in which to break news to Thea which would destroy her whole life as she knew it. One month in which to fulfil his promise to look after Thea for life. One month to convince her that marrying him wasn't lunacy, but necessary to ensure her financial security.

'Can I get you anything? A drink? Something to eat?'

She shook her head, refusing to meet his eye. Spying her canvas clothes bag, she made a relieved grab for it. 'If you don't mind, I just want to go to bed.'

'It's barely eight-thirty,' he noted with surprise.

'It's been a long day.' Thea shrugged. 'I figure I could try to sleep. Just hope that, if I do, when I wake up it won't be this day any longer.'

'Right.' He nodded quickly. He doubted she'd slept

much in the three weeks since he'd told her that Dan was dead. 'Of course. I understand.'

She was still standing there, as if waiting for him. Was he supposed to go with her? That wasn't the agreement they'd made.

'Um…which room is mine?'

She flushed a deep red and Ben cursed his lack of sensitivity. The sooner he was redeployed, the better.

'Oh, the second on the right. But we can swap later, if you prefer. I won't be here much.'

She gave an uninterested nod and, dismissing his words, turned swiftly to head up the stairs. He heard her moving around up there as he tried to still his mind with the banal task of unpacking some of the boxes. The kettle, some mugs, teabags for a start.

He opened the first box and came face to face with a photo of himself and Dan on their first tour of duty together. This was harder than he had feared. Slamming the box shut, he grabbed a sleeping bag and followed Thea's lead, heading upstairs to the other bedroom.

Ben lay rigid and motionless on his back in the bed, his hands locked behind his head. There was no way he could sleep. He watched the numbers counting up painfully slowly on the clock projecting the time onto the ceiling. Twenty-one hundred hours. It wasn't just the time. Normally he could sleep on a clothesline, and anyway he'd been to bed at more ridiculous hours in his time on tour. It was more the fact that on the other side of the wall he could hear Thea in her own bed as she shifted, coughed and sporadically sobbed.

He had no idea if he'd done the right thing by marrying her, but he knew he was honouring his promise to Dan and that was all that really mattered. Plus, even if their marriage was fake their friendship didn't have to be. Thea was grieving, and Ben knew just what she was going through.

Unable to lie there listening to her distress, he got up off the creaking bed and ducked out of his door to knock gently on Thea's. No answer, but by the sudden silence it was clear that she had heard him. She didn't respond.

He should leave. She obviously didn't want him there. But a little voice told him she needed him. He knocked again, then turned the handle, tentatively at first.

'Thea, is there anything I can do?'

Thea was sitting up, her knees pulled to her chest. Her tense features relaxed slightly as she looked up and saw him.

He crossed the room in a couple of long strides, scooping her up and pulling her into his arms, assiduously ignoring the pretty lacy lemon negligee. One hand secured her to him, the other smoothed her hair gently, and he let her cry it out. Holding her until she finally grew still.

When she did, he shifted as though to lower her back onto the bed.

'Don't go,' she whispered. 'Please, stay with me... just for tonight....'

'It's not a good idea.'

So why was he so tempted?

Lifting herself, Thea searched his face with red-rimmed eyes. 'Then at least talk to me, Ben.'

Talking. The thing he was least good at.

'What about?' he asked, faltering.

'Anything...' She hiccupped. 'Distract me.'

'Why did Dan always call you Ethel?' he blurted out, his mind having gone suddenly blank. 'I never knew your real name was Thea until our date. When I found out you were Dan's sister.'

Way to go, idiot. Talk about the very person she doesn't *want to think about.*

But Thea smiled. A small, fond smile which tore at Ben's heart.

'When I was a kid I couldn't pronounce Alethea, so I used to tell people my name was Ethel. Dan loved it. Even when I started to be known as Thea he still called me Ethel. It was our thing. No one else could share in it.'

'Right...' Ben swallowed uncomfortably. He wished he'd never asked. Somehow it had made him feel closer to Thea. He didn't *want* to feel closer to Thea. He clenched his fists as the image that had haunted him for the last three weeks swam into his head in high definition.

Dan...cradled in his arms as he lay dying on that hard desert ground.

Their two-man patrol had walked straight into an ambush and the two of them had been alone and pinned down by the enemy, with only a rocky outcrop for protection. Ben had tried and tried to stem the bleeding but it had been just too severe. Time had started to run out for the guy he'd fought alongside twenty-four-seven, for three hundred and twenty days of their last year's tour of duty. And for multiple tours over the last seven years before that.

Grief hovered in the back of his mind but he refused to let it in. There was no place in his mind for mourning—he had to stay strong for Thea. She didn't know the half of it. And he was never going to tell her. Besides, wasn't he the king of shutting out emotions? He'd been doing it well enough for the last decade and a half.

'Did you ever wonder how we'd never met before?' Thea asked suddenly. 'I mean, you were Daniel's best friend and I was his sister.'

'Not really.' Ben paused thoughtfully. 'Dan was always careful to keep the two sides of his life separate—his personal life and you, and his Army life. I think after your parents died he didn't have the easiest time of it in the kids' home. He never really talked about his past to anyone.'

'Except you?' Thea observed. 'Because he trusted you?'

'Right,' Ben answered bleakly.

'But still...' Thea shook her head, still confused. 'If he trusted you that much, surely you'd have come with him round to the flat?'

'No, I never came round.' Ben shrugged. 'You have to understand I'm a commissioned officer. Dan wasn't. Being part of a team and in each other's company twenty-four-seven is one thing, but socialising back home isn't that easy.'

'Because the Army don't allow it?'

Thea frowned, confused. Ben didn't blame her. The Forces had their rules, their protocols, and if you were a part of it then it all made sense. It could save lives. But to an outsider trying to understand it might seem strange.

'They don't encourage it,' Ben admitted. 'We have separate messes for socialising. But the Army *do* realise that the bonds formed in war time don't just dissolve when you get back home. So, like some of the others, Dan and I used to go on training runs together, and we headed into the mountains once or twice a year—but always off the base.'

'Right...' Thea hedged. 'But when you were deployed together he never even showed you a photo of me?'

'Having a photo of your wife, or girlfriend, or baby is one thing. But having a photo of your sister... There's no way Dan would have risked the guys seeing a photo of a girl like you. It would have invited attention…comments that a brother wouldn't want to hear about his sister.'

'Oh.'

Thea flushed a deep scarlet as the meaning of his words sank in. He found it surprisingly endearing—a reminder than she had never really appreciated just how stunning she was. Even now.

'Tell me what you thought the first time you met me,' she said. 'On that date we went on together.'

He stiffened. This wasn't a conversation he wanted to be having.

'Please, Ben. I need to hear something…*pleasant*… Everything's gone so very wrong. I just want to hear what you told me that night.'

Ben met her wobbly, pleading gaze. She wanted distraction, a better memory to offer some flicker of consolation at one of the worst times of her life. After the way he'd treated her, surely he owed her that much?

'I thought you were the most beautiful woman I'd ever met,' he said quietly. 'Not just aesthetically, but on the inside, too. You were fun, impetuous…you had a vibrancy about you which was wonderfully infectious to all those around you. You made everyone want to be near you, to be part of your group.'

He'd been on a rare night out with some other officers—at a crowded bar—when Thea had slipped into the space beside him. They'd started talking casually and that had been it—he'd never felt such an inexorable attraction to a woman before. He'd excused himself from his group as soon as he'd been able to, just to spend the rest of the evening in Thea's company.

'Oh…'

She sounded let down, and he knew why. She thought he'd understood her better.

He hesitated, then conceded. 'At least that's what you wanted people to see. But beneath that veil there was a quietness, almost a shyness about you when you thought no one was watching you. Judging you. I assumed it was a defence mechanism you'd created after your parents had died, to stop people asking if you were all right.'

'Really? You *saw* that?'

Her evident pleasure that he'd seen a part of her others had been only too happy to ignore made him want to kiss her and berate her all at the same time. And that was the damned problem.

'So the next day, when you told me we couldn't see each other any more…?' She hiccuped, clearly torn between not wanting to say the words and needing to know the truth. 'You didn't have feelings for me anymore?'

How was he supposed to answer *that*? From the moment they'd met he had been hooked. This spellbinding young woman had persuaded him to take her to a funfair. There had been a small group of them—Thea's friends—but he hadn't even noticed them after the first few minutes. He had only seen Thea.

They'd hurled leather balls at the coconut shy, laughed their way through the hall of mirrors and shared an incredible, intense first kiss at the top of the Ferris wheel.

In most of his life—even much of his childhood—Ben had never felt as happy and free of responsibility as he had that evening with Thea. And he'd known even then that she had an ability to make him fall for her such as no other woman ever had.

And now she wanted to know why he'd walked away from her. What could he say? He owed her something. Perhaps a variation on the truth was the safest option.

'We're just…weren't a good match. I'm sorry, Thea.'

Her body seemed to curl even more into his arms and

he felt worse than ever. But it was a necessary lie…no, a half-truth… They *weren't* a good match. Ben could recall tantalising glimpses of a real inner confidence and a love of life, rippling constantly beneath that artificially shimmering, vivacious exterior. He had seen them from the beginning. She was the kind of person who made people feel good, want to bask in her warm glow for ever.

He wished he could be the kind of person who made *her* feel good, who could inspire that hidden side of Thea.

Instead he knew that he was the kind of person who would eventually extinguish that dancing light in her soul. If he was the kind of man his father had been he would drag Thea down, as his mother had been dragged down. What kind a life would that be for a woman like Thea?

He'd known as he'd walked her home that night, wondering at the way she had made him feel about her after just one incredible date, that he needed to walk away from her before he *did* hurt her. But he hadn't been able to. Even as he'd walked up the pathway to her ground-floor flat his head had been telling him one thing whilst his heart had been making plans to take her out the next day. Imagining a future with her.

And then Dan had opened the door and demanded to know what the hell Ben was doing with his sister.

Dan—the guy who'd had his back through countless tours of duty. The buddy who would have given his life for Ben, and for whom Ben would have sacrificed his own.

Only Dan had and Ben hadn't.

So, just like that, the woman he had thought he might actually be able to fall in love with had been off limits. Still, Ben had to wonder whether Dan had been the real reason that he'd walked away from Thea.

Or just the excuse.

He could have fought for her. The thought slid, unbidden, into his mind. But would that have been fair? All the women he'd dated in the past…he'd never felt strongly enough about any of them. With Thea it was different. It had been even from that first meeting. But the closer you were to someone, the more hurt you could cause. Ben had learned that from his parents. If his father had taught him anything, it was never to get close to anyone. Or let them get close to you.

It was a lesson he'd do well to remember with Thea.

Lost in his own dark thoughts, it took Ben a while to realise that she was asleep. He heard her breathing ease and deepen, felt her heartbeat drop to a slow, rhythmic pulse. And for the first time in a long time—with Thea still wrapped in his arms—Ben fell into a deep, restful sleep of his own.

He woke to the sound of an unfamiliar phone alert. A text? An email? Not wanting to wake Thea, Ben squinted through the curtains to the darkness beyond. Years of field experience told him it had to be around four in the morning.

Nevertheless he felt her stir beside him, felt her raise her head up and then reach across him for her phone. He felt the skim of soft breasts and lacy fabric against his bare chest and fought to stop his body's primal reaction. He didn't stand a chance.

Thea froze.

For a moment Ben vacillated. Should he apologise? Leave? She had wanted him there, to comfort her. She had trusted him. Such a base reaction was the ultimate betrayal of that trust. He had no doubt she would consider it as unexpected as it was unwanted.

He was shocked when, instead of scooting off the bed away from him, Thea reached out and touched his face.

'Don't, Thea. It's not a good idea.' He gripped her wrist, stilling it and moving it away from him as he opened his eyes and came face to face with her direct gaze.

She still looked pale, drained; but there was a glint in her eyes which he hadn't been expecting—something he couldn't quite pinpoint.

It held him in her bed, motionless. Part of him knew he should leave. He had promised her this was a marriage on paper only, assured her she could trust him. Still, part of him wanted to stay. He couldn't deny his attraction to her, and all their talk last night had only made it harder to put his feelings for her safely away in their box.

'Why isn't it a good idea?' she whispered, gently twisting her wrist from his loosened grip, slowly returning it to his face.

She traced the outline of the scar which pulled at the corner of his eye. 'Some war wound, huh?' Her voice shook as she spoke,

Memories punched into him. The last time she'd asked that exact question had been on their one and only date, moments before they'd shared their first kiss. Could it only have been six weeks ago? It had been a gentle yet powerful kiss which had rocked him to his foundations in a way he'd never suspected a mere kiss ever could. It was the moment he'd realised he wanted more, so much more, from this woman.

She'd asked him how he'd got it—assuming, as others had done in the past, that it was something to do with the Army. Ben had always been happy to go along with their assumption—not that he'd dated a lot since his career had begun to come first. But instead he'd found himself telling Thea how the scar was a result of running into an open kitchen drawer when he was boy.

In fifteen years he'd barely even spoken to anyone about his mother. But that night he'd regaled Thea with the story of how he'd been running away from his half-furious, half-scared mum, having been found blown half-way across the room after jamming a kitchen knife into an electrical socket, trying to retrieve his wedged-in toy soldier.

Thea had been shocked and amused in equal measure, with no idea of the enormity of what Ben had just done in telling her something so personal. And now she was tracing his scar and asking him the same question again. Deliberately reminding him of that night.

He felt his willpower slipping.

He snatched his head away, jackknifing his body up-right to slide her off him and launching himself sideways out of the bed. But she slipped her arms around him, stopping him from leaving the bed completely.

'We can't do this, Thea,' he repeated.

If he didn't stop this his self-control would crumble, and at some point she would come to hate him for letting this happen She would never forgive him for not staying strong enough for both of them.

'I don't want to be alone. Not tonight,' she whispered hoarsely.

Grief was still etched into her expression. He felt torn. He was supposed to be here to look after her, to support her—how could he walk out on her now?

He had to get things back to where they'd been a cou-ple of hours earlier. He could hold her, comfort her, but nothing more was going to happen.

He moved back to the bed and sat down to pull her

into his arms and soothe her, as he had a few hours earlier, but Thea had other ideas.

Turning her head to his, she pressed her warm mouth to his skin, kissing his temple, his cheek, the skin inches from his mouth.

He moved his hand to stay her. 'Stop, Thea. Neither of us are thinking straight.'

'You're wrong…'

Her shaky voice should have told him more, but he didn't want to hear.

'I know you still want me. And it's precisely because we *aren't* thinking straight that we can do this. We need this. *I* need this. I need oblivion. Take me away from all this. Make me forget the last three weeks. Make me forget everything. If only for a short while.'

'It will still be there afterwards,' he said.

Resisting her touch was taking all his willpower. She was right—he did still want her. Despite the promise he'd made to himself six weeks ago, never to go near Thea again, he hadn't stopped wanting her or thinking about her. She had haunted his dreams.

'Just make me forget for a moment. Please, Ben, can you do that?'

She touched him again and his mental grip slipped further. He shouldn't give in, but he was losing control, his head was spinning. Grief, guilt, lust—all mingled together with his lack of sleep over the last month, and Ben struggled to pick his way through the tangle of emotions.

As if sensing his weakening resolve, Thea slid hesitant fingers under the waistband of his boxer shorts, looking to him as if for compliance. He should stand his ground, tell her that she was still grieving and scared and confused, that she didn't know what she was doing.

Except it seemed as if she knew exactly what she was

doing. She seemed to know what she wanted and just what effect she was having on him. And, as she'd already pointed out, she knew only too well how much he wanted her.

With a slight dip of his head he conveyed his acquiescence, sucking in deep breath as Thea slid his boxers off him and surveyed every inch of him. Then, almost shyly, she took his hand and moved it to her breast. Her nipple was hard against his palm.

The effect was instantaneous. Pushing her back into the middle of the bed, Ben moved to cover her body with his, and as she arched slightly to meet him every inch of their bodies was pressed into delicious contact. Slowly he lowered his mouth to hers, to claim it as his own, but she squirmed slightly beneath him.

'I don't need the niceties,' she said, flushing red at her boldness. 'I just need you to take me. To make me forget.'

Ben scanned her face. It must have taken some courage for her to say that. He hesitated. Since he'd met her, kissed her, six weeks ago, she had danced into his late-night fantasies, but this wasn't the way he'd imagined their first time to be. Still, there would be plenty of time for languid, indulgent exploration of each other's bodies the next time—and the time after that. If immediate release was what she wanted now, this time, then he wasn't objecting. He just wanted Thea—to touch her, to claim her.

He slid his knee between her legs, gliding his hands over her skin.

'Open for me,' he murmured, revelling in her immediate compliance, sliding his fingers between her legs and finding her hot and wet.

'God…' He gave a guttural groan. 'You're going to be my undoing.'

She gasped as he dipped inside her, finding her clit and flicking back and forth, knowing just the right amount of pressure to elicit a moan of pleasure from her. But before he could continue her hand pushed down between their bodies, her fingers latching around his wrist as she pushed him away, wrapping her legs around him instead and shifting her body so it was central to his.

The tip of his erection skimmed her damp heat and he heard another low moan. It took him a moment to realise it was his own voice.

'No niceties, Ben. Remember?' Thea muttered.

'This is all you want?' Ben asked. Holding back when he was this close was almost unbearable, but he had to be sure.

'It's all I want,' she confirmed, burying her head in his shoulder.

Unable to hold back any longer, he pushed inside her, feeling her stretch around him, tilting her pelvis up slightly to draw him in deeper and deeper. Her arms slid around his back, holding on to him as he rocked inside her. He knew he was close—six weeks of almost nightly dreams of Thea, and none of them had come close to the reality. And this wasn't even their best. But, if the way she was tightening around him was anything to go by, he wasn't the only one close to the edge.

Resting his weight on one arm as he continued his relentless rhythm, he reached for her thigh with his other arm, hooking his hand under her knee and locking her leg around his back. The action opened her up just a fraction more, and Ben heard her little sounds of pleasure as he thrust deeper, harder. Then she was arching up again, her breath quickening, and as she orgasmed she tightened around him—only moments before he felt his own climax crashing over him. His back stiffened and he groaned, spilling inside her, barely able to think but careful to hold his weight off her.

'Ben...?' she whispered, almost expectantly.

Was she waiting for him to say something? For a split second he wished he was good with words—wished he could tell her how he felt right now. Instead he froze, and reality hit him.

This was *exactly* why he'd needed to stay away from her. He would always be shutting her out, and she would always be fighting for him to let her in. He would never be able to give her what she needed. He was useless.

It was only when he raised himself up to look at her that he saw the tears spilling from her eyes. Horrified, he slipped out of her, rolling onto his side to pull her into his arms.

Thea resisted.

This was what he'd been afraid of.

'This was one of the three most horrific days of my life...' She stumbled over her words.

'I know.' What more could he say?

'I just thought it would make it better. Us. Together. Just this once.'

'And it didn't?' He felt sick. Of course it hadn't. Hadn't he told himself this would happen?

She shook her head, the tears coming faster now.

'If anything, it's made it worse.'

Moving quickly off her bed, he searched for his boxers. Found them. Slid them on as quickly as he could.

He had known she wasn't thinking straight. But *he* should have known better—saved her from herself. Instead he had taken shameless advantage of her. All because his own lust for her had let him believe her when she'd said it was what she wanted.

His brain searched for something to say—anything

which would express how very sorry he was. Nothing came. How could it?

The past—*their* past—his emotional distance…it was all bound to catch up with them sooner or later. Perhaps it was best that it was sooner. Before anything more happened between them. He needed to get away—put some space between them before he hurt her any more than he already had.

'You're leaving?' she asked flatly.

'I think it's for the best.' *So why did the words stick in his throat?*

'What now?' Her sad, wary eyes sought his.

He hesitated by the door. 'My compassionate leave is almost over. I'll be shipping out soon anyway.'

'So we go back to the original marriage agreement?' she asked urgently, as if seeking that security at the very least.

He wanted to say no, to tell her that he couldn't go back to anything after what had just happened between them. He wanted to tell her that he wanted more from her, from their marriage. But what had happened between them had only cemented his fear that she was already under his skin and he'd never want to let her go. He owed her more than that. He was no more able to be the kind of man she needed now than he had been six weeks ago. On top of which, his guilt at not being someone she could trust weighed heavily on him. Until he was able to make amends for that he could never ask more of her. So he owed her what he'd originally promised.

'Yes,' he confirmed at length. 'We go back to the original deal.'

She nodded once—a sad bob of her head.

Before he could say anything more—wreck things any further—Ben yanked the door open and escaped into the hallway. Forget a few more days. There was no way he could stay in this house with Thea for even one more night. He needed to get out of here. *Now.*

CHAPTER THREE

Present day

BEN WATCHED THE interns shuffle out of his side room. The habitual idolising smiles they gave whenever they saw him set Ben's teeth on edge.

'They annoy you, don't they?' Thea asked, suddenly appearing at his door.

He ruthlessly ignored the kick of pleasure at her presence. She shouldn't have to be here. He wasn't her problem.

'They treat me like some kind of...'

'Hero?' Thea smiled.

'I'm not a hero.' Ben ground out the words.

'Two weeks ago you were caught by two IEDs. The first one severed your left arm, yet you still managed to drag your men to safety before getting caught by a second IED. Geez, Ben, you were pinned under a Land Rover with a suspected crushed spine—it could have left you in a wheelchair for the rest of your life.'

'It *could have* but it didn't,' Ben growled. 'They couldn't tell because of the swelling so they suspected the worst. They were wrong,' Ben refuted flatly. 'It turned out I'm fine. I just need to get out of here.'

'You're hardly *fine*,' Thea scoffed. 'You still suffered

contusions of the spinal cord. You were lucky not to sever it. Not to mention you've dislocated and shattered a whole raft of vertebrae which have had to be pinned and bolted. Oh, and did I mention the replantation of your arm?'

'Really?' Ben arched an eyebrow at her. 'I hadn't noticed—other than the fact that my left arm is now two centimetres shorter than my right arm.'

If he'd thought to intimidate her then he'd thought wrong. If anything, she looked almost amused.

'Then you're damned lucky. I saw a girl last year whose right arm was not only severed, but crushed. By the time they cut away the damaged tissue and bone her arm ended up twelve centimetres shorter than the other. This year she underwent bone-lengthening surgery and she'll be over the moon if she reduces that to a two-centimetre difference. And did I say that she's right-handed, like you, but unlike you *she's* now had to learn to be left-handed?'

'Then, like I said before,' he pointed out, 'I'm fine.'

'You're lucky, Ben, but you're not fine. And pretending you are is only making you push yourself far, *far* harder than anyone else is comfortable with.'

Before he could respond Thea advanced into the room, ticking off her fingers as she counted the days.

'Let me break this down for you, Ben. Days one, two and three you were operated on, flown here, and put into traction until the swelling could go down and they could better assess the damage to your spine. That happened on day six. By day seven they were able to operate. By day eight you already had sensation in your lower limbs and were able to move your left big toe on command. Day nine your left toes and your right big toe. By day ten you could move both feet. By day eleven you could lift your left leg above the bed, and day twelve your right leg—'

'Is there any point to this?' Ben interrupted.

He shifted irritably in the wingback chair. He hated being in this thing almost as much as he hated being in the damned wheelchair. The sooner Thea left, the better.

'Yes,' she replied, unflustered. 'It's now day eighteen. By rights you should be up and about in a wheelchair, and you *might* be able to take a few steps around your room with the aid of a frame. Instead of which you're pushing yourself around in gruelling laps of the hospital like you think you're some kind of superhero.'

'I do *not* think I'm some kind of superhero.'

'Really? Then let me check your chart.'

She was right about one thing, though. He *was* desperate to get out of the room, away from Thea, and push his broken body to try another circuit of the floor. Even the pain was a welcome distraction from the nightmares which haunted his darkest thoughts. Nightmares of explosions and of IEDs, of flying debris and vehicles. The old nightmares too, of Daniel screaming out to him. And now, this last fortnight, inexplicable new nightmares— of Thea, looking on as he lay helpless and weak. In his nightmares he could never work out whether her expression was one of satisfaction or sympathy. Vindication that he'd finally got his comeuppance? Or pity?

No, the pain was good—it meant that he was alive.

So he forced himself to stay still, trapped as he was in the too-soft seat, and tried to the let Thea's words wash over him. He studiously averted his gaze from the detestable hospital bed—in which he tried to spend the very least time he possibly could—and attempted to conceal his frustration.

'Aha, nothing to indicate a problem on your readouts. However...' She glanced up at him before reading the notes. *"Visual assessment suggests breathing seems shallow, cheeks flushed and feverish—query possibility of infection."'*

'It's wrong,' Ben dismissed it.

'Of course it is,' Thea snapped. 'Since you know, and I know, and fortunately even Dr Fields knows enough to note that any potentially concerning visual indicators are nothing more than a result of the fact that you got up at around five a.m., and then spent the last couple of hours pushing beyond your body's limits in completing circuits of the hospital before hobbling here—probably in considerable pain—to beat Dr Fields and his interns back on to the ward before they started their rounds.'

'It's called recovery.' He gritted his teeth. 'I need to push my body to help it heal.'

'You need to *rest*!' Thea cried out. 'Ben, in all seriousness, you have done *incredibly* well—in no small part due to your grit and determination. It usually takes five weeks to get where you are now, and you've done it in under three. But you need to take things easy.'

'The sooner I recover, the sooner I can get out of here.'

'Ben, you *have* to know that's not going to happen. Not whilst you still refuse to come home with me. You need someone to take care of you during your recuperation.'

'I don't need *anyone*,' Ben snarled. 'Least of all you.'

He didn't want to hurt her, but it was the only way he could think of to chase her away. She shouldn't be here—he wasn't her responsibility. Not when he'd treated her the way he had. But, really, what choice had he had?

There's always a choice. The thought crept into his head before he could stop it. *You just made the wrong one.*

'That's why I need to push my body. Recover. Then I won't need to be discharged into anyone's care,' he spat out.

'That isn't going to happen, Major.' Dr Fields strode into the room, one of his interns by his side.

Dammit, that blasted smile of adulation again.

'Ben, this isn't just about your physical recovery. Even if your rehabilitation continues on this fast track you've put yourself on—and I highly doubt that it will, since I think you're pushing yourself far too hard and will end up doing your body more harm than good—I would still need to know you had someone to stay with during the last part of your recuperation. Someone to support you, talk to you, observe you and make sure they're on hand if there happen to be any unforeseen complications.'

'If you're talking PTSD, Doc, just come out and say it.' Ben shook his head. 'I'm fine.'

'You might not want to admit it...' the doctor spoke gently '...but the nightmares which wake you in the night, have you screaming out in a cold sweat, are a symptom of PTSD. It's still relatively mild at this stage, and only natural after all you've been through, but the longer you refuse to deal with it, the worse it will get.'

'There are men out there who have suffered a lot worse than me,' Ben growled, not wanting to be having this conversation. 'Buddies of mine who lost limbs or didn't even make it. I'm already back on my feet. I've nothing to complain about.'

'Which is the problem.' Dr Fields sighed. 'Still, we'll save that for another day.'

No, they wouldn't. Ben gave an almost imperceptible shake of his head. *He was fine, even if he didn't deserve to be. But he needed to get out of here.*

His eyes slid to Thea. For all her bravado now, he could still remember her standing by his bedside in those first few days, her face white with fear and concern for a man she hadn't seen in five years. He clenched his fists;

she'd been dragged into this out of some misplaced sense of obligation but it had nothing to do with her. There was no way he was about to let her take responsibility for his care. Her unfailing loyalty was her downfall.

He could only imagine how much she must have resented being summoned here. How much she must hate him—dragging her into a marriage in order to fulfil his own need to honour his promise to her brother. Only to give in to his baser desires, his long-standing attraction to her. So what if they had both shared the attraction at one time? He'd had no right—it hadn't been part of the plan. And, anyway, what kind of man bedded his dead best friend's grief-stricken sister?

'Ultimately, Ben, your body still has a lot of healing to do, and I am concerned that you're driving yourself too hard. You need to back up a little, or you risk doing permanent damage.'

'I hear you, Doc.' Ben nodded flatly. *No chance. He was out of here as soon as they all left him alone.*

Dr Fields turned away from Ben to the intern. 'Dr Thompson—since Major Abrams isn't feeling compliant, I suggest you run those tests after all. Time-consuming, yet non-costly,' he added pointedly. 'I may not be able to stop Major Abrams from destroying the body I worked so hard to repair, but I *can* slow him down. At least for a few hours.'

'Really, Doc? Pointless tests?' challenged Ben.

'They aren't pointless if they stop you from hauling your butt out of here the minute we walk out the door for another set of exhausting laps. Now, Dr Abrams—' Ben started, and then realised that Dr Fields was addressing Thea. 'Have you got a moment?'

Ben resisted the uncharacteristic compulsion to get up and throw the chair out of the window. For a start, he doubted he'd have the strength. And secondly he never let his temper get the better of him. He never let *any* emotion get the better of him—hadn't his father always drilled into him the need to keep a tight, unrelenting control over all his emotions as all times? He'd be ashamed of Ben if he knew how his son had used Thea five years ago. Not that his father had ever been proud of him—even when he'd followed in the Colonel's footsteps into the army.

Ben shut down the familiar sense of failure, but it had already got a grip, and as the intern began his nonsensical tests Ben couldn't deny that part of him was grateful for the excuse to take a break—if only for an hour of rest. It was probably the same part of him which was finding it so damned painful to put one foot in front of the other as he shuffled along at such an interminably slow pace.

Weakness, he thought with disgust, and his father's words echoed in his ears. *Weakness has no place here.*

Ben grunted with effort as he executed a one-armed pull-up out of the wingback chair and into the wheelchair which would allow him off the ward without attracting attention. Ever since Thea had visited yesterday that intern had held him hostage, running unnecessary test after test. He hadn't managed to get out once, and it had left him feeling irritable.

Yet he couldn't deny that his body felt stronger than ever after a full twenty hours of rest. Maybe today was the day to push himself to walk outside in the fresh air. Once he was outside, in the quieter areas of the hospital grounds, he could discard the unwanted lump of metal and force his body not to be so weak. Dr Fields was wrong. He needed to push harder, not less.

He propelled the wheelchair along strongly with his good arm, only stopping once he'd reached the peaceful gardens outside and found a quiet spot. With a deep breath he pulled himself to an unassisted standing position. So much for a walk. He didn't think he could even take a step. Thank goodness no one could see him like this—weak as a kitten and utterly tragic.

'So now you're trying to kill yourself trying to walk around outside the hospital, without even a wall to lean on?'

His head jerked up. It was an effort to stay upright, but he'd be damned if he fell over in front of *her*. In front of anyone.

He lashed out before he could stop himself. 'What the hell are you doing here? Are you following me?'

Thea blanched visibly at his hostility and he immediately felt ashamed of himself. Yesterday she'd been so strong, so unintimidated, he had forgotten how easily undermined she could be. The last thing he wanted was to hurt her, yet he had to stay resolute. Thea was only here because the Army had contacted her as his next of kin—as his wife.

His wife. The words echoed around Ben's head, taunting him.

For five years there had been no contact between them, and these sure as hell weren't the circumstances in which Ben would ever have chosen to have her back in his life. When he was helpless and unable to provide for her...to protect her. A wave of self-loathing washed over him. He wasn't even a proper man any more. Just a shell of a man who couldn't walk without leaning heavily on a wall, a rail, a walking frame.

Pathetic, he thought scornfully.

He needed Thea to leave. *Now.* And surely she *wanted* to leave, deep down? She couldn't want to be with him now. No one could. He had to convince Thea that her duty was done, that he was fine and that he didn't need her. Then she could leave, get on with her life.

He steeled himself. 'Hell, Thea, can't you see that I don't want you here?'

'I don't understand what I've done to make you hate me so much.'

As fast as the anger had arrived, it disappeared. *Hate her?* What on earth made her think that? If anything, it should be the other way around.

Suddenly he felt exhausted. He didn't want to fight with her any more. He just wanted her to feel free to go back to her own life whilst he concentrated on his recovery.

'I've never hated you.' Ben spoke quietly. 'But our marriage was never meant to be anything more than on paper. You shouldn't be here now—this isn't your responsibility. I was just trying to make you see that.'

'If you don't want me here, then answer me something.'

'Answer you what?' he asked, wondering why he felt as though he was walking into some carefully set trap.

'Why am I still listed on your Army paperwork as your next of kin?'

Ben felt his breathing stop, before exhaling with a *whoosh* of air. So he was right—she *was* only here under obligation, because the Army had called her. She resented him for it, and he couldn't blame her.

'I left you on the Army paperwork because we were married. If I'd put down someone else as my next of kin it would have raised questions.'

'I see.'

Something flashed across her face, but it was gone before he could identify it.

He'd also left her on it so that she would always have a

direct means to get in touch with him if she ever needed his help. He'd even hoped she would—especially in those first months after their wedding night. After all, they hadn't used protection. He supposed it was a blessing that nothing had ever come of it; in his experience an absent soldier never made a good dad. And yet he suspected a tiny part of him had once hoped otherwise. Not that he could say that now.

The silence hung between them.

'Now I see that it was a mistake,' he ground out eventually.

A mistake. Was that really how he thought of her?

Thea felt the nausea churn in her stomach, as it had been doing practically every day since she'd heard about Ben's accident.

She watched him edge painstakingly to the rock wall across the hidden courtyard, and resisted the urge to leap down and ram his wheelchair under his backside, just to stop him from punishing his body.

She spotted a movement out of the corner of her eye— it was the man who had been outside Ben's hospital room that first day. She'd thought he was some kind of Army specialist, but now she wasn't so sure. She'd seen him a few more times over the last few weeks, always observing but never making any direct contact with Ben. Perhaps he was some kind of counsellor—someone Ben could talk to. Someone who might be able to understand this irrational need Ben seemed to have to push his body to breaking point—and maybe beyond.

The first time she'd seen Ben in the wheelchair she'd felt a laugh of disbelief roll around her chest. It had been a welcome light-hearted moment in days of frustrating ignorance and gloom. Only Ben Abrams could have en-

gendered a posse of men from his unit marching down
to the hospital to present their hero commander with a
racing chair which had once belonged to a former Para-
lympic basketball champion.

And only Ben would have hurtled around the corridors
in it the following week as though he was in a rally car on
a racing circuit, pushing his one good arm past its limits.

Even she, who was impervious to him now—or at
least ought to be—hadn't been able to ignore the fact
that the simple white tee shirt he'd worn had done little
to hide the shifts and ripples of the already well-honed
muscles which had glistened, to the delight of several of
the medical staff, covered with a perfect sheen of sweat.

She could still remember the feel of that solid chest
against her body…the sensation of completeness as he
moved inside her.

*You, my girl, have all the resistance of a chocolate
fireguard.* She shook her head in frustration. Hadn't she
learned anything from that night? Despite his warnings,
despite his resistance, she had pushed and pushed until
Ben had ended up hurting her—more than she could
have thought possible.

Yet here she was. And she might have come for closure, but he was already shaking up her emotions. It was
difficult to keep hating a real-life hero who was prepared
to sacrifice his own life for others time and again. Not
just on an everyday basis, or even after Daniel had died,
but when he'd been so very badly injured himself in that
bomb blast.

According to some of the neighbourhood wives, all
the Army convoys used frequency-jamming devices—
which meant that the enemy who had detonated the IED
which had caught Ben's patrol had to have been close by.

Close enough to potentially have had a shooter to take individuals out.

Ben would have known that too. With all his training it would have been one of the first things he had realised. But instead of taking cover he'd stepped up anyway, to save the lives of five of his men. By rights he shouldn't be alive.

She had to admire this man who was so hell-bent on fighting his way back to full health, who refused to sit back and wallow in self-pity. Even his frustration, his anger now, was because he refused to accept the limitations his body was imposing on him.

She just wished he could let his guard down, even once, and let her in. But he never would. She wondered if he even knew how to.

There was no doubt that Ben's sheer grit had helped him achieve in a few weeks what other patients far more fortunate than him were still fighting to attain after months. She might have known Ben Abrams would be a rare breed… What was it her brother had once told her the men called Ben? Ah, yes, 'the Mighty Abs'. And indeed he was—by name and nature.

He even garnered attention in this place—not just as a soldier, but as a man. She wondered how much female attention he'd enjoyed over the last five years. It was none of her business, she knew that, and yet she couldn't seem to silence the niggling question.

Giving in to temptation, Thea allowed herself a lazy assessment of the man she had once thought herself in love with. Five years on and there were obvious differences, but he still resembled the young man she had known—if only briefly. Despite the dark rings around his eyes—testament to his recent experience—there was no mistaking that he was lethally handsome. Not *pretty-*

boy handsome—he'd never been that—but a deep, interesting, arresting handsome.

The nose which had been broken in the field a few times only enhanced the dangerous appeal he already oozed, and the scar by his eyebrow snagged at his eye, lending him a devil-may-care attitude. She remembered kissing that scar. The feel of his skin under her lips. The glide of her hands down that infamous torso. In her naivety she'd believed that if he gave in to her once, just once, he would realise that they could start again…redefine their relationship.

Sheer folly.

Now, at twenty-six, she understood what Ben had known all along. Things between them would never have worked. He was too entrenched in his ways and she was too idealistic. Still, even if she had realised that one night would be their only night, she wouldn't have changed it—even to spare herself the pain. But she *would* have taken her time that night. She hadn't been a virgin, but at twenty-one she hadn't had a wealth of experience either. She'd spent the last five years imagining how it would have felt if she'd let Ben do all the things to her he'd wanted to, let herself explore him more…

Heat suffused her body and, embarrassed, Thea dragged her mind from such inappropriate ponderings. Her emotions had been all over the place since she'd seen him again.

Because you still haven't told him your painful secret, goaded a little voice. She closed her mind but it refused to be silenced. *What about the baby you lost? Ben's baby?*

As long as he'd been away she'd been able to convince herself that it wasn't the sort of thing that could be explained over the phone. But now that he was back she no longer had that excuse. She'd have to tell him before he left again. But not now—and not here.

'Anyway, I'm not following you,' she said abruptly. 'Yesterday I was visiting you, but today I'm working in the area. I'm on my lunch break.'

'You work here?'

'The scrubs didn't give it away?'

Ben frowned. 'You were in your final year of medicine at uni when I left. Then you were going to be a junior house officer. I thought you wanted to go into paediatrics after rotations? That your goal was Great Ormond Street?'

She felt an unexpected rush of pleasure that he remembered. It shouldn't matter. But it did.

'It was. But then Daniel died and everything changed.' She shrugged, seeing the flash of sorrow in his eyes before his face closed against her, as she remembered it doing a decade earlier when she'd spoken her brother's name. Just another reminder of the fact that he could never open up to her.

'I realised I was better in trauma. Daniel had taught me some stuff over the years—techniques you guys use out in war zones which had yet to filter down to Civvy Street. I was able to adapt those things into my own work, so I started to gain quite a reputation. Before long I was getting offers to go and learn from Army trauma doctors who were coming back from Afghanistan. The more I learned, the better I became, and the more offers I got.'

'So now you work here? Nice scrubs… Blue always was your colour,' he said without thinking. The conversation topic had momentarily given them common ground.

'Actually, I work with the Air Ambulance as a trauma doctor. I just happen to be on secondment here at the moment.'

He saw through the excuse immediately, and the moment of connection between them disappeared as he glowered at her. 'You're playing with your career to stay here and check up on me?'

Dammit—she hadn't wanted him to realise. She'd been lucky that the Air Ambulance had been so under-standing from the moment she'd told them about Ben last month.

'I'm one of the doctors for the Air Ambulance. I don't *play* with my career,' she objected. 'They have set up a temporary exchange programme with one of the hospital-based trauma doctors for me.'

'Are you that good?' He looked impressed.

'Yes.' Thea nodded proudly and offered a cheeky grin. Typical of Ben to cut to the chase, and she wasn't about to disappoint him with false modesty. She was proud of all she'd achieved—especially after losing Daniel and Ben, albeit for very different reasons. 'I *am* good, as it happens.'

She'd worked hard for her achievements, and her past had driven her on—including Ben's abandonment.

'There'll always be more to learn—new procedures, research progress… That's the nature of medicine—you know that. But, yes, I'm one of the top in my field.'

'I'm pleased for you,' Ben acknowledged, and the sin-cerity in his tone gave her an unexpectedly warm glow.

She had been setting money aside ever since her first decent job, and now had enough to pay Ben back every bit of money he'd ever given her for her education. But some-thing warned her that now wasn't the time to mention it. Somehow they seemed to have struck the beginnings of an uneasy truce, and she wasn't about to jeopardise it.

'So, you've been here every day?'

'When I'm working here. Sorry, Ben, I don't have time to come and visit you all the time.'

Had her nose just grown about a foot? She had been surprised that he hadn't informed Dr Fields that they were estranged and got him to force her to stay away. But then, that would have entailed talking to a stranger about his private life.

Thea watched as he tried not to let her see he was leaning on the rock wall for support. The nurses had told her he'd long been refusing any pain medication, claiming it would prevent him from being able to tell whether his body was healing or not. She wasn't convinced—there had to be more to it than that. Still, it was little wonder that his brain was hazy if he was dealing with that level of pain. If so, was this her perfect opportunity to convince him that he should be discharged into her care?

Apprehension rippled through her. If she was honest, she wasn't sure she wanted him in her home again—it threatened to raise too many unanswered questions. She'd thought Ben was firmly in her past until she'd received that nightmare phone call a few weeks ago. Then she'd realised she needed closure. But the way he had her emotions scattering all over the place scared her. She couldn't afford to let him get under her skin again.

But if he needed someone looking out for him for the next few months then she owed him that much after all he'd done for her. Besides, as the cottage was part of Army married quarters, technically it was as much *his* house as it was hers.

'You've got your hospital stay and your initial rehab stay. After that you'll have a long-term rehab stay—*or* you can choose to come home with me so that I can help you through your recovery.'

'So that you can keep tabs on me, you mean?'

'Yes, if you like.'

No point in denying it.

'Look, Ben, you're going to push yourself—we both know that. Hell, the whole hospital knows that. But they won't discharge you to live on your own. They have a duty of care to make sure that someone is around.'

'Thea, I don't want to have this conversation with you.'

'Well, frankly, I don't want to have this conversation with you either,' she bit back.

He'd never listen to her if she buckled at his first objection. She'd been preparing her line of argument for the last week.

'Ben, the situation is ridiculous. It's your house too—married quarters because you're an officer. Don't you think that people are suspicious that they've never seen you there? Did you know that I've had to pretend to go away, stay in hotels, just to pretend we're together when you're on leave? If you don't come home now, being this injured, you're going to open us up to an investigation.'

She shrugged. Maybe that was what he wanted. For the Army finally to realise. Take the house away. Force them to face up to their sham marriage and divorce? She wasn't sure.

'I'm sure we can live there together on a temporary basis…*separately*.' She licked her lips, forcefully blocking any more memories of their night together in that house.

'Separately. Of course,' Ben echoed.

His voice sounded unexpectedly hoarse, as if his mind had taken him to the same place hers had. Which was ridiculous, she knew, and fanciful. She doubted Ben *ever* thought about that night, or else he did and cringed at the way she'd thrown herself at him.

Yes, she definitely needed closure.

'Consider it, Ben,' she pressed on. 'You gave me a

home, and you funded me so I didn't have to drop out of medicine at uni and take some waitressing job, or something, just to keep a roof over my head. Do you know how many people out there have the smarts but could never pay for the education *you* paid for—for me?'

'You achieved this by yourself,' Ben growled. 'Your success is nothing to do with me.'

'You're wrong,' Thea shook her head, wondering why he suddenly looked so angry again. 'I feel I owe you. If you come back home we can stay out of each other's way, but you can recover at your own pace and get back to the Army. Because that's your goal, right?'

His face said it all, and it was as if her heart plummeted to the uneven flags underfoot. What was it that drove him so that he refused to take care of himself and let his body recover? He seemed so hell-bent on getting back to the Army, being redeployed as fast as he could.

Or was it just that he was desperate to get away from her? Again.

She shook her head and faced Ben down.

'Fine. So you come home, recover properly, and then you're free to get on with your life. And I can get on with mine knowing that I owe you nothing. From that point on my successes *will* be my own. Deal?'

She waited, wondering what lunacy had made her think that Ben would agree.

Still, she couldn't help pushing… 'Deal?'

'I'll think about it,' Ben rumbled at length.

'Think hard,' she bit out.

He had at least four more months of recovery and procedures in the hospital—although at the rate Ben was going he'd be out much sooner than that—so she had some more time to work on him. But today was a start.

He might not have wanted her to be his wife, but after supporting her financially all these years she owed him something. And at least he wasn't refusing outright any more.

CHAPTER FOUR

'So, HERE WE ARE...*home.*'

Whether she meant her home, his home or theirs, Ben wasn't quite sure. But, despite the overly cheery demeanour, the slight catch to her voice, which she had tried so hard to hide, reassured him that she was finding this whole thing as awkward as he was.

He looked up at the familiar and yet alien house. It had been five years—hardly any wonder that he felt almost apprehensive about going inside. He stood there, his one solitary bag at his feet, and stared at climbing roses he didn't remember, a freshly painted fence which was so well bedded into the grass it had clearly been first built a few years ago. Even the evening sun seemed to be in on the act, picture-perfect as it set over the roof.

This wasn't his home. This was Thea's home. And he felt like an intruder.

What the hell was he doing here?

'Ben?' Thea walked over to him, holding out his walking cane.

He gave a single, sharp shake of his head.

'I don't need it.'

'Ben. Don't be too proud.' She reached for his bag. 'You've achieved in three months what it takes most patients five or six to achieve. But you still have a way to go.'

He stayed her hand and she jerked her head sharply to look at him.

'At least let me carry it for you.'

'Thanks, but I can manage,' he spoke quietly.

'Ben…'

'I can manage, Thea,' he repeated firmly, softening his words with a smile.

The hospital might not have been prepared to discharge him unless he had someone to take care of him, but he'd be damned if he'd let his presence interfere with Thea's life—even for a moment.

Slinging his bag over his shoulder and ignoring the flash of pain—less pain now…more an intense discomfort from his arm—he urged his reluctant legs to follow Thea through the door.

Was it really only five years earlier that he had handed the keys of this house over to Thea? Both of them had been in a daze of grief and shock, but he recalled muttering something about decorating it any way she liked, since he spent so much time away on back-to-back tours.

Even through the fug, he remembered he had seen the place through her eyes. Her small flat had been full of colour, and life and memories. The Army cottage had been bland mimosa walls, brown carpets and standard issue grilled-lightshades. Much like his Officer's accommodation in barracks had been before marrying Evie. Not to mention his abject lack of any personal effects.

That was something Ben had picked up as a kid. His father had loathed ornaments—dust-harbourers, he'd called them. Not even a photo of Ben's beloved mother had been allowed, because of the dust which would collect on the glass. And Ben had become accustomed to bareness, nowhere ever felt like a home—it was always just a place to lay his head.

Thea had changed the cottage. Army accommodation or not, this was like a completely different place. The walls were a warm colour and she had replaced the carpets with engineered floorboards, which made the place look clean and fresh, and somehow bigger.

'New curtains…nice…' He gestured, feeling he ought to say something.

The curtains were held back from the windows with pretty metal ties and light flooded into the downstairs room, bouncing off the two couches in the centre, one a vibrant purple and one a rich red. In his head he knew it ought to clash, but it didn't—it all came together beautifully. She'd injected colour and a real sense of fun into the place.

His sense of unease grew.

It felt like a proper home. Not girly or overly feminine, but somewhere he could instantly feel comfortable. And that made him feel disquieted. Yet what would he have preferred? That everything would be as it was the day he'd walked out? With boxes still in the hallway?

Whatever he'd expected, this wasn't it. He didn't like the way it welcomed him…suited him.

But Thea definitely wasn't the same girl he'd left. She had grown up a lot in five years, and her home, like her, was sophisticated and yet still with that irrepressible sense of fun and a zest for life. He was glad. His one regret had been that his actions might have crushed that vibrancy out of her. It was good to see that in some ways she was still the same Thea who had once so captivated him.

And that was what was most worrying.

'Um…do you want to sit down?' Thea asked abruptly. 'You're making the place look…'

'Look what?' he prompted uneasily. This was going to be even harder than he'd feared if she was so used to living alone that she thought he'd disturb everything in the place just by setting foot in it. 'Unsightly?'

'Not unsightly…'

Thea chewed the inside of her lip nervously. It was a trait he suddenly remembered from long ago.

'Ben, we're not going to get very far if you think I feel you're getting in the way. It's just…you're kind of filling up the door frame.' She wrinkled her nose, her cheeks flushing slightly. 'It makes the cottage look a little… small all of a sudden.'

'Right,' Ben acknowledged. *What was that supposed to mean?*

'It's a compliment,' she offered uncertainly.

'Oh, right. Thanks, then.' He tried to smile, but it felt taut on his cheeks. It hadn't *sounded* very complimentary. It had sounded definitively put out. 'Well, I'm pretty beat…it's been a long day. Mind if I hit whichever room is mine and freshen up?'

'Sure. I've set up the dining room.'

'Sorry?'

'The dining room.' She gesticulated, as though he might have forgotten where it was.

'Is there something wrong with the actual bedrooms?' He hadn't meant for his voice to sound so menacing, but he caught the nervous flicker of her eyes.

She licked her lips. 'I thought it you might prefer to avoid the stairs. You're healing well, and I know you're walking normally on level ground again, but the physios did say that stairs could still be a problem for a few months. I've ordered a temporary stairlift, so you can get to the bathroom, plus there's a downstairs toilet and—'

'Stop right there.' He held his hand up. If Thea thought him incapable of getting upstairs by himself, then she was mistaken. 'I'm not staying down here. I'll get myself upstairs and I'll sleep in a proper bedroom, shower in a proper bathroom. And you can cancel any damned stairlift. Now, which room can I use?'

'You're being ridiculous. You still need to recover.'

'Which room, Thea?'

She *harrumphed* in displeasure, and despite his frustration he thought it was so old-Thea-like that it almost made him smile.

'Fine. You can take your old room. I left it for you in case you ever decided to return.'

Ben frowned at the unexpectedly pointed comment. He felt as though he was missing something. When would Thea *ever* have wanted him to return? He narrowed his eyes at her, but she was already turning around, busying herself with rearranging the cushions of the couch. No, he had to be imagining it.

He inclined his head—redundantly, since she still had her back to him—and ducked out of the pretty living room. Climbing the stairs was still harder than he would like, especially with the added weight of his bag. He'd tried a short, slow jog around the hospital grounds the other night. Even though it had hurt like hell, it was still easier than climbing stairs, which tugged at the incision site on his back.

He reached the top landing gratefully. Would his room would be unchanged? As he'd left it? Did he want it to be? Or would he prefer it if Thea had worked her magic in there too, whisking away the memories of that last night together? Memories which had danced into his dreams over the years until he'd finally stuffed them away, locking them out for good.

He passed Thea's bedroom door and paused, standing motionless in the hallway for a moment. If only things had been different. If only *he* had been different.

But he wasn't different.

Shaking off the feeling, Ben moved to his own door and opened it. He was pleasantly surprised. Apart from the fact that Thea had taken away the old carpet, and sanded and varnished the beautiful floorboards underneath, as well as giving the place a dust and polish and a lick of paint, the place looked familiar. Fresh bedding lay folded on the clean mattress, and the empty drawer units smelled citrusy clean. When he opened the storage closet in the corner of the room he almost jumped as one of his old kit bags tumbled out. He'd go through that later.

Busying himself putting his few items away and grabbing a shower was unexpectedly satisfying, and it occurred to Ben that part of the problem was that he wasn't used to having nothing to do. Normally, if he wasn't deployed, he'd be on some adventure trip, learning new skills or honing old ones, or maybe planning training exercises and evaluating his men.

He felt bored—as if he was stagnating. He missed the exhilaration of successful trauma surgery, and his active mind was finding other areas to divert itself into. Dangerous areas. Like remembering their one night together. He couldn't afford to do that. However he tried to spin it, he'd betrayed her trust, and he wasn't the right man for Thea.

The dynamic between them had been irreversibly altered, and since a romantic relationship wasn't an option after he'd left her that night he'd bunked at a mate's house until he'd been shipped out. He'd been doing back-to-back tours ever since. Punishing duties in dangerous regions. Either he would pay off his dues or be killed.

His face twisted bitterly. Neither had happened.

Sometimes, in the beginning, Ben had wondered how things would have turned out if Daniel hadn't been his buddy. Hadn't been Thea's brother. Hadn't died. If he and Thea had been able to be together, would the whirlwind of that night have been sustainable? Would they have had the chance to explore a proper relationship slowly? In their own time? Maybe even got married for real?

He shook his head, as if to rid it of such pointless musings. Thea needed someone she could count on, someone she could trust, and he was neither. He hadn't even been able to bring himself to tell her exactly what had happened the night Daniel had died. All she knew was that *he*, Ben, been lauded like some kind of hero. Awarded a DSO—something which he certainly didn't deserve.

But he hadn't been able to bear to see either recrimination or pity in those dazzling sea-green eyes of hers. So instead he'd taken the coward's way out. Staying silent on the facts surrounding Daniel's death, and trying to make amends by fulfilling the promise he'd made to Dan. To provide her with a home, security and her education.

A gentle rapping on his door pulled him out of his reverie. Hauling the heavy wood open, he was surprised to see Thea in her coat and dressed to go out.

'Sorry, I didn't know if you were sleeping. I just wanted to let you know that I'm heading out, I've got a twenty-hour shift starting soon. I'm going in a bit early, and I won't be back until tomorrow afternoon.'

Twenty hours of focussed work to occupy the mind. That sounded really good right about now, Ben thought enviously. And he could understand her eagerness to leave the house early. This wasn't the easiest of arrangements.

'Sounds good.' He nodded. 'What is there to do around these parts these days? I might need something to do to-morrow.'

'Not a lot, to be honest' Thea pulled a face. 'Since you've gone all superhero maybe you could try the park. Or there's a little coffee house in the village up the road.'

Ben didn't answer. He'd deserved that. Instead he tried to smile and make it into a joke.

'So, what you really mean is, I have another day of nothingness to numb the brain.'

'Sorry.' She shrugged, moving quickly across the hall-way to the stairs.

Feeling even more deflated, he exhaled heavily and closed the door again.

Tap-tap-tap.

'I thought you'd gone?' This time his smile was less forced as he opened the door. She was doing that lip-chewing thing again.

'Do you want to come with me?'

'To your work?'

By the look on her face, she was just as surprised he was by her offer. Still, she rallied well.

'Why not? I mean, I can see how you might be going a little mad with nothing to do. I think I would be too, in your position. And from a professional point of view I think you'd find it really interesting. The base is quite big and there are quite a few teams on site. Plus we've got a couple of ex-Army trauma specialists with us at the moment. You won't be able to come out on any calls, of course, but you can see how things go down at the base.'

'And today just happens to be *Take an Estranged Hus-band to Work Day*?' Ben grinned. The offer was tempt-ing, but he couldn't see them letting him in.

'It might not be usual, but not *everyone* is the "Mighty

Abs".' Thea deflected his scepticism with aplomb. 'A decorated major and renowned Army field trauma surgeon? Oh, I think they'll make an exception.'

Ben suppressed a shudder. 'Thanks for that.'

Still, if it meant getting out of this place and having something decent to distract him he wasn't about to grumble too loudly.

He grabbed his bomber jacket and followed her into the hallway. 'Lead the way.'

Thea made for the live feed screen on the wall the minute she stepped through the doors. Returning calls of greeting absentmindedly, she scrutinised the screen. It streamed real-time information on all incoming 999 calls for potential call-ups. Already she knew it had the potential to be a pretty busy day, but for now she had enough time to show Ben around.

Ben! She spun around with a start, but he'd already been whisked away. *Dammit.* Coming to work had provided the mental distraction she'd been craving, but it had also made her forget the one thing she needed to warn Ben about. That nobody actually knew she was married.

She felt physically nauseous as she dashed through the base, pulling up short as she spotted Ben in the break room, already surrounded by her colleagues. Well, she'd been right to suspect that he'd be more than welcome here, judging by the way everyone was falling over themselves to be introduced to him.

In one way it was a good sign—it meant she could give him the basic tour and then let someone else take over. Inviting him to join her certainly hadn't been an altruistic gesture. Being around Ben was proving even harder than she'd feared. Her little cottage, her haven, was now thick with tension, memories and unanswered questions. All of which she'd thought she had laid to rest a long time ago.

Seemed she'd been wrong.

So she'd brought Ben here. Hoping to prove to him just how much she'd changed in the last five years and perhaps hoping that their mutual love of medicine might offer them some interesting cases which they could discuss back at home—instead of strained one-liners as they skirted awkwardly around each other.

Caught up in anxious thoughts, she suddenly realised that everyone at the base had gone deathly silent. Apprehension gripped her as nine pairs of eyes fixed accusingly on her.

'Ben is your *husband*?'

'You're *married*?'

Dammit, she should have warned Ben to keep his mouth shut.

'Got a family tucked away we don't know about, too, Thea?'

That last quip had Thea's heart plummeting to the soles of her rubber rescue boots. They wouldn't be so quick to smile at her if they knew the truth. *Ben* wouldn't be so keen to be around her if *he* knew the truth.

'I… We… I…'

Of all the eyes boring into her it was the pair of familiar battleship-grey eyes she was most conscious of. *Ben's.* The pair she was keenest to avoid meeting.

Confusingly, she sensed the greatest level of accusation coming from him…and something else she couldn't quite pinpoint… *Could it be…hurt?* He had a damned nerve, she tried to tell herself.

'It's called a personal life for a reason, guys.' She tried to joke, but even to her ears it came across as prickly and standoffish.

'What my wife is trying to say is that it isn't easy being married to a soldier.' Ben stepped in, somehow managing to unruffle feathers and smooth things over with apparent ease. 'I've been on a lot of back-to-back tours and that's always...difficult.'

A series of grunts and nods told Thea they were buying it, and it was all she could do to stop her mouth from dropping open. Aside from the fact that it wasn't remotely close to the truth, why the heck couldn't Ben be so apparently open and communicative when it came down to what was *really* the problem between them?

As her colleagues drifted back to work, affording Ben and Thea a degree of space, Thea marvelled at their acceptance. If had been up to her, she wouldn't have lived it down for at least the next year.

She supposed she should be grateful to him. But she wasn't. She couldn't help noticing the way he'd fitted so seamlessly into her life, as though none of the pain of the last five years meant anything. She was beginning to wish she had never brought him here.

'So, what's next on the tour, Boss?' Ben asked pointedly, as if sensing her resentment and trying to push past it.

She opened her mouth before spotting one figure, leaning on a brick pillar, watching them. *Nic*, she realised with a start. She'd forgotten all about him. But even as she turned towards him he ducked his head and moved away.

'Who was that?' Ben asked quietly, moving to her shoulder.

She hesitated. Perhaps it was her resentment, or maybe guilt, but Thea found herself almost challenging Ben with her tone.

'That was Nic, another trauma doctor. We once dated.'

The shock in Ben's eyes was almost gratifying.

'What did you expect, Ben? That I'd been sitting around for five years, waiting for you?'

It felt good, almost cathartic, to say the words. He'd married her, given her one precious night and then walked out on her. For five years there had been no contact, and even now she was only with him for closure. It was galling that he had dropped back into her life with such apparent ease, as if he'd never been away. This was her way of reminding Ben that her life *hadn't* just stood still whilst she'd waited for him to return.

'No,' Ben answered softly at length. 'Our marriage was one of convenience. A marriage on paper—nothing more. You had every right to date. I did too.'

The admission was unceremoniously delivered, yet ridiculously it felt like a body blow. Unwelcome tears pricked the corners of her eyes and Thea blinked them away in confusion. Why should she react this way? She didn't care.

'You've dated?' she choked out.

Ben shrugged. 'A couple of times. Not seriously—the Army always came first.'

Somehow that made her feel better. Part of her had secretly hoped Ben would return, but mostly she had been grieving for the baby she'd lost, and it had taken her years even to think about starting to move on with anyone else. Eventually she'd tentatively started dating again, but it had mostly been abysmal—until Nic. He had been kind, and understanding, and a good communicator.

After Ben—after the baby—Nic should have been everything she wanted, or needed. But even then the wounds had still felt too close to the surface and she hadn't been able to let Nic in. Like it or not, a relationship with him just hadn't been what she'd wanted. She was only grateful that Nic had been as private a person as her, and so there were no other colleagues to whom they had to explain themselves.

She searched Ben's face, looking for clues. Realising there was nothing more to be said, she forced herself to move on.

'We've got three helicopters across two regional bases,' she announced flatly. 'So, between everything, we're never more than a fifteen-minute flight to the nearest hospital.'

He whistled. 'That's pretty impressive,' he said, after only a beat of hesitation.

He looked around to take it all in. She felt another odd swell of pride as he turned back to her, more questions at the ready.

'So, what's your range?'

'About six thousand square miles.' Thea indicated the map on the wall, showing the area in question, grateful to have something concrete to focus on. 'Our helicopters can fly up to around two hundred miles per hour, and are fitted out with the most advanced lifesaving kit to give the patients their very best possible chance of survival.'

Great—now she sounded like one of the charity's donation request adverts.

'Is it usually single individuals, or do you get multiple casualties?' he asked thoughtfully.

'Both,' she confirmed. 'From a single jockey or a skateboarder to a multi-car pile-up. The most I've triaged in one go is nine. So…let me show you around the base.'

'Thea, we're up.' One of the paramedics hurried over. 'Motorbike accident—twelve miles out.'

With little more than a cursory farewell to Ben, Thea switched her mind from the complications and questions which had been dogging her all afternoon, and focussed in on her team.

Pulling her gear on, she listened as the base's switchboard operator relayed the details as they were fed to him.

'Two casualties—one rider, one pillion. High-speed collision with a car at a junction. There are two road crews already on their way to the scene but we've been called to attend.'

'We'll stay patched in. Keep us informed, Jack,' Thea said as she headed onto the Tarmac with the two paramedics on her team.

Her pilot, Harry, was already good to go, and as she jumped into the helicopter she brought up the crash location on her onscreen map, talking it through with him. Ultimately it would be his job to choose the optimal landing site.

As the helicopter ate up the relatively short distance to the crash site she kept an eye out for a clear landing location and potential hazards. A pass over the accident itself was an opportunity to take in as much detail as possible from the air—once on the ground it would be all go.

'There's a grassy central reservation—looks like we'll be able to land there. Just keep an eye out for power lines and street lights,' the pilot reminded her team, as he did every flight. It was part of their ritual, and it made sure they had their eye on the ball.

Thea drew in a few deep breaths as the pilot prepared to land the craft. This was the worst part. They were so close, and her adrenalin was coursing, but they had to be calm, patient. The pilot was lining the helicopter up between the street lights, with everyone systematically checking their own side, the rear, and below. It was always felt so painfully slow compared to the rest of the flight.

With an exhalation of relief, Thea felt the helicopter

touch down and she and her team jumped out. The road ambulance paramedics were waving her over to one crash victim. Even as she approached she could tell it was bad. The man's leg was open to the bone, presumably from his skid across the Tarmac of the road. But it was his silence which concerned her the most. She could hear his pillion passenger screaming in pain, but this man, the rider, was showing minimal response.

She hastily called in to update Jack, back at base, then turned her attention to their patients.

She couldn't assume the pillion rider was all right without checking, so she carried out a quick triage to confirm her suspicions.

'Stable, good SATS, broken leg and primarily superficial cuts and bruises.' She patched in the information to Jack.

But the other man wasn't so fortunate, and she suspected there would be a risk of amputation without immediate treatment—which was why her crew had been called out.

'Main casualty has open fracture on his knee. Suspected abdominal injury. Left side of chest severely compromised and he's in and out of consciousness. His SATS are down in the low eighties and I'm not happy that they won't drop out. I'm recommending ground ambulance, given the turbulence we experienced on the flight down and the short distance to the closest hospital. I'm going in the road ambulance—my guys too.'

If his SATS dropped again, or there were any other warning signs, Thea knew she would be able to spot them quickly and treat them. The fact that she was a trauma doctor was an advantage the air ambulance had over their road crew counterparts.

'You're clear for that.' Jack's voice responded immediately. 'Team Two are still on standby. I'll contact you if there are any emergencies.'

Giving her pilot a thumbs-up, telling him to return to the helicopter and follow the team to the hospital, Thea swung herself up into the ambulance with the critically injured rider and began to work.

Ben watched as Thea jumped smoothly out of the helicopter, striding out across the Tarmac back to the base. It was her third call-out in twelve hours. She looked exhausted. And beautiful, Ben realised in a tumble of emotions. Emotions he had no place feeling, which were now vying for his attention. He fought to hold them back. He'd been emotionally prepared for the old Thea. But this Thea— this strong woman who seemed to bulldoze through all his carefully laid plans—was a different prospect.

As she walked into the base and her eyes collided with his, however, he could have sworn he saw her face fall.

'You were listening in the whole time?'

Why did he get the impression that whatever answer he gave it would be wrong?

'It was an interesting case.' He shrugged.

'But you would have done things better?'

Ben frowned, confused. From all he'd heard, her last patient had been DOA. No one could have done anything about that. But he stayed quiet, giving Thea a moment.

Did she think he was going to challenge her? Nothing could be further from the truth. Thea was good. She was more than good. She had to know that. This sudden hostility didn't seem to fit with the Thea he knew.

But how well do you really know her?

Ben tried to ignore the niggling reminder that she had never mentioned their marriage, even to her close-knit crew. He told himself it was hardly surprising, given that their marriage had been a sham anyway. But still, he felt oddly hurt and sidelined. She was getting under his skin again.

'It was another motorbike rider in a high-speed collision—this time with a truck in the oncoming lane.' Thea pushed past him into the break room, making her announcement to no one in particular and flinging her helmet down in frustration. 'She was pushed into the central reservation when someone pulled into the fast lane to overtake and didn't see the bike coming up behind. She clipped the barrier and flipped over into the oncoming traffic. DOA.'

'I'm sorry,' he sympathised.

'Why don't these people realise what happens to the human body when you come off one of those things?'

'One in three are dead on arrival.' One of the other paramedics looked up at Ben from his newspaper. 'Thea takes it personally. She wants to at least feel she stands a *chance* of helping the victims she's flown out to see.'

Ben nodded. He could understand that—it was something he had felt himself many times in the past. Perhaps it was conceit to think that he *could* have done something if the casualty had been alive when he arrived, rather than accepting that they were so badly injured they would have died whether or not he'd been there.

Still, he could empathise with Thea's frustration. And it was a relief to find common ground. It was as though it helped him to understand the woman Thea was now. As though it somehow brought them closer together.

He let his gaze fall back on Thea. She'd looked so calm and poised, hour after hour, call-out after call-out. Now, suddenly, she looked sad and deflated. He wanted to comfort her but she wouldn't welcome him. And besides, she didn't need him. She probably never had.

Still, wordlessly he moved into the kitchen to make her some strong, sweet tea.

He'd listened to her interactions with Jack every time her team had gone out, had admired her professionalism, her composure, her confidence. She commanded her team with respect and she knew how to get just that little bit more out of them—and her colleagues returned double that respect. Thea had seriously downplayed her talent when she'd told him she was good at her job. He'd be happy to have her work alongside him any time. No, scratch that, he'd be happy to work alongside *her* any time.

He felt a swell of pride which he had no right to feel. It was as though *he'd* had something to do with her success, and he knew that wasn't the case. She'd achieved this all on her own.

Still, this grown-up Thea was a far cry from the twenty-one-year-old Thea who had captivated him with her flightiness and her lust for life, combined with the gentle, almost shy side she'd kept hidden. This Thea was confident, ballsy and sexy, but utterly dedicated and focused on what really mattered. And, from the various admiring glances he'd seen cast her way, he wasn't the only one to think so.

He briefly wondered what had happened between Thea and Nic, before pushing the question aside. Who she dated wasn't his business. But the fact that she wanted to *was*. She was right about the Army not letting her stay in the house if they knew they weren't really married. But at some point she was bound to find someone else she *would* want in her life. And she and Ben needed an exit strategy.

He clenched his fists. The very thought simultaneously sickened and angered him. *Jealousy?* What was he playing at? This had to stop. *Now.*

Because he was beginning to think that he'd never be able to let her go. Not really. He didn't think he could stay in that house with her for longer than was absolutely necessary. The sooner he finished his recovery and got back to Army life, away from Thea, the better.

And not just Thea. He was feeling inexplicably drawn to the life she led here. Once, back-to-back tours had made him feel proud—as if he was achieving something. But more and more over the years he'd begun to feel disillusioned. As though he was fighting the same war over and over again but never getting anywhere. As though he'd be more effective elsewhere. Somewhere like here.

But he couldn't come here. This wasn't his life—it was hers. A life which she'd carved out for herself despite him. And he had no business being in it.

As much as he suddenly found himself wanting to.

CHAPTER FIVE

THEA RETREATED TO her bedroom the moment they returned to the cottage. It was the only sanctuary she had left now Ben had catapulted back into her life. She flopped onto her bed, expecting exhaustion to claim her, as it always did after a twenty-hour shift. But today it proved elusive and instead she twisted and turned in agitation.

Ben! she thought resentfully. She could hear him moving about in his own room, and even that riled her. She should have known when Ben had agreed to be discharged into her care that he would fight any real attempt to help him through his recovery. She'd been nothing more than a means to an end—a way for him to get away from the hospital and away from people. Because heaven forbid anyone should ever get close to him.

The only person Ben had ever appeared close to had been her brother Dan. Best mates and Army buddies, they would have laid down their lives for each other. Dan had done so. No wonder she could never compete with that in Ben's eyes.

She *harrumphed* and jettisoned herself off her bed to go and stare, unseeing, out of the window, lost in her thoughts.

What on earth had possessed her to invite Ben to

work, to meet her colleagues, when she'd *known* it was bound to come out that she'd never told them she was married? Had she subconsciously *wanted* to create a confrontation? Neither of them had been prepared to be the first one to bring up their past, but now it was out there and she and Ben could no longer pretend to tiptoe around each other.

If it had been her unwitting intention, then it hadn't worked anyway. Ben didn't seem to care—not even about Nic. She didn't like to admit how much that hurt, but it *had* underlined things for her. She didn't want to keep avoiding their past—not when she still needed answers that only Ben could provide. They needed to have a conversation, at least once, which included the reason why he had *really* married her? The last time she'd asked him that he'd told her it had been the only way he could honour his promise to take care of her. But if that had been all there was to it then he wouldn't have slept with her.

She needed to understand. How could he have walked out on her that night?

And she wasn't the only one who was owed the truth. At some point she was going to have to tell him that she'd fallen pregnant that night and that she'd lost their baby. *But what if he didn't care?*

Thea turned around from the window. She was suffocating, trapped within the four walls of her room. She needed to get out of there.

She lunged across the room to the high chest of drawers and scrabbled for her running kit, but even now, as if taunting her, her eyes slid down to the bottom drawer. In there, tucked in a small brown envelope and slid out of sight under the maternity clothes she had bought in such excitement but which she'd never had opportunity to wear, was the scan image she had of the baby she'd lost.

She froze momentarily before wrenching her eyes away, focussing instead on the drawer crammed with sports gear. She needed to occupy herself, push herself to her limits, exhaust her body so that she might finally find the blissful oblivion of sleep.

Thea dressed within minutes and then ducked down the stairs and outside. She would stretch in the garden—it was a pleasant enough afternoon. A wave of relief flooded over her at her sense of freedom. But it was short-lived.

'Ben? You can't *seriously* be going out for a run?'

Instantly his expression of cautious greeting evaporated, closing down as he shut her out.

He sighed, as if humouring a small child. 'Look, I've jogged before—at the hospital.'

'Of *course* you have.' She snorted. *Why couldn't he just cut himself some slack?*

'Short distances, slow pace. I'll probably just jog down to the end of the road and back. How about you? How far are you going?

She bit her lip angrily. He was being foolish, but there was no way she was going to be able to talk him out of it. He was so stubborn.

'I was thinking five or six miles.' Thea stalled for a moment, contemplating cutting her stretches short. Ben couldn't afford to do anything to interfere with his body's healing process, but maybe she should jog away—stretch somewhere else.

Instead she stayed where she was, bending one leg up behind her, tucking her heel against her bottom to stretch her thigh. Refusing to be chased away.

Out of the corner of her eye she watched him move towards the gate. He was clearly pushing past his limits, against all medical advice. Suddenly she felt tired of telling him, tired of trying to be there for someone who clearly didn't want her help. So much for her hope that caring for Ben during his recovery would help her find the closure that she was so desperately lacking.

She took her time finishing her stretches, wanting to give Ben plenty of time to put some distance between them as he so clearly wanted to. She headed out in the opposite direction when she finally set off.

She wished it didn't matter. Over the years she'd almost convinced herself that she'd put Ben Abrams into her past. And then she'd received the news that he'd been blown up and was being shipped home. Her whole world had been thrown into chaos and she'd realised she'd never moved on from him, or from their wedding night, at all.

She'd been so silly in the beginning—racing home every day and hoping against hope that he'd be there, waiting for her. When she'd found out she was pregnant she'd believed that somehow he would sense it and come home. He hadn't. Just as he hadn't sensed it when she'd seen those first ominous spots of blood, or when the pain had hit, or when she'd lost their baby.

The loss had been visceral. And it had taken her so long to piece herself back together. How many times had she dialled the first few digits of Ben's mobile—wanting his strength, his comfort—only to terminate the call? She had needed him to come home because *he* had chosen to—not because she had compelled him. It had only been then that Thea had realised, deep down, that Ben was never coming back. She was on her own and she was always going to be on her own.

In the end she'd thrown herself into the last year of her degree, grateful for the long hours of exhausting work which had kept her out of the house and distracted her. A year to the day after she'd lost the baby Thea had finally picked up her first paintbrush and started the transitioning process, doing little bits of decorating on her few days off or when she'd found herself at a loose end.

Redecorating the house from top to bottom had been the only way she'd been able to occupy her thoughts and move on from what she had lost with Ben. It was no coincidence that her first—awful—date had taken place shortly after there had been no more decorating to do. Apart from Ben's room, which had remained untouched until last year.

If she looked back she wondered how she had managed to get through those dark, bleak days. So she'd stopped looking back, shut the memories away and pretended they belonged to someone else. And now she wasn't sure how to unlock them properly again, or even if she wanted to. What purpose would it serve to tell Ben about the baby after all this time? And yet somehow she felt as though he had a right to know.

It piqued her to realise that, deep down, she *wanted* to tell him. But she still couldn't shake the fear that he might not care.

Thea stopped running, her legs suddenly sapped of strength. She shook her head, but her doubts weren't so easily dislodged. Nor was her darkest and yet most precious secret.

Caught up in her thoughts, she didn't realise she had run for miles in a long circuit, eventually coming to the park where Daniel had used to train. Suddenly she found herself in front of the long, steep hill on which, as a kid, she had sometimes watched him complete hill rep after hill rep before they talked about life, school, and whether anyone was bullying her. Inexorably drawn there, Thea wished she had her brother to talk to now. But then if

Daniel had still been alive she wouldn't have been in this predicament with Ben in the first place.

Unexpectedly she felt her eyes prick with tears and took a step backwards, struggling for breath. Five years and she had pretty much come to terms with losing her brother. These days it rarely caught her off guard like that.

She suspected that her earlier thoughts of Ben had a lot to do with her scattered emotions. No matter what she did, she couldn't seem to get away from him.

Thea jerked her head up as sudden movement over the dip caught her eye. As if to prove her point, Ben came gradually into view, evidently pushing through every pain barrier. He saw her and, even from that distance the clenching of his jaw betrayed the little muscle ticcing in irritation.

'Daniel used to train here.' She wrapped her arms defensively across her chest as he approached.

'Hill reps—yes. I know.'

'You trained here together?' Realisation dawned. 'Daniel brought me here sometimes, to talk and to jog around the lake with him.'

'I never thought… Of course. You miss him,' Ben stated flatly. 'I'm sorry. I didn't mean to intrude on your memories. I'll leave you to your peace. See you back at the house, Thea.'

Abruptly Thea wondered if, like her, Ben's memories were what had drawn him here today. To her, Ben's accident sounded similar to what had happened to Daniel. Certainly the ambush and getting pinned down by the enemy. She wondered if Ben was feeling as disconcerted about their being back at cottage together as she was. She wasn't sure why that made her feel a little better, but it did. It offered her a new sense of courage.

'No—wait.' Quickly she put a hand out to touch Ben's arm, to stay him, but she wasn't prepared for the jolt that fizzed through her.

Snatching her fingers swiftly away, she forced herself to meet his eyes. *That wasn't supposed to happen.* It certainly wasn't what she *wanted* to happen.

Still, it was proving impossible for them to live together. As much as they had tried to ignore the problem, accusations hung silently around them every time they walked into the same room. She'd been right earlier. Pretending the issues between them didn't matter wasn't working. At some point they *would* have to talk. And now, here, seemed as good a time as any.

'Don't leave. We both came here for a reason.'

'This isn't the time.' Ben turned, ready to move away.

I think this *is* the time,' Thea argued. 'Don't *you* have questions? Because I have.'

So many.

'I know what your questions are, Thea.' He turned slowly back, meeting her gaze head-on. 'But I can't give you the answers you want to hear.'

'You don't know what I want to hear.'

'I think I do.'

It was like some surreal stand-off, neither of them wanting to blink first.

Across the lake a little girl threw oats onto the water. Ducks fought for them and other birds tweeted as they flew gracefully in from overhead. The little girl laughed and turned to her mother for more. She was four, maybe five. Briefly Thea wondered if that might have been her and their child, if things had been different. It all seemed so familial and idyllic—a stark contrast to the turmoil going on in her head and the thunderous pounding in her chest. It made her stand her ground all the more.

As if sensing the subtle change, Ben conceded. 'All right—what do you want to know, Thea?

It wasn't exactly encouraging a proper dialogue between them, but it was better than him shooting her down as he had in the past.

She sucked in a deep breath. 'Why did you marry me, Ben?'

The words seemed to hang in the stillness of the park. Ben stopped shifting but didn't immediately turn to face her. By the look on his face and the steel-shuttered set of his eyes it seemed his acquiescence of a moment ago had merely been his attempt to humour her.

'You asked me what I wanted to know,' she prompted urgently. 'This is it.'

'We've been through this. It was the only way to take care of you properly in a way the Army would accept.'

'Yes, but then you slept with me. And ever since I've wondered if there was something more to your offer.'

'I'm sorrier than you can ever imagine for that night.' Ben gritted his teeth, disgust etched onto his features.

'*Are* you?' Thea asked desperately. 'Only I think maybe you wanted me as much as I wanted you.'

His Adam's apple bobbed but he said nothing for several long moments. 'Of course I wanted you,' he ground out at length.

'Is that why you married me? Because even though you told me we weren't a good match you still...obviously you didn't love me, but *lusted* after me?' She flushed red, embarrassed by the words.

'I married you because Dan asked me to look after you and it was the only way to get Army approval,' Ben repeated flatly. 'He asked me to take care of you. He was my best friend. I agreed.

'As simple as that?' she snapped in frustration. 'Really?'

But Ben didn't bite back. 'As simple as that.'

She swallowed down the sarcastic retort on her lips. What was it about Ben that had her feeling like a desperate twenty-one-year-old again? She was a successful, respected trauma doctor, so why, after five years, was it still so important to her to know if something more than just a casual promise to her brother had driven Ben to marry her? Something more emotional. The same something which had sparked between them when they'd slept together, perhaps?

Surely it hadn't just been her imagination.

Judging by the way he shifted edgily, she was getting under his skin as much as he was getting under hers right now. Somehow it offered her some small comfort.

'For heaven's sake Thea.' He tugged his hand through his hair irascibly. 'What does this conversation gain for us? How we felt or didn't feel—it doesn't change anything.'

'It does for me,' Thea half-whispered. 'It matters to *me.*'

'Why? Why does it matter *now*?'

She faltered, licked her lips nervously. 'Because in all these years you've never really told me what happened between you walking me home and saying how *connected* we were on that first date and then, almost within hours, telling me you weren't interested.' She had never been able to help wondering if she'd done something wrong.

The seconds ticked by between them and she was sure he must be able to hear her heart beating out of her chest.

'Okay, I liked you,' Ben shrugged, as if it was no big deal. As if *she* was no big deal. 'But then I walked you up that driveway and Dan came to the door, bellowing his head off. The minute I realised you were his sister you were off limits, Thea. We'd just met, had one simple date—what did it matter?'

Thea shook her head. 'It wasn't just a *simple date*, though.'

Not for her—and, according to Ben, not for him either. He had been the first person she'd met who had seen through her bubbly façade to the uncertain, slightly bruised person underneath. Her brother had done an incredible job of making her feel loved, a secure and rounded person—but nothing had ever made up for losing her parents as a kid. Nothing had ever taken away the uncertainty that had brought. Not completely.

And Ben had seen that. She'd never met anyone with whom she'd clicked so perfectly—either before or since. To someone who had perfected the art of letting people *think* they were getting close to her, Ben had been the first and only person who had ever slipped past her defences—effortlessly—and *really* got to her.

Ben shrugged, again reaching for the easiest explanation. 'You were Dan's sister—'

'No,' she interrupted. She knew what was coming and she didn't want to hear it. 'Not that *"Buddy Code"* bull you and Daniel had about not dating each other's kid sister. Not this time. You won't trust each other with your sisters, but you'll trust each other with your life?'

'Out there we'll take a bullet for each other. It's not a game, Thea. It's war. Dating is the least of our problems. People *die* out there.'

His words were like a kick to the stomach. But she had lost too much to be fobbed off so easily.

'You think I don't *know* that soldiers die out there?' She gasped. 'You might have lost your best friend, Ben, but I lost my *brother*.'

He stared at her wordlessly for a moment, with a death-like pallor. He gave a sharp nod, as though acknowledging her point for the first time.

'Why don't you ever talk about him?' Thea asked suddenly.

He blanched, and it was like a door clicking open in her head. How was it that she'd observed Ben's avoidance in the past but never really *noticed* it?

Had she missed something fundamental all this time?

'Why don't you ever talk about *yourself*?'

'There's nothing to tell.'

He drew his lips into a thin line, refusing to be drawn by her. She couldn't remember ever seeing him look shaken or uncertain. If she really thought about it she could only picture the determined, closed-off, emotionless Ben of the past. A picture of him pieced together after their date, their few weeks together between Ben telling her about Daniel's death and the moment she and Ben married, and the many fragments of stories Daniel had told her about Ben.

Whatever had started this conversation, she felt the urge to push him that little bit harder before he had time to pull that impenetrable armour of his back into place. She might never get the chance again.

'Ben?'

'I *liked* you, Thea,' he suddenly blurted out. 'I liked you a lot. Maybe too much.'

'What does *"too much"* mean?' she asked instinctively, but Ben was already shaking his head, back-pedalling. Did it mean the Buddy Code was just an excuse—as she'd always wondered?

'It doesn't mean anything, 'Ben growled. 'Forget I said it. I just mean I thought you were incredible. But when I realised you were Dan's sister I knew we weren't a good match.'

'You didn't know anything about me.' She frowned.

He opened his mouth, as though he had something more to say, and then the shuttered look she knew so well came down over his face.

'You're right—we didn't know much about each other,' he conceded. 'But then I made a promise to take care of you, and that was what I intended to do.'

The moment was lost, Thea realised in despair. Whatever had made him drop his guard a few moments earlier, it was gone now.

'So because of that promise you ended up with a wife you'd never wanted? A bad match? No wonder you abandoned me.' Frustration tinged her words with bitterness.

'*Abandoned* you?'

Ben whipped his head around to stare at her, shock clouding his handsome features. Then it was gone, and the mask of indifference was back, leaving Thea wondering if she'd imagined it.

'When did I *abandon* you?'

'The morning after our wedding. The morning after...' She swallowed, suddenly nervous '...after *that* night.'

'I didn't abandon you. You told me to leave.'

'Sorry? I did *what*?' She was incredulous.

'I did what you asked me to do.' His voice was low, urgent. His eyes were raking desperately over her.

'That's ridiculous!' she cried.

He would *not* wriggle out of this. *But, God, it was humiliating.* She'd offered herself up to him that night, convinced that there had been more to his marriage proposal, that deep down he still liked her even if he couldn't admit it. Clearly her mistake, but if Ben had wanted to honour his promise to her brother surely he should have understood that she'd been grief-stricken and had made an enormous error of judgement? Not walked out on her, leaving her all alone.

'You left when I needed you most. I felt alone…deserted. I'd just buried my brother. I never thought *you'd* leave me like that.'

'You needed space.'

'I needed *support*!' she cried.

'You needed someone you trusted,' Ben countered. 'And after we slept together you didn't trust me. Why should you? I'd taken advantage of you when you were at your most vulnerable.'

'You didn't take advantage of me.' Thea shook her head.

'Of course I did,' Ben spat in self-contempt. 'You even told me that it was one of the most horrific days of your life,' he told her.

'You know it was,' Thea muttered. 'I'd just buried my brother, and yet I was getting married.'

Little wonder that her head had been a confused jumble of emotions. Even though time had passed, she still didn't like to dwell too long on the bitter memories.

'You told me that you'd thought us sleeping together would make it better,' Ben recalled. 'But that it had just made it worse.'

'Because I'd spent those six weeks between our date and the night we slept together hoping, deep down, that you would realise your mistake in ending things. I hoped you still had feelings for me and I thought our sleeping together would help you admit it. Instead you rejected me. *Again*. I felt more alone than ever.'

She watched the rise and fall of his chest as he absorbed what she was telling him, part of her hoping he'd tell her that it had all been just some big misunderstanding and they could have been with each other all this time if only they'd realised.

But that was nonsense, wasn't it? Because it hadn't been a misunderstanding. Ben was never going to talk to her, open up to her. There was some element of survivor's guilt too, which she couldn't afford to underestimate. But ultimately Ben would *never* be able to open up to her, talk to her about his emotions.

No misunderstanding could change that.

And what about *her*? She'd idolised Ben even before she'd ever met him, having fallen in love with the incredible war stories of him as brave hero which Daniel had told her growing up. In her head Ben had already been extraordinary. So even if he *had* been able to talk to her and reveal his weaknesses would she have actually listened? Would she ever have allowed him the hopes, the fears, the disappointments of any ordinary man?

Thea couldn't be sure. Unlike Ben, who hadn't known her when they'd met that first night and gone on that first date, *she* had known exactly who Ben was. So in some way perhaps she'd brought this on herself.

Not that she could ever admit that to Ben. If he ever realised that she'd known who he was that first time they'd met and not told him he would think she'd been manipulative, that her actions had been deliberate. But they hadn't. At worst she'd been naive, even foolish, but she had never intended anyone to get hurt.

When she'd first seen him walk into that club with his friends she'd been drawn to him, but she hadn't realised why. Not at first. She'd watched him for a while, liking the way he interacted with his group. He'd seemed as if was having fun, but he hadn't been rowdy, like some of the guys she'd known. She'd watched several girls approach him, and although he'd been friendly enough he hadn't seemed overly interested in any of them.

When he'd gone to the bar she'd taken her opportunity and slipped through the crowd to join him. The ease with which they'd struck up a conversation had seemed like a sign. Even when she'd found out his name she hadn't put two and two together, but as the evening had worn on she'd found their instant attraction developing quickly into something more—in one evening she had known she really liked him.

It had only been later that night—when he'd mentioned excusing himself from his Army buddies—that she'd asked him about his job and suddenly realised why he'd seemed so familiar to her, why she'd felt so instantly at ease in his company. She'd seen him before—in a rare photo Dan had from an early tour in Afghanistan.

Dan had told her so many stories about Ben as hero that when she'd seen him walk in—even though she might not have realised it—she'd already known he was a good guy. More than just a good guy. But she hadn't been able to bring herself to spoil the evening or have it come to an abrupt end by telling him she was Daniel's sister. She'd already liked him too much to risk him walking away before he had taken the time to get to know her.

Yes, she'd been foolish and naive, caught up in the myth of 'Ben the Hero', but she hadn't deliberately set out to deceive anyone.

Putting Ben on a pedestal, idolising him—that had been no basis for a stable marriage. And if he hadn't walked out on her she might never have realised how truly strong she was, how much she could achieve. She might never have become the successful, respected doctor that she was today.

In some perverse way she should be grateful to him for

abandoning her. For not loving her. It was a *good* thing. But it didn't feel like that.

She'd moved on a long time ago, so why did it feel as though a childhood dream, a girlish fantasy, had just died? That things were never going to be the same again? She had wanted to see Ben through his recovery in order to gain closure, but she'd never expected to gain it this way.

Well, she almost had closure—she still needed to tell him about the baby. *Their* baby.

But not today. Another day. When she was feeling stronger.

'I don't know what to say…' Ben began. 'I'm sorry.'

'There's nothing to say.'

Thea stood up abruptly. Her humiliation was almost complete and she'd brought it all on herself. She'd laid her heart out there for him and he still wasn't able to tell her he'd really wanted her.

'I've got my answer. Thank you for being honest with me.'

'Thea, listen…'

She held up her hand to stop him.

'Please, Ben, don't say anything. You've answered my questions. It's not your fault if I don't like what I heard.'

Quickly she turned and jogged away, before the tears which were pooling in her eyes could begin to fall.

CHAPTER SIX

BEN SAT BOLT-UPRIGHT. The blood was gushing in his ears, his heart was hammering out of his chest, his body was drenched in sweat. Nightmares. *Again*.

He forced his head to focus on the clock. Two-thirty a.m.

Pushing himself out of bed, he tried to escape his unwanted thoughts. But not even standing under the hot, powerful jets of the shower, almost too exhausted to raise his arms, could wash away the doubts which had long since lurked in his subconscious but were now beginning to break the surface.

The events of yesterday had played through his head all night—events from the moment Thea had left him at the park.

He felt mentally and physically exhausted, and he knew it wasn't just from pushing his body too hard yesterday. Although he had. He'd pushed himself too hard from the moment he'd got out from under the hospital's watchful eye—he knew that. Thea had been right about him pushing past his limits. The pain was almost constant now, rather than easing off bit by bit, day by day, as it should be.

But he almost welcomed it.

It meant that he was still alive when so many others were dead—his men, his friends, Dan.

He must never slack off—never let the injuries defeat him. He felt ashamed that only a few months ago, when he'd first woken in that hospital, paralysed and groggy, he'd closed his eyes and prayed that when he went back to sleep he wouldn't wake up again.

He was so very grateful he *had* woken again. And now he owed it to the memory of every soldier who had died out there never to let himself fall that far again. He needed to get his body back to full health, pass his Army Medical Board and get back to whichever war zone they wanted to send him to, save as many lives as he could.

He also needed to get out of this house, before he did something he regretted. Like giving in to temptation with Thea the way he had on their wedding night.

And right now that was proving harder than ever.

Her revelations yesterday had been a bombshell. He still couldn't quite get his head around it. He'd spent five years believing that he'd betrayed Thea, taken advantage of her in her grief, and he had hated himself for it. He'd left the following morning because he had genuinely believed Thea had wanted him to. His shame had been the only thing which had stopped him from making contact in all these years. He had believed she must abhor him even more than he loathed himself. Instead Thea was now telling him that he hadn't taken advantage of her vulnerability at all—that she had actively *wanted* him on their wedding night. As much as he had wanted her.

And that raised a whole other problem.

Thea's frankness yesterday had caught him off guard. She had his emotions starting to spiral out of control, and for someone who had always been taught to put his feelings in a box and shut them neatly away it was all a completely alien experience.

Slamming the shower off, hearing the *clunk-clunk* of water hammering through the pipes, he hoped it wasn't reverberating around the silent house and waking Thea. Still, the noise aptly mirrored his sour mood. He half-heartedly patted his body down with a towel and then shuffled across to his bedroom to flop, exhausted, back into bed.

He didn't expect to sleep, but the psychological impact of Thea's revelation was taking its toll on his still healing body. As soon as his head had hit the pillow sleep engulfed him, and he slept for four hours straight.

By the time he awoke the blinding pain of yesterday had receded to a dull ache and he felt somewhat revived, a little less tense. He listened carefully. They were going to have to build some bridges, but right now he could do without bumping into Thea. Reassured that the house was silent, Ben climbed out of bed and crept quietly out of the room and down the stairs to the kitchen.

'For crying out loud!'

As Ben stepped through the door he ducked just in time to miss a high-flying empty juice carton which a clearly exasperated Thea had just over-armed towards the swing bin. It hit the sweet spot and tumbled in.

Time to start bridge-building after all.

'Nice shot.'

It might have been weak but it was a start, although her grunt of response wasn't encouraging. Neither was the fact that she'd flushed bright red and was refusing to meet his eye, sitting straighter, more rigid on her stool. No doubt she was feeling raw and embarrassed after their last conversation. And that was his fault too.

He cast around for something else to say and noticed

the glass sitting forlornly on the countertop, next to where Thea was. There was barely a trickle in the bottom, but the same carton had been over half full when he'd taken it from the fridge last night. Hence the flying missile, he realised.

'Sorry about the juice,' he apologised. 'I meant to go out early this morning and pick another one up, but…'

She shot a sharp look his way and he realised she thought he was having a dig at her. His gut twisted. He'd had no idea he'd hurt her so badly; it certainly hadn't been his intention, and making amends was going to prove harder than anticipated if she was still smarting from their confrontation yesterday.

Now was his chance to say something. But the words wouldn't come. Instead he told himself that Thea had finally got a long-held resentment off her chest and he couldn't blame her for any of it. Raking it all up again in the cold light of today wouldn't help anybody.

Thea might not realise it, but she had changed so much in the last five years from the young woman he remembered. She was successful, settled and happy, and just because she'd taken the opportunity to vent it didn't mean she wanted to be dragged into his emotional baggage. What was it she'd said? *There's nothing more to say.*

Caught up in his musings, he almost jumped when the toaster popped up a teacake. He gave a wry smile. He'd forgotten how much she loved them. Dan had once told him that teacakes were the reason she'd dragged him to endless teashops—one of the many things he'd affectionately recounted about his kid sister.

What was he doing, reminiscing? There was no place in this scenario for such sentimental nonsense. Thea needed something more tangible from him. A matter of a few

weeks ago she'd asked for a semblance of friendship—
well, now was his chance to try it.

He glanced at her. She was ignoring the teacake, still
rigid on her stool. Reaching over, he took the teacake and
placed it on the plate she'd set by the toaster, then slid it
over to her with a smile.

'An olive branch?'

'Thanks,' she muttered. 'Um…could you please pass
me the butter as well?'

'Sure.' Surprised, he obliged.

Thea slipped off her stool and appeared to shuffle to
the cutlery drawer, careful to keep the counter in between
them. It was only when he leaned over to slide the butter
tray across the island that he understood her discomfort.

Just beyond the countertop he caught a glimpse of
the curve of her pert backside, peeking out from beneath a short, cheeky dressing gown. Unexpectedly desire
fired through him. He wondered what would happen if
he rounded the island and took her in his arms. Claimed
her mouth with his, reminding her of what she'd once
wanted with him. What they had *both* once wanted.

'Ben?'

He snatched his gaze up to see her staring at him,
her eyes wide, a horrified expression on her face as she
tugged desperately at the dressing gown, dropping the
knife in the process. It hit the floor with a loud clatter.

What was wrong with him?

Disgust flooded through him and he turned away,
angry with himself for letting his lust take over when
he was supposed to be focussed on making amends to
Thea. He still wanted her, after all this time, but he had
no right to.

Her flushed face turned an even deeper shade of scarlet and then she was scurrying around the island, head

down and mumbling something. *Hell*. That was his fault. *Again*. He'd made her feel uncomfortable in her own home.

He stepped into her path to block her exit. 'Thea, I'm sorry. That shouldn't have happened.'

'I thought you were asleep when I came down...'

She paused for a moment, shaking her head, biting her lip. Then she stepped forward placing her hands flat on his chest as if to gently move him out of her way. Reaction fizzed through him, and by the way her head jerked up and she looked him in the face Thea felt it too.

They stood motionless for several moments, unable to break whatever spell momentarily bound them. Then he moved his hands to cover hers and took a step closer. She didn't back away. He could feel her breath, soft and warm on the back of his hand. He wondered if she could feel his heartbeat accelerating beneath her touch. It was practically hammering its way right out of his chest, and the desire to kiss her was overwhelming.

Ben dipped his head, then paused.

He wasn't sure who pulled away first, but in an instant they were stumbling awkwardly away from each other, snatching their hands back as if they'd been burned and muttering incoherently.

And then she was gone and Ben stood alone, fumbling to regroup. He glanced around the kitchen, wondering what had just happened between them.

'You're early,' Jack noted as soon as Thea walked onto the base for her shift. 'Your shift doesn't start for an hour. What's up? Trouble in paradise?'

'What?' Thea looked at him sharply.

'Difficult to get used to being around each other again?' Jack shrugged. 'When a soldier comes back to civilian life after a long time away at war? The readjustment period, isn't it?'

'Oh. Right. Yes.' Thea forced herself to smile.

If only it was that. She had no idea what had happened between them this morning. Except that she'd let her emotions—her desire for Ben Abrams—get to her again. She knew better than that—at least her head did. So why couldn't her heart toe the line as well? There could be no future for them—especially after she'd laid everything out to him, spilled her heart, and all he'd been able to say was an unsatisfactory *sorry*.

She wondered if deep down she'd been holding out for some declaration of love—if only to restore some of her bruised sense of pride. She didn't *want* a romantic relationship with Ben—they had too much painful history and logically she knew it would never work out between them. But clearly he'd never once regretted his decision to leave, never once thought about her or wondered what might have been. And that hurt more than she would have thought possible after all this time.

She ought to be resolved to it. But she'd woken up this morning wondering if maybe they *could* salvage something out of this mess, if she *could* set aside her wounded pride. The beginnings of a tentative friendship, perhaps?

Instead she'd made another spectacle of herself.

Even now her cheeks burned when she thought of what she'd been wearing when he'd walked in. She'd thought he would sleep longer. Through the wall she'd heard his bad night, so she hadn't expected him to come down to the kitchen until she'd left, but he hadn't known that.

She could recall the look of pure disgust on his face with humiliating clarity. He was going to think she was throwing herself at him all over again—especially after wearing her heart on her sleeve yesterday. And then, as if hell-bent on making matters worse, she'd hung on to him like a limpet when *he'd* been politely trying to lift her hands from his chest, unable to shake off the deep, longing desire which had flooded her body as soon as the two of them had come into contact.

'Thea? Did you hear what I said?'

'Hmm? Oh, sorry...' She cast Jack an apologetic look.

'I thought not.' He sighed, then warned her, 'I was telling you to watch out—Sir James has been after you.'

'Sir James? What does *he* want?' She could do without any added stress today. The man never called in without a reason, and it wasn't usually good.

'Not here—on the phone,' Jack reassured her. 'You probably need to call him sooner rather than later. The office should be free.'

'You're probably right.' Thea pulled a face as she trudged to the door. 'The last thing anyone wants is to be caught in Sir James's sights if he comes down here to reprimand me in person.'

'Thea?' Are you okay? You look white as a sheet.'

Thea was startled when Nic walked into the office. How long had she sat staring at the phone after her call to Sir James had ended? She stared bleakly up into Nic's concerned face.

'What's wrong, Thea?'

'That was Sir James.' Her voice sounded hollow. 'About Ben.' She stopped, shooting Nic an apologetic look. 'I'm sorry. You're probably the last person who wants to hear about Ben.'

'You mean the husband I never knew you had?' Nic answered wryly. 'And the fact that I dated his wife—presumably you *were* married when we dated?'

'God, I'm so sorry. I should have told you. I just never… I shouldn't have…'

'Thea.' Nic pulled her hands gently away from her face. 'It's okay.'

'Is it? How can you be fine about it?' Thea asked incredulously. 'I mean, I'm grateful that you are, but I feel like I lied to you.'

'No, you didn't.' Nic pulled a wry face. 'Don't you remember turning me down twice before finally giving in to my charms? And even then you warned me that it was just a taster date between friends.'

'I remember.' Thea blinked. *How had she forgotten that before?*

'I always suspected that there was someone else—or at least that there had been someone.'

Thea was silent. She couldn't tell Nic that it hadn't been because she'd still been in love with Ben, more that the wounds had still been too close to the surface. Especially the miscarriage.

'So…' Nic gently broke into her thoughts. 'What did Sir James say to upset you?'

'They want Ben to work here.'

'Ah.'

'You don't sound surprised.'

'Honestly? I'm not. You know how tight-knit our medical community is. I'd heard about Major Ben Abrams even before you rolled up here and shocked us all with the revelation that he's your husband. He's one of the most pioneering trauma surgeons in today's war zones. Some of his techniques have already filtered down to the likes of you and I. Plus…' Nic grinned again. 'He's the hero who miraculously survived *two* IEDs and is back up and walking in almost half the time of any most other patients.'

'Jogging, actually.' Thea arched her eyebrows at him, still trying to calm her racing thoughts.

'You're kidding?' He stared at her, as if waiting for the punchline. 'You're not kidding. The man must be a machine.'

The man has demons, she thought. Ben pushed himself and pushed himself, and even now she didn't fully understand his reckless drive. If he didn't confront his fears soon then he was likely going to self-destruct.

And if he was here, working with her every day, wasn't there a chance she would let herself be dragged down with him?

She dropped her head into her hands. How was she supposed to work alongside the man?

'Okay,' Nic continued eventually, 'tell me what Sir James said.'

Thea drew in a deep, steadying breath, trying to still her spinning head.

'He said what you've just said—about Ben being a cutting-edge trauma surgeon, skilled in field techniques which will really benefit us on Civvy Street. He reminded me that the Air Ambulance is a charity, and that someone like Ben could really help to raise our profile and secure us extra funding. And he informed me that there are many other interested parties trying to court Ben in the event that he doesn't return to active duty.'

'So far, so Sir James,' Nic muttered. 'But surely the idea of Ben not returning to active duty appeals to you?'

Thea snorted. 'Ben would *never* give up an opportunity to return to full Army life.'

'He might. For you.'

She opened and closed her mouth a few times.

'That's lunacy. And anyway... I'd never ask him to do that.'

'I didn't say you would. So, let me guess. Sir James threatened your place here if you don't talk to Ben.'

'Not in so many words. But he implied that he would have to think twice about someone who didn't have the best interests of the charity at the forefront of her mind,' Thea agreed.

'Why doesn't that surprise me? Okay. Forget Sir James and his threats—look at it another way. If it was anyone other than Ben, would you be in favour of it?'

'I… Well…' Thea blinked at him, for the first time really stopping to think.

'For what it's worth…' Nic spoke again '… I have to admit I wouldn't mind learning from a trauma guy of Ben's calibre. Imagine the potential to save lives we might otherwise lose.'

'That's what Sir James said. *"Imagine if the Major's knowledge could help you save just one additional life you might otherwise have lost."'*

'The old guy's devious, but he has a point,' Nic conceded. 'Even one precious life.'

Thea felt a shiver creep over her back. *One precious life.* She knew the value of that. She was a trauma doctor. But just for a moment she'd been ready to become a mother. What wouldn't she give to have a happy four-year-old running around now?

Her heart flip-flopped. She had no choice. Somehow she was going to have to try and forge a friendship with Ben. Until she did they wouldn't possibly be able to work in the tense atmosphere which surrounded them when they were together.

'You're right. I'll speak to Ben tomorrow.'

CHAPTER SEVEN

IT WAS JUST after midday when Ben heard Thea moving in her room. She'd got in from her shift at six a.m. and had crashed out for the last few hours. He waited impatiently for her to shower and head downstairs. If they were going to make this arrangement work then it was time to re-establish some basic ground rules—especially since that unexpected moment between them in the kitchen yesterday morning.

However much he wanted to deny it, there was still some spark between them, and they needed to address that. They couldn't afford for it to happen again.

Thea had moved on with her life without him there to complicate things and was now a successful trauma doctor. And in a few months he would be returning to his Army life, able to bury his feelings for Thea once again.

'I want to apologise for all the drama since I came home,' he announced, once she'd come down and they'd dispensed with the small-talk. 'I can imagine it hasn't been easy having me here, bursting back into your life and disrupting your routines. So I'd like us to try and start over.'

'Start over? How?'

He could hear the caution in her tone and forced himself to smile brightly. 'Try to forge some kind of a friendship. Like you suggested.'

She licked her lips and a fresh wave of lust coursed through him. *Get a grip,* he chastised himself, but the image of those long, slender legs of hers, and that perfect backside, popped into his head.

This was exactly why he needed to confront things. Put a stop to this unwelcome lust now.

'I've made you some breakfast, by the way. Plus I bought you two fresh cartons of cranberry juice. Can I get you a glass?'

She looked around the room, her eyes scanning everything, her nose sniffing appreciatively and her stomach offering a low grumble despite her reservations.

'Well, it's not cereal,' she quipped, clearly attempting to meet him halfway.

He couldn't help being surprised—and pleased. He hadn't thought it would be so easy to convince her.

'Pancakes,' he confirmed, gesturing to the array of syrups, jams and fruit he'd bought. 'Listen, Thea, I need you to know how sorry I am. This is all new to me. I know how to be a good field surgeon, I know how to be a good commander, and I know how to be a good soldier. But I don't know how to do *this*…'

'Normality?' Thea suggested when he floundered.

'Domesticity,' Ben confirmed. 'I'm out of my comfort zone. I'm sorry if this seems corny to you, but this is me trying to make amends.'

'So you made pancakes?' She raised her eyebrows, sliding in at the breakfast bar and watching him slide a fluffy disc from the pan onto a plate. 'I didn't even know you could cook.'

'I like to eat—the two go together. Besides, pancakes aren't really cooking.' He shrugged, grateful for her acceptance. 'But they're my Achilles' heel—especially with maple syrup, a handful of berries and dollop of cream. They're why I have to train so much—just so that I can keep eating.'

He tapped his chest, as if to prove his point, and saw Thea let her gaze drop over his body. She snatched her eyes away, two spots of colour flushing her creamy, smooth cheeks.

She was still attracted to him despite what she'd said last night, he realised abruptly.

His reaction was instantaneous and he shifted uncomfortably. *This* was what he had to avoid. He'd allowed his desire for her to drive his actions once before, and he'd ended up having to walk away from her, having to—what had she said?—*abandon her*. And nothing had changed. He still couldn't give Thea what she needed, provide emotional support the way she wanted. He was still broken—perhaps now more than ever. He could never be the man Thea deserved.

He was stalling. If he didn't speak now would he allow himself to back out?

'I owe you an apology,' he said quickly. 'The things you said at the park the other day…'

'Oh, Ben, please don't…' She backed up immediately, waving her hand around as if she was trying to swat a fly. 'Could we just pretend all that never happened—?'

'No.' He interrupted her embarrassed stuttering firmly. 'You were honest and open yesterday, but I wasn't. I'm sorry.'

She narrowed her gaze uncertainly at him, her voice tentative. 'What weren't you honest about?'

'You asked me what I meant by liking you *too much*, and if the Buddy Code was just an excuse. I didn't give you a straight answer.'

'No, you didn't,' she said nervously.

'I think maybe it *was* an excuse.'

Simple. Direct.

He would have needed a serrated knife to cut the tension. He hated this kind of conversation, talking about his feelings, but if they were going to get past their baggage he needed to make himself do this. Just this once.

'I should have told you that the night I first met you—that one spontaneous date—you made me feel the most alive and yet the most relaxed I've ever felt outside of a field hospital.'

'Coming from you, that's quite a compliment,' Thea murmured, pouring herself some juice.

'It might not sound like it, but it is,' Ben told her. 'That was the only place I'd ever felt comfortable. As though I belonged and was happy. Until I met you. You had me telling you things I'd never told anyone before…about my childhood…my mother…'

'You miss her,' Thea said simply.

Ben felt his jaw lock. He never said the words—even in his head. It was difficult even hearing someone else say them. Still, he forced himself to nod.

'Yes. But we never talk about her—my father and I. We don't do this…*touchy-feely* stuff.'

He pulled a face. This incredible woman had lost both her loving parents at such a young age, and yet she still believed in love. How could he explain to her that the relationship between *his* parents had been so different? Even before her death his father's too-serious nature had stifled his mother's vibrant spirit. After she had died the last fragile threads of the relationship between Ben and his father had been irreparably ruptured.

What if Ben damaged relationships the same way? After all, it was all he'd ever known.

He wrenched his head from his black thoughts and back to Thea.

'When you and I had that one date together you completely blindsided me.'

'How?'

He'd had a feeling she was going to ask that.

'If I'm honest with you, you scared the hell out of me,' he admitted reluctantly. 'I'd only met you a few hours earlier and you'd already had this unimaginable effect on me.'

He still didn't understand how one person could have such an impact on another in so short a time.

'But surely that's what made it all the more exciting?' Thea frowned. 'It *was* intense—and unexpected, and a little scary—do you think I wasn't feeling just as overwhelmed as you? But I just ran with it. I wanted to see where it would take us.'

Ben shook his head. 'I don't *do* overwhelmed. I set a goal in life, put my head down, and work to achieve it.'

'So what about the passion, the spontaneity, the *fun*?'

'They're overrated,' he answered simply. 'That's why when I was walking you home I was telling myself I needed to back away from you. Instead I found I was wanting to meet you the next night, willing the time away before I could see you again. And then Dan opened that door and bellowed his head off.'

'That was just Daniel being Daniel—he'd have come around quickly enough,' Thea objected.

'I know. But it was the excuse I needed. That's why I had to walk away, there and then. And Dan knew me well enough to suspect why, so he let me do it. It was for your sake more than mine. Like I said, I wasn't a good match for you.'

He met her eyes, holding them steady, ignoring the

look of disbelief which chased across her delicate features. Features which he could trace in his dreams—had reconstructed in his dreams even when he'd been redeployed. Even when he'd reminded himself that his life wasn't on Civvy Street—wasn't a safe life like Thea's. *His* life was working in war zones. And being the partner of someone who did that that was not a pleasant life.

He knew that from bitter experience.

Watching one person love with all their heart while the other stay closed off and unreachable was the most soul-destroying thing he knew. He could never have done that to Thea. He could never have made her happy. He would never have deserved her.

He hadn't banked on Dan dying less than two weeks later. Lying in Ben's arms as the life drained out of him, choking out his last words to make Ben promise to take care of Thea. His best friend had gone, and for a short while he'd struggled to keep his emotions in check. The grief had almost overwhelmed him. It had taken every ounce of willpower to rein himself in, to stuff those feelings down and carry on with his life. What good would talking about it do?

'How do you know we weren't a good match?' Thea asked at last. 'Maybe I could have helped you. Aside from one date, you didn't really know me.'

'That's not true,' Ben told her. 'True, we'd never met before, but I already knew what kind of a person you were. How strong you were. Dan used to talk about you all the time. He was so proud of you.'

Ben stared out of the window, as if remembering.

'I knew what you'd been through with your parents' death, and yet how caring, how open, how loyal you were. In no small part due to how close and supportive you and your brother were to each other. How much you share. *Shared.*'

Thea struggled to control an unexpected wave of sorrow. 'You mean unlike the way you *never* talk about your feelings?' she said sadly, worried about breaking this fragile moment.

'It's not what I do,' admitted Ben, seemingly lost in his own head.

'Why not?' She spoke gently, but he either couldn't hear her or didn't want to hear her.

Still, he was right, she realised. Physically, he might push himself way beyond anything his body should be doing at this stage—but *emotionally*? Emotionally was a whole different ball game. Ben barely even acknowledged his limitations to himself, let alone discussed the accident with her.

Had he always been this way? Was it something to do with the childhood Ben had had? From what little she knew of it, in his childhood he had been instilled with almost impossibly high expectations and a heavy sense of responsibility.

'You'd been through so much, and yet you'd managed to grow into a rounded, caring person.'

Ben continued to face out of the window, but she doubted he actually saw anything there.

'You supported your brother's career even though he told me you hated it, worrying every time he went to war about if he would come home. So I knew you deserved someone who could make you happy, and that certainly wasn't me. You didn't need the uncertainty, the instability, of a boyfriend who was a soldier too.'

'Wasn't that *my* choice?' Thea asked incredulously. 'And when we decided to get married anyway, wasn't that a good excuse for us to re-evaluate? See if it could be more than just a marriage of convenience?'

'We weren't meant to *be*, Thea. I'm not good at all this…*talking*.'

'You're not doing badly,' she noted. 'It's more than I've ever heard you admit before.'

'But you've had to push and push. We both know that would have grown old quickly—we'd have eventually grown to resent each other for it. And you would have been stifled in a cold marriage and never blossomed into the confident, successful doctor you are today.'

He'd only appreciated the truth of his words as they came out, and he was surprised when Thea nodded her head sadly.

'Funny, but I thought the same thing last night. I would never have realised how strong I really am.'

'So now we need to look to the future.' He changed the topic with forced brightness.

'Okay…' Thea acknowledged hesitantly. 'How do you propose we do that?'

'We try being friends—like you offered back at the hospital. We still have to live together whilst I'm recovering, so we need to find some solution—however temporary.'

She nodded slowly in agreement.

'Obviously there's still an attraction there,' he stated. After that spark the other morning there seemed little point denying it. Better to confront it head-on. 'But it's just a physical thing. We can ignore it if we really want to.'

And if he exhausted his body with physical exercise and took plenty of cold showers. But he didn't have a choice. He couldn't afford to let Thea get under his skin again or give in to temptation only to hurt her all over again when he backed away emotionally. And he would.

She looked as though she was going to object again, but then she closed her mouth and offered a tense smile.

'Sure we can ignore it. It's not as though it's even *real*, is it? Probably it's just a residual effect of a long-overdue conversation which, now we've had it, will go away by itself anyway. We've both moved on in five years, right?'

'Right,' he agreed, wondering why he felt as though a tiny black hole of emptiness had just opened up in his chest at the way she could dismiss it—*them*—so easily.

'Okay, so…friends,' she confirmed, licking her lips before chewing nervously on the inside of her cheek. 'And now, in the spirit of friendship, can I ask are you still going to push your recovery so hard? Push your body past its limits?'

'I don't know.' He didn't want to talk about it, but he forced himself to face her.

'You still think you'll return to active duty when you recover?'

'Sure.'

'I thought so. I said so to Sir James on the Board, when they told me to ask you to consider coming to work with the Air Ambulance.'

Not what he'd been expecting her to say.

He glanced at her sharply. Her feigned casual air wasn't fooling him.

'You want me to work with you?'

'The Board have asked me to present the offer to you. It would be on a consultancy basis. As they understand it, even though you're physically healed enough to re-turn to work, you still won't be ready for deployment to a war zone again for quite a while. So working with the Air Ambulance would be a great way to keep your skills sharp.'

And it would keep him in the game if he was never cleared by the Army to return to active duty. He'd be damned if he was going to let his injuries defeat him. But he had to admit it *would* keep his skills honed. *Plus he'd get to work with Thea every day.*

He hastily pushed *that* thought to the back of his mind. 'What do you think?'

She shot him a penetrating look. 'You want to know what *I* think?'

She sounded so shocked it surprised him. It was as though she thought her opinion didn't matter to him. It couldn't be further from the truth.

He frowned at her. 'Of course. We'd be living together as well as working together. And you have to admit that it hasn't exactly been the easiest ride so far.'

'Of course,' she murmured.

For a moment he thought he caught an undercurrent of something. Then she went on.

'You're right. It hasn't been easy,' she began. 'But I can't imagine that being around the house all day, with little else to do but physio and more physio, is helping your medical brain. Plus there's no doubt you'll have trauma skills from being out there which we could really benefit from in Civvy Street.'

All of that was true, but it wasn't what Ben was interested in. He knew he was approaching dangerous territory—they were only just trying to forge a friendship—but he pushed the question anyway.

'What about the living and working together bit?' he prompted.

Again that tongue darted out to moisten dry lips, and

Ben had to refocus before his brain started going down the wrong path once more.

She coughed, clearing her throat. 'I think it hasn't been easy, but we've been more open and honest with each other in the last two days than I think we've managed in five years. We're mature, successful professionals, and working together on a professional level should be fine. Plus my contract might not be renewed if I seem opposed to the proposal.'

'They *threatened* you?' So that was why she had been prepared to ask him. He felt disappointed, as well as angry. 'I'll have a word with them.'

She paused and swallowed hard.

'Best not to. Anyway they're right—you *would* be an asset. I think we ought to be able to put our personal feelings aside for medical gain.' She shrugged. 'There's only one other sticking point.'

'Which is…?' He didn't understand quite why it galled him that she should be so unemotional about it all.

'They all think we're…*reunited*, I suppose you could say.'

'We'd have to play a happily married couple,' Ben realised. 'How do you feel about that?'

'That bit…' She pulled a face. 'I'm not sure we could pull it off.'

He resisted the uncharacteristic impulse to suggest that they might have fun trying.

'You can tell them I'll think about it,' he told her at last. 'When are they thinking I would start?'

'How about during my next shift?'

'Jack, there's no way.' Thea felt panic rising, already bubbling in her throat. 'That's just *not* a good idea.'

'Sorry, Thea. That's what the boss said. Ben's on *your* team whilst you show him the ropes.'

'No!' She could have cried in despair.

'C'mon, Thea, I know you think that working with a partner can split your focus, but for what it's worth I've never known anyone as professional as you. And Major Abrams... *Ben*...has a formidable reputation. I don't think it's going to be as bad as you fear.'

Thea stared at Jack. His sincerity would have been touching if the entire situation hadn't been so terrifying. There was no way she could tell him the truth. She couldn't tell *any* of her colleagues. She and Ben had started their 'happily reunited' charade last week—now they had to live up to that.

Talk about impossible.

She had never taken a sick day in her life. Never missed a single day of work. But right now it was all she could do not to drop everything and run straight through the door to the car park and freedom.

She'd hoped to call Ben's bluff about not having any problem with him working there, and she'd been surprised when he'd accepted the temporary role. But she'd taken comfort in the fact that at least they wouldn't be working together.

That, she'd decided, would be a step too far.

And yet here he was, on his first day, assigned to her team. How were they possibly meant to work together when neither of them could bear to be in the other's company for long? Ever since the pancakes, and their agreement to give friendship a go, they'd made a concerted effort to make small-talk and go out running together. Their strained conversation had been painful and draining. Work had been a welcome escape.

But now they were expected to work together.

Anything else she might have said to Jack stuck in her throat as Ben rounded the corner. She squared her shoulders, conscious of Jack watching them, and strived to regulate her laboured breathing. She had to keep it together.

'What do you need me to do, Boss?'

Polite and deferential—all part of his Army training—but her throat was nevertheless too dry for her to answer. The idea of being boss to Dr Ben Abrams would have been a daunting prospect at the best of times, let alone given all the baggage between the two of them.

'Boss…?'

She heard the gentle prompting in his tone. Jack didn't know Ben well enough to pick up on it, but she knew Ben was trying to encourage her. She was both grateful and resentful at the same time.

'You remember Ron and Andy? My paramedics?'

'Yeah, and Harry, our pilot,' Ben confirmed. 'I've just been to introduce myself to them all again.'

Of course he had, she bristled. He might appear deferential, but he was used to running the show. How was he going to respond to taking orders from *her*? Because she *would* be giving them. That much *had* changed in five years. This was *her* team and *she* was responsible for what went on in the field during her watch. She took that responsibility seriously and she had her own way of doing things. A way which suited her guys.

Two bosses vying to take charge. Now what? How was this possibly going to work?

'Thea—new call-out,' Jack cut in with sudden efficiency as he slipped his headphones from around his neck to cover his head. 'Sounds like a horse rider fell—the road ambulance have requested our assistance.'

Well, it seemed as though she was about to find out. With a rush of adrenalin lending her strength, Thea turned her focus to the screen to read the incoming transcript. There was an open fracture to the ankle, hence the request for a trauma doctor. It didn't take her long to make a decision, and she spun around to Ben.

'Alert Andy and Harry and grab the gear. There won't be enough seats if we have to transport anyone, so tell Ron he can monitor from here. Meet you at the heli.'

'Understood.' Ben issued the automatic verbal confirmation before ducking out of the door.

'Send the co-ordinates to the chopper, Jack, and update me with anything as we're in flight.'

'Roger.' Jack dipped his head.

Racing out into the corridor, Thea grabbed her own kit and headed out onto the Tarmac, swinging up into her seat just moments behind the others.

'Harry—you've met Ben already, I understand? He's a military trauma surgeon, recently returned from Afghanistan,' Thea stated, as soon as Harry had completed his checks and they were airborne. It was a discreet attempt to establish herself as team leader.

'Yeah, turns out we served in the same region a couple of years ago.' Harry smiled. 'Although we never met out there.'

Another veteran who no doubt knew of Ben's reputation. Thea couldn't help another small stab of apprehension. If Harry knew Ben in a professional capacity she might have to work even harder to ensure she didn't end up losing control of her own team. It was almost out of her hands. The dynamics of the team largely depended, whether she liked it or not, on how well Ben could take orders from her.

'Keep a look-out as we approach the scene and stay alert,' Thea advised Ben over the headset. 'The rider was apparently on a hack alongside a canal, so when we get closer we'll follow the canal and look for somewhere to land. By the map it looks like there are some accessible fields nearby. You can learn a lot from the scene with a bird's-eye view like this.'

'Acknowledged.'

No doubt he already knew all that, from his military training, but so far he didn't appear to be trying to take command—subconsciously or not.

'Approaching scene,' Harry confirmed about ten minutes later.

'Rapid response vehicles, eleven o'clock,' Thea observed.

'Noted.'

As Harry checked the area for safe landing sites and brought the chopper gently down, Thea waited for the thumbs-up before nodding to her team and jumping to the ground.

She covered the distance to the casualty quickly, taking in everything around them as she introduced herself and her team to the patient and offered some brief reassurance. A quick visual confirmed the leg injury.

'Open fracture above the ankle.'

'Right.' Ben nodded grimly.

His jaw had locked, and she knew he had the same concerns as her. Open fractures to the ankle were often associated with a lack of blood supply to the foot, which could result in the loss of the foot itself. Like her, he must be running through ways to protect the blood supply.

Still, before focussing all her attention on the obvious injury she wanted to ensure that there wasn't another, less obvious but potentially more life-threatening, injury to prioritise. Distracted by the open wound, the road crew might have missed potentially fatal internal bleeding into the patient's chest, his pelvis or his stomach.

To her surprise Ben, as though anticipating her immediate priority, stepped away to the rider's girlfriend, to ask what had happened, as she took the opportunity to ask the rider himself. Her account might shed light on something the patient himself had missed—like the angle of his fall. It might help Thea to decide if there was another test she needed to carry out.

After running through her checks Thea stepped away to discuss a treatment plan with Andy. Ben quickly joined them.

'A startled duck took sudden flight off the canal, spooking his horse. The horse bucked and the rider fell onto the gravelly, tree-root-riddled path,' Ben advised.

'I got the same account.' Thea nodded. 'Plus he was clear, concise and calm. My gut says that although he's in some pain, there are no underlying issues. He's stable.'

'Agreed.'

'That blood supply concerns me,' she murmured. 'I want to try an open reduction before we move him.'

'Good plan, but you're going to need some strong pain relief if you want to get that bone back under the skin,' Ben noted.

'I'll get the Ketamine,' Andy said, jogging back to the helicopter.

'That's a pretty powerful drug.' Ben looked surprised. 'I didn't know emergency vehicles carried it.'

'The road ambulances don't,' Thea agreed. The drug could effectively unplug a patient's sight, hearing—the lot. 'But it's another advantage of the Air Ambulance having trauma doctors. We can carry a range of equipment and drugs other rapid responders can't.'

'Nice.' Ben looked impressed. 'So is that why the road crew called us out instead of just packing the rider into the ambulance and taking him to hospital?'

'Yep.' Thea busied herself getting her kit together to perform the reduction procedure. 'The road crew can only scoop and run, whilst with our knowledge and our kit we can, as they say, stay and play. Treating an injury like this in the field can mean the difference between the foot needing to be amputated and saving it.'

'Right…' Ben nodded in agreement. 'It's a very battlefield-orientated approach.'

Thea blushed. Of course he would already know that as well as anyone. Still, he wasn't rolling his eyes or complaining at the lesson. Perhaps her initial fears about them working together were unfounded. And it felt good to be in control of something—of Ben—when up until half an hour ago she'd been feeling as if she was drowning.

'Exactly. Right, I'm going to update them back at base. Do you want to go and explain to the rider what we're about to give him and why?'

'Sure.'

Ben jogged off immediately and Thea contacted Jack. She couldn't help noticing a slight stiffness in his gait. The cold weather, she realised instinctively. She'd noticed he always seemed to be in that bit more pain when the temperature dropped, or if a storm was brewing. He was like a human barometer.

As she checked in with Jack she took the opportunity to snag a high-vis puffer jacket from the helicopter, and she tossed it to Ben as she returned to the rider.

'I need you to go to the end of the lane when you've finished with the patient and flag down the second road crew who are on their way. Put that on and they'll see you better.'

She studiously ignored Ben's sharp look as she administered pain relief to the patient, but noticed that he was quick to wriggle into the jacket's cosiness. The pain must have been twisting into his bones.

She sat back thoughtfully for a moment whilst the drug took effect. Ben had turned towards the rider, and his reassuring voice was repeating information to ensure the guy understood.

'Okay, so Ketamine's what we call a dissociative drug. It's going to make you feel a little strange, maybe a little spaced out, and you might not remember any of this— all right?'

The patient muttered something which she didn't catch, but Ben was clearly completely in control.

'It's going to take your pain away and enable us to do our job. We're going to try to save that foot.' Ben glanced up as Thea took the ankle and gave him the nod. 'Okay, are you ready?'

Confident that Ben had the rider's trust and attention, Thea knew all she needed to do was get on with her job. With any luck she would have five, maybe six minutes to reduce the open fracture. If the patient wasn't compliant, she would have to administer a second dose.

'Just try to relax,' Ben soothed the rider. 'This stuff will work much better if you're relaxed.'

Andy and Ron were both good, and she was proud of her team, but there was no doubt that Ben had an extra edge. It wasn't just his Army training, or his skill as a trauma surgeon, it was something essentially *Ben*. He was still talking to the patient, looking up to give her a brief nod when he saw the drug was starting to work at the same moment as she was already moving in to work on the ankle. They seemed to be completely in sync.

Working carefully and quickly, she tried the proce-dure, but the man was becoming agitated, and with only a look to Ben Thea was able to confirm that the rider wasn't responding adequately to the drug. She wouldn't be trying a second time.

Ben left to flag down the second road crew whilst she stabilised the rider for transportation to hospital, since they had been unable to reduce the wound on site.

As they flew back to the base Thea couldn't help admiring Ben. It was odd, but the ease and harmony the two of them lacked in their personal relationship had appeared automatically within the first hour of their professional one.

CHAPTER EIGHT

FOR THE FOURTH time in as many minutes Ben tried to read an interesting article in his newspaper, but he found his eyes wandering back to the glass wall which separated himself and Thea. Just as they had been doing more and more frequently since he'd started working with the Air Ambulance less than a week ago.

If he'd thought their working and living together would drive a much-needed wedge between them, dampen his emotions and desires, then he'd been completely wrong. All it had shown him was that Thea really was incredible. Dedicated, focussed and skilled, with a knowledge base a doctor twice her age would be proud of. She quietly commanded loyalty and respect from her team—and the other teams, too—and gave it back in spades. And Ben knew he wasn't the only one to think so.

In spite of all that had happened to her—losing her parents as a kid, losing Dan, and then his own actions—Thea had held tight to her resolve and grown into a kind woman and an extraordinary trauma doctor. And he felt proud of her even though she'd done it all on her own. It was getting harder and harder to keep his distance, but he knew he had nothing to offer her and she deserved so much.

He watched as Thea reappeared from the kitchen,

making her way to the rec room area, where various other team members sat relaxing. She flopped down sideways onto an easy chair and threw her legs—long, sexy legs, even clad in her flight suit—over the chunky chair-arm, before tucking into a yoghurt with a sense of relief.

'Voracious appetite!' Nic teased her, and despite himself Ben set down his paper and sauntered casually over, just as Thea replied.

'Yeah, well, having had nothing but paperwork to do all morning, the very second I decided to grab lunch there was, of course, a call-out. Now I'm starving.'

'And *that's* the extent of your lunch?' Ben frowned as he sank down with careful nonchalance in the chair next to Thea.

'Are you kidding?' She snorted, jerking her head back over her shoulder. 'I inhaled a pulled pork sandwich before I even left that kitchen.'

'Hey, that was mine!' Harry stopped tapping on his phone long enough to look up.

'Sorry, mate—first come, first served.' Thea grinned. 'You were on a call-out.'

'Oh, yeah…' He pulled a face. 'A fourteen-year-old swimmer at a meet—bad dive, landed on her head. Probably permanent spinal injury, unfortunately, poor kid. I'm kidding about the sandwich, by the way. I brought enough in for everybody.'

'Yeah, I know.' Thea smiled. 'I heard you tell everyone this morning.'

The banter continued and Ben smiled at the easy camaraderie. It was what had made it so easy for him to slip into his new role—feeling instantly accepted and welcome. It would be a shame to leave. He'd thoroughly enjoyed his first couple of days with Thea, and now working with Team Two was proving almost as enjoyable.

When he'd first realised Nic was the trauma doctor in charge of Team Two he'd had his reservations, but it turned out Nic was a good leader and a skilled doctor, with the same strong ethos as the soldiers Ben had worked alongside in combat. Working with the new team was proving enjoyable as well as informative; it was clear that whatever had happened between Thea and Nic was firmly in the past—for both parties.

He knew it shouldn't please him that Thea had no love interest. It wasn't his business and it shouldn't have any bearing on him whatsoever. Yet whenever he watched her Ben couldn't help feeling...what? Contentment? Pride? Maybe even a hint of healthy possessiveness?

He shook his head. He had no business feeling either of them. His Army Medical Board assessment was a matter of weeks away and then he would be shipped out to another combat zone. Back to actual trauma surgery in the field, to that rush of adrenalin, the pressure, the buzz.

Funny, but the thought of it seemed to have lost its ability to give him that same high it once had.

He glanced across at Thea. No more having to feign being a happily married couple in front of everyone. That should be a *good* thing. Only over the last few days it had felt less and less like such a charade. The air had been significantly cleared between them, and ever since he'd admitted to his old feelings for Thea it seemed to have paved the way for them to cultivate the beginnings of a real friendship, much to his surprise. If only he could keep control of the lust, which seemed harder to resist with each passing day.

Thea was intelligent and fun and witty, as well as being stunningly beautiful. He enjoyed being around her to listen to her, talk to her, work with her. The feelings had crept up on him, slowly at first, and now he found himself actively seeking her out, feeling pleased when she seemed to come looking for him, too.

He tuned back in to the conversation just as Ron was urging Thea to join them at the pub.

'Sorry, Doc, no crying off—this one is mandatory.'

'Since when is going to the pub mandatory?'

Thea tried to laugh it off, but Ben could see those tiny stress lines of hers—imperceptible to anyone else—tightening around her eyes.

'Since we've been working together for a couple of years, and not one of us here knew you were married.' Ron feigned hurt. 'Let alone to *sod-that-for-a-game-of-soldiers* Major Abrams, here.'

Ben would have laughed if Thea hadn't suddenly gone so tense. Unexpectedly he experienced an instinctive urge to protect her.

'You know what it's like with us soldiers...' He reached casually across Thea to the fruit bowl and snagged an apple, temporarily creating a human buffer for her. 'You never know where we are, what mission we're on, when we'll be coming home—and you know what people are like for asking questions. Even well-intentioned. Sometimes you can feel a bit daft when the only answer you can give is, *I don't know.*'

Ron looked thoughtful. 'I never thought of it like that. I suppose you *would* feel a bit like you were always in the dark. Can't be pleasant.'

'It isn't,' Thea confirmed.

She cast Ben a grateful glance, which filled him with an unexpected warmth. Lots of the little things that Thea did were causing that reaction these days—from a shared, knowing smile to a grateful glance like that one. He knew he should be taking it as a warning, forcing more space between them. But instead he was doing the opposite.

'Well, that aside, the guys were talking before and we want to know what *else* we don't know about our devilish Doc Abrams, here.' Ron unpeeled his banana and gulped down half of it in one mouthful.

'Hmm, well, let me think… I'm a whizz in the kitchen,' retorted Ben promptly, and the group chuckled.

'Sorry, mate, we mean the *other* Doc Abrams.' Ron chuckled, polishing off the rest of the fruit.

'Right,' said Andy. 'We reckon it's time to find out.'

'I'm not sure I like the sound of this…' Thea feigned a frown at her friend.

'Nah—you will,' Andy assured her. 'We've got a couple of days off from tomorrow night—how about we all go for a drink after work?'

'Plus it's time for you guys to tell us what's been going on,' Ron added pointedly. 'And, Ben, we'll tell you all the little fun stories we've got about your wife here.'

'What stories?' Thea wrinkled her nose.

Ron smiled broadly. 'Like the fact that the first time she travelled on the chopper she threw up!'

'Really?' Ben turned to Thea as she turned beetroot-red. But at least she was starting to relax a little now the very personal questions were over.

'Thanks for the loyalty, guys. *Not.*'

'Come on, Ben, you're new to the crew,' urged Franco, another paramedic. 'It's a good way to get to know everyone without the stress of call-outs.'

Ben turned to Thea. 'I reckon a night out would do us both good.'

He knew it wasn't really her thing, and it wasn't really his either, but it seemed like a good opportunity to try and create that distance he was considering. It would certainly beat going back to the cottage together and tiptoeing around her in the kitchen in an effort not to simply drag her into his arms and pin her back against the kitchen island.

'Then tomorrow night it is,' Ron confirmed, pleased when everyone nodded their agreement.

But when nobody was watching Thea shot Ben a confused glance, as though somehow he'd managed to upset her again. Before he could catch her attention to find out, another paramedic came running around the corner.

'RTC just called in, guys. Big one. They're asking for both Air Ambulances.'

'Two? Hell, must be bad.' Nic was up and moving before the paramedic had time to say more. Everyone else was right on his heels.

'I want my whole team,' Nic instructed as the two teams raced out onto the tarmac. 'Franco, don't stay behind this time—and, Ben, you're coming too. Sounds like we could do with an extra trauma doc, and one of us can always ride in the road ambulance if necessary.'

Thea stood up from her fourth collision victim, circling her arm and stretching her neck from one side to the other. She had been working non-stop for the last few hours, first triaging, then tending. Her latest victim had a collapsed left thorax, both clavicles and numerous ribs broken, and Thea had been particularly concerned about internal aortic bleeding which might ultimately prove fatal. Until the other trauma team returned to airlift the woman to hospital Thea had been draining the chest cavity, but she knew she was just fighting to buy the woman enough time to get there.

With even a third team now here, she should transfer the woman to their care, and move on to the next casualty who urgently needed her help. Ron had already called her over a couple of times for the next one on their priority list—a list which just kept getting longer as they care-fully extricated more victims from their cars. She, Ben and Nic were staying on site to stabilise as many as they could either for air transport or transfer by road crew, but it felt like a losing battle.

As she signalled to another trauma doctor she averted her eyes from the black bags dotted around. The acci-dent had been horrific. Multiple cars—or what had once passed for cars—were scattered over a good mile of mo-torway, along with debris, people screaming for help, and those who were ominously quiet.

As they'd approached from the air the sheer scale of the collision had been evident, with the police struggling to close all six lanes of the motorway and clear the way. The biggest threat, however, was the two cars still smoul-dering despite efforts to control them. The fire brigade was still fighting to reach them up the packed motorway.

Both air teams had got to work as soon as they had landed, assessing and operating in tandem with the four rapid response vehicles which *had* made it through the traffic, with more on their way all the time. Working quickly, Thea had confirmed a spinal injury, a dislocated knee, a hip injury and a head injury, continually com-municating with both Nic and Ben in order for them to assess the priority patients.

She prepared herself now to move on to her fifth ca-sualty.

'I think I've got the driver of the van,' Thea calcu-lated. 'They've managed to get him out of the vehicle now, and initial assessment shows he has definite inter-nal bleeding.'

'I'm still with my motorcyclist.' Nic ran across the motorway. 'Ben took the woman with the head injury.'

'Acknowledged.'

'Whoever finishes first should move on to the passenger of that second car, though. They're getting her out now, and I don't like the way she's progressing.'

'Understood,' Thea nodded, jogging to her driver and treating him as best she could before she bumped him to the top of the medevac list.

Ben appeared at her side without warning.

'Take over my patient,' he instructed, his voice oddly quiet.

'Where are *you* going?' Obediently Thea headed over to take his place, but Ben didn't respond. Instead he raced towards the evacuated area where small fires still burned as the fire engines inched closer and closer through the backed-up traffic which was blocking even the hard shoulder with damaged vehicles hit by debris earlier on.

Where a car had been smouldering before, Thea could now see flames jumping and dancing and she realised it could blow at any time. *What the hell was Ben thinking, running in there?*

She ran forward to intercept him, thinking he mustn't have realised, but he almost mowed her down as he sprinted past her and into the danger zone.

'Ben!' Thea shouted. 'You can't go in there.'

He ignored her, seemingly oblivious. It was useless. Ben either couldn't—or wouldn't—hear her. But the look on his face as he'd run past her had chilled Thea to her core. His expression had been one she didn't recognise. A dangerous look, almost as if he hadn't even seen her. Hadn't necessarily even seen what she was seeing.

Dr Fields had said months ago that Ben's PTSD was only mild, but was this an escalation? She saw the body bags with fresh eyes, through *Ben's* eyes, wondering if they had triggered something for him.

Bang.

Thea screamed as a piece of flying debris landed a couple of metres behind Ben. He launched forward to protect her body, pushing her further away from the demarcation line and, mercifully bringing himself out of the danger area.

'Stay out of here,' he ordered, his voice oddly strangulated.

'Ben, we don't have time for this,' she argued desperately. 'You have your head injury casualty, and I have to get to my van driver.'

Boom.

One of the cars exploded and the sound was deafening. Thea barely had time to react before Ben threw her to the ground, his body covering hers. She heard the sound of metal slamming into the ground. Felt the Tarmac vibrate. But with Ben over her she had no idea how near or far the debris had fallen.

Then he was up, lifting her bodily into the air and throwing her well clear. The haunted look was more pronounced than ever. Then he was gone. Racing to the exploded car and dropping to the ground as he got closer to the intense heat. He began to move forward on his belly and elbows.

'Ben!'

He crawled closer and closer to the flames. A loud *bang* came from the burning engine. There was going to be another explosion and there was absolutely nothing she could do to save Ben.

Nic ran to the edge of the zone, his hands cupped around his mouth as he bellowed Ben's name.

'What the hell is he *thinking*?' Nic sounded frantic.

'I think its PTSD,' Thea whispered. This was why she'd needed to be there for Ben when he was discharged.

Someone to talk to. But she hadn't helped him. She hadn't encouraged him to open up enough.

Why did the idea upset her so much? Because she'd thought they'd been getting on so well lately? Because she'd genuinely thought he was changing in the way he saw her, how much he trusted her?

And now he was in there, in the danger zone, risking his life. *For what?* She *still* didn't understand him. It scared her.

'I don't know.' Thea bit her lip. 'He was working on that woman with the head injury one minute, then racing over there looking like death the next. A paramedic is still with her, and another is with my van driver, but we needs to get over there.'

Nic nodded grimly. 'Right, I'll go with you and check on them.'

Tearing her eyes from the last spot where she'd seen Ben, Thea ducked her head and raced after Nic. She didn't have time for emotion, or these thoughts. She had patients—people who needed her and who *wanted* her help. Not like Ben. She needed to focus on them.

Nic looked up at her as she approached. 'She keeps slipping in and out of consciousness. Apparently she was thrown clear of her car, but she had a two-month-old daughter in the back. Ben's risking his life trying to save that woman's baby.'

'She has a *baby*?'

Thea felt numb. The irony wasn't lost on her. It was as if all the fates were taunting her that she was judging Ben right now, but she still hadn't been entirely honest herself. She felt a gurgle of hysterical laughter bubble up, *so* unlike her, and hastily swallowed it back down.

It must have been all over her face because Nic suddenly grabbed her hand, snapping her back into focus. 'Yeah,' he squeezed her hand quickly, as if to offer her comfort.

He didn't know about the baby, but could he read her thoughts? See the guilt etched in her face?

'If Ben's going to give his life trying to save the baby, the least you can do is fight to save the mum. I'll take your van driver.'

Nodding, but unable to speak, Thea took over.

'Try not to worry. Ben must know what he's doing— he's a soldier. He's trained to risk his life for others. I understand how scared you must be right now, it's obvious how much you love him, but put it out of your head and focus,' Nic advised gently.

He was right. She *was* still in love with Ben. After all this time she was no closer to getting over him than she had been five years ago. Well, she was damned if she was going to let fear take her over. Shutting out the black thoughts, Thea forced herself to work, to concentrate on the casualty in front of her, who had passed out again.

Head down, forcing herself not to be distracted, she worked steadily on the young woman, relieved when she'd alleviated the pressure in the patient's chest and the mother of the baby finally regained consciousness.

'Van driver's stable. I'll take over here.' Nic suddenly appeared and drew her to one side. 'Go and check on Ben. See if he's saved the baby. If not try to get him out of there. Then move on to the next casualty.'

'Understood,' Thea choked out, hoping her legs wouldn't buckle under her as she stood up.

He was still over there? How long had it been?

Thea gratefully passed the reins on to Nic and raced to the edge of the danger area. The remaining vehicle creaked and groaned distressingly. It sounded as if it was about to blow up at any moment. She resisted the urge to vomit.

'Ben, you have to get out of there!' she cried again. *'Ben!'*

She waited for what seemed like an eternity, and just as she was about to run to her next victim Thea saw his feet, then his legs, as he emerged painfully slowly.

'Get out of there!' she yelled.

Finally free of the wreckage, he stood up—and only then did she see the baby wrapped in his arms. Emotions tore through her without warning. Fear, relief, and the searing agony of the loss of her own baby—*their* own baby.

'There's a pulse!' Ben shouted this confirmation, tearing out of the area as another bang—louder this time—could be heard. 'Didn't you say Nic had extensive paediatric experience?'

'Give her to me.' Nic had already raced over and Ben willingly handed over the bundle. 'Nice going, Ben. That baby's only alive because of what you've just done.'

Words froze in Thea's mouth. She wanted to tell him how stupid he had been. But watching the tiny baby being raced safely away in Nic's arms stopped the words from coming out. Instead she pressed her palms to her eyes, stemming the tears.

'Are you okay?' she managed, just as they heard a *whoosh* followed by a *boom*. Ben swept her into his arms and charged them both backwards. By the time he released her the car he'd crawled out from, carrying the precious bundle, was a fireball, and smoke was billowing out around the scene. All the debris, however, was still within the danger zone. A metre-long shard of metal had been driven into the ground exactly where Ben had been standing with the baby a few moments earlier.

'I'm fine.'

Ben had dismissed her concerns. It felt as though he was dismissing *her*, in a way he never did with anyone else.

'Who's left to triage?' he asked.

CHAPTER NINE

'To Ben,' Franco announced quietly, raising his pint glass. 'If it hadn't been for his actions yesterday that baby wouldn't be stable in hospital with his mother now.'

'Ben,' chorused the remainder of the two teams soberly.

Ben grunted but said nothing, trying to temper his displeasure. They had no idea how much he hated this. The undeserved praise. They had no idea how many lives he'd lost, how many dead bodies on the battlefield, men he'd failed to save. He was just lucky he'd got to the baby in time. Which was more than could be said for Dan.

He downed his drink in record time and took the opportunity of going to the bar for a refill just so that he could slip away for a few minutes to clear his head. He'd barely got his drink when a soft, female body pushed against him.

'On the hard stuff, I see,' Thea murmured, looking at the glass of water in his hand.

The crowd around the bar was three rows deep, and she didn't exactly have the physique to push her way through. He pointed out as much.

'Elbows.' She smiled, holding them up as if for him to inspect. 'And stop deflecting.'

'I just don't like the accolades,' he admitted. 'I don't deserve them.'

'Yesterday was horrible—we lost a lot of patients. We don't even know if those we got to hospital will make it,' Thea pointed out gently. 'But you're the one who risked his life to crawl into burning wreckage for a baby who might not have even been there.'

'So we cheer that and forget the bad?' Ben pulled a face.

'No, we find a small victory in a hellish situation and celebrate *that*,' she told him quietly. 'Are you telling me that you never did that in all your time out in Afghanistan?'

Yeah, they'd definitely done that. *He'd* done that. Until it had been *him* they were celebrating. Then it hadn't seemed so…appropriate.

Still, her calm reminder had eased the tension he'd been feeling. She'd made him feel stronger again. The crowd surged slightly and Ben pulled her towards him protectively, concerned about her getting pushed too hard. She barely resisted before slipping neatly into his arms.

Too neatly. As if she was meant to be there. They both stayed still, taking comfort in the closeness, the crush and clamour fading away until all he was really aware of was himself and Thea. It felt particularly intimate, and he knew that the tension of the day, the memories, meant he'd let his guard down. Suddenly he didn't care.

'Can I get you a drink?' he asked softly. *Could she hear his heartbeat accelerate?*

'I have one.' She shook her head, but her voice sounded unusually throaty and he wondered if she was as aware of him as he was of her.

'Thea—'

'Can I ask you something—?'

They spoke at the same time, both stopping and offering a nervous laugh.

'Go ahead,' Ben said eventually, not caring about the crowd surging around them.

It occurred to him to ask Thea if she wanted to go somewhere quiet to talk, but he didn't want to break the spell, and thought that maybe the crowd was somehow making her feel more secure than if it had just been the two of them. Too much pressure.

'What happened yesterday?' she asked tentatively.

He huffed out a hard breath. It wasn't exactly a surprise question, but that didn't make it any easier. Still, he was determined to be honest with her. They'd come so far he didn't want to mess it up now. He cast around for the right words before realising there were none. There was just the truth.

'Your PTSD is triggered at night, when the house is silent, right? What triggered it at that crash site yesterday?

He assessed her thoughtfully.

'I think seeing everything from the air definitely reminded me of my own accident. But instead of making me freeze it cut out my fears and drove me to act on autopilot, without really knowing what I was doing.'

'But you ran into an evacuated zone; you could have been blown up,' Thea objected, still concerned.

'I know that. I knew it then. But when my patient told me her baby was still in there... I couldn't *not*.' How could he explain it any other way? 'Standing back just isn't *me*.'

'And if that car had blown up and you'd be in there you'd have both died.'

The shake in her voice touched his heart. Without thinking he pulled her into his arms and held her close.

'And if it had blown up and I hadn't even tried how could I have lived with myself?'

'At least you'd have been alive,' Thea muttered against his chest.

But he could tell by her tone that she was glad he'd saved the baby. Glad he was the kind of soldier who was willing to make that sacrifice if it was the right thing to do.

He pulled her in even tighter for a moment, breathing in the crisp, clean scent of her shampoo which he recognised so well from the shower room. Everything about Thea was like a breath of fresh air. And now she was opening up more to him, just because he had been honest with her. At least partly. He wasn't sure how to be completely honest without letting her down, but for the first time in five years he wanted to change, to find a way to be in her life.

Ben frowned as darker thoughts crept into his head. His memories of that IED hadn't been as controlled as he'd led Thea to believe. The motorway crash site had triggered other memories of his accident. Memories which had crowded his brain, gripped his chest, almost making him incapable of breathing. Even now the images were sneaking back in. He wasn't ready to face them yet, and before they could take root he hastily shut them down.

But he couldn't afford to do that because that meant shutting Thea out too, and hadn't he just decided he wanted to change—for her? Which meant he needed to talk to her, to tell her. Yet he didn't know how. He only knew he'd felt utter fear and panic when Thea had been standing so close to that car when it exploded.

'I couldn't cope with anything ever happening to you.'

It wasn't until he caught sight of her face, flushed with

pleasure as she stared up at him, that he realised he had uttered the thought aloud.

'Really?'

It made him feel good that his words affected her so positively.

'Not like you to be lost for words,' he teased, raising his hand to push a few stray tendrils of hair from her face. 'Anything else you want to know?'

She shook her head.

'Anything you want to tell *me*, then?'

She shook her head again, her eyes flickering to his mouth and back up to his eyes. As if she was waiting for him to kiss her. As if she *wanted* him to kiss her.

His gut kicked harder than a fifty-calibre machine gun recoil. Only it felt much more pleasant.

'Nothing at all?' He tried to tease her as he fought to slow his accelerating pulse.

'Okay…well, for the record, you cook really, *really* well.' She laughed softly. 'I never knew that before.'

'There's a lot we don't know about each other,' he reminded her gently. 'But I'd like to change that.'

Her eyes widened for a moment. 'I'd like that too.'

'Good.'

Before she could say anything else he cupped her cheek, dipping his head down and brushing her lips gently with his.

Her response was tentative, and then she was sliding her hands around his back, but not holding too tight.

He cautioned himself about pushing her too fast. He took his time pulling her closer to him, all the while exploring her mouth delicately. Afraid of startling her.

But a few moments later Thea seemed to have her own ideas. Her hands were sliding up his spine with confidence, holding tighter as she pulled herself in closer and pushed her body up against his.

He deepened the kiss, feeling lust jolt through him as she met his tongue boldly with hers. The kiss became unhurried, and boundless, and sensual. It reached deep inside him, making him for one long moment forget everything else. Around them, all the bustle and revelry faded away.

It was several long moments before they surfaced, but he couldn't drag his eyes from her face.

'So, where do we go from here?'

'How about straight home?' she couldn't help suggesting, her cheeks flushing slightly at her own audaciousness.

The whole way home Thea could barely believe her boldness. But it had been as though Ben was deliberately holding himself back, trying to be gentle with her, and she didn't want that at all.

She'd only slept with three other men besides Ben. One before him, which had been her fumbling, cringeworthy first time—and second time. Then two after Ben. But whether it had been because of Ben, or the miscarriage, those relationships hadn't stood a chance, and although the sex had been fine it hadn't been all fireworks and crashing waves.

She'd been beginning to wonder if there was something wrong with her. But just that kiss with Ben had set her body on fire, from her toes up, and now she felt more daring than she'd ever wanted to be before.

The taxi ride was like a lesson in pure torment, as Ben drew lazy circles on her arm and her back, occasionally dropping gentle kisses on her lips, but not letting them get too close for fear of losing control and giving the driver an X-rated show.

By the time she tumbled out of the taxi she was shaking with lust and pent-up tension. It was only as she was walking up to the door that she felt a momentary pang of nerves, but then Ben slid his hand to the small of her back and guided her into the house, closing the door behind them. He pulled her against him, one hand sliding into her hair to tilt her head up to his, his lips claiming hers with all the confidence and expertise she expected from him. Her nerves forgotten, Thea gave herself up to him.

She felt his reaction hard against her thigh, and a bubble of impatience popped inside her stomach as she reached down to fumble with his belt. She'd never felt this impatient with anyone before, but right now all she wanted was to take him in her hand, feel that velvety smoothness against her palm.

'You're sure?'

Ben broke off for a moment to pull back, and Thea felt the beginnings of a confidence she'd never had before.

'Will you just shut up and kiss me?' she muttered, slightly abashed, reaching for his jeans and undoing the buttons until he sprang out, revelling in his low moan of appreciation when she slid her fingers around him.

Following her pace, Ben divested her of her tee shirt and bra in a couple of smooth movements, before snaking one arm around her waist, the other hand expertly caressing her breast. Then, arching her back slightly, he bent his head to bestow a trail of hot kisses down the line of her neck to one hard nipple, before taking it in his mouth and sucking deeply until she gasped aloud. His tongue slipped in and out, deftly flicking over the bud before taking it into his mouth once again. Then he turned his attention to the other breast, and she could

feel him flexing in her palm as she threw her head back
to push her nipple further into his mouth.

'Let's take this next door,' Ben murmured, shifting out
of her hand and lifting her up, wrapping her legs around
him so he could carry her.

'Not upstairs?' Thea felt uncertainty creeping back.

'Too far.' He shook his head in mock contrition and
she felt any doubts dissipate.

Lowering them both swiftly down onto the rug, he
slid her jeans off, hooked a finger under her lace panties
before running it between her legs. She moaned, sounding out his name, and he repeated the action, this time
dipping his finger in, making her squirm with pleasure.

He didn't even have his tee shirt off and hazily Thea
reached for it, wanting him as naked as she was. Wanting to feel his skin slide across hers. But he'd already
ducked away, his mouth moving down from her straining nipple to her stomach.

'I want to taste you,' he murmured, his tongue leaving a gentle whorl on her belly button, his kisses weav-
ing lower and lower down her abdomen.

Filled with lust, her bottom shifting against his touch,
Thea didn't even realise he'd slipped her panties off until
his tongue chased up the inside of one thigh, gliding over
her and flicking through her wetness, making her pelvis
jolt in response.

'Ben…' Thea gasped. 'What about you?'

'Relax,' Ben murmured against the sensitive skin,
making her throb and swell with need. 'Right now this
is about *you*.'

Something jarred slightly in the recesses of her head,
but before she had time to think Ben was cupping her
backside with his hands, pushing his tongue inside her,
drawing back only to suck before sliding in again.

She grasped the rug for traction. It had never been like this for her before, and her head was swimming with building need.

'Thea, you're perfect. So hot, so wet...' he murmured. 'So close...'

'Don't stop,' begged Thea, arching up to him, loving it that he so obligingly returned to the task in hand.

He pushed his tongue in deeper, then moved back to suck a little harder, and instinctively she tilted her hips up to encourage him. Her hands moved to touch his shoulders, frustrated by the feel of fabric instead of bare skin, and she slid her fingers into his hair instead.

His tongue moved faster, making her catch her breath, wanting more, then demanding more. She instinctively opened her legs a little wider and he groaned, the sound vibrating against her body. It was her undoing.

The orgasm started slowly, with her fingers and toes tingling first, then quickly picked up pace as it spread through her veins like fire and tore through her, making her cry out as her body was caught up in waves of bliss. But Ben wasn't stopping. He held her writhing hips in place, his tongue never leaving her as he kept up his relentless pace, and Thea gave herself up to a return wave which ripped through her abdomen and made her body tremble. Even as she came down the aftershocks kept pulsing through her, leaving her fighting to breathe and unable to speak.

She'd wanted fireworks—he'd given her a New Year's Eve grandstand. How was she ever to repay the debt?

It was going to take her a few minutes longer to regain her breath, and she was grateful when Ben came up to lie beside her and pull her into his arms. Her hand crept over him, grazing down his front to where his jeans were still open. She slipped her hand inside.

His reaction was immediate, and the guttural sound he made turned her on again. Already.

Thea smiled shyly at him, barely able to believe they'd turned such a corner. Hardly daring to think this might be the start of something else.

She pushed herself up, swinging one leg over to sit astride him, trying not to let her nervous anticipation show. She should have taken his jeans off first, but there was nothing for it now. She curled her fingers around his tee shirt and lifted.

Immediately his hands slipped around her wrists, locking them in place, twisting them gently away from his tee shirt. He sat up, Thea still across his lap. She felt a stab of apprehension, her eyes flying to his, wanting him to erase her fears. Instead, he refused to meet her gaze.

'Ben?'

He shook his head. She didn't know if he couldn't, or simply wouldn't find the words to explain. She just knew that anger was swiftly replacing the sense of contentment and completeness she'd been feeling only moments earlier.

'What the *hell*, Ben?'

Her eyes were pricking with tears of shame, and she felt utterly vulnerable and exposed. She fought to hold on to the building rage. Anything was better than crying in front of him.

'It's not what you think. Just…leave the shirt, Thea.'

'Leave the tee?' She shook her head, bewildered. And then it dawned. 'The scars?'

He raised his hand to cup her cheek but she batted him away, afraid that the gesture would start the crying. Once she started she didn't think she'd stop.

'We can have sex as long as I don't see your scars?' She could barely see through the tears.

Jackknifing off him, she stood up, grabbing the throw from the couch in a belated attempt at modesty, fervently ignoring the little voice in the back of her head which was trying to remind her that she, too, had her own trust issues. She might be upset with Ben now, but how upset would *he* be if he found out the secret she'd been keeping?

Her arms covered her abdomen, as if protecting the memory.

'I can't do this with you, Ben.' She bounced her head from side to side. 'Not any more. Every time I think we're taking a step forward I let my guard down and you hurt me again.'

'I know, and I'm sorry, Thea.' Ben stood up, buttoning his jeans and reaching to pull her into his arms.

How she dodged him, blinded as she was, she didn't know, but she bolted for the door.

'Please leave, Ben. Not just for tonight. For good. I can't be hurt any more.'

'Thea, just give me time.'

She shook her head. They'd messed up exactly the way she'd feared they would, she thought bitterly.

'I'm sorry, Ben. I've no more time to give you. Please. Just go.'

CHAPTER TEN

BEN WATCHED AS Thea skied down the last section of the run which led off the mountain and down to their private log cabin—practically to their door. His heart thudded as she drew to a stop next to his snowboard, lifted her ski-glasses up and offered him the same wary look she'd been sending his way for the last week.

And he only had himself to blame.

He was grateful that he'd managed to convince her to come here with him. Although he regretted the fact that his convincing had mainly taken the form of admitting that he'd arranged this time off with her colleagues weeks ago, as the honeymoon he and Thea had never had, and reminding her that if she still wanted to keep up the 'happily married' charade she was going to have to come on this so-called holiday after all.

Now he could only try to ensure that he used this as an opportunity to prove to Thea how sorry he really was.

'Good run?' He kept his tone deliberately upbeat.

'Sure.' Her mouth formed the right shape for a smile, but her eyes didn't reflect the sentiment. 'Yours?'

'Yeah. Great.'

His gut twisted every time he thought of that night back at the house and how much he had inadvertently hurt her. *Again.* He'd had no idea that he would suddenly feel so self-conscious about his scars or he would never have initiated such intimacy with Thea in the first instance—however much he'd wanted to. He would never have knowingly put her in a position where she would feel made so completely vulnerable by his actions. But that was exactly what he'd managed to do.

Damn idiot.

He'd gone over and over events in his head, wondering what had prompted that moment of reservation from him, but there was nothing he could put his finger on. He kept picturing Thea's face when he'd emerged from that car with the baby. She had been frightened, angry, relieved—he knew that. But he couldn't shake the sense that there had been something else in her expression...something which didn't fit, which he simply couldn't identify.

He shook his head. *Ridiculous.* And it was wrong of him to try to offload his guilt and his problems onto Thea. He knew what that moment at the crash site had been about. He understood the triggers and the way his mind had shut down. He hadn't seen his surroundings. That burning car might have been an Army Land Rover, the injured passengers his wounded soldiers and the baby an Afghan child, for all he had known at that precise moment.

Thea had been right in her suspicions, so it was hardly any surprise that her face had been such a patchwork of emotions. He was reading too much into it.

'I thought we might eat out tonight,' he suggested casually as Thea flicked her boots out of their ski-clips.

Her wary look cranked up a notch and she narrowed her eyes suspiciously. The casual approach clearly wasn't working.

'I promised you honesty. I think it's time we talked.'

He seemed to be saying that a lot lately. But after decades of stuffing down his emotions perhaps it was only right that he should start to be honest now—with Thea, the person his actions had hurt the most.

She blinked slowly at him, as though she was trying to work out the depth of his sincerity. Then she inclined her head. 'I think you're right.'

The resort staff had been into their cabin and a fresh basket of fruit sat on the table, a fire roared in the hearth. Thea made her way straight to it, warming her hands and avoiding his gaze.

'Shall we say half an hour?' he suggested.

'No problem.' Her voice was clipped, taut, as she ducked her head and made for her suite on the opposite side of the log cabin to his. Briefly he wondered if she, like him, was fighting to still the questions which swirled around his head.

Now he had finally forced himself to own up to his motivations Ben knew he was never going to be free of his ghosts until he told Thea what had really happened with her brother the day he'd died. She needed to know the truth but he'd never given her that luxury—it had been too hard for him to talk about. But every time he looked at Thea he remembered, and it was this inability to open up—to anyone—which had stopped him from being with Thea.

If he could talk to her about Dan's death he knew he could talk to her about all the ghosts of his past. And that meant he would no longer be emotionally closed off from her. He could be the man she needed him to be. And she could finally, *truly*, be his.

Standing under the jets in the shower in his own suite, Ben tried not to think about Thea in her shower, less than fifteen metres away. Knowing he had acted out of lust, without thinking through any consequences, hadn't stopped him wanting Thea. He could still recall her touch, her taste, her smell, and he felt an aching need for her in the pit of his stomach.

It had taken every ounce of his determination to convince Thea to give him one more chance, to persuade her not to let his moment of uncertainty lead them to discard all the progress they had made in their relationship until that moment. It had come at a cost—he'd finally had to admit to her that there were things he hadn't yet told her—and he'd asked for just a little more time to get his head straight.

Choosing a ski-break—the honeymoon they'd never had—had been his way of proving to her that he really was trying to change. As well as a way of giving them something to talk about and lessening the tension of being around each other—especially when it was just the two of them in their private log cabin, tiptoeing around each other as they had done in the early days at the cottage.

Ben suppressed his frustration. For every two steps forward they seemed to take together it seemed that there was always something to send them a step backwards. But, he rationalised, at least it was *some* kind of progress. However, whilst the choice of location *had* provided a much needed buffer for the last few days, it had perhaps made it *too* easy for them to avoid the real issue, and Ben was determined that tonight they would talk.

By the time she walked back into the living room he was already in the kitchen, downing a pint of water in the hope that it would ease his cracking voice. He turned to face her and instantly his mouth went dry again.

She had left her hair to dry naturally into the loose natural curls he loved. They tumbled around her face and past her shoulders, and even now his fingers itched to slide into their silky depths and pull her lips to his.

A soft, body-hugging lilac cashmere jumper show-cased her breasts and slim waist, and tight black jeans curved lovingly over a pert backside which had his body responding like a teenager. The knee-high boots only heightened his reaction—even if they were flat, so that she wouldn't slip in the snow.

What the hell is wrong with you? he berated himself silently. This evening was all about finally telling her what he should have confessed five years ago. Using sex to create an artificial sense of intimacy between them might make him feel better in the short term, but until he could move past that and *really* open up to her they were never going to have a long-term future.

If they could *ever* have a long-term relationship.

Wresting himself from the moment, he strode across the room, snatched up their parkas and, gently throwing hers over her shoulders, opened the door. He ushered her outside to where a horse-drawn sleigh waited patiently outside the cabin. Two inky black horses stood quietly, their breath forming little clouds in the cold air, and Ben heard Thea's nervous intake of breath.

'It's not a big romantic gesture,' he hastily reassured her. 'The restaurant is a couple of valleys over, and this is the best option as it can go cross-country.'

Not entirely a lie. The horse-driven sleigh *was* the most practical way to get to the restaurant. Its long, wide sleigh-skis allowed it to travel easily over the snow-covered countryside, and they could be raised up to allow thick snow-wheels to carry the carriage easily over roads and paths, too. But Ben hadn't been entirely unaware of the romantic connotations and had deliberately chosen it with Thea in mind.

The yellow sleigh was decorated with flowers picked out by gold braiding. Ornate bridles peeked from beneath the blankets which had been temporarily slung over the horses' backs. The lanterns, which adorned the carriage would be lit once night fell.

'Oh.'

Was that good or bad? Ben wondered.

The driver offered them a friendly smile as he jumped down, opening the half-door to the open-topped sleigh and patting the warm rugs which were folded neatly on the seat. Then, moving away, he busied himself with removing the horses' blankets whilst Ben made his way over, offering his hand to Thea as she approached.

He helped her in and swung up afterwards, deliberately sitting on the same side as her, but not too close so as to crowd her. He took the blankets the driver had indicted and opened them up, resisting the urge to brush across Thea and tuck them in. *Another delaying tactic,* he reminded himself, and he wasn't going to create another excuse to put off his confession to another day.

At the driver returned to his seat at the front, and signalled the horses to move off, Ben caught the tilt of Thea's lips. Despite herself, she couldn't help but enjoy the gentle lurching movement and the sound of crunching snow under the horses' hooves and the sleigh's snow-wheels.

This first part of their trip took them around the old town while the driver gave them something of a historical tour of the place. Ben felt Thea relaxing more and more as she engaged with the driver, learning about the area and asking questions. It was so typically *Thea*, Ben was beginning to realise. Although it ruffled him that Thea could be more at ease with a stranger than she was with him right now.

Their tour of the town over, the sleigh made its way out of the central area and towards the lower slopes. The slow, mechanical ratcheting noise of the sleigh-skis coming down was the only sound to punctuate the stillness. The next part of their journey, heading over to a neighbouring town, was about to begin, and as the buildings fell away behind them Ben felt Thea edge forward to talk to the driver about the region itself. Anything to avoid feeling as if she was alone with him, it seemed.

The daunting prospect of their conversation later this evening began to creep up on him, and as Thea learned about the area he leaned back into the soft blankets and listened, distracting his mind.

Finally the sleigh dropped down out of the countryside and into a large, busy town, and soon they stopped outside a non-descript-looking building with heavy, ornate, chunky wooden doors.

Elden Huset—The Firehouse—by name and by former nature.

'We're dining *here*?' Thea glanced up, surprised.

She felt torn. She'd been itching to eat here ever since she'd seen it on a popular cooking show back home. With their 'back to the Stone Age' birchwood fire cooking, the chefs had been lavished with praise, and the whole experience had looked wonderfully sensational. But things with Ben were as awkward as ever, and she couldn't imagine enjoying the experience with such a cloud hanging over them. The sleigh ride had been difficult enough.

He'd told her they were going to talk tonight, but instead of making her feel better it had only made her feel even more on edge. He might not realise it, but Ben wasn't the only one with a confession. She still had to tell him about the baby. *Their* baby. And she didn't relish the thought one little bit.

Allowing Ben to open the door, Thea stepped inside, and the sounds, sights and aromas which instantly assaulted her senses promised her that she was in for an incredible experience.

Despite her initial apprehension, for a while all her concerns receded into the background. With a growing sense of excitement, she moved further inside. The place was all leather, copper and stone, the chefs in flannel shirts, working in an open kitchen where the occasional burst of flame *whooshed* up towards the thick, oak-timber-beamed ceilings in a blaze of glory which ignited her sense of smell and her tastebuds with tantalising delight.

'This place is incredible...' She inhaled the smoky scent with deep, appreciative breaths, hearing the sound of crackling birchwood and clanging copper pots, which lent an exciting edge to the atmosphere.

Thea's eyes were drawn to the smooth grace of the chefs, working in such harmony, and she watched as one chef took a generous piece of salmon, wrapped it in hay, and thrust it onto the bars above the fire. The flames took hold of the hay and the fire blazed over the salmon in seconds, leaving it apparently black and burned-looking. Then the chef turned it over to repeat the action, before taking the fillet out and sliding it onto another tray, which he slid into what looked like a wood furnace.

Remembering Ben, she turned—only to find he was also watching the proceedings with the same look of intensity on his face that she'd had. Somehow it helped her to relax a little, and she was able to enjoy watching the chef pulling the tray out of the oven. In one slick, efficient movement he peeled the blackened skin off the salmon to reveal a pink, perfectly cooked piece of fish. Her mouth practically watered even as he finished serving it up, and she swallowed once...twice.

'I'm having *that*,' she declared, as soon as she'd regained control of her mouth.

The spectacle of the restaurant had changed the atmosphere between them—if only temporarily. And by the time they'd ordered and their meal had arrived Thea was beginning to feel comfortable enough to just enjoy this part of the evening without being wrapped up in what happened next.

'My mum used to love to cook,' Ben said suddenly—unexpectedly.

She opened her mouth, then closed it again. When he had promised her they would talk tonight, this wasn't what she had expected. Ben had *never* talked about his family—not to her, at least. She'd gleaned from Daniel, before she'd ever met Ben, that Ben's mother had died when he was young—maybe the same age Thea had been when her own parents had been killed.

'It must have been hard for you when she died.' She knew exactly what he must have gone through. 'Isn't your father in the Army, like you?'

'Yes, he's in the Army—but he's not medical, like me.' Ben answered her question, then reflected for a moment before continuing. 'And you're right—it wasn't easy. Although it must have been worse for you, losing *both* your parents. After Mum's death my father cleared out all reminders of her from the house. Photos, jewellery—*anything* she had loved and valued. We never spoke about her again.'

'Never?' Thea replied, shocked. It was so different from the way Daniel had helped her when their own parents had died. He'd made a scrapbook of photos and memories, so that she'd felt she would never forget them. He'd talked to her as often as she had wanted, answered as many questions as she'd asked, and almost always found some way to make her laugh again.

Her brother's endless support and love had nurtured

her spirit, influencing her to become the person she was today. She couldn't imagine how it would have affected her to have been forbidden from talking about her parents. If Ben had been almost *conditioned* not to think talk about his mother from a child, was it any wonder that he found it so difficult to open up to her...to *anyone*...now? He and Daniel had been close, but she was beginning to understand why Ben was so closed off.

'What else do you remember about your mum?' Thea asked tentatively.

'Plenty.' His voice was thick, loaded. 'My father might have taken everything tangible of hers which I wanted to cherish—photos of her, the emerald necklace I always remembered her wearing, even the damned sofa cushions she loved to sew—but he couldn't take my memories.'

Couldn't take my memories...

The words punched through to her stomach. How many times had she thought the same thing about her baby? She might have lost the one thing she had cherished the most, but the love was still there, the memory of that feeling of knowing a life was growing inside her. That single scan.

'She used to teach me how to bake cakes as a kid,' Ben continued hesitantly, as though he was fighting to speak. 'Then how to cook.'

'Is that where you learned to make the pancakes you cooked me that time?' Curiosity crept over her.

'Yes—and thanks to her I can rustle up something a bit better if I want to. I can even make a mean Madagascan vanilla bean soufflé. I once dreamed of becoming a chef when I grew up.'

'Really? What did your mum think?'

Ben hunched his shoulders. 'She encouraged it. She never wanted me to become a soldier—she was frightened she'd lose me. I've always wondered, if I hadn't gone into the Army, if I might have made it as a chef. I'd have loved to start something like this. It's right up my street.'

'I can see you as a chef…' Thea murmured. 'Why didn't you do it? Too many memories?'

'No. My father didn't encourage it, and I always wanted to please him so I followed his lead.'

'And *did* it please him?' she couldn't help asking.

Ben pulled a face. 'There was never *any* pleasing him. But I didn't find that out until much later on, and by then I'd already chosen my path. So I made it work for me and decided to have nothing more to do with him.'

Thea stayed quiet. She missed her family. They weren't around to talk to and she'd have given anything for one last conversation. It was unimaginable to her that Ben should be in a position where he *could* talk to his father, but that things were so bad he didn't want to.

Her heart suddenly ached for him. His relationship with his father wasn't something she'd ever thought about, but now she couldn't stop wondering what kind of a father Ben would have made himself. Even given the circumstances, somehow she didn't think he would have abandoned her—or his baby. Or put them through whatever *he* had been through.

The guilt pressed in on her with even more force.

'Would you ever leave the Army and try?' she asked, trying to jog the thought from her head.

'What? Becoming a chef? No chance. Too old now!' Ben laughed.

'You love being a Major?' She struggled to keep her tone light, to betray none of the sadness she felt for him. Or her self-reproach.

A shadow crossed his face. 'Not any more. I've worked

hard, I've done my duty, I've given my all. But now I don't think I have any more to give.'

'But you would never *leave*?' She held her breath in shock.

'I'd like to, but... I still feel tied in. I'm working on it.'

Thea knew she was staring. Hastily she averted her gaze, but her mind was swimming. She'd thought the Army was his life—she'd never thought he would consider leaving.

Ben moved his hand across the table to take hers, turning it over gently and rubbing his thumb on her palm.

'I'm sorry.' He looked her straight in the eyes. 'About the other night.'

Was it only such a short while ago? It almost felt a lifetime earlier.

'It should never have happened.'

She could only stare at him. It was happening again— *another mistake.* She was such an idiot.

But he was pressing on uncomfortably. 'After that motorway call-out I finally admitted to myself I still had feelings for you—I was driven by some need for you. I should have controlled it—waited until I'd addressed the issues which had kept us apart in the first place. I hope I haven't ruined it between us.'

'So you still...want me?' Her mind was reeling.

'Yes. And I'm sorry for not trusting you, Thea, for not wanting you to see my scars. You've only ever been supportive and that was unfair of me and so very wrong.'

'*Why* didn't you trust me?' Thea asked quietly, still trying absorb the fact that he wasn't rejecting her. *Again.*

'I don't know. I know that you'll be there for me, no matter what. You've already proved that. There's no one single thing I can pinpoint. But I guess the day before had been a traumatic day for everyone, and I don't find it easy to talk anyway. With memories of my own accident, it all came to a head. And maybe I felt as though you were holding back a little.'

'Do you really believe that?' Thea's heart lurched with guilt. 'That I was holding back?'

'I don't know.' Ben shook his head apologetically. 'No. Probably not. I was trying to deflect. You were right. I wasn't exactly thinking straight during that RTC. Anyway, I'm sorry.'

'Don't be.' Thea swallowed. After seeing him save that baby her head had been all over the place—it was no wonder Ben had picked up on that.

'No. I am sorry. I should have trusted you enough to tell you. I didn't, and that wasn't right. You deserve better than that from me.'

Thea felt her eyes prick—couldn't look up from the remnants of her meal. He thought she deserved better but he was right—she *had* been holding back. She was *still* holding back. Ever since he'd walked towards her with that baby she'd been fighting to shut out the painful memories. And Ben was a part of them. With every new confession he made to her it only made her feel more conscience-stricken. It was time to tell him the truth. Because—really—didn't *he* deserve better from *her*?

'Thea? Are you all right?'

His evident concern only heightened her gnawing guilt. She pushed her chair back and rose to her feet. Words were lodged in her throat and she had to force them out.

'Can we get out of here?'

He frowned. She didn't blame him for being confused. Still, he nodded and stood up too.

'I'll find someone and pay.' He glanced around for a waiter, signalled to him, then turned back.

She couldn't bear the way he was looking at her.

'I'll wait outside,' she muttered, turning swiftly and doing all she could not to run for the door.

The cold night air made her bury her head in her jumper. In her haste she'd forgotten her coat, and it was freezing out here. She stopped, half turning back to the restaurant, knowing she would have to go in but unable to bring herself to do so. No—better to find their sleigh and grab one of the blankets from there.

Before she could go any further the door to the restaurant opened and Ben appeared. He jogged over to her, wrapping her in her coat so solicitously that she batted away his hands before tears overwhelmed her.

'Don't, Ben, please. I don't deserve your kindness.'

'You're wrong.'

His certainty only made her feel worse.

'Please—just let me say this.'

He hesitated for a long moment before taking a reluctant step backwards, as if to give her space. Oddly, it made her feel alone. She stared down at the slush-covered cobbles, unable to meet his eye. Then, somewhere deep inside herself, she found the edge of her forgotten resolve and dragged her gaze up to his. She owed him that.

'The night we… Our wedding night,' she corrected hastily. 'Oh…there's no easy way to say this. There was a baby. *Our* baby.'

CHAPTER ELEVEN

BEN STARED AT her for several long moments.

Their baby?

His chest started to constrict acutely. *Where was she... he...? Why hadn't Thea told him before?*

His head fought to catch up with the words she'd used. 'There *was* a baby?' he asked urgently.

Thea nodded, and her head bounced madly around as though it wasn't even her own, as if it had been let loose on some kind of out-of-control spring.

'You...terminated?'

The words made him feel nauseous, even though his head, trying frantically to keep up with his racing heart, was desperately trying to caution him. He was in no place to judge Thea, or to censure her. But why hadn't she told him? He could have supported her, made sure she knew all her options before making that momentous decision.

'No!' She jerked her head up.

Everything seemed to stop for him.

No? No, what?

'But you didn't have it?'

He heard the catch in his voice, berated himself for it. But he was powerless against it.

The look she darted at him was evidence that Thea

was frenziedly trying to work out what he was thinking. He opened his mouth but no words came out.

'I lost it.' She stopped abruptly. That just made it seem as if she'd been careless. She cleared her throat and met his eye again. 'I miscarried.'

Her voice cracked but her emotion, the look in her eyes, told him all the things she couldn't say.

'When?' he asked, struggling to keep his voice from betraying any emotion for fear of upsetting her further. Inside he was in turmoil. 'How far along were you?'

'Three months. It was ten days after the first scan. I… I started to bleed.'

'Were you…okay?' It wasn't what he meant, but she seemed to understand anyway.

She squeezed her eyes shut.

'It's been five years, but even now, remembering that day, I can still recall exactly how I felt in that instant. Blind fear and…and…utter sorrow. There's no way to properly articulate that.'

He should have known—should have been there for her.

'I'm sorry. I'm so, so sorry,' he whispered, but he didn't think she was even hearing him. 'Time heals,' he offered helplessly, but it sounded hollow to his ears. It hadn't healed the loss of his own mother, and it hadn't with the loss of Dan. Or was that his own guilt?

Thea shook her head, swallowing hard.

'I'm not so sure about that. With my parents, with Daniel, certainly the edges have dulled. Slightly. Given enough time. But the pain has never gone away completely.'

Ben nodded. He knew that feeling well.

'But with a baby it's different, somehow. Every year I think about what could have been. Every year, when I see a child the same age as…as ours would have been, I imagine whether it would have been crawling, walking, talking, playing, jumping, laughing.'

A sob suddenly escaped from somewhere deep inside her, tearing at Ben's gut.

'I can't even say *he* or *she*. I have to say *it*.' She looked up at him with an expression of pure anguish as she asked helplessly, 'Does that make it better or worse?'

He shook his head, unable to speak. Reaching out, he placed his hands on her shoulders and pulled her, ignoring her resistance, until she was in his arms. Rigid. Unyielding. But there, none the less.

'It doesn't make it anything,' he whispered hoarsely. 'It just *is*.'

They stood like that for a few moments, Thea still stiff in his embrace, before she pushed herself out of his hold, crossing her arms in front of her chest protectively.

He wanted to stop her…wanted to offer her more support, more relief—*more*. His head felt as if it was too small for his swirling emotions.

He took a step back. 'You never called me. You should have called.' He hadn't intended for it to sound like an accusation.

She squeezed her eyes shut, willing herself to keep control.

'To say what?' she asked flatly.

'To *tell* me about it. To say you needed me, that you weren't okay—*anything*.'

He practically shouted the last word and Thea winced as people in the street turned in their direction.

'Thea, I didn't mean that—sorry.' He raked his hand through his hair as he turned in a circle. Then turned to face her square-on. Her eyes were filled with torment.

'You should have called me, Thea. I would have come back in a heartbeat.'

'What would have been the point?' She hunched her shoulders. 'We weren't together. You'd walked out on me.'

'I didn't abandon you,' he hissed. 'We've been through this. You *told* me to leave.'

Why were they attacking each other? He needed to end this. *Now.*

'I take that back unreservedly,' he said immediately. 'We've been through that already. But, Thea, you still should have called me.'

'And said what? That I *had been* pregnant, but not to worry because I'd lost it?'

'Thea…' he growled in warning. 'You should have called me before then. The moment you knew you were pregnant. You should have called me *then.*'

'You were…busy,' she muttered weakly.

He felt the brush of disgust. 'You're better than that, Thea.'

She glared at him, then drew in a deep breath.

'I'm sorry. Maybe you're right. Maybe I should have called as soon as I knew. But I *thought* you'd walked out on me—I believed you didn't want anything to do with me—and I didn't see the point in involving you in something you wouldn't want to be a part of. Or at least something I *thought* you wouldn't want to be a part of.'

He stared at her in disbelief. Realisation dawned.

'Wait. You thought I wouldn't want it? That I'd suggest you terminate it?'

He felt physically sick.

'I didn't know!' she cried, spreading her hands helplessly. Then she stopped to fix him with her direct gaze. Her voice was calmer, firmer. 'I just didn't know, Ben. You *must* see that.'

He felt as if he'd just been punched in the solar plexus and was struggling to draw breath. Was that really how she felt about him?

'I see.'

They both stood, motionless. Neither quite sure where to go or what to do.

He wanted to say more.

There was nothing left *to* say.

Ben turned around, looking for the sleigh. If the journey over here had been strained, the return leg was going to be excruciating. But there was nothing else for it.

His arm felt like a ten-ton weight as he signalled the driver and marched over. Thea followed behind, reluctance emanating from her with every step. As before, he offered her his hand, but unlike before she took it awkwardly, trying to maintain as little contact as possible while still accepting his help with cold politeness. He practically vaulted up into the sleigh behind her, watching her scoot as far away from him as possible, and tugging a blanket up around her neck, her face turned away.

Even in the moonlight her profile looked so full of misery that he was hit with remorse. This evening was supposed to have been about him opening up to her. Now his head was roiling and tumbling and he was unable to work out how he felt, let alone comfort Thea. He knew he was angry. He just didn't know at whom or about what.

He had a feeling it was himself.

Thea stared at the ceiling. The bed was a jumbled mess from where she'd been tossing and turning for the last five hours.

Tonight had been absolute purgatory. She'd expected it would be—that was exactly why she had dreaded telling him, had put it off again and again. However, she had never once imagined that it would be such a nightmare because he would feel so hurt. She had expected panic, anger, relief. She had never considered devastation, anger, loss.

Now that she was beginning to come down from the peak of her rampaging emotions she wasn't sure what to make of it. Turning over to her right side and then back to her left proved no more satisfactory. Sleep wasn't to be her friend tonight. She threw off the covers and grabbed her fleece jacket, hoping that she could resurrect something of the fire from its smouldering embers, and padded out into the living room.

She saw that Ben was staring into the flames of a roaring fire the moment she walked through the door. She froze, but it was too late.

'Can't sleep either,' he murmured. 'I've just made coffee. Do you want one?'

'Please.' She matched his tone, grateful that they didn't appear to be about to start arguing again.

She sat on the other couch, the warmth of the fire seeping into her bones and making her feel better—if only a little bit. Then Ben was back with her coffee.

'I'm sorry. Maybe I should have told you...'

'I'm sorry. I shouldn't have reacted like that...'

They both spoke, and stopped, in unison.

Thea flushed. 'Go ahead.'

'I'm sorry, I shouldn't have reacted that way,' Ben apologised. 'Just the idea of you not telling me, going through it alone—whichever way it played out... Either an absentee father, or a man who leaves the woman he got pregnant to deal with everything alone—that isn't the man I would ever have chosen to be. And then to think of what you had to go through... It just isn't the person I want to think of myself as.'

There was no doubting the sincerity of his words, and Thea nodded awkwardly.

The silence was slightly less taut than it had been before and they sat sipping their coffee as logs crackled in the fire. Thea even unzipped her fleece quietly.

'I have a picture,' she said suddenly. 'A scan.'

Ben's head snapped up. 'Of our baby?'

Our baby. She'd never expected to hear those words drop so easily from his lips. She nodded, ducking into her room to fish her purse out of her bag. She almost hesitated by the door, but then she drew together whatever courage she could and propelled herself forward.

Ben took the scan picture without a sound. His eyes never left the black and white image, and his finger almost imperceptibly twitched, as if to stroke the tiny peanut shape.

'You can keep it. If you like,' she offered tentatively. 'I have another.'

He nodded, slipped his wallet out of his pocket and slid the image inside.

But as he went to close it Thea's hand stayed the movement. A single photo had caught her attention.

'May I?'

He looked as though he was going to object, then abruptly handed the wallet to her. She turned the image towards her, her heart thudding. The man in the photo was younger than he'd looked on the two occasions she'd seen him observing Ben's recovery in the hospital, but it was definitely him—the man she'd assumed was some kind of psychiatrist or counsellor. But what would *that* man be doing in this old photo, with his arm around Ben, and next to them Daniel, looking proud. She peered closer at the man's rank.

'This is the Colonel who commanded you and Daniel?'

Ben stayed silent.

She was pretty sure the answer was obvious but she needed to hear it. 'Ben?' she pushed.

'Yes, that's the Colonel when he was younger,' Ben said eventually. 'And, yes, to what you're thinking. He's also my father.'

That wasn't what she'd been thinking, and now the wheels were spinning in her head as she tried to catch up. So this was Ben's father—the same man who had commanded Ben and Daniel, and of whom Daniel had always thought so highly. The father Ben had cut out of his life on any personal basis. And yet he still kept this photograph in his wallet.

'Have you ever thought about talking to him?' she offered tentatively. 'About what happened? How you feel?'

Ben snorted. 'About Dan's death? Me getting blown up? No. He wouldn't care. His only priority is for me to get on with my recovery and get on with the next mission.'

'His only priority? How can he not care? You work together every day.'

'It's not like that. You don't understand.'

Ben sighed, as though the whole topic of his father was too tedious for discussion.

'When I say he's my Commander, you think we work together in the field hospital like some cosy father-and-son duo. We don't—we never have. I'm a trauma surgeon—one of around two hundred medics out there, with a Lieutenant Colonel as my direct Officer in Command. My father is a full Colonel—IC of the whole battalion, with up to four thousand men under his command. My unit of two hundred is a drop in the ocean. Granted, we might cross paths occasionally out there, but he would never go out of his way to talk to me. He probably wouldn't even know if we were at the same base. The last time I saw him was about a month before my accident. He was holding a command briefing for the Lieutenant Colonels on our camp and he conducted a quick check of my field hospital with my Commanding Officer. But we barely saw each other, let alone exchanged pleasantries.'

It would seem for all the world as though he didn't care. Only Thea knew Ben did care, deep down, whether he realised it or not.

Thea thought back to the times when she'd seen his father in the hospital when Ben had first been brought home. 'And what about him coming back here?'

'And leave his command to someone else? He wouldn't consider it for a moment,' Ben refuted flatly, then added dismissively. 'Even if he wanted to he couldn't.'

She wavered. *Ben needed to know. He carried a photo of the man in his wallet.*

She licked her lips. 'You do know he was at the hospital, don't you?'

Ben jerked his head up. The look of hope that flashed through his eyes, if only for a fraction of a second, was heartbreaking.

'When?' Ben peered at her, then shook his head. 'No. I told you—he was in Afghanistan. He wouldn't have returned.'

'He did,' Thea insisted. 'I saw him several times outside your room when you were first flown back, consulting with your doctors. They definitely seemed to be deferring to him. The other time was in the gardens, the day you decided to take your souped-up wheelchair for a test drive into the hospital bushes.'

'You've got the wrong man,' Ben said flatly.

'No. I haven't.' This was harder than she'd thought,

but she couldn't let up now. 'He's older now, of course, and his hair is grey, but the cut is still the same and the face is clearly his.'

Ben shook his head.

She needed one last jolt.

'He was definitely the Colonel from the photograph in your wallet.' She steeled herself for the next bit. 'The one with Daniel.'

Even then Ben refused to believe her. Drained, she had no choice but to let it go, and when he changed the subject she let him. But the very fact he'd told her who the man was gave Thea even more hope.

'Anyway, thanks for the scan pic,' he muttered, finally slipping his wallet into his back pocket.

'Sure,' she managed awkwardly, sipping her coffee again and watching the flames lick over the logs.

'Would you have told me?' Ben asked suddenly. 'In the end? If you *had* had the baby? Earlier? I mean, say, four years ago?'

She'd often wondered about that. The answer had always been the same. 'Probably.'

'You think so?'

She nodded. 'I think probably just before I was due. I couldn't have imagined the baby being born and not giving you the chance to be there. I still... I still loved you back then. And I couldn't have faced my child in the future and told it I hadn't been able to put aside my own pride to give it a chance a relationship with you.'

He stared into the fire again, then said simply, 'Thank you.'

It was odd. His entire reaction to the news of their baby had been unexpected. For the first time Thea didn't feel quite so alone. But she still felt raw, exposed, and she knew Ben's revelations about his father had left him feeling equally vulnerable.

Tentatively they began to make small talk, but she wasn't really surprised when Ben suddenly leaned forward and took her face in her hands, then kissed her.

The kiss conveyed all the raw emotion that had been circling around them all evening. Tonight the flimsy veil had been lifted on the void which was always inside her, and his deep, searching, almost fervent kiss let her know he was feeling just as vulnerable and exposed.

His kiss was almost desperate, and it mirrored every fear and emotion in her gut. She responded to it on a primal level, allowing Ben to pull her to her feet so that they could get closer, and his hands moved quickly over her back, around to her front, grazing her breast through the fabric.

She wanted to let him carry on, take more from her, give her more. But she couldn't—not yet. She stilled his hand uncertainly. As much as her body was crying out for them to make love, to give that empty feeling some relief, if only temporarily, her mind couldn't quite let go of the last time. She didn't want that rejection again.

Suddenly Ben pulled back from her, leaving her feeling momentarily bereft, before she realised he had lifted his jumper and tee over his head in one movement and now stood, unmoving and wordless, in front of her. Slowly she took in the long, thin scars which circled his arm, from where it had been reattached, the thick, circular splodge of a scar under his armpit, from where the surgeons had entered his chest cavity, and the criss-cross of scars over various parts of his torso from where metal debris and bullets had grazed his skin. Silvery and light in some places and angry red welts in others.

Her raw sadness was dulled slightly, somewhat eased

by the enormity of the step Ben had taken in letting her see them. She took them all in, her eyes raking from one to another to another and back. Finally she took a step forward, reaching a tentative hand out to touch them, half expecting him to pull away, surprised when her fingers ran softly over his skin and still he didn't reject her. But his body was taut, his apprehension spilling out in his body language, and Thea longed to set him at ease.

Dipping her head down, she only hesitated for a fraction of a second before letting her lips make contact with the damaged skin. She dropped little kisses at first, becoming bolder when he remained motionless, his hands clenched by his sides as if he was fighting an internal battle. She trailed kisses down the criss-crosses, lower and lower, until they dipped out of sight beneath the waistband of his jeans.

She leaned back to look at him in silent question. Was he ready to trust her completely?

His hands moved to unbutton the jeans, stilling as she covered them with her own, her eyes never leaving his as she stripped him of the rest of his clothing. Finally he was standing naked and proud in front of her, the trust she had wanted at last in evidence. As well as something more.

Sensing her ultimate capitulation, Ben pulled Thea to him and swept her into his arms as he lowered them both quickly to the rug. Despite herself, Thea knew that tonight was about losing themselves in each other. Masking the grief they were both feeling. In some ways she could see Ben's actions as progress. But what was driving them might be a step forward, or it might be another scurry backwards.

CHAPTER TWELVE

BEN CONCENTRATED ON the slope, acutely aware of Thea skiing so close next to him, acutely aware of *everything* she was dong. After last night things should have been good between them. Better than good. He had finally trusted her enough to let her see his scars—the unmistakable evidence that he'd survived a war which had indiscriminately taken the lives of others. Taken the life of Dan.

But showing Thea those scars was only part of it. He bore other scars. Scars which couldn't be seen. Emotional scars from the bomb blast, from Dan's death, and until he let Thea see those—as incredible as the sex had been between them—there was no shaking the truth that things had happened out of sequence. As a result of raw emotions. And they both knew that.

Thea's revelation about their baby had sent him reeling. Last night it had been an incredible shock. But in the cold light of day the shock was receding and he felt as though a hollow emptiness was tearing a hole inside him. How could you miss something, feel such pain and loss, for a baby you had never even known about? And yet he felt as though he was grieving that, too.

Somehow Thea's secret had given him the excuse of avoiding telling her about Dan—yet again. But he knew that until that final obstacle was removed, once and for all, there could be no future for them.

He hurtled around a bend, lost in his thoughts, until a movement in the next valley caught his eye.

'Are you trying to kill us?'

Thea almost skidded into a snowbank as she edged her skis hard into the ice to avoid a collision. Breathing hard from her exertions, she made her way up to him, her voice loaded with shock.

'Look over there,' he instructed, ignoring her fury. Then, as she failed to react to his order, he moved to stand behind her, lining up her eyes with his arm. 'Across the valley.'

It didn't take her long to realise what he was trying to show her.

'An avalanche.' She sucked in a breath. 'And a skier? What's he even doing there?'

'From the bright yellow jacket, I'd hazard a guess he's Mountain Patrol, checking the slopes. He'll probably be okay.'

'Right…' Thea nodded, watching the skilled skier racing down the piste, trying to outrun the avalanche. There was a gap in the treeline to the side of the piste, which he was clearly aiming for, and Thea watched as the patroller reached the gap and practically did a one-eighty turn on his pole to drop back on himself, off the piste and onto the narrow, tree-free path twenty feet below, just as the avalanche thundered by above.

She exhaled a *whoosh* of relief, but even as she did so the skier either caught a hidden rock or slid on the ice. He had fallen, and was now hurtling down the slope on his stomach, his skis flying into the air with frightening sprays of snow.

'He's not going to be able to stop himself!' cried Thea as the skier headed straight towards a wooded embankment.

Sixty feet into the slide, the skier slammed straight into a tree—head-first.

Time stopped for Ben, and it was as if his surroundings spun around him. Snow, desert, skis, tanks, bodies. He ripped his snowboard off and threw it into the webbing on his back. Through the fug in his head he vaguely heard Thea scream at him, but her words were indistinguishable. Something about a death wish. At some point she might have grabbed his arm, but he threw her off without a glance and then he was jumping down the steep embankment, letting himself fall and fall into the valley, hoping he'd land on soft snow and not hard rocks.

Wading through thigh-deep snow, he felt his back screaming at him, already on fire, but he ignored the pain and pushed on towards the immobile body. His mind kept switching the figure of the skier on the snowy slopes for Dan, bleeding out on the rocky mountainside. There was no way he could leave him there.

He had no idea how long the interminable trek across the valley took. The relief when he finally reach the skier and saw the man had his eyes open was indescribable. The guy was alive. Even better, the man's eyes widened slightly upon seeing him. A trickle of relief crept down Ben's spine. At least it meant the man still had some cognitive function.

'Don't try to nod or shake your head. Try not to move at all for the moment. If you can't talk, just blink.'

'I can talk,' the man rasped, clearly having trouble breathing.

'Okay, that's good. I was on the run down the mountain to the village and I saw everything. I'm Ben, by the way. Can you remember what happened to you?'

'Ben...okay. I'm Tomas. I was patrolling the unmarked slopes, looking for any extreme skiers. I triggered a snow slide and I was trying to outrun it. I thought I dropped down safely...but maybe I fell? I don't recall much after that.'

'Good—that's good.' Ben nodded encouragingly. 'Can you move your arms and legs?'

'I don't know.' Tomas was clearly having trouble concentrating. 'Are you a doctor?'

'A trauma surgeon.' Ben nodded again.

'Both of you?'

Ben froze as Tomas's gaze lifted to just over his right shoulder. He turned slowly but he already knew what he was going to find. Thea, white-faced but resolute, stood behind him. His stomach slid away in fear. She'd only come because of *him*. If she got hurt it would be *his* fault.

He moved away so Tomas wouldn't hear him.

'Are you crazy?' he hissed. 'You could have killed yourself.'

'No more than you could have,' she countered angrily. 'You shouldn't have come over here. You *know* the snow is probably unstable. There was a heavy snowfall last night, and it must have landed on a layer of compact ice. The whole lot is probably ready to slide at any moment. You could be just the provocation it needs.'

Fear clawed at him. 'Dammit, Thea, if anything happens to you I'll never forgive myself.'

'Then you'd better hope nothing does happen to me.' Thea jutted her chin out determinedly, but inside she was shaking. 'I couldn't just leave you to it, Ben. Odds are it'll need two of us to stabilise him. Then I'll ski down to the town.'

'You need to get out of here,' he argued in desperation. 'You know how time-critical this is.'

'It's only time-critical if there's a stable patient,' countered Thea. 'It wouldn't matter how fast I got down there if you can't stabilise him. He wouldn't live long enough for rescue to arrive.'

She had a point. Ben shook his head, hardly daring to say another word.

Sensing she was gaining ground, Thea pushed her point home. 'We're the eyes and ears for the local trauma unit. The more information we can gather and pass on, the more pinpointed their subsequent care can be.'

His glower raked over her. He looked exhausted and scared.

'You've got some nerve…' His voice shook but he said nothing more.

He turned back to the skier.

'Tomas, our priority right now is to get you comfortable while we assess your injuries.'

Tomas fought to draw a deep breath. 'I was sliding, and then I remember a hot, searing pain travelling from my head to my toes.'

'Yeah,' Ben confirmed. 'You hit a tree—good job you were wearing a helmet. So, have you got your patrol two-way radio?'

'Should be in my pocket… If you call in, they can send another patroller with a toboggan. Then they can take me to a landing zone a bit further down, where a chopper can land to medevac me.'

Ben checked Tomas's pockets, then looked at Thea. The radio had been lost in the slide.

'Tomas did have a toboggan though,' Thea murmured quietly.

'Understood.' Ben nodded. 'Okay, Tomas, I'm just going to pinch your thigh—you tell me if you can feel it.'

'No…' He closed his eyes for a moment. 'But I think I can move my hands.'

Ben watched carefully as only two fingers on one of Tomas's hands twitched. Thea cast him a sinking look, they needed to stabilise Tomas fast and go for help.

Thea kept her voice deliberately neutral, clearly not wanting to lie to the man but needing to offer some reassurance. 'There is *some* visible movement—try not to worry. I'm just going to prep you for when they arrive with the full transport.'

She had barely finished speaking when Tomas went into cardiac arrest.

Uttering low curses, they started chest compressions, relieved when Tomas came back relatively quickly.

'Wait, there's his rucksack,' Thea spied suddenly. She waded through the snow and retrieved a small pouch, opening it… 'Space blanket, water camel, emergency medical kit—that's something.'

Before Ben could answer Tomas went into cardiac arrest again, and with barely a glance between them they resumed their places to work together. It took longer this time, and the look Thea cast him confirmed Ben's apprehension.

They made Tomas comfortable before carefully retreating a small distance.

'He won't cope with continually going into cardiac arrest,' Ben murmured. 'I'm pretty sure it's the paralysis which is causing the problem. I think it's causing his diaphragm to stop rising and falling and that's what's knocking his heart out.'

'That makes sense.' Thea nodded. 'But there's nothing here to help him breathe in the interim, is there?'

Ben paused. 'Maybe…'

She followed his eyes to the water camel.

'It's not ideally sterile, but the long tube could be put into cold snow to harden it slightly.'

Thea grunted, not keen. 'Might be hard to intubate without a sedative but he will need to be stable enough for me to go for help.'

'Then there's nothing else for it,' Ben confirmed. 'If Tomas goes into cardiac arrest a third time we'll use the opportunity to intubate before starting compressions.'

'And then?'

'If we can't get Mountain Rescue to Tomas, we'll just have to get Tomas to them,' Ben ground out.

'How?'

'Find his rescue toboggan. He had it right up until the last moment. It can't be far away.'

It was a long shot, but they both searched the landscape in silence.

'Over there,' Thea cried out.

Ben swung around, following the direction of her outstretched arm. The toboggan wasn't too far away, but the slope wasn't a used one and the snow didn't look bedded in.

'Don't move,' he commanded as Thea edged her skis towards the slope, preparing to ski up the mountain. 'I'll go. You stay here with Tomas.'

Thea shook her head. 'I have skis. I can side-slip up there. If I feel the snow start to give, I can ski out of there before the slide starts. You only have a snowboard—you can't do it the same way.'

'Makes no difference.' He shook his head.

She snorted, half-angry, half-frustrated. 'Of *course* it makes a difference. What makes your life any less valuable than mine? No—don't answer that. Like you said, this whole thing is time-critical. I need to go, and you need to get back to Tomas in case he arrests again.'

Before Ben could say anything else she was off, carefully edging up the mountain, step by step, until she could traverse across to the toboggan. She knew he wanted to stop her, wanted to send her for help, but he also had to know that she was right. If they wanted to save Tomas and give the man any chance at a halfway decent recovery then they needed to get that toboggan.

He stood and watched her for several moments, inching very carefully up the treacherous slope, her heart in her mouth. She was relieved when his focus had to be split between the man lying on the snow in front of him and her, as she inched her way further and further into danger. She knew he'd be worried that she was too far away for him to do anything about it if something went wrong. This was exactly why he hadn't wanted her here. It was also exactly why *she* hadn't wanted *him* here. But he hadn't listened to her. She didn't think he'd even registered her.

Her heart hammering, she reached the toboggan and dug its metal arms out of the snow. Then, pulling it behind her, she skied carefully back down to Ben and Tomas. Ben practically snatched the handles out of her hands.

'How is he?' She kept her voice low.

'Slipping in and out of consciousness,' Ben murmured. 'We need to get him down.'

'Right.' She checked the rucksack she'd recovered. 'We can stabilise his neck, then get the scoop around him.'

Working quickly and carefully, they manoeuvred Tomas into position. He was barely conscious, and they could feel time slipping through their fingers.

'You need to ski into town now,' he told her when they were finished. 'Be sure to stay well ahead of us in case the toboggan dislodges anything and it rolls down to you. Thea, remember this isn't a designated slope—it isn't safe. Be careful.'

She frowned. 'Wait—you're on foot?'

Ben shrugged, and she realised that of course it wasn't as though he could pull the toboggan on his snowboard. Quickly releasing herself from her skis, she circled around him to grab his board from the webbing he'd thrown on to the snow earlier.

'I'll take the snowboard—you take my skis.'

'You can't snowboard,' Ben objected irritably.

'No—I don't *enjoy* it as much as skiing. Doesn't mean I *can't*. I'll get down faster than if I'm trying to ski through the snow anyway. And there's no way you can walk and pull a toboggan.'

'That's an impossible maze of trees and rocks to try to navigate,' he argued.

'And I won't be trying to do it whilst pulling a seriously injured man on a scoop.'

He closed his eyes for a moment. 'I just want you off this dangerous slope. I want you safe. I don't want an argument keeping you on this damned mountain any longer.'

'So put on the skis and do what I'm suggesting.' She stood her ground.

'Fine.' He gritted his teeth. 'Thanks.'

She flipped the board around, clipped her ski boots in, and started off slowly down the wooded, rock-littered slope, trying to quell the rising terror. How was Ben possibly going to navigate it without causing more injury to Tomas? Alone, with only his ghosts to keep him company?

All along he had refused to entertain the idea of losing the skier. It meant more to him than just the rescue that it was. She'd seen the haunted look that had veiled his eyes the moment he'd seen the skier lying prone on the snow. Another of those PTSD triggers...

Thea wondered if he would ever be able to open up to her about that darkness he carried with him. She wanted to help him, but she wasn't sure she could. Not until he wanted to help himself. She had a feeling that unless he did there was no hope of a future for them together.

Tonight she was going to push him. Tonight would be his final chance to let her in.

Lost in her thoughts, she was down the mountain safely before she realised it. She raced to the Mountain Rescue centre and alerted the team. Then, explaining she was a trauma doctor, she convinced them to let her on the helicopter to show them where she and Ben had agreed their Emergency Rendezvous point would be.

Finally, she spotted him, painstakingly picking his way through the trees, near to the lower treeline and close to where the helicopter was now landing. Ben approached them smoothly, quickly, his body betraying nothing of his own pain. But Thea knew his body had been pushed too far today. However there was no disguising his fury at her return as she jumped down from the chopper.

'Your wife briefed us,' the rescue team leader acknowledged, taking the scoop from Ben and prepping Tomas for the flight.

'Good.' Ben nodded. 'Tomas went into cardiac arrest a third time. I had to improvise, using a water camel as a breathing tube. I'd recommend administering a sedative for the flight, and using a bag valve mask to force air into his lungs.'

Accepting the team's hurried gratitude, Ben and Thea moved out of the way as the helicopter took off, the snow around them swirling in a mass of chaos. Then the chopper flew away and the snow dropped down silently, deadly, as an equally heavy silence shrouded the two of them.

Wordlessly they exchanged skis and snowboard. Thea felt exhausted. The rescue had been draining and all her body wanted to do was make it back to the cabin and crumple into bed. But trepidation stayed her.

'Are you going to tell me what that was all about?' she asked at last, as she skied slowly away.

He remained silent.

'I only came on this trip with you because you asked me to. You promised me honesty and you asked for my help,' she reminded him desperately. 'Well, I'm here, fulfilling my promise. Now you need to fulfil yours.'

'Fulfilling your promise like the fact that for five years you kept our baby a secret from me? You've had a chance to mourn what we lost. But you denied me that chance.'

The words hit her with such force she struggled to breathe. He couldn't *really* be throwing that at her now, could he?

'I'm sorry.' He shook his head, devastated. 'I shouldn't have said that.'

'This isn't about the—the baby,' she managed to stutter out. 'This is about *you.*'

'What do you want from me, Thea?' His voice was low, deep, uncompromising. Yet his eyes were ringed with red, glistening.

It took her by surprise. He was a soldier—he saw war, saw lots of things. That he should be so affected by the loss of their baby caught her off guard.

'I don't know.' Thea closed her eyes to hold back her own tears.

He dipped his head. Saying nothing. Busying himself with the snowboard.

Then, in silent unison they skied back down to their cabin.

'You're leaving, aren't you?' Thea asked as they headed inside.

'I have to,' he told her. 'I'm sorry.'

'You can't protect everyone. Even though you might want to,' she whispered as he turned to face her. 'Just don't go getting yourself killed out there.'

'I don't intend to,' he replied gruffly, tilting her head up and kissing her salty tears. 'But I *do* intend to come back for you.'

Her throat felt closed. 'Then you know where to find me.'

But deep down she knew he never would. What Ben needed to do was the one thing he could never do. To open up. To talk about his emotions. But he was Army— through and through. Bottling everything up and hoping he never got shaken.

They stayed in each other's arms for only minutes, but it felt like hours, and she clung to him for as long as she could. When he tore himself away to pack up his belongings and leave the cabin she knew she couldn't watch him leave. Their final embrace would be the memory she held on to—not the sight of him walking out through the door.

Quickly, she stumbled back and into her room. She didn't hear Ben leave, but she felt it when the cabin was suddenly empty. Deep down she knew she would never see Ben Abrams again.

CHAPTER THIRTEEN

BEN EYED THE solid wooden door and, squaring up to it, offered three deep, uniform raps with his knuckles.

'Enter.'

The rich, commanding voice threatened to send him walking away. Instead Ben placed his hand firmly on the door and stepped determinedly inside.

'Hello, Dad.'

Ben knew it would wind the old man up—him marching into his barracks office, in uniform but without an appointment, and not addressing him as Colonel. It wasn't intentional but it was too bad. This wasn't about his dad. This was about *him*. And about Thea.

This was the next crucial step in his plan to win her back. Not that it was much of a plan. Despite being in the military, he'd spent much of his career winging it, making up his own medical procedures as he went along in the desperate need to save a life. The only difference this time was that by winning her back the life he would be saving was his own.

He stared across the desk, prepared to see the inevitable disappointment. However, the man behind the desk looked surprisingly drawn, unusually thin beneath the dark tan from the Afghan sun. He peered over his glasses, and Ben registered a flicker of shock as he made himself stride in confidently.

'I heard you weren't in Afghanistan.' Ben stood in front of the desk. The etiquette drilled into him from childhood even now precluded him from sitting down until invited. 'I didn't believe it.'

'I came back a while ago.' His father gave an imperceptible gesture and Ben pulled out a chair and sat down accordingly.

'You weren't planning on being redeployed the last time I spoke to you,' Ben challenged.

He had crossed paths with his father at their last camp, a couple of weeks before Ben had been caught in the IED blasts. Yet Thea said she'd seen his father at the hospital soon after Ben had been transported back.

'Things…changed.'

Could his father really have given up his command for him? No, he was being fanciful, caught up as he was in his drive for information. There had to be a more logical explanation.

'I understand you passed your Medical Board Assessment today, clearing you for active duty? Congratulations.'

'Thank you.' Ben inclined his head.

He'd been in there less than an hour ago, but why should he be surprised that his father already knew the results? The Board probably had the Colonel on speed dial.

'However, I won't be returning to active duty. Tomorrow I'm going to tender my resignation from the British Army,' he announced quickly, without fanfare. 'I'll be handing my official letter to my Commanding Officer.'

'I see.'

The Colonel looked grim, and Ben felt a rush of irritation.

'I'm only coming to forewarn you now as a courtesy,

Dad.' He intended to emphasise that it had nothing to do with his father's position as Battalion IC.

'May I ask what has precipitated this decision?' his father asked stiffly.

'This isn't the life for me any more,' Ben answered simply, surprising even himself with his confidence in his decision. 'I've enjoyed it for twelve years, but it's time for me to move on to new things. I'm not running away.'

He wanted to get that in before his father leaped to his own assumptions. He knew it was true. He was running *towards* something. Towards a new life, a new future, and the only woman he'd ever loved. He just had to convince her that he'd changed enough for her to love him too. Not that his father would ever understand any of that.

'I have *never* known you to run away, Benjamin. Not in the twelve years you've served your country and not as a boy.'

Ben certainly hadn't been prepared for his father's apparent acceptance. He sat, shocked, as his father continued. Awkwardly, but with the resolute glint in his eyes that Ben recognised so well.

'I know you better than you realise, Benjamin. So I understand why you waited to pass your Medical Board before tendering your resignation. You wanted to see your recovery through and you were determined to pass. Because now you can be satisfied that the decision to leave is all yours—no one else's.'

'Right...' Ben frowned. 'Thank you.'

Of all things, his father's understanding, his acceptance, was the last thing he'd expected. He stood up to leave, almost forgetting why he'd wanted to come.

Abruptly he stopped. Turned. 'Did you visit me in the hospital?'

His father hesitated. 'Yes,' he acknowledged after a moment. 'I suppose your young lady told you?'

So Thea *had* seen him. Ben was shocked.

'She's Daniel Fletcher's sister, I understand?'

'Yes,' Ben ground out.

He didn't want to discuss Thea with his father. Didn't want any shadow cast over her. Not by his father—not by anyone.

'She has nothing to do with my decision to leave the Army.' It wasn't strictly true, but he wasn't leaving *for* Thea. He was leaving for the life he wanted away from the Army, which happened to include Thea.

'Sir James tells me she's a very accomplished young trauma surgeon,' his father continued levelly.

'She is.' Ben felt a rush of pride, momentarily loosening his tongue and making him forget who he was talking to. 'She's one of the most gifted trauma doctors I've known.'

She was also caring, compassionate and strong. *So* strong. And he might have thrown all that away just because he had thought closing himself off emotionally was the *only* way to be strong. She'd shown him how wrong he was. She was the reason he was now able, for the first time in his life, to ask his father questions he would never before have been able to. She had made him realise that this was where he'd learned to suppress his emotions— from his father. But he still didn't understand *why* his father had shut them out.

'Was I the reason you returned from Afghanistan? Gave up your post?'

'Benjamin, I don't think this is the right time for this conversation…'

'*Was* I?' Ben pushed, refusing to back down.

'I… I thought I'd lost you, son.' The Colonel jutted

his chin out defiantly but suddenly, if only for an instant, he stopped looking like the driven, emotionless, inflexible Army Colonel Ben knew, and Ben caught a fleeting glimpse of a shaken, frightened, uncertain father.

And then it was gone.

But still, it had caught Ben off guard and unsettled him.

'Where has all this compassion, this emotion been for the last twenty years?' he bit out in frustration. 'Where was all the grief when my mother died?'

He expected his father to shout, to reprimand him for his insolence. Instead the old man offered him a sad smile.

'I was trying to do what was best for you. For us.'

'By getting rid of all traces of her?' Ben shook his head. 'By never discussing her?'

Thea was right—it *wasn't* healthy for anyone to bottle things up. His relationship with his father was a mess. He had no idea if it could ever be repaired—or if his father would ever *want* to repair it. But Ben *did* know that he was going to do everything in his power to salvage his relationship with Thea. She was good for him. She'd helped him heal when he'd never known he was broken. He was never going to find it easy to express how he was feeling, but he now knew he had to try—for himself as much as for Thea. She made him want to be a better person.

'How did you think pretending she'd never existed would help?' Ben urged.

For a moment he thought his father was going to shut down, he could see the old man struggling, but—incredibly—the Colonel met his glower.

'I thought keeping the past behind us would help you to move on. I thought it would help me too.'

To Ben's horror, his father faltered. He had never

seen the old man struggle to control his emotions—*any* emotions—before.

'I was wrong. I'm…sorry.'

So Thea had been right along. He needed to tell her that. Needed to tell her how he felt. Everything. Before it was too late.

If it wasn't already.

'I have to go. There's someone I need to talk to.' Ben stalked to the door, hauling it open and striding outside just as his father's parting words reached his ears.

'Perhaps one day you'll allow us to start to rebuild our relationship?'

Ben turned back, the closing door still giving him a visible line to his father.

'One day.' He nodded. 'I'd like that.'

CHAPTER FOURTEEN

THEA SANK DOWN onto the bench to change out of her flight gear. Exhaustion was a daily occurrence these days. She'd told her colleagues nothing more than that Ben had returned to active duty, but as though they'd sensed the depths of her sorrow they had sent as many call-outs as they could her way in order to keep her busy.

She was grateful for the work. It kept her distracted, draining her physically and mentally, so that when she went home to her empty cottage she barely had the energy to sleep, let alone mope or cry.

Deep down she knew Ben was never coming back. As much as he loved her—and she now knew he did—she couldn't compete with the ghosts of the men he had lost, the ghost of Daniel. But it wasn't just the ghosts. It was more about the fact that Ben could never open up to her about it, that he was so emotionally closed off to her even after everything they'd shared. It meant that there could be no future for the two of them.

Stepping out of the shower, she started drying herself. It was an effort to get dressed. If she could have stayed here, slept in the rec room and waited for her next shift, she probably would have done.

She stepped out of the locker room and straight into a solid, well-built body.

'Ben?'

She felt her chest start to bubble and expand as hopeful anticipation jangled wildly. She ruthlessly stamped it down. She'd been here before with Ben. Twice. She couldn't put herself through it a third time. She had to be absolutely certain.

'What are you doing here?' She was proud of how even she'd managed to keep her voice.

His response, however, wasn't as measured.

'Looking for you.'

Her traitorous heart gave a leap of joy before she muffled it into submission.

'I was also signing some paperwork with Sir James.'

'What paperwork?' she asked suspiciously.

'My release forms. From the time I spent here on a consultancy basis.'

Of course he was. He'd need to be cleared in order to go back out on tours of duty. She was an idiot. Thank God she hadn't given in to the urge to race to him.

'When do you ship out?'

He fixed her with a look.

'I don't.'

Thea felt her legs start to weaken but she held her ground. She was relieved. Knowing he was back out there was her worst fear. Still, she felt sympathy for him.

'I'm sorry,' she said sincerely.

Ben frowned. 'What for?'

'The Medical Board? You weren't cleared for active duty?'

His slow, wide smile made her heart falter. It was genuine, but gentle.

'I *was* cleared for active duty. My recovery is better than textbook.'

'You've been incredible.' She'd seen it for herself but

it was still impressive. And so typically Ben to make such a startling recovery. She bunched her shoulders. 'But you're not shipping out?'

'I quit,' he said simply, his eyes never leaving her face.

'You…*quit*? The Army? For good?' She was having a hard time getting her head around it.

'For good,' he confirmed patiently.

It was the news she had been longing for—the news she'd never expected to hear. 'What changed your mind?'

'You did,' he answered honestly.

She shook her head. She needed more than that.

'Shall we talk in private?' Ben asked, indicating the main office.

With a nod of acquiescence Thea managed to make her legs move towards the quiet room. Stepping inside, she sat down on a chair and looked at him expectantly.

'What I have to tell you…' Ben sat in front of her, taking her hands in his as he leaned in. 'Well, it isn't going to be easy to hear.'

'Because it's about Daniel?' she acknowledged.

'Yes.'

'I don't think you have a choice, Ben.' She tried to quell the anxious jangles. 'I think you *need* to tell me— whatever it is. I think everything inside you is all hopelessly bound together, and until you actually say the words you've no chance of ever untying it in *here*.' She tapped the side of his head, as if to illustrate her point.

He nodded, but stayed silent, his hands still holding hers.

Thea watched their two sets of hands, together but not quite entwined, unable to draw her gaze away. Eventually the silence weighed too heavily.

'You *have* to tell me, Ben. Whatever it is, I can handle it—as long as you're the one who is telling me.'

'Are you really sure you want to do this, Thea?'

She swallowed hard. *No turning back now.*

'I'm sure.'

Ben nodded, taking a moment as if to compose himself, then starting.

'You once asked me why I *really* married you. I told you that part of it was a promise I made to Daniel.'

Thea nodded.

'You never quite understood—never could see the significance—and I don't blame you. But the truth is I made that promise to him the day he died.'

Thea felt as though wheels were spinning in her head.

'The day he died?' she repeated slowly.

'I'm sorry, Thea. I should have explained it to you a long time ago. When he made me make that promise Dan was dying.'

It sounded as though Ben was trying to talk with a tongue too thick for his mouth. As if it was an effort for his mouth to form the words.

'Pardon?' Thea swallowed hard. A deathbed promise? Had she *really* been prepared to hear this?

'We'd been heading to the front line. There had been a battalion manoeuvre and there were thousands of soldiers out there. Hundreds wounded. They couldn't get the injured back through the lines to our field hospital fast enough. A few two-man medical teams chose to advance, to try to help as many as we could in the field—stabilise them until they could be moved back.'

'You and Daniel were one of those teams?' Her heart was practically battering down her chest wall.

'Yes. We were ahead of the other teams. There was a small enemy section closing in on one flank that no one had seen. We got pinned down and Dan took a bullet. He couldn't move. I was trying to drag him behind some rocks for cover when we fell into a foxhole in the dirt. We stayed there whilst I tried to stem the bleeding, but…he was badly hit.'

'He was dying?' Thea whispered, lifting her head to look at Ben.

'I'm sorry.' His eyes pinned her in place. Sincere and full of apology. 'You asked for the truth.'

So help her, she had.

'I was concentrating on stemming the wound. Trying to see if there was any way I could possibly get us out of there. But they were all around us. Searching for us. We could hear them passing less than a foot away. It was all Dan could do not to make a noise.'

No, Thea realised, *because even if he'd known he was dying he would never have wanted to risk his best friend's life.*

'When he realised he was dying he made me promise to take care of you. I think, deep down, he knew I hadn't got over you. Just as I told you he knew that I'd used our "buddy code" as an excuse to back away.'

'Yet he still trusted you enough to ask you to take care of me…as he died?' she said, feeling rattled.

So this was why Ben had never been able to talk about it. The more he revealed, the more she understood why he found it so hard to talk about himself. She almost laughed at the absurdity of it.

Instead a tear escaped and slid down her cheek.

'Thank you for telling me. It was…*is*…important to me.'

'It doesn't bring him back, though,' Ben stated sadly.

'No, it doesn't.'

Aside from the promise, none of these facts about Dan's death were a great revelation to her. But she could see the strides forward Ben had made in order to finally tell her all that. To finally begin to face up to the emotional toll it had taken on him.

'Because he'd trusted me that much I was determined to set aside my own fears and support you whenever you needed me. Instead we slept together. I felt as though I'd failed even in *that*. I couldn't talk to you about it—I couldn't talk to anyone. So I did what I believed you wanted and I left. I let you down…over and over again. Just as I'd feared I would.'

'I wanted to help you, when you were first injured, but you wouldn't let me.'

'How could I? I'd let you down and I'd shut you out—time and again. How could I accept your help and be so indebted to you when I couldn't even tell you how I felt? It's taken time, and an incredible amount of patience on your part, but you've begun to change all that.'

'Really?'

She clearly desperately wanted to believe him, but he couldn't blame her for holding back. It was almost ironic. She had helped him to open up about his emotions and his actions had caused her to become more guarded.

'Yes,' he said earnestly. 'You *have*. And not only that you've taught me how to love, unconditionally, for the first time since my mother died.'

'I have?'

Ben dipped his head in confirmation.

'My father and I have had a…complicated relationship. Growing up, I learned that people weren't capable of loving each other without hurting each other, or letting them down. So I overthought everything, always calculating the risk. But then you came along and taught me that love isn't about risk calculations or logic. It's about taking a leap of faith and trusting my heart. And I trust my heart when I'm with you.'

It took every last bit of Thea's self-control not to let him gather her into the strong arms which she remembered too well. She wanted so much to believe Ben, but doubts still lurked.

'I thought you were getting there on the ski trip, and then...' She tailed off helplessly.

'I *was* getting there,' he assured her. 'But things were so close to surface back then, I suppose. Then you told me about the baby and I think it just tipped things again.'

'I'm sorry. I shouldn't have said anything.'

'Of course you should have. I needed to know as much as you needed to tell me. I just wasn't prepared. I hadn't quite processed it. I was still reeling. Every time I turned around it seemed that my inability to open up to you had just caused more and more ripple effects, each one more devastating than the last. You'd lost a baby, *our* baby, and I'd left you to deal with it all on your own. The one person I was meant to look after and protect, and instead I'd made things worse for you.'

'So when you saw that skier the next day you just reacted?'

'I thought—stupidly—that it was one thing I could control. One thing I could do right and help someone.'

'So what's changed?' It was difficult to believe it had been that easy.

'I lost you,' he answered simply. 'You'd been there for me and I let the best thing in my life slip away from me. I knew I had to win you back, and the only way to do that was to deal with all the issues I've spent years—some *twenty* years—bottling up. And that's because of you. You have helped me to heal.'

'But your Medical Board...?'

'I realised I didn't want to go back on active duty a long time ago. I wanted a different life. A life with you in it. The only reason I took that assessment was so that I could turn it down. Simply to prove to you that making a life with you was my first choice. Not a fallback. The minute I lost you, out on that mountain, I knew I'd messed up. You are the only thing that matters, and I'm willing to do whatever it takes to win you back.'

'So you passed the Board so that you could leave the Army?'

'Yes,' Ben said simply. 'And, for what it's worth, the assessment was intensive, rigorous, and full of questions. Yet nothing fazed me. I didn't have flashbacks, or moments of anxiety or anger, and I didn't shut down. I just told the Board what they wanted to know. I recounted what had happened factually, but not with any need for clinical detachment. And that's all down to you. Getting me to talk, to open up, to acknowledge how I was feeling. You've helped me to heal what I didn't even know before was broken.'

Thea couldn't help but begin to believe him as she considered the man in the chair opposite her. Sitting back comfortably, his hands resting together, his eyes meeting hers easily, he was a far cry from the man of several months ago who had sat ramrod-straight, his fists clenching and unclenching on his knees, refusing to meet her eye but staring fixedly out of the window as each word was wrenched from him.

'So you've really left?'

'I've really left,' he confirmed. 'I've given the Army twelve years of my life. I've served with honour and I've loved almost every minute. But now it's time for a new chapter in my life. A chapter that includes you and hopefully our children.'

'I'd like that too…' Thea bit her lip.

He saw she still wasn't sure about him, and the realisation felt like a punch in the guts. He focused on the hope flickering in her eyes.

'But you still don't believe me?'

He felt as if it was all sliding away, and he was frantically grasping at the remnants of what might have been.

'I believe that you're sincere, and that you've turned a corner. But, Ben, you don't have to be in a war zone with the Army to find ways of risking your life. You ran towards a burning car when you were with the Air Ambulance. You crossed an avalanche-struck slope on a *ski holiday*.'

Ben stared at her incredulously. 'To save *lives*. You and I both know that if I hadn't that baby, and Tomas, would have been dead by the time anyone else got there. If someone's life is in danger I have to help—that's just who I am.'

'I know that,' Thea assured him. 'And I would never expect you to walk away from someone in need. But the *way* you do it—running blindly in, with no regard for your own safety—that scares me.'

'Then what do you propose?' He held his hands out desperately. He couldn't lose her. Not now.

'A trial period,' she said at last. 'For our relationship and for the Air Ambulance.'

'What does that mean?' Ben asked carefully.

'At work you're always going to be the one who risks his life for others—look at your Distinguished Service Order, look at the men you pulled to safety after that bomb blast even when you only had one arm. I'm not trying to change that. But just take a moment—one minute, thirty seconds, fifteen seconds—that's all I ask. To talk to me, or anyone, so that I know you've assessed the danger. So that I know you're taking calculated risks, not reckless ones. So that I don't feel so helpless.'

'I can do that,' Ben agreed slowly.

He understood exactly where she was coming from, and he respected her strength of character. He was impetuous, she was right about that, and he needed someone who cared enough about him to pull him up over it. He knew Thea was that person.

'And as for our relationship...'

This was the bit he really wanted to know. He had to convince Thea that she was all that mattered to him. Without her, his life was empty.

'We spend time together,' she said simply. 'We get to know each other. Sometimes we do boring, mundane things, like going to the cinema, instead of you wanting me try base jumping or something equally adrenalin-fuelled.'

He nodded. He'd always used that kind of stuff as a distraction—especially around anniversaries—to avoid having to think about how he felt. But with Thea he didn't feel he needed those safety nets any more.

'Learning about each other...talking,' he agreed with a grin. 'I can do that.'

'It doesn't mean we can't have fun together.' She smiled.

'Does this trial period include separate bedrooms?' he asked, suddenly straight-faced. 'Because if it does, I can tell you that's a deal-breaker.'

'It does *not* include separate rooms.' She laughed softly.

'OK, then.' His gaze never left hers as he became serious again. 'I'll give you as long as you need. Until you know that you have nothing left to fear. I intend to put you—our family—first from now on.'

'Then I think you'd better sign some new paperwork,' she choked out, tears spilling over as Ben crossed the divide between them in one smooth movement and lifted her up from her chair into his arms, his mouth coming down to claim hers.

It was a kiss full of hope, full of promise, and one day soon he hoped it would turn into one free of any lingering reservations.

'And when you finally trust me completely I promise you I'm going to carry you over that damned threshold, Mrs Abrams.' His lips rumbled against hers as they finally came up for air.

'I hope you can fulfil that promise, because I'd like that, Mr Abrams,' Thea murmured. 'I'd like that very much.'

EPILOGUE

Five years later

'HAPPY TENTH ANNIVERSARY, Mrs Abrams.' Ben kissed her gently awake as the first rays of dawn poured through a gap in the curtains.

'Happy tenth anniversary,' she mumbled sleepily, wrapping her arms around his neck and getting ready to pull him back into bed for a proper good morning celebration.

But Ben quickly detached her grip with a rumble of amusement.

'Sorry, my love, but no time. You'd better brace yourself.'

'Brace myself…?'

'Happy Mummy's day to you, Happy Mummy's day to you…'

Their three-year-old burst excitedly into the room with a delightfully out of tune, improvised rendition of 'Happy Birthday'. She stopped, glancing at him for guidance, and Ben was only too happy to jump into the fray and sing along with his daughter.

Then, waving a handmade card with a colourful, splodgy footprint on the front, she leapt onto the bed, and Ben felt a burst of pride as he watched his little girl snuggle up to her mummy, almost shoving the card up Thea's nose in her eagerness.

'I made it for you, Mummy. It's my footprint—see?'

She waggled her foot in the air, as if fearing her mother wouldn't recognise it otherwise, and Ben was amused to see Thea actually checking the foot. Mercifully, it was clean—which was more than could be said for the bathroom floor right now.

As Thea shifted up the bed to wrap her daughter in her arms Ben lurched forward to help her.

She batted him away good-naturedly. 'I'm pregnant. I'm not ill.'

'I know that, but you're over a week overdue and you look ready to pop,' he chastised her as a fresh surge of love crashed over him.

'Which is why they'll be inducing me on Wednesday if he hasn't been born by then. I'd say he's definitely *your* son.' Thea shot him a wicked grin. 'He won't arrive until he's good and ready.'

'A brother, a brother... I'm getting a brother,' came a sing-song cry of delight. Then the little girl stopped, a look of concern clouding her perfect features. 'Do you think he'll know that it's my birthday next weekend?'

'I'm pretty sure he will,' Thea reassured her, with a quick glance to Ben.

He nodded in confirmation. He had collected a couple of gifts and some party supplies yesterday, knowing that it would reassure Thea. She was adamant that this would be the first party their three-year-old daughter would remember, so they were going to throw one this year.

With all the attention she knew was bound to be lavished on their new son by well-meaning friends, Thea was determined not to let their daughter feel even a little bit left out.

She was an incredible mother. An incredible woman. After the bad start their marriage had suffered, those first five years, Ben had been determined to ensure these last five years had been the best years of her life. They had certainly been the best of his.

They worked alongside each other occasionally, but staggered their shift patterns so that one of them was almost always home with their incredible little girl. He couldn't be happier. Except, perhaps, when their new son joined them properly and they would be a foursome.

'Come on, munchkin.' Ben leaned over the bed and swung his daughter up. An excited shriek came from the little girl. 'I promised you a morning in the park whilst your mummy sleeps. She might have a busy day ahead of her soon.'

'Um, Ben—'

The catch in her voice made him spin around quickly.

'I think that day is now. I've been having light contractions all night, and my waters have just broken.'

'We're going in?' Ben confirmed.

Last time Thea had taken a bath and baked her favourite carrot cake before finally letting him drive her to the hospital.

Thea pushed herself out of bed and took her daughter for a last cuddle. 'Phone the Colonel first.'

'Colonel Grandpa! Colonel Grandpa!' The little girl jiggled, delighted at the fulfilment of a long-standing promise of a day or two exclusively with her grandfather.

Ben grabbed her and tickled her, before she could kick Thea to bits in her excitement.

Funny how the term *Colonel* was now used affectionately to refer to his father. Ben had never expected to have a good relationship with him, but things had changed a lot over the last five years. And the old man positively doted on his granddaughter.

'I'll be back in a few minutes,' Ben said, placing the wriggling three-year-old on the floor, She raced out through the door to find Ben's phone. He cast Thea a glance. 'And then we'll get ready to welcome our son into the world.'

'Our new bundle of joy.' Thea smiled softly.

'To go with our beautiful daughter.' Ben beamed proudly. 'Have I told you yet today how much I love you, Mrs Abrams?'

'No,' Thea teased. 'So tell me now.'

* * * * *

MILLS & BOON®

MEDICAL ROMANCE™

THE ULTIMATE IN ROMANTIC MEDICAL DRAMA

A sneak peek at next month's titles...

In stores from 16th June 2016:

- **Taming Hollywood's Ultimate Playboy** – Amalie Berlin
  and **Winning Back His Doctor Bride** – Tina Beckett

- **White Wedding for a Southern Belle** – Susan Carlisle
  and **Wedding Date with the Army Doc** – Lynne Marshall

- **Capturing the Single Dad's Heart** – Kate Hardy

- **Doctor, Mummy...Wife?** – Dianne Drake

Available at WHSmith, Tesco, Asda, Eason, Amazon and Apple

Just can't wait?
Buy our books online a month before they hit the shops!
visit www.millsandboon.co.uk

These books are also available in eBook format!

0616/03

Lynne Graham has sold 35 million books!

To settle a debt, she'll have to become his mistress...

Nikolai Drakos is determined to have his revenge against the man who destroyed his sister. So stealing his enemy's intended fiancé seems like the perfect solution! Until Nikolai discovers that woman is Ella Davies...

Read on for a tantalising excerpt from Lynne Graham's 100th book,

BOUGHT FOR THE GREEK'S REVENGE

'Mistress,' Nikolai slotted in cool as ice.

Shock had welded Ella's tongue to the roof of her mouth because he was sexually propositioning her and nothing could have prepared her for that. She wasn't drop-dead gorgeous... *he* was! Male heads didn't swivel when Ella walked down the street because she had neither the length of leg nor the curves usually deemed necessary to attract such attention. Why on earth could he be making *her* such an offer?

'But we don't even know each other,' she framed dazedly. 'You're a stranger...'

'If you live with me I won't be a stranger for long,' Nikolai pointed out with monumental calm. And the very sound of that inhuman calm and cool forced her to flip round and settle distraught eyes on his lean darkly handsome face.

'You can't be serious about this!'

'I assure you that I am deadly serious. Move in and I'll forget your family's debts.'

'But it's a *crazy* idea!' she gasped.

'It's not crazy to me,' Nikolai asserted. 'When I want anything, I go after it hard and fast.'

Her lashes dipped. Did he want her like that? Enough to track her down, buy up her father's debts, and try and buy rights to her and her body along with those debts? The very idea of that made her dizzy and plunged her brain into even greater turmoil. 'It's immoral... it's blackmail.'

'It's definitely *not* blackmail. I'm giving you the benefit of a choice you didn't have before I came through that door,' Nikolai Drakos fielded with a glittering cool. 'That choice is yours to make.'

'Like hell it is!' Ella fired back. 'It's a complete cheat of a supposed offer!'

Nikolai sent her a gleaming sideways glance. 'No the real cheat was you kissing me the way you did last year and then saying no and acting as if I had grossly insulted you,' he murmured with lethal quietness.

'You *did* insult me!' Ella flung back, her cheeks hot as fire while she wondered if her refusal that night had started off his whole chain reaction. What else could possibly be driving him?

Nikolai straightened lazily as he opened the door. 'If you take offence that easily, maybe it's just as well that the answer is no.'